A. N. Homer

Hernani the Jew

A Story of Russian Oppression

A. N. Homer

Hernani the Jew
A Story of Russian Oppression

ISBN/EAN: 9783743399457

Manufactured in Europe, USA, Canada, Australia, Japa

Cover: Foto ©Andreas Hilbeck / pixelio.de

Manufactured and distributed by brebook publishing software (www.brebook.com)

A. N. Homer

Hernani the Jew

HERNANI THE JEW

A Story of Russian Oppression

BY A. N. HOMER,

AUTHOR OF "THE RICHEST MERCHANT IN ROTTERDAM," ETC.

CHICAGO AND NEW YORK:
RAND, McNALLY & COMPANY,
PUBLISHERS.

HERNANI THE JEW.

BY A. N. HOMER.

CHAPTER 1.

Early in the year 1861 General Hourko stood within his palace at Warsaw watching some Jews and Poles driven back over the Praga Bridge by a handful of Cossacks. Titus Popoloff, his secretary, was with him, and a couple of aides-de-camp were discussing the political situation in the ante-room.

At the General's feet stretched the terraces of the palace gardens, fringed with straggling trees already denuded of their leaves; beyond, the placid volume of the river Vistula; and a little to the right the bridge upon which the lean and shaggily-mounted Cossacks were proving their zeal and devotion to the Tsar.

From his point of vantage, and with the aid of his field-glasses, the General could see clearly what was going on.

"Come here, Popoloff, and tell me if you can make out what the rascals are doing," he suddenly exclaimed, as they quitted the bridge and approached to within a stone's throw of the palace walls. "Whom have they got hold of amongst others? A woman for certain, but no peasant, I should say."

"Eh, your Excellency; she seems to be respectably dressed, well-looking, and of fine presence. Ah! now I can see plainly."

"Of course she is, man. A Polish lady, and handsome. This won't do, Popoloff. I thought my instructions were clear. We must not quarrel with the women. Send someone to rescue her, and bring her to me."

Popoloff hurried into the ante-room, and General Hourko squared his shoulders before the window again, muttering to himself, "If I only knew what to strike at; if there were armed troops in the field against me instead of unarmed conspirators, I could act decisively. Officialism is corrupt because the officials are Poles. The Church is corrupt because it is not Orthodox, and the Rabbis are not slow to grasp the hand it stretches out to them. Fancy Roman Catholics and Jews talking of exchanging presents! Strong measures should be taken, I am confident. The place should be declared in a state of siege, then powder and shot poured in, and all would be quiet. But what would they say in Petersburg? Ah! they send me here and handcuff me. Alexeieff!"

"Yes, your Excellency."

"Does the crowd in the square gather?"

"It does. But the people are collected in groups, and they talk and gesticulate wildly."

"Let them. How many of them are there, do you think?"

"It is difficult to say, sir."

"Three or four thousand people?"

"Perhaps; but then there are the approaches which are crammed. All Warsaw is on foot."

"What do they want, eh?"

The aide-de-camp smiled sarcastically.

"The freedom of Poland, sir; nothing less will satisfy them."

"An insane idea. And for a rabble like this to talk of petitioning his Majesty for a constitution. Ah! here is Popoloff."

The sudden opening of the door of the apartment revealed Popoloff's spare bent form on the one hand, an aide-de-camp on the other; between them, a young, dignified, and at once remarkable woman. She was clad in deep mourning, and this sable costume heightened the distressed pallor of her face, the fine features of which were lighted by clear, fearless eyes. Even Hourko, who considered himself a judge of feminine beauty, scarcely concealed his surprise and admiration.

"Madam, I trust you have suffered no personal inconvenience," he remarked, in a firm voice which drowned Popoloff's whispered "Madam, this is his Excellency the Governor of the Kingdom."

"I have been put to considerable inconvenience and annoyance, sir, though no bodily harm has been done me," was the calm answer, although evidently her pulse was beating wildly.

"I sincerely regret to hear it; but soldiers, like other mortals, are apt to exceed their instructions, to become over-zealous, madam." General Hourko's voice had changed slightly; it was colder and more dignified. Was he not the representative of his sovereign? What reason was there for him to be conciliatory—above all to a person who, his keen Russian eyes told him, was not a Pole after all, but one of a people it had been part of his training and education to look down upon, even to despise? He had been under the roof and in the camp, with those who had followed the world's teaching, and had turned their hands against the whole Hebrew race. Yet this woman was certainly not purely Jewish. In the distant past, Polish blood had intermingled and left signs which to him were as plain as the letters of the alphabet. But then, too, she was refined, and elegantly though simply dressed. It had never occurred to him that a Jewess could possess any of these perfections of manner or style. However, he was prepared to accept two incontrovertible facts—that a female, and a beautiful one, was before him; and accordingly he added with a smile, "War is never waged upon women; but in such disturbed times as these, and for your own personal safety, I would remind you that it is not well for ladies to go into outlying districts alone and on foot. The Praga quarter is, I understand, inhabited by the dregs of the population, who——"

"Are Jews, your Excellency, like myself," interrupted the lady, crimsoning, for, having watched Hourko's face attentively, she had read his thoughts, and blushed with what she deemed righteous anger. "Amongst my own people I am safe. Why should they hurt me? I only try to help them in their sickness and misery."

The General was slightly irritated, but he was insensibly becoming more interested. If it had not been so—that is to say, if he had not found her beautiful—he would have dismissed her with a few suitable words, but it pleased him to allow himself to be attracted by beauty when he had the time to spare. The acknowledged admiration of it was one of his most amiable weaknesses. It was true that Warsaw was in a most disturbed state, that the social and political condition of affairs were rotten to the core, that the educated classes were believed to be hostile to the government he represented, almost to a man; there was nothing in all that to prevent him from feeling horribly bored at times. It was well to lighten the heavy burden of the official day when a good opportunity presented itself, and it was part of his duty to pacify and please people.

"To offer a helping hand, madam, to people in distress of any kind, is noble, and the reward will come in affection and respect. Such amiable actions would meet with the approval of my august master, who can only be grieved when there is sickness, poverty, or any kind of unhappiness amongst his people. His sentiments on these points should be well known to all. May I ask how you came to be annoyed in the way you seem to have been, because my instructions are peremptory: no peaceable person is to be interfered with?"

Popoloff pricked up his large ears at this juncture, and, adjusting his spectacles, remarked gravely—

"I am told that this lady was discovered in the house

of some people who have given much trouble, your Excellency. Some rifles, a small package of saddlery, provisions, and a banner displaying the Polish eagle, were found and seized; and money—I won't say a large sum —had been supplied to them by her."

"Ah! is that so? Such a statement is serious; yet, pray, don't distress yourself, madam. Thank you Popoloff—this will be explained." And, bestowing upon him a look which that individual quite understood, next moment General Hourko found himself alone with this woman who had begun to interest him so much. His manner instantly became more affable. He planted his back to the huge stove and, with his hands crossed behind him, inquired gently—

"May I first know to whom I have the pleasure of speaking? I don't wish you to think me a kind of ogre, or to be the least bit afraid of me. I am here to see that justice is done to everyone."

Instead of allaying her fears, the mildness of this speech excited them. Why did he wish to talk to her—to question her in this way himself? Already she had refused to give her name, hoping to escape the necessity. Now she must do so, and she was alone in this huge palace with a man whose power was absolute, who could dispatch her to Siberia as easily as to her own home; and who, moreover, in addition to his reputation for harshness, some alleged brutality, was believed to be morally weak and unscrupulous. How far her information was correct she did not know, but the situation she found herself in was one which began to try her nerves and arouse her fears. Not naturally timid, she already felt painfully so. Her eyes swept the apartment as though seeking some means of escape, and as though to say, "Your desire is hopeless." There were the walls, lofty, paneled, elegant. No hope in that direction. There, too, was the figure of Hourko, strong, apparently inexorable in his tightly fitting General's uniform, which rendered his shoulders squarer, his neck stiffer, his heavy, resolute features and thick iron-gray mustache most awe-inspiring. At length, feeling that she must reply to this demand made upon her, she allowed one word to escape her.

"Hernani."

"Your name is Hernani, madam?"

"Yes."

The General reflected. The name struck some note—sounded, in fact, perfectly familiar to him. Ah! he remembered.

"Are you related to a banker in this town of that name?"

"I am his wife."

"Indeed! What a pity you did not tell me sooner. Your husband is well known, above suspicion, and I understand is much respected." Then he added laughingly, "You are not likely to have been guilty of aiding these refractory people." Receiving no reply, he thought, "So this is Sara Hernani, wife of Kasimir Hernani, the great Jew banker; Sara Hernani, as famous for her beauty as he is for his wealth. What a fortunate scoundrel, a millionaire and with such a wife!" Aloud he added, "You will be good enough to explain to him, please, how I regret the inconvenience you have been put to, but the Government has a difficult task before it—to deal firmly with those who would defy it, without wounding the tender susceptibilities of those who respect it, and are honest in their support of law and order."

Pondering over his former remark about aiding the disaffected, and knowing her husband to belong to the White party,* Sara was disturbed, and, barely hearing him, vaguely answered—

"Indeed, it must be a hard task"—not without a sense of hypocrisy mingled with fervent prayer that the interview might terminate speedily.

General Hourko saw that she longed to escape from his

---

*Moderate party.

clutches; but all the same, before she left him, he was keenly desirous of making a better impression; of letting her know something of what he felt, and that he would like to see her again, if only to feast his eyes on a face which charmed him so. He made a last effort to prolong the conversation.

"This disturbance to-day is to be lamented. It can be productive of no good. Why won't people be contented?"

"With what, sir?" inquired Sara, daringly, though with the sensation that she had impressed him too well to offend him.

"With the good things his Majesty, my Imperial master, lavishes on them, and the recollection of the tender solicitude they know him to take in their welfare. Then, too, so much more trust might be reposed in them would they but prove themselves worthy."

"I fear I am incapable of discussing such great questions," replied Sara, in despair at still being detained.

"Then believe what I tell you," replied Hourko, a little pompously; and, further disconcerted at the small amount of headway he was making, he added, "If I can be of use to you in any way, don't fail to apply to me, and remember, too," he blundered, "that I think your husband most fortunate."

"Why?" demanded Sara, not seeing the drift of his remark until she had spoken.

"To be the happy possessor of so much beauty," was Hourko's prompt answer, accompanied by a look of admiration which could not escape her understanding.

Instantly the defenselessness of her position was before her in full force. She experienced the sensation of being wounded, insulted, of having an attack made upon her—when, considering that she was virtually a prisoner, such an attack was almost brutal. How dare he pay her compliments, when, having dragged her before him, he dismissed his attendants and interrogated her as he chose! But then, too, she ought to have remembered that this was the treatment she should have expected from him. Was he not the Governor of the Kingdom of Poland, and was she not—worst thing of all—a Jewess? With the warm blood dyeing her cheeks and surging through her, leaving her hot and cold in turn, she rose to her feet, determined to regain her liberty at once.

"I have already been away from home a long while, your Excellency, and my good looks which you have so graciously admired will be missed there. May I return, please?"

General Hourko saw his mistake and made an attempt —the best he was capable of—to repair it. Reassuming his polite and serious manner, he said—

"Oh, I forgot. Of course. A carriage must be ordered. You shall be driven where you wish."

"Thank you; I know every step of the way, and I prefer to walk."

"But it is not safe. The crowd blocks the square. Listen to the shouts and uproar."

"Your Excellency, you are very kind, but the crowd will do me no harm, I assure you." Advancing toward the door, the General could do no less than open it, and Sara Hernani passed down the grand staircase and so out of the palace, Popoloff, who had been on the lookout, escorting her to the entrance.

Left to himself, the General passed to and fro before the stove, in which wood and coal crackled merrily. The sensation of being lonely as well as irritated stole over him. Sniffing the atmosphere, in which it seemed Sara had left a trace of some fragrant scent she affected, his eye fell upon the chair in which she had sat, and memory placed her there again, in all the rare perfection of her form and face. On the long pile of the Turkey rug there even appeared to be the faint impression of her foot, which he now remembered had peeped from beneath her skirt sufficiently for him to pronounce it small and shapely. He regarded that imaginary mark fixedly for an instant, and then with a savage kick sent the chair spinning under the table, and, stamping upon the rug, exclaimed—

"What an old fool I am, and worse than ever—worse than ever!"

Ringing a hand-bell with a crash, there appeared upon the scene Tit Prokofievitch Popoloff, or, as the English tongue would render it, Titus Prokofievitch Popoloff, with his habitual stoop which suggested weak lungs, and added to his ill-shapen legs, increased his aspect of ungainliness; with his lean, irregular features, wrinkled and yellow skin, pale, almost colorless eyes, and strange stealthiness of movement—Titus Popoloff, in fact, with nothing to recommend him so far as one could judge. Yet consider what he had done. In a few years he had succeeded in raising himself from the position of a small tchinovnik* to that of secretary—trusted adviser really—to Ivan Nicholaevitch Hourko, who, it may be added for the benefit of those who do not remember, had played an important part in the rebellion of '30, had been conspicuous for his bravery at the battle of the Alma, and, in addition to being considered one of the most resolute and sagacious officers in the Russian service, was known to have gained the approval and confidence of his sovereign. All these wonders Titus Popoloff had worked, or, rather, the whim of a woman he had contrived to please had enabled him to work them.

Olga Pavlovna Hourko, the General's wife, had discovered him one day quite by chance, ink and dirt begrimed, dishevelled, and meanly clad, sitting in his poky office somewhere in the Ukraine, where she had large estates. She had been insanely jealous of the General at the time, and Titus, in his post of tchinovnik in the service of the Provincial Crown Domain Office, had proved

*Civil servant.

himself discreet, in fact invaluable. The General, being easy-going, a warrior, and not a cautious diplomatist, had not troubled himself to make any inquiries about Popoloff, but, accepting his wife's recommendation without a murmur, had placed this deserving person's feet upon the ladder of ease and security, after which Titus had taken care to mount upward.

Conscious that he was no longer alone, but without taking further notice of the fact, the General assumed his favorite position near the stove, and some minutes elapsed, during which time Popoloff silently busied himself with polishing his spectacles with a large colored silk handkerchief, and holding them up to the light. He had just placed them on his nose, when the General said suddenly—

"Can you tell me anything about Hernani the banker, here?"

"What do you want to know, your Excellency?"

"Everything. His temperament. How and with whom he lives. Exact nature of home ties—yes, mark that—and political bias. Now I shall be glad to have this information soon, for he may be dangerous enough to be worth the trouble of watching. Do you know who that woman was?"

"Who has just left, sir, and who is so beautiful?" he added slyly.

"Ah! those old eyes of yours have discovered that, and what else?"

"That she is Kasimir Hernani's wife."

"And how did you learn that?"

"I recognized her at the first glance, your Excellency. She refused to give her name, but I make it my business to know."

"And you do your business well. Ah! Popoloff, good looks don't mean good brains."

"Not always, sir."

"Well, be thankful you have the brains and I can pay

you for them. One word about Hernani: set your wits
to work at once and let me hear the result quickly. Why,
what is this—the square almost clear, the mob dispersed?
Look, Popoloff! Now that is good—that is good; the
noise they made was a frightful nuisance." And crossing
over to a writing-table, with a sigh of relief, the General
became absorbed in scanning and sorting some papers,
occasionally pausing to make corrections and annota-
tions. A little later Popoloff noiselessly withdrew, and
when the neutral tints of the winter evening had deepened
into the blackness of night, when the stars were ablaze
overhead, he entered another apartment in the huge palace, an apartment small in size, octagonal in shape, paneled with rare wood, cozy with soft mats and replete with
every luxury which a fastidious, selfish, and wealthy
woman could crowd into her boudoir. In the midst of
all this finery a little lady with sharp, mean features, faded
yellow hair, and tired-looking eyes, which struck one as
being too large for her small, oval face, was reclining half
buried in cushions. The atmosphere was that of a hot-
house, and even Popoloff, through whom any keen wind
blew, found himself perspiring; while she, with a little
dog curled on her knees, and some tea at hand, com-
plained querously of the cold, asked twice over if it was
freezing, and only seemed to forget about her chilliness
when Popoloff got deep into the events of the day. For
this was a part of his duty—to recount to Madame
Hourko all that had transpired, all that her husband had
done and deemed secret proceedings, if need be. But
then Popoloff was always so obliging, and might not
have retained his position if he had not been large-minded
enough to consent to a little harmless gossip now and
again. And this was the kind of woman the General had
chosen for a wife; physically weak, often ailing, by no
means beautiful, but doting on him sufficiently to be jealous of a shadow if it bore any resemblance to a female.
How strangely people marry!

CHAPTER II.

Once outside the great gloomy walls of the palace, Sara found herself in the square, the space of which was now but thinly sprinkled with the moving forms of people looming large in the blue mist of the gathering darkness. Torches were being kindled and brandished, and the smoke and blaze of them lent a savage aspect to the scene, begirt, as it was, by towering gables and turrets. Snow was beginning to fall in large flakes, and as they struck upon her face, half blinding her, the shrieks of women's voices, the angry tones of men, the sharp cracks of Cossack nagaikas* sounding clear above the sullen roar of the dispersing mob, assailed her ears and made her shrink and cower under the dark walls. She had but one wish —to reach her home unmolested. But her nerves were shaken, and her dress, though black, was costly enough to betray her. Ladies were constantly being accosted and insulted, and, in spite of the brave words she had spoken to Hourko, her mind was full of such stories.

In the Faubourg Cracow some Cossacks opposed the further advance of a drunken and infuriated droshky driver, and one of them lashed the face of a poor beggar who was slinking along in half-clad wretchedness. There was a piercing shriek, a volley of oaths, and, with the smell of unwashed clothes and vodka in her nostrils, Sara fled into the quiet shelter of the Jardin de Saxe, and, still breathless, arrived at the entance of a mansion which formed the whole side of a square, scarce two hundred yards from the Place de Saxe. This was her home. This was the palace of the famous Jew banker, Kasimir Hernani, and within its walls loans were advanced to Euro-

---

*Whips.

pean monarchs and nobles, vast business obligations were entered into, and millions of rubles sped out over the world, guided by the wisdom and foresight of this financial genius. Here in this splendid home Sara worshiped, and had been worshiped, ever since she had come to it out of poverty and want, hardships innumerable, the alarming existence the daughter of a poor and persecuted man must lead.

Hernani doted upon her. She was the apple of his eye, the breath of his nostrils. Here he had delighted to see her, clad in costly clothes, to satisfy her slightest whim, to greet her with his fondest word, his warmest smile, to lavish upon her the luxuries and refinements, the delights which his affection and wealth could supply. Here, amidst a subdued light, with the perfume of flowers, the gentle lullaby of falling water and the soothing cadence of singing birds, no matter how the world shook and was troubled, there was quiet and peace for this idol he had set up.

And the moment she entered he hastened to join her, to reassure himself that she was safe; for he had been anxious, disturbed beyond measure by her long absence; the report that the people were astir having reached him. Her wraps were upon her still when she heard his step and voice.

"Ah! you are safe; but what has delayed you? You have given me such a fright."

"I couldn't return sooner. The streets were blocked," she answered, endeavoring to speak as though nothing had happened.

"Blocked—and you in them? But why did you not drive out to-day? I told you—I warned you. You must never do this again, dearie. You must promise me. I knew something had happened. But what is the matter? Ah! something else has occurred; tell me."

His kind words had affected her. She could still see the rough Cossacks and hear their strange voices and coarse oaths. The people she had been herded with, poor and dejected, were about her again, and then the picture of Hourko, his words and looks. Overwrought, she leant upon his shoulder and sobbed.

"Come—I insist," he went on, her tears salt upon his lips. "Now, pull yourself together and tell me."

Struggling to regain her composure, she said at length, "You know I went to the Bieloi's over in Praga?"

"Yes—well?"

"They were making a search."

"Who—the Cossacks?" he demanded fiercely.

"Yes."

"While you were there?"

"Yes."

"And you—come—I must know. What is there to hide from me?"

"Nothing, of course. Well, they found arms and things. Isaach Bieloi was wrong."

"To let them find them, the ass!"

"Yes; and I was ordered out of the house like the rest."

"You—ordered out of a hovel where you went to aid starving people! Curse them!—the dogs! Is there no freedom in the land? And what else?"

"Oh, nothing! Kiss me and do not worry me into going over it all again. It will only excite you and do no good, and I want to forget. Here I am, safe and sound; we shall be quiet together for the rest of the evening and I will sing to you, so you must do as I tell you." And she clung to him so that his face was hidden in her auburn hair.

"But I won't be put off in this way."

"Not if I wish it?"

"No. How did you get out of the grip of the brutes, and what did they say?"

She stood before him, her head tilted to one side, the sweetest and most provoking little smile upon her lips.

"Well, you see," she said slowly, "I never got into it,

and they only—well, they only—smelt. Oh!" she added, mimicking a shudder, "bad tobacco, vodka and filth equals asafœtida. Dearie, what a relief it is to find one's self back, to feel a little tired, to sit down on something soft, to be cold, and for the dry heat to·put warmth and life into one. Those poor Bieloi's hadn't a crust—not a kopec left. Besides them, I saw six other families worse off if possible—and to think of them all, this bitter night! How will they get through the winter? Oh! if I could only build a great house where they could all find food and warmth and rest. They are no longer fit to struggle. It is terrible."

"You have done what you can," Hernani answered gravely, "and God, blessed be He, will do the rest."

"But the children——"

"Ah! the children," interrupted Hernani in a hollow voice, and his eyes sought hers with a hungry look in them, then softened to their usual expression as he added, "Well, the children will be taken care of, and, after all, they can't suffer as acutely. But now I must go to my work; when I return you will be rested and less gloomy. You see, no one is free from trouble." And without saying more he left her, still with a trace of the sad look in his face, and she watched him away with pain in her own.

Her allusion to children—a natural enough one—had stirred up the family ghost, and a moment after she had spoken she could have cut out her tongue.

Hernani was strong, rich, and respected, but he had no children, and of course he would have given all he had in the world in exchange for them. He wanted a son to bear his name, a son to whom he could leave his wealth, and when exasperated by some new act of oppression—some evil tidings which told of his people being wrongfully used—he had been heard to declare that he wanted a son whose heart he could set against those whose hands were turned upon the whole Hebrew race. Hernani knew that, compared with the blood of the multi-

tude of those who had allowed his kindred no resting
place, who had driven them from land to land, that in
his own veins was as the pure stream to the puddle in
the street. He knew that Benjamin of Tudela—a learned
and great traveler two centuries before Maundeville and
Marco Polo—had mentioned in his writings that he had
met a great merchant prince named David ben Hernani,
whose ancestors had acquired their wealth and influence
at the court of the Caliphs of Baghdad, that he had found
this same David, with some thousands of his kindred,
living at the city of Bussorah, situated on an island in
the river Tigris; but of the actual existence of members
of his own family at Damascus, Cairo, and afterward at
Constantinople, he—Hernani—possessed positive proof.
Within his own house were stored quaint stones in ancient rings, bearing inscriptions, curious relics as well as
documentary evidence, which proved that the long line of
dead from whom he had sprung were not barbarians, but
had played their parts as men of culture, wisdom and refinement, through the long ages of the past. Part of the
wealth he had inherited had thus come to him from such
men, who, as renowned doctors and persevering and
astute merchants, had fought their way in these ancient
cities of the far east. Always scattered and oppressed
these men of old had battled against overwhelming odds
with the most superb courage, and, like them, Hernani
had the desire to grapple to the death rather than tamely
submit to be swept from the face of the earth. This lack
of children, then, was the plague spot in his life to which
his eye often turned darkly. His wife was so beautiful,
but beauty was dear, bought at the price of barrenness,
for any hag in the streets could bear children—too many
of them, as he knew to his cost. True, he suppressed
these feelings as much as he could, but every now and
then the demon of dissatisfaction would up and declare
himself. Some trifling and innocent allusion of the sort
related, some chance remark about other people's chil-

dren—their beauty, ability, the trouble they gave or the comfort they were—and the slumbering volcano in Hernani's breast became active.

With these thoughts again astir, he returned to his bureau, which was situated so as to place him in instant touch with his employes, who had been accommodated with quarters so arranged that a great business could be conducted without in the least affecting the domestic arrangements and general comfort of the establishment. Massive and built of stone, having passed the principal entrance to the building, which was in the center, a lofty hall was gained, upon either side of which were doors, opening into suites of apartments commanding a view of the square. These suites of rooms were thus on the ground floor, and were furnished as offices. A couple of ante-rooms passed, and you were in the midst of the clerks and cashiers. Several smaller rooms abutted on this general office, and upon the doors of these were painted the names of the leading officials, heads of departments. Once in the central hall again, a flight of steps conducted to folding doors whence the mansion itself was entered. Then the luxury of the place burst upon one. Alabaster columns supported galleries and staircases lighted by a dome, beneath which exotics reared their crowned and feathered heads, seeming ever green and flourishing midst the harmonious tinkle of water which rose from and fell into a silver fountain, a miracle of goldsmiths' work. And no harsh sound disturbed the repose which reigned amidst the tree ferns and palms, the pomegranates and oleanders, for the feet sank in soft rugs and carpets brought from the famed looms of the far east. Amongst the priceless walnut and pearwood furniture were gems which had decorated the salons of those whose voices had reverberated over Europe. Gold and china from which princes had drunk, brocaded lounges upon which they had flirted, pictures they had feasted their eyes upon, ivory cabinets finer than the

Pope had bestowed upon Sobieski for his conquest of
the Turks at Vienna, and which had held documents deciding the fate of empires. All these things were collected about this man, whose gold had gathered them
together, only that he might beautify the home he had
made, the nest to which he had brought the woman of
his choice.

And now he had become as famous for them as he was
for the beauty of his wife, for his untiring industry, his
financial genius, and, not least, his innumerable acts of
charity. He had built a synagogue, and an institution
to alleviate want and misery, by enabling those who could
and would work to know where to find it. At all times
he had opened his purse wide, proud and thankful that
it was in his power to do so by reason of the intellect
God had given him to fill it.

Perhaps the knowledge that he was of so much use
in the world inspired him with the strength and energy
he displayed, for he scanned his vast correspondence, dic-
tated replies, and had set the many and minute wheels
of the machine he controlled revolving, while the bulk
of other men slept.

And at night he seemed to know no fatigue, for his
dark eyes flashed as brightly, his tall form and broad
shoulders knew no stoop; he was still fit to enter into
anything, though the darkness seldom found him far
from his wife and his beautiful home. Sometimes he
would entertain, and then unconsciously his knowledge
of life leaked out, for in his younger days he had wandered through the crowded towns and bazaars of India,
Persia and Asia, where his marvelous capacity for acquiring languages—a gift common to many of his race—
had enabled him to enter into and understand the lives
and characters of those he met, instead of passing
through the country forced to be content with seeing
only. He had attached himself to caravans and had journeyed through the desert, smoking the pipe and lying

down to sleep with men who valued a life at less than the price of a she-camel. His grasp of Arabic was so thorough that he could have passed for a native had he chosen, and had thus been safe in the midst of perils to which a less gifted and capable person must have succumbed. As much at home on the deck of a ship as on the back of a dromedary, he had once fitted out a vessel in which he had sailed along the African coast, putting in at every strange and interesting port, making long journeys in-land and only returning when his mind was stored with curious information, his body hardened by exposure and exercise, his cheek bronzed and his eye as clear as those of the eagles and vultures who had fought over the car-cases he had shot.

Beloved by all who came in contact with him, his re-appearance on his own deck was but the signal for shouts of welcome, and for the sails to be set, the course given for some new place of wonder, toward which when the winds blew fiercest and the waves leapt high, Hernani would himself steer, as cool at the helm with the lee rail buried, and the Mediterranean waves hissing and foam-ing about him, as he had been when his life had hung upon a death-shot from his rifle. And then his wealth had never made him selfish or overbearing. One of his own crew or some poor devil of a black, sick or staggering under a burden too heavy for him, were equally sure to receive the best medicine or help he could offer.

He seemed to remember that all men had souls like himself, that one day he must lie down when it pleased God he should, and be as one of the least of them. Of course these adventures and journeyings—that strange, wild, changeful life in which he had delighted—were as a dream, a page of his past in which Sara had played no part, having been lived before he had met her, as he had, in the hey-day of her maidenhood, though in the very thick of the poverty and trouble, which had en-shrouded her father, and been her only birthright. One

of his acts of charity had brought about his first sight of
her.

At his hotel in Cracow a heart-rending story had been
told him of a learned doctor who, on account of his anti-
Russian views, had incurred the displeasure of the authorities, had in fact been driven out of one town and then
another, always upon some unreasonable or harsh pretext, until at length his means had become so limited
that he found it difficult to support himself and daughter.
The mother and two other children were already dead,
the beauty of this remaining one being indeed marvelous. The older her clothing and the less food she had
to eat, the more ethereal she appeared. Her face was like
that of an angel in a fresco. The sun had kissed her
hair and had painted it forever, and her eyes, they were
large and spoke—never the like of them in Cracow before—their color oh! the heavenliest gray that seemed
violet or black, as the light might shine. Some artists
—foreigners—had begged to paint her, offering large
sums and declaring in despair that if they might, their
fortune would be made. But these requests the good
doctor had frowned upon and refused. He would have
none of them or their gold. His daughter's honor was
more precious in his sight than pearls. And then the
girl was so clever, thanks to her father's teaching—for
he was wise, though he had little money. Had they no
friends? Oh, yes, in a sense, but people had grown tired;
it was natural. But to see her eyes and hear her voice—
she could sing like the saints in Heaven—was worth
a visit, well worth a visit; and there was a droshky at
the door—ten minutes' drive and he could judge for
himself. And Hernani had gone, a little curious, and
a little sad that such things should be, but his sense of
pity astir in him. He had found them as described to
him—in the midst of poor surroundings: the old doctor
in a dirty caftan, Sara attired in much worn, ill-fitting
clothes, tongue tied, and the blood in her cheeks at sight

of such a stranger. For to her Hernani seemed a prince such as she had only read of—with his tall form, well-molded features, long curling moustache and sunburnt complexion. It was winter, the snow thick upon the ground, and in his handsome fur coat and high leathern boots he looked so big and beautiful that he filled the tiny room. This was Sara's first impression. Afterward, when time had passed and her father had said to her, "He is a good man, he has done much. Not a penny do I owe, except to him, and may the God of Israel bless him and help me to pay him back," her young heart had gone out to him, so that she grew to blush and tremble when he came near, and at length, when she learned that he desired her and that she might be his wife if she pleased, it seemed as though heaven had descended upon her—her ears tingled, they were not to be believed, and she could have leapt with joy. The wife of this man whom she loved to be near, and whose footfall made her pulse quicken—who could take her where she would be free from anxiety, and where she could sit and think, with as many books and flowers about her as she pleased! Oh! the Holy One—blessed be He!—was good to her, too good. Meanwhile, Hernani, foreseeing how it would end, had ordered the most extensive preparations to be made in Warsaw, and when Sara entered his house as his honored wife—the very raiment which touched her soft white shoulders having been paid for by him with the look of love in his eyes—she could have screamed with delight. Even in her dreams she had never conceived anything so beautiful. The marble columns, the tessellated pavement, the cozy lounges beneath palm leaves and blossoming pomegranates; with the water showering its crystal drops upon the arching greenery and then sinking to rest in the marvelous silver fountain; the central ornament upon which was an oasis in the desert—a well, surrounded by date palms, which overshadowed an Arab horseman, dismounting, breathless, dying of thirst, rushing to drink with the fierce expression of a fiend upon his face; and from the spot upon which his agonized gaze was bent—the well—burst this delicious spray, so suggestive of refreshment, luxury, sleep. Then she had gone into ecstasies over the bright bits of color, the frescoes upon the ceilings, the alcoves with ancient Moorish lamps glowing like huge emeralds or rubies; and beyond all that—away from the furniture and pictures, the objets d'art, beautiful as they were— was something which had filled her soul with delicious tranquillity—a garden—only a garden, but one green and cool, designed in terraces, where, amidst some yews and cedars, pigeons cooed and goldfish sported, while the sun told the time on an ancient dial which had stood there mutely for centuries, as a part of the building had done, being very old.

Many years had passed since her arrival at this, to her, veritable Aladdin's Palace, but then she had been only a child, though old enough to know that her heart had gone out to Hernani; now, in the fullness of her beauty, in the perfection of her womanhood, she understood better how she only lived for him. And was it wonderful? Had he not rescued her from trouble, and from her father's faded cheeks had he not tried to smooth the wrinkles, until the Angel of Death had become impatient and had taken him? Ah! he had been very good, too good, but if only she could have given him what he yearned for, what she yearned for—if only she could have borne him a child, then she could have been quite happy. And yet it was not right to grumble. So she dressed as she knew pleased him, and waited for his return, glad that she had told him nothing of her enforced visit to the palace. It would only have increased his deep-rooted hatred of Hourko, and made his blood boil, and she wished of all things to soothe him, being fearful that he would be rash in some way, even to joining in the threatening rebellion, so risking his position.

perhaps life. Of Hourko she thought with loathing, hating him as she had never hated anyone—in quite an unnatural way, in fact. His request that she should seek him, if he could be of use, recurred to her. How terrible to be driven to entreat him, but then that could never happen, being out of the bounds of possibility. Smiling contentedly to herself, secure in her surrounding, she thought this just as Hernani approached her with a letter in his hand.

"Dorozynski has written to me," he exclaimed.

"Count Andrew Dorozynski?"

"Yes; you seem surprised."

"He is a Pole."

"Well, and I am a Jew. Were you going to add that I ought to feel honored?"

"Kasimir!" she exclaimed reproachfully.

"This is what you meant then. That we have not existed on the best of terms. That the Pole has looked down upon the Jew, perhaps cursed and spat at him. What of that? The whole world has done the same. By this time we should be used to it, and yet," he added, passionately, "that same world might have learned the lesson we have tried to teach it for so long now—that it may hang, burn, and do its best to destroy us, but it will not succeed. We shall spread over the earth and flourish, for the God of Israel fights for us. But why do I become excited? There is nothing to excite me, at least not yet; though there is that ahead which will do so, I fear. Ah! I have distressed you; forgive me. So——. Now to consider this Pole's letter. There should be no enmity between us because we are not of the same race. There is a similarity in their fate as a people, and ours, which should draw us together. Some few drops of their blood, at least, are in your veins, and still you know I love you. Well, they have been oppressed and so have we, but they stretched out their hand to us long years ago. Here in Poland we were permitted to live, pro-

tected, in comparative safety, and I say that at the least
we owe them gratitude; more than that, my feelings are
shared by others, and already an understanding has been
arrived at—of such a nature, too, that should war break
out, should these people who are brave and generous,
attempt to throw off the yoke of the oppressor, when they
have taken the field, they will find us there with them.
But Dorozynski's views are moderate at present, though
he knows, as I do, that the very foundations of Warsaw
are honeycombed by those who are preparing for the
strife. The streets are empty at night, strangely so, but
it is because preparations are progressing underground.
The town may seem deserted, but there is not a bed to
be had at the hotels."

"But how do you know that?" exclaimed Sara, apparently startled.

"How do I know that?"—and then with stern satisfaction, "I am informed, well informed, of all that goes
on. Yes, if I chose to turn traitor, I could feast the Russians on fat things. I promise you I could tickle their
palates. They would give their ears to hear the words I
could pour into them, and on the strength of them would
take care to hang, shoot or exile, half the nobility of this
down-trodden land. But the Poles are safe in my hands,
which is more than I will say for their conquerors, should
the chance come my way, for I have a score against them
and am on the lookout for a day of reckoning. In the
event of an outbreak, if I could only bring myself to believe that France or England would come to the rescue,
I should not hesitate long."

"Why, what would you do?" demanded Sara, with
feverish eagerness.

"Openly join the Poles," replied Hernani resolutely.

"You! Risk your life, and if the attempt failed, have
your possessions confiscated, your wealth seized—be ignominiously shot, after being flogged and insulted; or be

dispatched to Siberia, which would be worse than all! Don't even speak of it. I should be——"

"Your safety would be my first consideration."

"I was not going to speak of my safety, though you would be as incapable of securing it as of protecting your own life."

"My life has often been at stake before. I fear nothing."

"Oh! I don't mean that; but what can you do against overwhelming odds, against swarms of Cossacks and gendarmerie—a price set upon your head, a——"

"And do you think that if I pretended not to be interested, took no part in what will assuredly happen——"

"What is that?"

"A rebellion."

"It will come?"

"Yes. Listen, Sara. It would be useless to deceive you; the gravity of the situation cannot be exaggerated. The storm has gathered and is on the eve of bursting. Those who have decided to bear a hand and abide by the result of it, are prepared to play a desperate game. The match is already alight that will set Poland in a blaze. Read the signs. What sounds do you hear in the streets? The national hymn or prayer for liberty ascending heavenward, mingled with the shouts and turmoil of public demonstrations like this of to-day. What sights do you see? The white eagle of Poland once more fluttering in the breeze, the theaters empty, no dancing, no entertainments, no light-heartedness—instead of all this, heavy looks and mourning, the churches filled with prostrate forms, the women pale and anxious, the men flushed, angry, and spitting upon the jostling soldiery and police, while flaunting the national costume. No! the strife must come, and do you think that as a Jew, and one of substance, I shall be suffered to sleep while the tempest howls around me? I tell you—no, again. My rubles have been counted, an inventory of my goods has been made. They would plunder me to feed their troops, to liquidate their debts, to furnish their palaces. Which is the best—to stand up and fight manfully in defense of justice and freedom, or lie down to be robbed and maltreated? The one must be done or the other suffered. Perhaps not now—not now—a little time may elapse, but it must come; only to-night it is all before me. The Count's letter has stirred me up, though it is moderate and full of wisdom; for the writing of a young man, strangely so. He clings to the hope that the Tsar will show mercy; suggests that he cannot know; that matters may be smoothed by means of patience and petitions. So it may be; for my part I have not much faith either in the one or the other at this juncture."

Hernani had risen as his feelings gained the mastery over him, and with restless strides paced to and fro before Sara, from whose cheek the color had fled more than once, and whose beautiful eyes had flashed and sparkled in spite of herself as the disturbing words were uttered. On their cessation her animation died away. She saw that it would be well to calm her husband, and with an air of easy incredulity, almost of apathy, she said, "But Count Dorozynski may be right, and you, for once, wrong. Who knows? Let us hope so. It will be much better. As for me——"

"As for you, not a hair of your head shall be hurt. Have you no faith in me?"

"Faith?—yes, but you frighten me when you become so vehement. Ah! the love of adventure in you is not extinct. The mere mention of the horrors which you say must come makes my flesh creep, my blood curdle. This home, of which we are so fond, in which we have been so happy, fades from before my eyes, and becomes one of thousands, broken up, desolate, a heap of ashes. Already I seem to see the hateful Cossacks and police crowding the rooms, their clumsy, ill-washed hands laid upon the things I prize; the very smell of their vile tobacco and

vodka oppresses me again, as it has already done once
to-day. A straw caught up by the hurricane is not more
helpless than I suddenly feel myself. Upon you a different effect is produced. You are no longer the peaceable citizen, the business man, the husband, happy with
his little wife. Your eye kindles, you are a man, you
seem to enjoy the idea of a fight and would like to try
your hand at it——"

"But you forget I——"

"Listen! I was once friendless, poor and miserable,
and the horrid dread that I might become so again, has
often seized upon me in the midst of the happiest moments I have ever known. I have cried, and you have
asked me why; implored me to tell you and I have not
liked to; it seemed so stupid of me. Now, surely, trouble
is coming upon us and we are about to pay for these long
delicious years we have spent together. However, if it
is to be, you will see, the little wife can be brave—she
can fight, too. One has only to harden one's heart. Yet
as I have said—you may be mistaken."

"Perhaps, as you say, it may be so. Prayers fill the
churches. The most High—blessed be He!—may decide
in favor of peace."

Sara stirred restlessly. She had not done with the
argument; she wished to say a little more.

"Should this attempt be made, has it occurred to you
what a hopeless one it must be?" she inquired, without a
quiver in her voice, and as though she did not know that
she herself must be drawn into the vortex of it.

"Not if the peasants could be depended upon?" he
answered.

"But they cannot."

"Who can say? It is impossible to judge. But all
would be well without them if France or England would
come to the rescue; and already good news has arrived
from Paris. I understand that the Emperor himself

favors the cause, and information of a later date fills me with hope that there is truth in the rumor."

In spite of Hernani's brave words and confident manner, Sara remained unconvinced.

"In my opinion the opportune moment has gone," she replied; "a few months ago a sudden attack upon the citadel might have met with success, but already the garrison has been strengthened, and fresh regiments will soon be advancing from every part of Russia; there must be more than enough men here now to render any such attempt hopeless."

"Nevertheless, it will be made," replied Hernani grimly, though visibly affected by Sara's remarks, over which he pondered in silence for a few moments, lifting his head at length and inquiring forcibly: "But who informed you of all this? I thought I was supplying you with news, breaking something I ought no longer to attempt to keep from you. The tables appear to be turned."

Sara hung her head and blushed, just as though she had been detected in some act of deception. Then, having made up her mind to speak as she felt, she replied vehemently—

"But surely you must credit me with a little sense. I have known all you have told me long ago. Should I be a woman if I were not curious, and do you suppose that such great changes could occur without my knowledge? Ah! let me tell you. I have lain awake night after night while you have slept, thinking—thinking till it seemed as though my head would split. I know you detest the Government, and you are passionate—very—and I have been beside myself."

Deeply affected, Hernani exclaimed—

"I am not surprised—I understand; but, dearie, how needlessly you have tortured yourself!" Then, as if recollecting something, he added, "But why were you so

much distressed this afternoon? I know the Cossacks——"

"Was that not enough?" Sara interrupted, with nervous fingers pushing some rebellious hair from her forehead.

"Well, yes, perhaps," answered Hernani, doubt expressed in his voice, his fine dark eyes questioning her.
Sara understood. He had been thinking, and in his
opinion she had not quite confided in him. This was an
opportunity for so doing. However, she had determined
that she would say nothing about her interview with
Hourko.

"Certainly enough, I think. How unkind of you! It
having dawned on those brutes who I was, I was at liberty
to fly, and I did so in terror of the mob, arriving here
breathless."

"Well, child," replied Hernani somewhat wearily,
"don't trouble to go over it. It won't happen again, will
it? You will take my advice and be more careful for my
sake as well as your own. As for me, you need have
no fear. I shall act, remembering that the days when I
used to search for excitement will never come again, and
I shall not forget that I am a peaceable citizen, a business man, as you describe me, with a little wife whom all
men envy me the possession of. Now, will that set your
mind at rest? You shall see my reply to Dorozynski,
and I assure you I have no intention of being mixed up
either with Poles or Russians, unless they drive me to it.
Come, sing to me—sing something sweet and pathetic,
and then I shall forget."

Sara rose to do as he bid her, and Hernani followed her
movements, admiring the color and quantity of her hair,
her delicate skin, the firm, full suppleness of her figure;
then as the first notes of her voice rang through the room,
as if recollecting, he repeated softly to himself, "Unless
they drive me to it."

3

CHAPTER III.

Usually calm, deliberate, and most methodical, from about this time Hernani's habits underwent a change. The confidences with Sara were not renewed, owing to a feeling of restraint and helplessness; a silent, almost unconscious decision that no good could come of talking. He slept at odd and unusual times, on the whole badly, and was at his place in the office earlier than ever. His confidential clerks received instructions which frequently brought them to their posts at an hour which made them growl in chorus. They were being led a nice dance and for nothing. The chief was made of iron, but all the same he was killing himself, which was his lookout—why should they suffer? Oblivious of such trifles, Hernani certainly labored as though the demon of unrest had entered into him. Had he received an official warning that the doors of his prosperous concern were shortly to be closed, that these were days of grace allowed him to arrange his affairs, he could have worked no harder. He was dressed and waiting to open his correspondence before the early post had arrived. The envelopes were torn open, the contents read, instructions given, and his own clerk would distribute the sorted letters arranged in little baskets to the various heads of departments—who had but just arrived upon the scene—as expeditiously as though he too had caught the fever which preyed upon his master. Then, as if not satisfied with commencing early, the work went on at night, Sara the while thinking of him, waiting for him, sitting opposite his empty chair, as though in expectation of his appearance, dismayed and distressed, but not daring to speak for fear of annoying him. Without doubt the burden he bore was heavy, the situation he found himself in, one to try the stoutest heart. Already he stood on the very edge of a precipice, and was incapable of measuring the depths into which he might be forced to plunge at any moment. These depths or abysses being represented by political events, which were shaping to a head at a furious pace.

Patriotic manifestations against the Government were of daily occurrence. The national hymn was sung in general chorus throughout Warsaw, and in the light of day. Large numbers of people were being arrested. Patrols of cavalry surrounded the churches, the streets were kept clear by detachments of infantry, and the Russian lieutenant was at length confronted by armed rebellion.

Sara now scarcely ventured out unless driven and attended; Hernani, owing to his numerous engagements, but seldom; all the same he returned one day black with fury.

"What has happened?" Sara cried the instant she saw him.

"More than enough," he shouted, beside himself; "the accursed brutes have fired upon the crowd, who were unarmed. Jewish blood has been shed. I myself saw it. Ah! God, how I longed for a rifle. The bullet pierced his heart—he fell stone-dead at my side, and I—I could only wrench a stick from someone and beat a Cossack to the earth."

"You—you, Kasimir!" she shrieked. "Do you know what you have done?"

"Done, woman!" he exclaimed, his anger terrible to behold, and for the instant becoming almost brutal. "Ah! why have I no sons to tread these vermin under foot?"

"You must fly, or you will be arrested," she sobbed, ignoring the allusion, knowing that he was only cruel as the waves are—in their wrath.

"Fly—do you think so? I shall not budge. Arrested

shall I be? Let them try it, let them come—they will find me prepared." And he shut himself up, to mourn and think, ashamed of his vehemence, and cooling, after he had been alone a little. But when really calmer he could talk of nothing but the aspect of the mob, gathered about the dark Monastery, of the Bernardines; of their fortitude, and the horrors of the scene, inasmuch as they were unarmed and so at the mercy of the troops, who had fired volleys upon them, riding them under foot and flogging them with their nagaikas.*

In the evening time, when Hernani was still desperately agitated, Ivan Nicholaevitch was composedly sipping some fine tea flavored to a nicety with lemon. A samovar and a box of choice cigarettes stood near and Popoloff was at his elbow.

"Have you found out who knocked the Cossack down?" he asked, helping himself to a cigarette.

"Yes, your Excellency."

"Who was it?"

"You will be surprised, sir."

"How do you know? Nothing surprises me."

"I only think so. It was the banker, Kasimir Hernani."

"Hernani? H-u-m-m!" Lighting the cigarette, he inhaled freely, blew the smoke out in rings, and with his eyes fixed on Popoloff, repeated, "Hernani?"—adding, "Do you know, Popoloff, I am surprised! He seems to be a dangerous character."

"Yes, your Excellency."

"We must not forget that."

"No, sir."

"But do nothing at present. The Cossack may have been insolent, and to be lenient is good sometimes. Remember what I say. Have you got the information I required about him? My hands have been so full that the matter has quite escaped me."

---

*Whips.

"I have it here, sir." And Popoloff handed him a paper.

Reading attentively for a few minutes, Hourko at length exclaimed—

"Let me see—ah! rubbish! Of course I knew that—religiously, not strictly devout. Attached to the White, or moderate party—looks so by his conduct; wonder what Zamoyski would say to that? This is more to the point. Home relations of a happy nature, the pair being devoted to each other, but for the absence of children, which is a source of great regret to Hernani. His sentiments on this subject are the common property of the household, and the relations between the couple are, in consequence, strained upon occasions. Very concise and yet exhaustive. I am obliged, Popoloff. Take care of the report. Good; now this is interesting. A gap is here which cannot be filled up, a rent exists which must widen, unless—how long have they been married?"

"I do not know, your Excellency."

"Some years, doubtless, and wife last resident in Cracow. How young she must have been, and what a delicious morsel; of a very affectionate disposition, too, I should say. So Hernani desires children, and, having none, upbraids her. What is his remedy, Popoloff?"

"How do you mean, sir?"

"Come, you lawyer. What can he do, given that he wished to take action in the matter?"

"Get rid of her, sir."

"Ah! How—poison?"

"You are jesting, your Excellency."

"Well, seriously, tell me."

"I will consider the question and let you know, sir."

"What—can't you state now? You will get no extra fees for the delay, eh?" And the General laughed.

"I would rather think it over, sir."

"Very well, but answer me this. If he got rid of her, she would be free, of course?"

"Certainly, sir."

"Would she be disgraced?"

"Not necessarily, but she would sink to a certain extent in the estimation of those who were aware of the facts of the case. Women would——"

"Oh, never mind about what the women would think. They must always be jealous of her, for she is beautiful —eh, Popoloff?"

"Very, your Excellency; but—a Jewess."

"Under some circumstances such an unpleasant fact may be overlooked. You see Esther was also a Jewess, yet King Kasimir adored her. Now although it would never do for me to be lenient to the Jews as that famous King Kasimir was, in consequence of his affection for Esther, yet I will own that I am interested in Sara Hernani just as he was in Esther, if I may draw such a parallel. Do you understand me, Popoloff?"

"Perfectly, sir."

"Well, then, think; I want this acquaintance, so oddly —one might say inauspiciously commenced—to ripen."

"Your Excellency's hands will be full with this insurrection, which draws to a head."

"Oh, I know—I know, but not so full as all that. Do as I order you. There will be plenty of spare moments which I intend to spend pleasantly, in spite of the restlessness of these pestilent Poles. Carte blanche is all I want to crush them in a week, instead of telegrams from St. Petersburg arriving at dead of night, conceived at that distance, without the knowledge procurable upon the spot —and so disjointing all my plans. But why did you drag it into my head again? I want to forget my worries for the moment, and so gain the strength to meet more of them. Where was I?—oh, yes, this Jewess. Well, think; see to it. I have belief in you, as you know."

Popoloff bowed with a gratified smile, polished his spectacles, and then peering craftily through them, said—

"I have not been idle. Aware of your inclinations, sir,

I have already thought, and have managed to see and come to terms with a servant Kasimir has had a long while in his employ, so that from time to time, in consideration of a judicious disbursement of rubles, I shall be informed of all that transpires in his household. This method of procedure is one which, as you know, I have found effective, with political issues at stake, and in that sense it may prove useful again; his wealth, coupled with his violence of temper, being a possible source of danger, as your Excellency has suggested. If I choose, he can scarcely leave the house now without my knowledge."

"Capital! That is good."

"And," continued Popoloff, with unshaken gravity, "already I possess copies of a correspondence commenced with Count Andrew Dorozynski, who figures on the list of those suspected of treason. Perhaps you will remember that the father, Count Thomas Dorozynski, has twice fallen under his Majesty's displeasure."

"Yes, I think I recollect something of the matter. He made himself conspicuous in the '30 affair."

"He did, sir."

"Had some of his estates confiscated and altogether was a source of great annoyance."

"Quite right, sir."

"Well, you have done marvels, Popoloff, and are wise to keep a watchful eye on such men as this young Dorozynski. What news did these letters contain?"

"Mild expressions of discontent run through them, sir."

"Written by Count Andrew, you say?"

"Yes, Excellency."

"What kind of a person is he? Likely to prove as troublesome as his father, I suppose?"

"I am afraid so, sir. I understand that he possesses the looks and temper of the old Count, who in his day was as handsome as he was proud and rebellious. But he shall be well looked after."

"There is wisdom in that. Is the family a large one?"
"Only Count Andrew and a girl, sir."
"Then there are the less to reckon with. Now don't
forget what I have said, Popoloff. Be mindful of my
instructions. By the way, I can see no one—I want
to be quiet."

Popoloff took the hint and disappeared, serving up for
Madame Hourko's nightly dish of gossip, only a few
choice morsels which he thought he might safely dis-
close.

Helping himself to some more tea, Ivan Nicholaevitch
stretched out his legs and began to think, selecting one or
two remarks of Popoloff's, which pleased him because
they concerned Sara. For example, he chuckled at the
recollection of Popoloff's evident appreciation of her
beauty, and was glad to think that his wits were at work in
support of the increasing intimacy he meditated. She
had been in his mind constantly, but he had not spoken
about her to Popoloff, knowing that the hints he had
thrown out would be remembered by that sagacious individual. Then he began to think how he should act
should she prove obdurate, and, as a guarantee of heading her off in that direction, he contemplated with much
satisfaction the immense strength of his position. With
the power of life and death in his hands, Hernani could
be swept away to Siberia, in spite of his wealth and standing. He would simply be numbered and lost sight of—
that was all; then, with Madame Hourko cajoled into
visiting her beautiful estate in the Ukraine, the coast
would be clear. It would then be easy to see Sara constantly, and to exert what influence he pleased over her
by promising to extricate Hernani from his terrible position. Already the banker had done enough to warrant
his arrest, and, if let alone for the present while events
took shape, in the end was sure to compromise himself
even more deeply. To watch and see him do so would be
best perhaps. Anyway, Sara must not suspect his hand

in whatever might be done. It would be well if she came to him and said, "Help me—I am in distress." Then he might seem magnanimous, in reality doing nothing beyond establishing himself more securely in her favor.

So for the hundredth time Hourko told himself that he was in love, and that he was not the man to be balked; in this cheerful frame of mind betaking himself to bed, and on his way there getting greeted by a cunning question from his little faded wreck of a wife.

"Do you know who attacked the Cossack? People are full of it," she inquired, as she tucked herself up, the light playing upon her sharp features and pale eyes, showing, too, how thin and like wire the remnants of her yellow hair had become.

"What if I do?" he answered grumpily.

"They say he was a Jew," she persisted, noting every change in his expression, every movement he made.

"Do they?"

"Yes; so he may go free, I suppose?"

The General wheeled upon her.

"Why?"

"You favor them, don't you?"

"No."

"Oh! I thought you did; but you needn't be so cross."

"Woman, don't worry me!" he roared. "I have enough on my hands. I have to forward a dispatch to St. Petersburg."

"Aren't you going to ask his Majesty to advise you how to deal with Jews who assault the troops?" she inquired, her eyes sparkling like a ferret's as she curled herself up.

"Damn the Jews and the troops too!" he retorted.

CHAPTER IV.

The violence Hernani had been guilty of in assaulting the Cossack weighed Sara down with anxiety. A tap of the massive knocker, or a peal of the bell, sent a shudder through her. She imagined that the police had arrived at last, empowered to arrest her husband—to carry him off despite her tears and entreaties; and at the thought she was torn with anguish. She did not blame him for his display of anger, but she lamented it as an act of extreme rashness. When all likelihood of the immediate enforcement of such stringent measures had passed, she became a prey to doubts, which were even worse to bear. Her nervousness was pitiable. She was certain that silence on the part of the police meant mischief, that they were employed in getting up a case against him, and were waiting only that they might act with more telling effect. Hernani's temperament even was a source of constant terror to her. She knew him to be fearless, but such a quality, though noble, when united to a quick temper, became a danger in itself.

As a Jew too, the laws he had lived under, the indignities to which he had been subjected, had irritated instead of crushed him. Though he was rich, in fact on account of his riches, he had been mulcted ingeniously and tortured slowly. The battle he had fought had been a hard one, and had rendered him keenly susceptible. So that whenever he was out of her sight the dread lest he should foul the authorities was always hot upon her. She would invariably escort him to the door herself, and with her last kiss would add, "Come back soon, and do be careful for my sake. Remember that the little wife is waiting for you." And the strong man would go away

with the tears in his eyes at this proof of her affection,
and would turn to look at his home wistfully, for he might
not "come back"—who could tell? Poland was such a
strange country and such funny things happened in Warsaw; besides, this was a time in which no man could contain his soul in quiet—least of all a Jew. With the
presage of a great conflagration aglow in the sky, the
gloom and horror of approaching strife cloaking the land
like a pall, none could gauge the closeness of Siberia, and
ruin or death might be very near at hand; for the laws
were severe, the swarming troops eager and vigilant.
Hernani himself was consumed by the bulk of these
thoughts. He knew that his wealth was a danger rather
than a guarantee of security in such days as those he
had come upon. With a wife to consider, had he been
free to choose, his first act would have been to quit the
country, but he was bound up in it, since his rubles were
laid out and at stake. What—abandon his fortune to his
foes by realizing at a frightful loss? Never! It would
be puerile, even cowardly. For although he could scarce
lay his finger on a soul he could trust, being like many
another man in that respect, there were those about him
who looked to him for moral support, took courage from
his energy and dauntless front, and would have been
plunged in despair had he turned his back upon them;
for his travels, knowledge and varied experience, added
to his known substance, made him a popular pillar of
strength. Months back, and seeing what was ahead, he
had seriously contemplated flight, but only for a little
while and because of Sara. Whether wise or foolish,
such an idea had been finally abandoned, leaving him resolved to face and fight whatever might come upon him.
So he worked and watched, getting up just as early and
retiring as late, his conduct being such as could give no
offense to the authorities; political gatherings and demonstrations being cautiously avoided by him.

Now and again he received letters from Dorozynski,

chiefly interesting to him because of the young Count's knowledge of the peasant question, which he shrewdly regarded as the kernel of the insurrectionary movement. "Would they rise? Indeed no." He even went further and said, "Those peasants who have anything to lose will, when the time comes, appear as enemies. But without some help, nothing is possible, so we must look to France, I think. The Emperor's attitude is, I hear, most favorable."

The young Count wrote from his father's estate, situated some twenty miles out of Warsaw, employing a messenger whom he no doubt fancied he could trust, Hernani doing the same, neither of them therefore imagining that there was any danger in the correspondence, and so tumbling into it—Dorozynski, because it kept him in touch with events when not in Warsaw, supplying him too with fresh ideas; Hernani, because of the young Count's frankness, ability, and shrewd common sense.

Between Sara and Hernani the touching God-speed and delight on safely meeting again was a perpetual evidence of the gloom and anxiety both were a prey to.

The incident of Sara's late return and evident distress on the day upon which she had been taken before General Hourko had been almost forgotten by Hernani, when of a sudden it was revived, and a new side of it turned to him, by a man whom he met quite by accident, and who loosed his tongue without thinking. She had been compelled to go to the palace and had, he stated, been detained there. Once upon the subject, Hernani extracted this information without showing how profoundly ignorant he was of the whole affair. Surprised and annoyed as well as doubting, he lost no time in applying dexterous questions to others, receiving much the same story over again. The tale, then, was common property and must be true. Of course, such ideas as these followed upon the discovery. Why had she omitted to tell him—refused to, in fact? What could it mean?

He blundered on with his reasoning, making nothing of it, and as if to provoke him further, later in the day he was informed by a Rabbi—who had been requested to represent his class in the famous Delegation which had been appointed—that General Hourko had himself spoken of and made inquiries about him. There was nothing wonderful or even strange in this, seeing that he was perhaps the most influential Jew in Warsaw, but—he became a little suspicious—was this the beginning of some delicate overtures on the part of the General, and if so, what was his object? Sara was beautiful—in his sight, wondrously so. A few pangs of jealousy were added to his suspicions; and the more he thought the keener they became. All at once he made an enormous mental leap. The Russian Governor had seen her and it had been enough; she had attracted him at once; perhaps the whole affair had been a carefully arranged plot. What more simple than to have noticed her in the town, perhaps shopping, admired her, had her watched, at length seized and conveyed to the palace. Hourko would run no risk by such an act; he would say to himself, "She is only the wife of a Jew; it will not matter— I am safe." It was a horrible thought; but there was a worse one to come. He had never known Sara refuse point-blank to tell him anything before. The terms upon which they had lived had been too happy to admit of secrets, however trifling. And clearly this was more than a small matter. Whatever had induced her to act as she had then? What was he to think? Was it possible that Hourko's rank, added to the splendor he maintained, had dazzled her, so that the attentions he had forced upon her, instead of proving odious, had pleased her? Was she silent because she wished them to be renewed when chance offered? Women are vain, Hernani argued.

Next moment he hated himself for thinking so ill of her. His little wife—impossible! What a fool he was!

She was not like that, and as pure as the driven snow. Love a Russian? What a mistake! Love anyone but himself in fact—he to whom she had surrendered herself! What madness to think such things! Really he would soon be fit for an asylum. His little wife—well! But he went home and said nothing, treasured his doubts as though they were gold, more precious to him even than fine gold or rubies.

Disguising his twinges of jealousy, his cruel and detestable speculations, as closely as he would have guarded the knowledge of some new-found and fabulous mine, the keen eyes of love looked into him and found something amiss.

"What was the matter with him?" Sara inquired. Had anything happened? No, nothing—Nothing! Well, then, they could be jolly together for the evening. No, he had work to do. Come—she could not hear of it. She—Sara—had a right to his evenings—they belonged to her. She was ready to devote herself to him, to sing, to amuse him, to make herself charming; and could any man wish more? This last remark was accompanied by a smile that made Hernani shiver; feeling how she affected him, and thinking how weak any man would be if it pleased her to make him so. She clung about him with her soft, warm touch, full of love, as she often did, but he loosened her hands, put her from him, and went away disturbed and sulky.

Later, when he rejoined her, a little ashamed of himself, horribly miserable, he attempted no explanation, said nothing kind—she hungering all the while—but with consummate coolness remarked that General Marquis Paulucci had been placed at the head of the police. She could have struck him.

"What do I care about Paulucci?" she replied snappishly. Was that all he was thinking about? Had he come there to annoy her?

"But it is a great matter, and the Government is obviously so weak. These concessions, the Delegation, the promise of even more extraordinary favors, is a positive proof. They are driven to it; or they would yield nothing."

Goodness! Was that all he had to say to her? All—and was it not enough? She should be delighted. Sara was thoroughly put out.

"Oh! I am sick of the whole affair!" she exclaimed petulantly. Then she suddenly relented, such a show of temper being foreign to her. She became again affectionate, tender, nestling against him. "Come, dearie, be like yourself," she said; "let us forget these horrid affairs which we cannot control, and with which we are always being bothered. Let us talk of ourselves, of old times; we were not so worried then; and you were so kind—you loved me so."

She had bid for a reply, which she did not get.

"Am I unkind now?" he asked coldly.

"Oh, no; probably we are neither of us quite ourselves. Do you know I begin to long for the spring, real spring weather; not like this, warm and muggy, with the streets full of mud, but fine and sunny. The trees beautifully tinted, and the birds singing in them as though they were just beginning life."

"It will come soon enough," he answered grimly; "a few days will decide all that."

"And will it not be nice? You will take me into the country; we can drive to Villanov, and sit in the shade at the little white Inn, where the birds chatter so in the chestnut trees, and we will have some of those cakes—do you remember? We might even go upon the river when we are tired of the gardens. Ah! how I love it—the cattle browsing in the meadows, and the stream so deep and placid, reflecting everything, the banks, the trees, the sky—how I love it!"

"And yet you are only a little town girl; you have tramped more pavements than fields."

She looked at him, startled and frightened, as though his words had recalled some hideous vision, and her eyes filled with tears.

"Ah! how cruel. The pavements—yes, I was poor, and I had to walk. One often has to do things one hates, and I hated the streets; but—do you want—do you want to remind me how much I owe to you? God knows——"

"Hush!" he said, and he put his hand upon her lips. "I am sorry, and I am not a cur."

She blushed and brightened at the tenderness in his voice; her tears were gone, her face radiant as a beautiful landscape after an April shower. The sun itself, the sun she loved so well, seemed to gild her bright eyes as she said softly, in a hushed voice, as though his instant kindness still rang in her ears, and by no harsh sound would she drive it away—

"Well, then, a day out there with you would be worth anything, and you can leave your business for once. It will be so nice—so nice."

But Hernani could only sigh. This forced gayety, as he thought it, was out of place and jarred upon him. Besides, could he quite believe her? Would it delight her so, or was she acting? Ah! he feared, he doubted. How absurd to talk about Villanov, the gardens, the river, a nice day spent there, when by that time he might have to fight for his life—who could tell?

Before going to bed he said suddenly—

"General Hourko spoke about me to Rabbi Nathan-sohn, so I heard." And watching her face narrowly he became furiously jealous, as he thought he detected a certain uneasiness in her manner.

CHAPTER V.

A little while afterwards Sara received a note from Hourko, signed by Popoloff, requesting her to see him on the ground that it would interest her to hear of, and to discuss, the merits of some benefits he proposed to confer upon the poorer classes of Jews. Perhaps, since she was so deeply interested in their welfare, she would have some useful suggestions to offer; therefore he should be glad if she would call any day about twelve.

Sara's first idea was to treat the request with indifference, doubting the genuineness of it; her next one, to write a brief line, courteously refusing; finally she decided that it would be well to be cautious, if not for her own sake for that of others.

Here was a letter from the Governor of the Kingdom, and the reason of it she well knew. She had influenced him, could influence him, if she set herself to try. Why should she not gain an ascendancy over him that would enable her to make better terms for her down-trodden race? He had proposed it himself; it was for her to manage him, for her to see that the suggestion he had set down bore fruit.

Would it not be selfish, almost criminal, on her part, to neglect such a chance of doing good to a vast body of sorely-tried, hard-working, and deserving people, whose lives she knew so well, and with whom she could sympathize as few could, having actually lived as thousands of them were living? They had no one to put in a word for them, no one who cared whether the ready-made collar about their necks was tight or no, or, if caring, could get it loosened. Perhaps she had some such power in her hands, if she would only exert herself and conquer the

4

repugnance she felt for the task.   Why should she hate
General Hourko so much—shrink from approaching him
as though he were an adder?   He must have his good
qualities, and had shown himself polite and reasonable
enough, though perhaps that was because he had been
affected by her beauty.   But for his one remark about
her, and the expression of his eyes, which was wicked,
she could find no fault with his reception and treatment of
her.   Then came another and a last thought which decided her.   She could remember ridiculing as an impossibility the idea of begging anything of General Hourko.
Already she saw reasons why those views should be modi-
fied.   So sure as she lived, Hernani would put his neck
under the heel of the Government, hating the existing
officialism as he did, writhing under the cruelty and injustice he maintained it had already been guilty of; ready,
despite his coolness and judgment in other matters, to
leap to arms should the least chance of success offer.
She might well look ahead and prepare a chance of escape for him, should failure attend him as she dreaded.
As matters stood, any day he might have to answer for
his furious attack upon the Cossack.   How well then if
she could buoy the course he was taking, since she could
not direct it, and so by her own judicious behavior, find
him, when the storm burst, an anchorage in which he
could lie safe.   What a wife she would thus prove herself.
The reason why he had not already been roughly dealt
with was perhaps due to her influence, for how many
thousands had gone to Siberia for a much lighter offense!

On her own account she must not be nervous; she
could take care of herself well enough, and for the present, certainly, there was nothing to fear.   For the best
possible reasons she must continue to be silent to Hernani, for to take him into her confidence, detesting Hourko as he did, would be to abandon her projects and in-
furiate him, since she would have to speak of the visit

she had already been compelled to make to the palace, which would be summed up by him in one word—insolence. No; she must keep her own counsel and act as seemed best, redoubling her caution to prevent him from discovering what she was about.

There was, however, just this difficulty of which she was unaware: Hernani had met Hourko's messenger by chance, as he was going out; had actually fingered the letter and recognized the official arms upon it; when questioned, too, the man had admitted that it was from General Hourko. Hernani had turned it over and wondered. Should he take it to his wife and ask her the meaning of it? No. He was proud. She had secrets. Very well; she might keep them. What was the use of trying to keep pace with a woman who wished to deceive. So he ground his teeth and suffered it to be delivered to her without comment, feeling the while as though his home were collapsing about him.

When Sara's reply reached the palace the General gave full vent to his satisfaction.

"So the Jewess is coming, Popoloff!" he exclaimed. "Ah! you were right, you were clever. She has swallowed the bait, and now I must be profoundly wise and sympathetic on the question of lightening Jewish burdens. Ha! ha! do you hear?"

Never known to laugh or to be enthusiastic about anything, Popoloff replied with the utmost gravity—

"Is that so, sir?"

"That is so, man. You have read the letter."

"Yes; but now let me tell you something I wanted to speak about, sir. I have not been idle in another direction."

"No; what have you done?"

"Renewed my acquaintance with Kasimir Hernani's lawyer, Hermann Bloch, sir."

"Is Bloch his confidential man?"

"He is, sir."

"Haven't I had some dealings with him? That mort-
gage on the property in Lithuania—you will remember."

"Quite right, your Excellency."

"Ah! I only saw him once, when I signed some papers, but Bloch might be a useful man, I should say.
Fond of rubles, eh, Popoloff?"

"Very, sir, as I have reason to know; he is, besides,
much about Hernani, and in delicate matters it is necessary to have the right tools to hand. Yes, I think he is
worth cultivating. Now, on the matter of the law we
spoke of."

"Ah! How does that stand?"

"Kasimir Hernani can divorce his wife, on the ground
that she is barren, if it should please him to do so, since
she would probably offer no opposition. When you put
the question to me at first, I could not reply, because I
did not know how long they had been married. Now I
only say he can do this. As a rule, divorce without consent is only resorted to by the lower classes of Jews."

"Still it might suit him."

"It might, as you say, your Excellency; of course it
depends upon the nature of his regard for her. Bloch
says that he has often lamented his childless condition,
and is, he assured me, irreconcilable."

"What an ass he must be, though, after all, I suppose
it is natural——"

"To men to long for something they don't possess—a
common failing."

"True."

"When is she to be here, sir? It has escaped me."

"The day after to-morrow. Not in a hurry, eh? But
now, Popoloff, when she comes, take care that I am
not disturbed. These Jewish questions are ticklish, you
understand."

"Perfectly, sir."

"Good; now tell me—what is the outlook? Are the
people less agitated?"

"Perhaps, since the appointment of the Marquis Wielopolski as Chief Minister. But it won't last; he has no following, and is detested, as your Excellency is aware."

"I believe in him, though. He is the most able man in the country. Count Zamoyski hasn't half his brains."

"But he is popular, sir."

"Ah! A great matter."

"The bulk of people assert that the Government is weak; that is one reason for the lull. The instant the notion is fully digested, their importunities will begin, and increase in proportion to the clemency shown them."

"The Government weak? They think that, do they! What d——d impertinence! They shall see in good time. We can eat them up at any moment. And yet there are few visible signs of disturbance."

"I have been told, sir, that a white squall—a storm much dreaded by sailors—scarcely signalizes its approach."

"From which simile I suppose you mean to infer that this Polish madness is ripening beneath smiles?"

"Exactly; the smiles of a villain when meaning to be most deadly."

"I daresay; I incline to agree with you, though you are a bit of an old croaker, Popoloff. Any news from the Ukraine?"

"A letter to-day——"

"Ah! Is it much warmer there just now?"

"Much, sir."

"Of course it is; I reminded Madame Hourko. The cold of this place kills her. A run down there would set her up. You tell her about it." And the General sauntered to a window, while Popoloff went away with a cunning grin of understanding and a folio of papers tucked beneath his arm.

CHAPTER VI.

With the light of the morning upon which Sara was
to see Hourko, came a load as of lead upon her heart.
A sense of approaching calamity, as though an irretrace-
able step were being taken, was blended with a tumult
of doubts which she thought she had set at rest. Was
she acting wisely in going? Would her visit be productive of the good she expected; and was it safe for her
to trust herself inside that great palace, with a man of
whom such stories as she had heard were told? She
distrusted and detested him; then why should she vol-
untarily put herself in his power? To end this mental
conflict which threatened to become interminable, she
asked herself one question: "Am I trying to do right?"
and the answer was an emphatic "Yes." Then what
disturbed her so unnaturally? If on the side of right,
what had she to fear? She was going to sacrifice her
own feelings for the good of others, and in so doing she
should have experienced a sense of restfulness, of quiet
pleasure, as though an angel had crept into her heart
and made its abode there.

Perhaps the anxiety she had felt about Hernani had
upset her. Never had he been so cold, so preoccupied,
seeming to avoid her, even to shrink from seeing her
during the last day or so. That was it, and no wonder,
when through the whole of their married life they had
been so happy together: perfectly so, but for the occasional uprising of the ghost—this question of children.
But his mood would pass, the old days would return;
likely enough some troubles of his own—business worries—were at the root of the matter.

"Patience little wifey," she said to herself over and

over again; "as Riva is fond of reminding me, to be patient is sometimes better than to have great riches." And as the time came to go she put on her hat and warm wraps, Riva Krein waiting upon her and fastening her boots; and when she was ready she breathed more freely and her heart became light again.

Riva Krein was old and peaked and yellow; half the size she had once been, owing to time, poor food, and trouble. But she still possessed the eyes of her youth, dark and piercing; and her hair had retained its color, for, though very thin, it was still black.

Sara had no secrets from Riva, for she had clung to the family in sickness and health, through good and evil repute, until grinding poverty had forced her away for a while. When Sara's fortunate marriage had come about, she had sought her out, and given her a home and wages that the old woman could never have got elsewhere. For Sara was not one to forget faithfulness and kindness. Riva Krein knew that, and her love for her amounted to worship; otherwise she was cunning and a little unscrupulous. Perhaps the world had made her so, for her legs had trembled always under the load she had carried from her cradle.

"Riva," Sara said, last thing, wishing to leave some trace of herself if need be, "I am going to the palace to see General Hourko. It is to do good to people like the Bielois, you understand. And you are to say nothing unless you have cause to be anxious. Mind now, not a word to a soul."

"Very well, my lamb; I will count and think, but will be as silent as a sepulchre. What says the law—'Silence is the fence round wisdom.'"

With a nod and smile of approval, Sara set off, quickening her step in the cool bracing air, and feeling refreshed and invigorated by it. She was anxious to escape observation as much as possible, yet she stopped to give a few kopecs to a little girl whose appearance pleased her, but who made her sigh as she remembered that she had no little baby face of her own to cheer her. It was so strange, since she was so well formed and so robust. But she was not disposed to look sadly upon anything just then; she could do good, and if some things were not as she wished, she had her use in the world. Besides, since she had not been out for days, the scenes so familiar wore a refreshing aspect of newness cheering to her. It was as though she had been ill and was taking her first walk. As she entered the palace her pulse quickened, and it occurred to her how strange it was to be calling upon a man who, in Cracow, but a few years back, might almost have flung her a few kopecs, had he been in a mood for giving alms; and she shuddered as she remembered how weak and faint she had often felt in those days, and how the bleak winds used to pierce her clothing, while the snow and rain had soaked through her boots and chilled her feet. Ah! it was all very strange, strange too and tragic, that the man who had lifted her out of such suffering, who had clothed and fed her so well, should at that instant have his eyes fixed upon her—eyes in which wrath and anguish fought.

Had she glanced back with keen enough vision to recognize who had tracked her, she might have saved herself the bitterest suffering, and the loving heart she owed so much to, an ache like unto death. But she went on without once turning, and when she had disappeared, Hernani, muffled in a great coat and fur cap, came to a standstill in an archway, watching. Occasionally a tear rolled down his cheeks, and he was very pale, but he scarcely moved for a good two hours, after which time she reappeared, passing within a few feet of him as he shrank back from her sight.

CHAPTER VII.

"And what have you been doing with yourself?" Hernani inquired when they met, hours after, his voice ringing true as though no mental conflict had shaken him.

"I—oh! I have been out," answered Sara.

"Yes; well, and who did you see, and what did you buy?"

"I saw scarcely anyone to speak to. Old Bloch came puffing along, looking as fat and red and funny as ever. I always laugh when I look at him."

"Do you—what, Hermann Bloch, the notary?"

"Yes—our Bloch. Don't you think he is odd looking?"

"Perhaps. I have never thought of him but in connection with business. He is very clever."

"So he ought to be."

"Why?"

"Because he is so ugly."

"Well, brains are better than beauty."

"Some men have both." The compliment was apparent, but Hernani let it pass. "I know someone who has big eyes for a pretty face," continued Sara playfully, expecting Hernani to say, "Yes, and that someone has eyes only for you," instead of which he said coldly—

"Wisdom and understanding are better than good looks, and virtue better than the three."

"How dull and grumpy you are," answered Sara, with affected petulance.

"I, my love?"

"Yes, you; and I have been buying something very nice for you—something you have long wanted and that we have often talked about. Now guess."

"I can't; tell me."

"No, you must guess, or I shall keep it a secret until it is made."

Hernani did not answer. How could he be in a mood to chatter? It was wonderful that he was able to pretend as well as he did.

"Oh! And who else do you think I saw besides Bloch?" resumed Sara, anxious to engage him in conversation, so that she might have him to herself for a little while.

"Eh!" stammered Hernani, roused from thoughts which cut him like sharp knives—"what did you say?"

"Why don't you listen to me, dear? Who else do you think I saw?"

"I have no notion."

"The Marquis Wielopolski, dashing along with his mounted guard—alone, haughty, and reserved-looking, as though his resolutions were fixed, and that was enough. How strange for a man to go about surrounded by soldiers in the heart of his own country."

"It is because his own countrymen don't trust him."

"Of course; but why?"

"Why are people distrusted? Really, Sara, how droll to ask me. Because of their conduct, I suppose." And the hateful reflection followed: "Politicians may well be doubted if men doubt their own wives."

"Oh! Well, I saw Wielopolski, and not ten minutes afterward, General Paulucci, whose appointment you raved about."

"Right—I did; but you seem to have encountered quite a throng of notables. General Hourko, now—did you see him?"

Hernani scarcely dared to look at her as he put the question—by which he meant to afford her another chance of confiding in him—and her answer, which was really a ready one, seemed ages in coming.

"I seldom see General Hourko; do you?"

Ah! the hussy; she had circumvented him; walked round him, indeed, without moving a muscle.

"No," he answered snappishly, and rose to leave her.

"Are you going?"

"Yes, I must. You forget that I have work to do—a dozen letters to write yet."

"Kasimir"—his name, spoken by her, made him tremble, so sweet did it sound—"you always make some excuse to avoid me. I have remarked it. You scarcely ever have time to talk to me now. What is amiss?"

"With me?—nothing," he answered gravely. "I am very busy; there are many things to disturb and occupy me just now; as for avoiding you, that is absurd. If you had your hands as full as mine are, such fancies would never enter your head." And as he went away he added to himself, "What impudence to ask me what is amiss! And yet, when she called me Kasimir, I shook! Ah! what a fool I have been to place my happiness in her keeping—what a fool." And, with a face distorted with anger and indescribable sorrow, he shut himself up amongst his papers.

After seeing Sara leave the palace as he had done, he scarcely knew where he had gone, what had become of him, how he had found his way home. Contrary to habit, for he was most abstemious, he dimly remembered entering several restaurants and drinking vodka freely; restaurants where he was known, and yet he could not recollect being addressed or noticed in any way. He wondered how he had conducted himself and whether any change in his manner had been observed. There must have been one, he was sure, for he had wrestled with his wrath and anguish, his feeling of being stricken to the earth, of being deprived of the only affection he prized and which constituted his whole interest in life; finally he had returned to his house with certain resolutions, having said to himself, "If a woman intends to deceive,

she will, in spite of one." It was her intention to deceive.
Very well; he was too proud to extract, compulsorily,
or by diplomacy, what she would not yield him of her
own free will. In short, he would seek no explanation.
Her very intention to deceive him, proved that he would
hear nothing genuine by questioning her. He would
save her the trouble of telling lies; of wheeling round
him by some tricks of the tongue which would leave him
no nearer the truth, though in his own estimation, with
shattered pride and injured dignity. In a haughty
silence he would find the only consolation he could hope
for. If this woman, whom he had delivered from many
trials, and had elevated to the honorable position of wife,
to whom he had devoted himself, bestowing upon her
all he had, his substance and his love ungrudgingly, and
in whom he had confided absolutely—if she could desire
to keep from him such amazing and important news
as two visits, to his certain knowledge, paid to the Governor-General of the Kingdom, she must have reasons
he had better not seek to know, unless he had decided
to part from her. Her race, her religion, her position
as his wife, his known hatred of this exalted Russian, not
to speak of the man's blood and creed, vetoed all intimacy, and increased the enormity of her offense in his
eyes. What had she to do with the Governor—what
could she have to do with him—she a Jewess—unless
her position was a wrong and ignoble one? The battle
he had fought, then, all through his life had been a vain
one. His existence made harder for him than for many
other men, he had withstood the scorching temperature
of the seven-times heated furnace in which he had
been tried—to what end! Only to find himself worst-
ed at last, defeated in matters dearer to him than success in life, than life itself in fact—only to find that after
all he had built everything upon the sand of a woman's
regard. Fool that he had been; and with his knowledge
of life, too, he might have known better. And what was

before him now? How was he to act? In no way
harshly, of course; rather play the mild if torturing
game of watching and waiting, with his heart on fire,
his head racked with the misery it had suddenly become
full of, occasionally suffering with such acuteness that
his mental equilibrium trembled. He must look upon
this woman, with whom all his latter days had been
spent, and with one agonizing wrench tear himself from
her; force himself to recognize that for him she had
ceased to exist. Ah! could a man be more cruelly
dealt with, for in addition to this woe, in itself sufficient
to crush him, there was the terrible, the incalculable
weight of this public calamity, this rebellion hanging
over him. When all men's lives and fortunes were at
stake, to what extent was he likely to be the sufferer?
His religion and his riches made answer. Whichever
side won, in the end he would lose. And at such a crisis
the consolation, the inestimable boon of close companionship with Sara, was denied him. For how could he
make a confidant of a woman whom he could no longer
trust, whom he more than half suspected of dealings
which maddened him to think of? Well, he would sit
down, he would watch and wait, whatever it cost him.
Clearly this was the moment for him to prove his worth
and strength to endure, and let none know what he
endured.

As a Jew, was he not familiar with the sensation of
the world in arms against him? Was he not an Ish-
maelite in this country of his adoption, and a thousand
times (like every Jew who keeps his head above water)
had he not proved himself victorious? But this plague
at his hearth, this canker within—this wife whom he
doted on—great God! It was hard, it was terrible.

In calmer moments he would endeavor to grope for
consolation, and, convincing himself that there was room
for hope, would whisper, "Patience, courage; time will
show, will prove, will even heal."

The hours dragging, Sara, in happy unconsciousness
of the storm she had so innocently raised, went and got
old Riva Krein to sit with her, since she could not come
by her husband, and outside her home had not a friend
in whom she dare fully confide. Glad of such a chance,
Riva, with her skinny hands folded upon her knees, and
her piercing eyes fixed upon the charming face of her
young mistress, sat as though at the feet of an oracle.

Knowing how curious and ignorant she was, and
though a little out of spirits, feeling mischievous, Sara
said—

"Riva, the palace is grand."

"Finer than this, my lamb?"

"Finer than this! This is small. There, the ceilings
are lofty, twice as high, with clouds and angels painted
on them, so beautifully that you would fancy that
heaven had opened and was smiling upon you. Then
there are great grand staircases, and halls and corridors
all of marble; rooms, Riva, with a dozen windows on
one side; the walls hung with paintings of battles and
warriors, or paneled with precious wood, sometimes
draped with tapestry. And there are marvelous gilded
clocks that revolve and chime and send serpents and
soldiers, all in the brightest and richest clothes, hurrying about their duties."

"Ach! And the great Russian—is he ablaze with
jewels, when quiet at home, as you saw him?"

Sara laughed a little. The old woman's lips were
parted, and she was beginning to lean forward, so as not
to lose a word.

"No; but he is big and grand looking. You've seen
him in the street."

"Yes, but my old eyes were too slow. He tore past
so quick. But to think of you, my lamb; your mother
would be proud, that would she. And did he treat you
nobly and honor you? Never woman with your beauty
has been seen by him before."

"Oh! Riva, how foolish you are."

"No, my lamb, no; as I live it is true."

"Nonsense. Yes, he was polite and dignified," she added, thinking how courteous and ceremonious Hourko had been.

"And will good come of your talk with him? Will he be kind and considerate, and help folks to food and work—folk, as you said, like the Biclois—that the Lord —blessed be He!—may make His face to shine upon him?"

"Food and work, Riva? No one could expect that. But I don't know; I talked to him, and he may not grind them so hardly."

"Then it was some good to see him?"

"Perhaps—I am not sure. Riva!"

"Yes, child."

"He loves me."

"He—what—the Russian—the Governor Hourko! Lusts after your beauty, my lamb."

"Hush!"

"No one is near. The master is in his bureau and the doors are shut. Loves you! Yes, as a Russian would love a Jewess. But you must go near him no more. You would tempt an angel. Were I a man and young, I should know no rest without you. What did he say?"

"He said nothing. He looked."

"I know—I know. With eyes like coals aflame—the wicked one. You must go near him no more. Ah! and the master would kill you."

"No one knows but you, Riva."

"It is well so. To serve you, for your own sake and your mother's, I would cut out my tongue. You know that."

"Yes, but listen. I would never see him again were it not for two reasons. First, that I may influence him to ease the burdens of hundreds—thousands, if he pleases; and secondly, you know that we are on the eve of trouble; any moment it may come. Your master is hasty, his blood hot and full of hatred for the oppressor. Already he has transgressed in striking a Cossack, and it may be through me he has been spared. Now I fear for him in the future. Well, should he do wrong —I mean, should he place himself in the power of the authorities, and should Warsaw be given over to fire and sword, as I dread—to have secured the Governor's friendship might mean saving him from indignities and pillage, perhaps death. Do you understand me?"

"Who could fail to? Ah! but you are shrewd, wise and good, as well as beautiful. You're your mother's child. Would that she could see you now! Yet she is best off with our Father Abraham; and she may be near at hand as we speak—who knows? But think— how is his protection to be bought? For, never fear, he will be satisfied with nothing short of ample payment. Gold will be useless. Do you know what he will ask, my lamb? He will require you."

"How dare you say such things!"

"As I live, it is true."

"But I would rather die—a thousand times rather. No—I think I understand him, and can make him useful without risk."

"Don't think it; the knife or the poison were safer than the mood of a man like that. Was there no dread in your heart when alone with him?"

"I suffered horribly; I could have fainted, but I meant well and that strengthened me."

"Ah! the Lord was with you in the midst of the Philistines. But if you will see him, mark me, you will make him mad for you; and as I live, when the strife is upon us and—who knows?—the master away, he will carry you off. There is nothing to protect you. The creatures he can send at dead of night, will raise the cry of 'Open to the police!' The doors will be rent asunder

and you will be lost. Turn aside, now, while there is
time. Your honor gone, would be to him and his flesh,
a victory won. With wine in his head he would boast
of it."

"Hush! It is not good to speak such words. You
may misjudge him. Where is your charity?"

"Dead to him and his race. What of your father?
They killed him—worried him into the grave—ah! and
thousands like him, skilled and law-abiding, only praying to be let live in peace. When you are as old as I
am, and have suffered as much, you will think as I do."
And Riva panted from excess of feeling, her black eyes
glittering, her long bony fingers working nervously, as
though clutching the throats of these foes of her life,
these oppressors of her race.

"Yes, I know—I can understand you; the same fire
burns within me. Do you think I have forgotten my
father's unhappy end? No; but such feelings are best
in bondage at times. I would be as good as I can, and
that too is best. How foolish of me to get excited; there
is no good in it. Ah! now I am better. Then your advice is, don't go near him?"

"You should not see him, my lamb. It is like playing with fire."

"I must give up all hope of helping these poor people,
then?"

"Whatever he has proposed to you, if there is truth
in him, he will fulfill."

"Besides abandoning the idea of being able to count
upon him in an emergency."

"Count on the Lord."

"Oh, yes; but we must help ourselves, Riva."

"I think it is a trick on his part," Riva answered,
ignoring the remark; "he wanted to have you to himself, to influence you."

"What!" exclaimed Sara passionately—"you think he
will do nothing for all these starving people, our own

5

kindred? And after writing to me as he did? You say
he wished to talk with me, to fill my head with hopeless
ideas, that time and opportunity might be gained for
his own base ends! Oh! you are wrong; it cannot be
so. A man in his position would not stoop to such
actions. If I thought it——"

"You need think nothing else. I feel sure of it. You
have stirred him, and that is all. Such a man as the
Governor is said to be, passionate and cunning as a
fox."

"Well, I will consider."

"Do, my lamb, and you will find me right. The
blessed Book says, 'The best teacher is time;' now I am
old and I may have gained a little wisdom."

"You're a good soul, if ever there was one. Mind, not
a word to anyone, Riva. When I act, it will be with
caution."

Riva nodded. She would have liked to have heard
more about the wonders and splendor of the palace, but
that would all come, and Sara had talked as much as she
cared to just then; besides, this was astounding news
about the Governor Hourko. It might bring evil too.
Bewildered and excited, she hobbled away to turn it all
over in her own way, and Sara, stepping from the room
in which they had been talking, seated herself under the
lofty glass dome, beneath which clustered the graceful
foliage of the bamboo, reminding one of the much prized
feathers of the ostrich; tree ferns of tender green with
serrated fronds, strilligias, philodendrons, delicate spikes
of orchid bloom, rare and exquisitely varied in hue,
amidst which, as though struggling for the mastery, the
bright scarlet blossom of the pomegranate and paler
oleander appeared; and in this truly sylvan light, half
religious and uncertain, but wholly soothing, amidst
the rhythmic cadence of the falling water and the mystic
shadows of those great silent plants, Sara was disposed
to think. It was the hour Hernani had often chosen for

joining her. Drawn from a handsome samovar, he would drink delicious yellow tea, there or in the garden, and they would talk over it of all that concerned them; but now there was no sign of him, and she began to call to mind the changes that she had observed in his conduct of late, speculating upon their cause. The greatness of her love for him enabled her to see such alterations with strange clearness of vision, and it was cruel of him, she considered, to make her feel gloomy and sad without any reason. What had she done that her mental condition should become overcast, through this unaccountable turn in his behavior? Why should he shut himself up amongst his papers with such persistency, by so doing breaking down long-cherished habits? He was rich enough without such hard work, without work at all in fact.

Was this another proof that his love for her was cooling? Ah! if only a child had been given them, what a tie it would have been. She need have had no fears then. So many of their acquaintances had ample families, and doted on their children, simply living for them, in so doing only exhibiting a feature, marked, amongst those of their persuasion. Such spectacles of marital bliss were always more or less painful to her. Was the sight of them, and the longing thus nourished, beginning to wear out his regard, which had once been all she could have wished for? She knew that this trait, this capacity for loving children, hereditary to so large an extent, was in Hernani's case even more strongly developed than was usual, amounting almost to a mania. While she was his wife, it seemed as though this keen desire must continue unsatisfied, his life remain uncrowned with happiness, for that happiness was just what her existence denied him. She had grown to magnify all that tended to tell strongly against her, and when in her worst spirits could see nothing before her but loss of influence, in the end of his love. Her head was con-

stantly full of the belief that her condition was fast becoming a pitiable one; and what could she do, poor
woman, but exert herself in all directions, and when
tired, again pity herself? If Hernani was not pleased
with her, it was through no fault of her own, for the
creed of her whole married life had been that to lose
him would be to lose the desire to live. To die would be
better than to linger on alone. She knew that he had
become part of her being, and she never attempted to
shirk the knowledge. He was her all, and it was all or
nothing with her.

So there she sat and cogitated, looking so charming
as the ideas flashed through her mind, that could she
have seen herself with the eyes of others, she would no
longer have dreaded that her power to captivate and
retain was waning; though the spectacle of Hernani,
alone in his study, would have done little to reassure
her.

For the moment his mental distress had assumed the
proportions of outward calmness. He was simply smoking and eating himself up with silent fits of smothered
anger and despair; yet had she approached him suddenly, he would have wreathed his face in smiles, accepted her caresses, allowed her in fact to consider herself happy, if she chose. At times he thought himself
cruel for practicing this deception, for letting her imagine—as he believed she did—that between them all was
as it had been. He had a mind to confront her, insist
upon being told the truth, and by such means cover her
with the confusion she merited. Yet he always shrank
from such a step. When doubts of her guilt assailed
him, as happened constantly, he swept them aside by recalling every particle of the evidence against her, which,
thanks to his jealousy and suspicion, appeared to be
utterly damning. If he, lulled by his senses of security,
had discovered quite by chance that she had visited
Hourko twice, and had received a letter from him in

addition, how often had she really seen him, and how
many unintercepted notes of his had reached her? It
would certainly be foolish of him to imagine that all that
had happened was known to him. He had been so busy,
so close a prisoner to his work, that Hourko might have
spent hours in the very house, and he would have been
none the wiser. No, no; there was more in it than he
had courage to lay bare, and further proof to that effect
would be forthcoming in a little while. There would be
no need for him to do more than wait. It had occurred
to him to cross-examine Riva Krein, who, as he well
knew, enjoyed Sara's entire confidence; but Riva was
devoted to her, not to him, and would sooner be hewn
in pieces than say a word against her. If his suspicions
were just, Riva would be mute, and if groundless he
would have placed himself in a false position, and cruelly
wronged the only being he loved in the world. But
though thus harassed and perplexed, with all these ideas
and suspicions clashing in his mind, he adhered rigidly
to the course he had first decided upon, the result being
that in a little while the dire calamity which had befallen
him seemed to have had the effect of nerving, even
steadying him. He succeeded in resuming to exactitude
his methodical existence, compassing the routine of the
day by sheer force of will. With clenched teeth he appeared to begin life again—setting his face against any
distractions, however trifling; toiling as though his existence depended upon his efforts; turning neither right
nor left and parrying all Sara's strictures upon his conduct with a set smile, almost a set phrase—"Ah! rubbish; you don't understand. Business absorbs me; I
must attend to my work. Any day the police may step
up and close the doors of my counting-house; and what
could I do? Is there any justice here?" And the large
sums of money he made by the extra strain he put upon
himself, he said nothing about, experiencing a sort of
melancholy pleasure in being more generous and char-

itable than ever, relieving every genuine case of destitu-
tion discoverable, and saying to himself, sometimes with
tears in his eyes, "Perhaps if I am good, good will come
to me." And the tears would be brushed away and he
would work harder.

Experiencing intense relief from this heroic effort to
forget himself, he took up the threads of two gigantic
schemes, long talked of, and to some extent developed,
but laid aside by reason of the threatening outlook and
the pressure, at the time, of other affairs. One was the
establishment of an ingenious system of banking upon
a colossal scale, the other the deepening and widening
of the Vistula, so as to admit of swift and specially-con-
structed steamers plying between Warsaw and Dantzic;
the gain, to be the development of trade to an enormous
extent, by the closer connection of those two important
places. Of course neither of these great ventures could
be actually floated until the political atmosphere had
cleared, but Hernani recognized that much might be
done toward putting them in trim, to begin when the
right moment should have arrived. Attaching great importance to Hermann Bloch's opinion on both these
huge undertakings, he had consulted him some time
back, awakened his interest and obtained his unqualified
approval. The shrewd notary, in whose abilities Hernani had such faith, expressed himself with confidence.
Large sums would be needed for the completion of such
great schemes, but Hernani was a power, and could
command the minds and purses of others as rich and
energetic as himself. There need be no doubt of the
ultimate success in both instances, should he really take
them in hand. And on the strength of such advice,
backed by his own unerring judgment, Hernani had
labored, so that on handling the reins again he found
much of the work already cut and dried. Appreciating
Bloch to the full, he sought his advice more than ever,
and at the end of a long discussion one morning, in

which an unusually confidential vein had been struck, they ended by drinking some vodka together in one of the smaller reception rooms, the door of which, abutting on the central hall, was like the rest, protected from draught by the folds of a heavy curtain. Smacking his lips in approval of the delicate flavor of the fine old Polish vodka to which he was being treated, Bloch observed that if he were of an envious temperament he should certainly covet Hernani's good fortune.

"And you can't wonder at it, can you?" he added. "You are the possessor of everything a man can wish for."

"Appearances are sometimes deceptive," replied Hernani, refilling the glasses as he spoke.

"Oh, come, now—how deceptive? You don't mean to tell me that there is anything of the kind about you and your surroundings?" insisted Bloch, his keen eyes playing upon Hernani from out a million puckers and wrinkles; for he was getting on in years, as he was constantly reminding people, and his hair, though so coarse and short that it stood on end, was almost white.

"Much," answered Hernani with some solemnity. Bloch pricked up his ears. Evidently Hernani was not jesting as he had thought on the instant.

On the other side of the curtain, in the hall, beneath the great dome, Sara was at work amongst the flowers, tending and watering them. It was a delightful self-imposed task, which she undertook at odd hours each day. At the moment she was quietly absorbed in cutting off a large dead strilligia leaf, being at the same time careful not to injure a choice spike of orchid bloom.

His reflections puzzling him, after rather a lengthy pause, Bloch could only say, naturally enough—

"Nonsense, my dear friend. You imagine things. All Warsaw envies you. Do you hear?"

"Why?"

"Well, to begin with, you are rich."

"And again?"

"You are respected and admired."

"Is that so?"

"Yes, and deservedly so."

"Possibly."

"No, without doubt."

"And what else?"

"You are still in the prime of life; you have a splendid constitution, and you are clever—better say a genius—financially speaking."

"And is all that worth envying me for, admitting your statements to be true?"

"All that? Well, how absurd! Why, to think of it makes one's mouth water. Here have I been laboring all my life, without any of your mental and physical advantages, and having arrived at the end of my tether pretty well, I find myself with only a competency in addition to the most modest position. And then you grumble. Really, something will happen to you if you are so wicked. What would you have? Do you aim at becoming the Governor-General, or what?"

"I aim at being happy," answered Hernani, in a voice so solemn that Bloch was not only startled, but convinced that something really was wrong. His curiosity was excited. An admission of weakness from the great man would be well worth listening to. Changing his tone of unbelief and banter for a more sympathetic one, he replied—

"I am very sorry to hear you speak so sadly. Of course, to be happy is the legitimate aim of everyone."

"Exactly, and you for instance have succeeded?"

"I, my dear sir? By no means. Practically speaking, I question if happiness is attainable. Owing to the strange molding of our minds, most of us have to content ourselves with the counterfeit, which in the long run we are thankful enough to accept. Plenty of people haven't even that offered to them. Take the case of myself, since you have alluded to me. Beginning in poverty, no sooner had I made a sum which far surpassed my first desires, than I became again dissatisfied; no sooner had I acquired a small house than I longed for a large one—a short, stout, dark-haired wife, than I was cursed with the desire for a tall slim one with flaxen locks, and so on, ad infinitum. Very well; now I have learned that I cannot get my flaxen-haired damsel, or the money, or the house—that, in fact, I shall never get any of these things I had set my heart on. The sensation was intolerable at first; the more firmly it laid hands on me, the more I writhed and rebelled; gradually, however, I grew tired, I became passive, I was broken in, and so with the wisdom I have bought so dearly I cheerfully accept the inevitable. It is only when all possibility of alteration has fled, that we settle down to the counterfeit of happiness—contentment."

"A nice compliment to someone who shall be nameless, eh?" interrupted Hernani, smiling in spite of himself.

"My wife? Well, if you put it that way, it looks ugly; but—what was I going to say? I have it. You have been put through no such mill as I have described. You——"

"How do you know?"

"I am sure of it. You are one of the favored few—the man in the million. Your ambitions have been satisfied—to a very great extent, I take it—and, to crown your existence, you possess a wife whom all men must agree in calling beautiful and accomplished."

"Beauty and accomplishments are well in their place, but a wife must have other virtues."

"Of course, of course."

"Or she may put to dangerous use her wit and good looks."

"Precisely. But look here—it's all very fine—any day

you may wish yourself back in your old shoes, though they seem to pinch a bit now."

"You hint at the approaching struggle. Ah! I have little doubt of that. But mind, I am not unthankful now."

"It seems to me—shall I say it?—that you are inclined to be."

"That is because you don't quite understand me. You must remember this, Bloch—as I daresay I have said to you before—I have no children."

"Ah! That is a trial indeed. I forgot that. I don't know what I should do without my little ones. I live my young days over again in them. Yes, my friend, I can sympathize with you."

"Thanks—I know that. Now, perhaps, no man ever longed for them more than I have done, and that longing I find impossible to destroy—difficult even to control. As a father, you may be able to understand me thoroughly."

"I can."

"I wanted to have my own flesh and blood growing up about me, learning from me, comforting me; inheriting my wealth, as well as my name—my own flesh and blood, of whom I could be proud, in whose triumphs I could triumph—and on whom I could rely—if need be—to do battle against the Philistines"—lowering his voice at the last words, then continuing abruptly, with growing excitement: "No; men may envy me what looks to them like good fortune, but I tell you they would not care to be saddled with my griefs."

"Come, come—you are never despondent. It isn't a bit like you. If you give way, what am I to expect next?"

"I am not despondent, I only face facts, and I never give way. It is not my nature. I endure," answered Hernani proudly, and they continued to talk in this strain, Bloch waxing sympathetic, Hernani perceptibly affected by the kindliness, until at length, as he spoke, his lips quivered beneath his long dark moustache and his voice occasionally shook. Suddenly his pent-up feelings got the better of him, and with a gesture of desperation, and passion he exclaimed—

"Look here, Bloch—listen to me. Any day I may have to divorce my wife. Divorce her—do you hear? It has come to that."

Astonished beyond measure, Bloch leaped to his feet, in doing so, knocking over the vodka and glasses with a crash, the noise he made drowning another and more startling one.

Riva Krein had been buzzing about her young mistress as usual, and had been near enough to clasp her in her arms as she was about to measure her length amongst the ferns and flowers. Then, with the tenderness of a mother, she supported Sara's trembling form, getting her away so that the two men remained undisturbed.

The vodka being set in its place again, Hernani continued—

"You are surprised; well, perhaps now you will agree with me that appearances are deceptive?" His burst of feeling had spent itself; he was cooler than Bloch, cynically so, as he added, "You are my solicitor, to whom I have a right to speak. And you won't envy me any longer, eh? Would others, do you think, if they knew?"

"Is it possible?" gasped Bloch, his face like a peony, his little eyes gleaming, his white hair really bristling, while he found it necessary to mop his forehead with his handkerchief.

"It is."

"What—give her gett?"*

---

*Writing of divorcement.

"Yes"—and then more solemnly, "give her gett. But it is not yet done."

"You—the model husband and wife!"

"Alas!"

"Idolizing each other, as we thought."

"Well, yes, but this becomes too painful. Let us say no more. I was carried away by my feelings or I should not have spoken."

"I understand, my dear fellow. But, as you say, it is not yet done. There is hope. It will not come to that. Courage, my friend—it will not come to that."

"May the Lord grant it," replied Hernani in a whisper. And old Hermann Bloch bent his white head as though in prayer, the two men grasping each other's hands amidst a profound silence.

"I will come and see you again soon," Bloch murmured as he went away, and Hernani merely nodded.

CHAPTER VIII.

Riva Krein had induced Sara to lie down on her bed, where she tended her as though she had been her own child; loosening her dress, applying various restoratives, and chafing the cold soft hands with infinite gentleness and affection. When she had done all she could think of, and her oft-repeated "Come, my lamb—look up and take heart. Tell your own Riva what ails you," had only been answered by sobs, she thought it time for her to cry, so tears began to disfigure her faded cheeks, descending in hot drops upon her red and bony fingers. Sara's distress wrung her heart. She had never seen her weep since the old days in Cracow, and the sight carried her mind back there, to the home that had been little better than a hovel, but where they had all been together; understanding each other, sharing the suffering and living in harmony, though they had been so miserably poor. Again she could see Sara's father, the old doctor, with his shriveled, bloodless features, rounded shoulders and poor, hollow chest, attired in his threadbare caftan; she could hear him, amidst the wheezing and coughing, explaining how his ideas and discoveries would one day make them rich. It was all certain—a question only of time. And he had been so kind and gentle and good, though he could never make a penny scarcely; and now he was under the sod with his knowledge and his unrealized hopes, poor broken life that it had been.

Sara's mother, too, was at rest, feeling no longer the snow and the rain, and the frightful anxiety. But she and Sara—they were still left to fight for a little while, and trouble had found them out again. And it

will have enemies if he does this thing. And the woman
—who is she that he has in his eye?"

"The woman!" gasped Sara.

"Yes, the woman, for there must be one if he thinks
such ill."

"Yes—oh! horrible—I had not thought——"

"Ah! but this will nerve you; this will turn your heart
to steel." And Riva's black eyes flashed fire. This is
no time for sore eyes. Dry them, or he will ask to know
what is amiss."

Sara started up, ablaze with wounded pride.

"He shall never know, though I die for it. He has
worked to deceive me—talks of me behind my back.
He shall see. I will begin from now. What is the time?
In a few minutes I must go down to him—we must
meet. Riva, do my hair—quick, and give me that
sponge. He shall never know."

Twenty minutes later and they were together. Nervous and sensitive to a degree, trembling from the shock
received, she was horribly afraid lest he should notice
some signs of the grief she had so hastily attempted to
obliterate. Her eyes and cheeks were hot and sore; she
felt ill—not up to her part in any way; and he who knew
her so well could scarcely fail to discover that all was not
right with her. In momentary dread of this, she took
care to be ready with an ingenious explanation which
would have disarmed all further inquiries, had he made
them. Surprised and relieved to find that she provoked
no criticism, was not even looked at pointedly, and that
he ate and drank with a good appetite and an unruffled
exterior, after a little while she forgot herself in her contemplation of him.

His perfect composure gave her courage; she became even interested in watching him and receiving his
customary delicate attentions, offered as though nothing
had occurred to disturb him. She knew one thing—he
could not feel as he looked; the tones in which he had

thundered "Any day I may have to divorce my wife" decided that. Yet here he was, having made use of expressions which were fatal to her happiness, and must
affect his own—calm and apparently in full enjoyment
of the luxury surrounding him. The sight of such composure gradually enraged as well as frightened her. If
he could be so calm, it was a sufficient indication that
she had lost the game already. He would not spare her.
All the same, she became furious—such insolence—she
could have struck him, as he commenced to chat glibly
on a variety of topics.

At length, itching to make a plunge—to have her say,
to convince herself that she was no brow-beaten woman,
given over to listening and silence, she demanded daringly—

"Tell me about Bloch; what had he to say for himself?"

"Bloch?" he answered unhesitatingly. "Oh! he talked
just as usual."

As usual? Then they were in the habit of discussing
her. What impudence!

"But was he clever as you say he is? Did he interest
you—had he any news to tell?"

"Bloch is always clever. To-day only in a business
way, because I made him stick to business. As for
news, I don't think he had heard anything fresh. The
suppression of the Agricultural Society has aroused his
indignation as much as mine. He shares my belief that
it will precipitate matters, stir up the worst possible feeling against the Government. This immense demonstra-
tion denouncing the act, and covering the closed doors
and windows of the building with flowers, convinces me
that I am right."

"But has all this happened?" inquired Sara, feeling
compelled to say something; "shut up here, I seem to
be ignorant of what is going on."

6

"Yes; but I spoke of it only yesterday. Vast crowds are now collecting before the palace."

A grim expression crossed Hernani's face as he alluded to General Hourko's official residence, but it fled as he added—

"In order to show that they resent this fresh step on the part of the Government as another national wrong, and to fully estimate the importance of the action the authorities have taken, you must bear in mind that the most powerful of the nobles and proprietors were members, and that in consequence the people looked upon the society as an institution through which, as through a mouth-piece, they could make themselves heard. However, it has ceased to be, and another act has been committed and added to the list of those for which a reckoning will be demanded."

"Was that what you were discussing with Bloch?" inquired Sara, as though the question barely interested her.

"In part," Hernani answered, unflinchingly meeting her gaze, and then, with a sense of pride in his own ability—outraged pride, since she no longer valued him sufficiently—he entered into an elaborate description of his two great schemes, about which he had never spoken to her before.

"You see," he went on, "this business I am conducting here, is not large enough to absorb anything like my whole attention, so that I shall have plenty of time to devote to the operations I have described."

"Yet it is the largest business of the kind in Warsaw." exclaimed Sara, becoming interested in spite of herself.

"Unquestionably."

"Then what need have you to tax your strength further by increasing your responsibilities? Is it wise?"

"I think so. You see, we are living upon a mine, the time fuse of which is already lighted. The explosion may occur at any moment, and I want to forget such an unpleasant fact, since I am powerless to avert the catastrophe. Work is the only remedy for forgetting one's self and one's troubles. Every day I grow more restless, more ambitious; stronger even it seems to me; though the strength may be due to the increasing excitement to which I am a prey. I am already rich, I have the desire to become great; not only by reason of the millions of rubles known to be at my command, as at present, but, with that power at my back, by launching enterprises of a magnitude the world must acknowledge and I myself be proud of.

"As Bloch said to-day, I am in my prime—the possessor of a grand constitution. What I shall do with it remains to be seen. This is the country of my adoption, and in my own way I love it; moreover, the nature of my ambition is summed up in two words—universal benefactor. If I could set in motion this system of banking, which I am confident must be a success if launched and conducted as I propose, I should be entitled to such an epitaph at least. They might thank me then; it would cost nothing. Bah! but what care I for what is said? The best preacher is the heart. I want to feel that I have done something worth doing. Then it will be all right. It will be well with me. And I have not even taken into account my scheme for the development of the Vistula. By means of that, don't you see how the cost of bringing goods—all imported stuffs—into the country would be cheapened, and that thus, by one magnificent stroke, the importance and financial prosperity of this, the capital of Poland, would be secured. A direct and thoroughly serviceable waterway connecting us with the ancient and wealthy port of Dantzic—that's what is wanted. There are boats you would say now; but what sort of boats? If you want to make a place great, let the sea in."

"But you can do nothing in the face of disturbances

such as are in progress and to be expected," insisted
Sara, now absorbed in interest and admiration of him.

"With the country bristling with troops and the people ready to leap to arms, I can take no active steps—
that is so—it would be madness, but I can make preparations; I can go into and arrange matters, so that when
the time is ripe there will be no delay. If we would reap,
we must sow. Ah! if I were only living in a country
where there were none of these accursed upheavals,
what headway I should make, how I should progress
by leaps and bounds!"

"But you have done so," she exclaimed enthusiastically.

"What I have done is nothing to what I will do," he
answered proudly.

Though the strong personality of the man, the
strength of old associations, the toughness and durabil-
ity of old ties, had caused her to enter into and interest
herself in this recital of his bold projects, forgetting herself when she could, the cuts and thrusts of his words
were all the sharper for the hold he had over her. Every
hope she possessed was left buried beneath what he had
said. He was to be greater than ever, but amidst his
triumphs there was to be no place for her; she was to
be left behind. He had done with her, as he had done
with the past. And he was doubtless getting everything
in readiness to put her from him, with the same patience
and method that he was employing in the steady development of his vast projects. In a loud, determined voice,
and no doubt with flashing eyes and quivering lips, she
herself had heard him say so; very well—he had never
given her cause to doubt his word. So to her it seemed
as though her doom was fixed, as unalterably as the fact
that she must die. She could have shrieked in her agony
as this idea forced itself upon her.

With his chin resting upon his clenched fists, his eyes
regarding space, Hernani was indulging in thoughts of

a very different kind. Mixed feelings of despair, rage, and jealousy had impelled him to speak of himself. He fully intended to attempt all he had said, but he meant to lash her with the information. He was not exactly a ninny, and just then he took a savage pleasure in letting her know it. He dilated upon the number of successful undertakings in which he had been engaged of late. Everything touched by him had turned to gold. His good luck was marvelous; even his dreams had been surpassed. If he told her all, she would scarcely credit him. Channels long closed had opened up again, and to an extent there had been no reason to look for. In short, money had simply poured into his coffers. She had thought he was working hard—ah! but it had been worth it. As a proof: if he had burnt the midnight oil, amongst a number of other charities, he had been enabled to forward five thousand rubles to the society in Cracow, for the aid of their poorer co-religionists. Now was she pleased? And having fired this last shot, made this last crushing allusion—as she understood it —to the straitened circumstances in which he had found and from which he had been good enough to extricate her, he left her; and not a moment too soon, for had he stayed to witness the effect of his remarks, her defensive armor would have failed her, and her tears have flowed.

As it was, he returned to his bureau as usual, and she went sobbing to her room, where old Riva soon found her out.

Sara was only like other women; she was being cruelly treated—kicked, in her opinion—yet she loved all the more.

It was scarcely possible for her to realize fully what had happened; whenever she seemed to, in spite of her efforts to remain calm and to think, she could only weep afresh. To decide upon her future conduct in the condition in which she thus found herself, was altogether

out of the question. Beyond the already fixed resolution that Hernani must know nothing of her feelings
and sufferings, she had not had time to go. With staring, vacant eyes, she lay full length, her ideas flowing
slowly as though she were half stunned, and through the
mists of weakness could neither think nor see with clearness. Growing stronger, she became conscious of
where she was, and that she was looking about her as
one looks upon things one has got to leave. There
were curious turns and twists on the carved ceilings,
familiar marks, the pattern of the wall paper, counted
and studied until she had felt dazed and had had to close
her eyes once when she had been ill; also the position
and character of the different articles of furniture his
taste had chosen and placed there. For this had been
one of his first ideas, delicate, and a delicious proof of his
affection; everything in her own chamber, everything
she wore, as near as could be, must be of his choosing.
She was his from head to foot; everything around and
touching her must be his also; then the delightful sense
of possession was complete. Exquisite and costly trifles
lay thick about her. One by one he had given them to
her, discovering them by degrees, paying fabulous sums
for them as gems of their kind, and each one had its little history, treasured and complete, and was indescriba-
bly sweet and priceless to her. What would become of
all these dear toys? Who would dust and polish, finger
and delight in them, as she had done? Assuredly they
must all be left behind, said farewell to, for when driven
out, when told that he no longer had use for her, she
would go, as she had come, with nothing. She would
put on a simple black dress, and not a ruble, not a ring,
would she take with her, but out into the world she would
go, as poor as she had been when he had asked her to be
his, leaving no trace, being to his future life only a recollection. Well for her now had her father been alive—
well for her, but not for him; and at this thought she al-

most broke down afresh. However, if she had no one to go to, no one who would stretch out a hand to help her, if there was not one corner in the great cold world where she would have the right to rest, perhaps death would seek her the sooner. There was always dying room to be found. As for Hernani, he would do what he had said. Clever and vigorous, patient and persevering, he would climb to the height he had foretold. He would meet with the recognition his abilities merited, he would be sought after, honored and admired, far more than he had ever been, in spite of being a Jew. A Jew —one of the chosen of God. Would the Gentiles have possessed their crucified Savior but for a Jew, or some other chosen instrument? Should they be reviled and maltreated then? Could logic propose and religion support such conduct? Surely not. But even as a Jew, with all the odds against him, Hernani would work as he willed, though she might not be near to watch or hear of him—might never know, in fact. Ah! someone—someone—oh! maddening thought, someone else, another woman would be about him, would take her place, the place that she lived but to fill. This being, this creature, would look into his eyes, feel his touch, hear his voice, council him and share his triumphs in place of her. Every fiber, every nerve, tingled and rebelled at a prospect endurable only had she loved less—just only—had she been false to her vows. Her cup of bitterness was full, full to overflowing.

"Yes, he will put me from him," she moaned, "because I have borne him no children. It is the law, as Riva says, and he will have it of me."

And downstairs, Hernani sat and smoked and thought. He had signed some letters and cheques, and then had issued orders to his people not to disturb him, the afternoon being still young.

Though in a sense irritated at his own weakness, he felt a little easier since he had told Bloch, and was drowsy, having fed well and taken wine. From sheer weariness and familiarity with the subject, he was beginning to think that divorce was really the only way out of his difficulties. He had been just and would be so, but between a woman beautiful as Sara, and a man like Hourko, there could be but one kind of intimacy, and the existence of that—such an accursed stain upon his honor—could be remedied in but one way. When the time came, he must steel his heart to old memories, the feelings that were knit in old days; he must be blind to Sara's beauty, he must forget what her kisses were like, since they were not for him alone; and though he could never love again, as he had loved, and God help him, did love, someone else must fill the place she must quit —someone who, perhaps, might prove bearable, when the children he had dreamt of came and dwelt in the heart that would be empty and waiting for them. Perhaps he might live through it all, endure, and in the end replacing the passion he had for Sara, a nobler, calmer, and less selfish joy might spring up, enabling him to die at least in peace. And so, thinking these things, he slept for a few minutes, yet lightly as a watch-dog does, being feverish and overwrought. Roused suddenly, and as soon fully awake, the dropping crackle of musketry rang in his ears.

Sara heard it too, and on the alert, as he was, heard him quit the house, saw him cross the square in haste, and followed as swiftly as the delay in putting on a cloak would permit. There was no need to doubt which way to go. The detonations again reverberated sharp and harsh above the dull sullen roar of the people in anger and in their thousands. Hernani had disappeared, and her feet flew over the rough stones and pavements as she pictured him in peril, exposing himself needlessly, courting danger even. Ah! if it could but be her lot to save him, rescue him, at risk of her own life, he might think of her with kindliness, even forgive her for a failing that was not her fault.

Many a time, in years gone by, well-wishers had said to her, "May the Lord bless you with children," but such expressions of good-will had, in time, become rare, and then ceased altogether. It was better so, perhaps they thought; silence saved breath, and, though significant, could give no offense. And added to these generous desires for her, had been her own prayers, and they too had remained unanswered. Well, would he forgive her if he owed his life to her? Fortune might favor her, the chance might come—who could say? It seemed to her that she could never again tell him of her devotion in words, but it was open to her to prove it in acts. All her spleen, her sense of wrongs, the great sorrow that had just come to her, vanished before these generous impulses, this inextinguishable love of hers, as chaff before the wind. On and on she sped, unconscious of fatigue, her little feet keeping pace with her thoughts, until at length she burst upon a scene that, she was never likely to forget.

There lay the cold and cheerless façade of the Imperial Governor's palace, against the gloomy walls of which a sotnia of Cossacks had backed their lean mounts, so as to give place to long lines of infantrymen, who in their mud-colored uniforms were again preparing to fire upon the vast concourse of people, who, standing and kneeling without arms, exhorted each other to remain firm; mothers, fathers, and children, clasping each other's hands, and with eyes cast heavenward wailing forth their national hymn or prayer for liberty. There was no sign of wavering, no thought of it, and at sight of their help-lessness and courage, the stones might have shed tears, the most heartless have admired, pitied, and shown mercy. Attracted by the dread sounds, ignorant of what fear was, new-comers, flushed and breathless, wedged themselves into the already compact mass of defenseless beings, while overhead, that wondrous and silent witness, the sun, in saffron streaks, had struggled through a dingy shroud of flying vapor, coloring the savage picture with that peculiar and beautiful hue which the great Dutch painters loved so well to copy. Hourko and his aides-de-camp, decorated, brilliant; the stern, meanly-clad infantrymen, like great children, rigid, expression-less, obeying; the motionless Cossacks, grim and cruel as the whips they held in readiness; the crowd of all sizes, castes, and conditions, young and old, poorly and well clad, comely and plain, menacing and despairing,— were all illumined by this delicate, clear-cutting light, to which the tall, dark, encircling buildings lent a solemn almost weird effect.

With a half-suppressed cry of joy Sara descried Her-nani, and with an exclamation of horror he saw and forced his way towards her. Sara—his wife, exposed to the Russian rifle fire! At that instant he understood how much he loved her.

"God of Israel, you here!" he exclaimed, when at length he had his hands upon her shoulders, his body between her and harm.

"And you?" she inquired, as calm now that she had found him, as though they had met at a *bataille des fleurs.* She had come there to be near at hand, to give her life for his, if necessary; she might have arrived to buy some bon-bons or a few bunches of violets. His an-swering words died upon his tongue, as a stern command produced a clicking of rifle locks, then a withering vol-ley. Into the vault of heaven, away amidst the swift drifting scud, rolled the groans of the wounded and dy-ing, the sobs of the bereaved, the shouts and execra-tions of the thinned and exasperated mob, while amidst the infernal din, like mere machines, the second rank stepped forward to collect the dead and maimed, who were to be seen plainly enough, after the smoke had cleared away, pallid, bloodstained, and leaden-looking past rough human aid. Sara, in swift, agonized glances cast over and between the bowed and kneeling forms, saw enough of all this to make her turn away sick and dizzy. Boiling with anger and hatred of the act, and in despair because of the risk she ran, Hernani caught her in his arms and strove by sheer strength to bear her clear of the throng. It was a useless attempt, one that the people were in no mood for; they would stay where they were, die where they were, no one should go, as their clasped hands testified. Summoned to disperse— why should they? They had a right to make their griev- ances known, a right beneath God's sky, and in the face of day to pray and sing for the recovery of their lost liberty. And again came the rattle of arms, the brief, sharp orders, the echoing volleys, the groans and shrieks and curses, finally the scream of Sara, as a huge Pole with a fur cap fell doubled up over those about him, be- spattering them with blood. Hernani was as tall as this man, was her first thought. He would be shot too. In an agony of fear and on her knees, she implored him to kneel as she was doing. To see her so hurt him; she was so pale, with the fear of death upon her face, for his sake as it seemed. He would have liked to do as she wished, but the thing was impossible. What—because these people amused themselves with shooting unarmed men and women in cold blood—was he to bend as he only bent to his God? Surely not, and bullets of such firing would do him no harm. So he set his broad back to the pealing volleys and shrugged his shoulders con- temptuously as the bullets whistled about him, the light of battle in his eyes the while, and his strong hands clenched with the wrath he suppressed. The old days were back upon him, days when the hot blood had rushed through his body, every fiber in him tingling with health and vigor, when his life would have been lost but for straight shooting, coolness and pluck; the desert sun overhead, the crisp invigorating air of the desert in his nostrils. Ah! how his fingers itched to grasp a rifle again.

In glorious freedom, and as if in mockery of his fierce reflections, some pigeons, scared by the firing, whirled and circled above him with sun-gilt flashing wings, and Sara, fascinated into staring at his angry face, became conscious of their presence, and wondered for a second how she could notice such an insignificant thing as a pigeon, at such a moment.

At length, sick of the storm of lead, the nauseous odor of powder, the crowd broke and swept out of the square, carrying Sara, with Hernani's arms about her, with it.

When they were at home again, safe and glad to be there, and she had recovered in a measure from the fright and fatigue of it all, he said to her—

"Why did you come?"

"And you?" she again murmured, pale and troubled-looking where she lay amongst some cushions.

"I—I knew what they were at, what I should see, but I was curious to——"

"So was I," she answered eagerly, preferring that he should deem her guilty of curiosity rather than of love.

"But you—you have no right. Look at the figure you cut, tearing through the street. What would people think?"

"I have no interest in knowing. What are people to me? Were they of use when I was poor in Cracow? Had I been seen tearing through the streets, as you phrase it, then, would it have mattered—and why should it matter now, since I might starve again to-day for aught they—people—would care? The right, the luxury of freedom, is worth more than public opinion."

He agreed with her; but she disputed with him so seldom, and that afternoon he had resisted the temptation to shriek in her ear, "Your lover, that d——d Hourko—why doesn't he stop the firing? You are here; isn't that enough?"

"There is no question of being poor or of starving," he continued haughtily, remembering the desire he had crushed.

"Not to-day, that is true, but to-morrow there may be," she said bitterly.

"What is the matter with you, Sara?" She had never spoken so strangely before. "You are never to run such a risk again. Remember, I forbid it. What I do, is one thing; what you do, another."

"Who cares what I do?" she had it on her tongue to say, petulant and weak, and having suffered enough in one day to last for a life; but by closing her eyes she hid the tears that filled them and only murmured wearily—

"I am overdone, very tired, that is all. I will do as you wish."

It seemed her lot to be corrected, misunderstood and ill-treated. From his lips she had heard words that were to her the most brutal he could ever speak; yet she had forgotten them at the first sound of danger to him, and here he was chiding her. She had admired him more than ever, if that were possible, as she had crouched at his feet imploring him to stoop. Was he not the youthful image of what a stately patriarch must have been in the old days; that great, splendid looking fellow, with his deep, wonderful eyes, his fine bronzed features and dark curling moustache? Again, he had been to her the handsome traveler, enshrined in romance, the mysterious Crœsus of the little hovel in Cracow. Was there anything he could not do?—smile with the bullets whistling about him, handle her like a child and protect her with his own body. Could she ever forget the beautiful light in his face as he had snatched up a little one who would have been trampled under foot, and held it tenderly in his arms, though its face was unwashed and its feet dirty, relinquishing it only when a place of safety seemed gained.

Then, too, was it not wonderful to contemplate this

success of his as a financier? The most intricate business problems were clear to him. He had only to think, to understand. And not content with the ordinary methods by which wealth was attainable, he imagined, invented and speculated, always with the same penetrative and unerring judgment, the same result—success. And after she had dwelt upon all these perfections, these admirable qualities, to her mind, another gift remained to him which perfected them all and was above price—the blessing of the Eternal, which was with him in his going and coming, an ornament about his neck, an amulet in the face of danger.

The good he did, too, would live after him, for to help those who were past helping themselves, the desolate and unfortunate, the sick and starving, was a pleasure in his life which grew and flourished and which he had taken in exchange for that common error men make—heaping riches on themselves. Was it to be wondered at, then, that she adored him, and that in consequence the fiat she had heard him pronounce assailed her with the more crushing force? On the evidence of his own lips, she was to lose him who was to her so admirable, so well worth loving, and to whom she had dedicated the beauty and freshness of her girlish years. How could a heavier blow have been dealt her, and how was she to endure the effect of it and retain her reason?

With half-closed eyes, she reclined amongst her cushions and watched him as he paced the room, apparently a prey to excitement produced by the bloodshed he had witnessed. But for this home trouble that had come upon her, she would have felt the same, her mind would have been full of the cruelty and horrors she had been compelled to see, but the actual destruction of others, shrank into insignificance beside the loom of the shadow which threatened destruction to herself. It was selfish of her, and she would have liked to have been good and great enough to forget her own woe in the sufferings of others. But after all she was only human, intensely so; a woman, weak, and with her heart full of the keenest longing for love and sympathy. Perhaps he was a little like her, and the distress she saw in his face was not entirely due to the inhuman acts he had been helpless to prevent. There was at least one circumstance that pointed to it. When he had found her in danger, he had made no secret of his distress and anxiety. If he felt as he had looked then, how could he turn his back upon her in cold blood, thrust her from him without one crime to record against her? Surely in the depths of his heart some of the love she had inspired must still linger. Ah! if but a chance of retaining him remained to her, how well she would do battle. How surely she would win with this great love nerving and strengthening her. But the dead weight of doubt soon crept in upon the thought, knocking the life out of it, leaving her with head propped up, swaying and splitting where she lay.

"What are you thinking of?" she demanded, when the desire to speak had grown too strong to resist.

"Thinking—er—I?" he stammered, startled into himself by the directness of the question. Then more collectedly, "Has to-day brought nothing fresh to think about?"

"It has brought too much," she answered simply and solemnly.

"You ought never to have been there," he retorted, the real meaning of her words conveying nothing to him. "Such blood-curdling sights are not for women. Why ever did you come? Had I dreamt that you would leave the house, I would have warned you. It was bad enough for me, to whom death is not unfamiliar—but you—you will dream of it, you will never get it out of your head. My poor girl, I am sorry. And yet, perhaps, it is as well; a baptism of some kind could not have been averted for long, for such fine doings will be thick upon the ground presently, and you may as well begin to harden your heart now as later. It only shows what one has got to look forward to, and increases one's respect for and confidence in the authorities. But what is one to do? There will be no peace in this accursed city very shortly, and for myself, I have the sensation of being caught in a trap from which I shall not be freed, until I have paid and suffered to the utmost. There will be no mercy shown me, you may be sure. I begin to feel as though time and money would be well spent in organizing and arming a few brave fellows, if only to avenge those who have been murdered in cold blood. Besides, is one to sit still and await one's turn, without making an attempt in self-defense, thankful if one escapes butchering? I tell you, my patience is becoming exhausted. Aware that life and property may be lost any day, I should like, at least, to have a fight for them. As I live, they will want money ere long, and then the usual proceedings will take place—a raid will be made and the wealthiest of us will be robbed. Did you see Hourko rigged out in his best? He should have whetted his appetite for dinner, but may it choke him, the villain!"

Narrowly though he watched her, he got nothing for his pains. Her innocence was her safeguard.

"Is General Hourko responsible for what has occurred?" she asked quietly, and without even so much as lifting her head to look at him.

"Responsible? Of course he is. He is empowered to act as he thinks proper. There can be no doubt of that. I dare hold the Tsar is practically blameless in the matter. Deceived by the unscrupulousness of his ministers and advisers, he never knows more than it suits their policy to tell him. He is fenced about by machinations, and, thinking he pulls the strings, looks on while they are pulled for him. Hourko?—I should think he is to blame!"

"Then he will be punished sooner or later," she answered wearily.

It disappointed her to find him full of the day's doings and apparently without thought of her. He could speak as she had heard him do to Hermann Bloch, and yet keep his mind clear to talk glibly on whatever topic turned uppermost. She could hear him thundering forth, "Any day I may have to divorce my wife," and the words buzzed in her ears as it seemed to her they would do till she died; yet, apparently, how little he was affected by them, or rather what had called them forth. Could he care for her then—did the dregs of his love for her still remain? The question died upon her tongue; she was without strength to answer it. To her, at that moment, there seemed to be a great contrast between them; he was so strong and vigorous, with the hue of health in his cheek, the fire of energy in his eyes, and she was weak and weary—tired—oh! how terribly so. "Well for me if I could die now," she whispered to herself, her eyes still closed and hot with tears—"he has done with me, and I would have done with life."

And with Riva about her, touching her tenderly, she said to her, "Riva, but for the sin of it, I would not live beyond to-night."

7

CHAPTER IX.

Youth and hope, sleep, awakening to the springtime,
revivified, again inspired—how comforting! Plunged in
despair one day, but cheered and strengthened another,
Sara watched and waited and fought to keep what
seemed to her—all—her husband. Glad of anything that
gained her time, she no longer discouraged the interest
he felt in the insurrectionary movement. Rather than
that he should think of and plot against her, she had best
fill his mind with it. Evidently his schemes were not
enough to satisfy his voracious appetite for work and
excitement; besides, they must hang fire, remain in
abeyance, as things were. Hitherto she had done her
utmost to restrain 'his ardent patriotism, but since he
would not be permitted to stand still, and according to
his own showing must be drawn into the vortex created
by the great movement, she would no longer be a wet
blanket. Where was the use? It would be better for
her if his mind ran on fighting and freedom rather than
on her and the children her existence denied him. Yet
again, she felt that if by her counsel or even neutrality,
ill befell him, she would be unable to forgive herself, and
would be in a worse plight than ever. She was thus
between two fires. And never in her life had she experienced anything approaching the restlessness and in-
decision, the unhappy vacillation and despair she was
now a prey to. At one moment she was for facing it
out, trusting to what might be the remnants of her influence, but what, since she was still with him, must
amount to influence, also to time and the secrets hidden
in the morrow. At another, she could scarcely continue to remain beneath the same roof. Anything rather

than this frightful uncertainty, this crushing weight
which his words had suspended over her head, and which
might fall upon her when least expected. The indignity
also of being told to go, would be agonizing. What an
insupportable affront! The contemplation of it, from
which she could seldom free herself, seemed to turn her
sick, to take her breath away. She watched him, too, so
closely, and weighed his words with a mind so completely impregnated with doubt and suspicion, that whenever they met, she fancied she had discovered some new
phase or development of the situation. There remained
no rest for her, and to succumb, to die, or disappear,
was apparently the only solution, the final termination.
When he was not with her, when out of her sight, she
was racked with doubts and dread of what was happening, what he was doing or thinking; and when they were
shut up together, her nerves were excited and strained
to such a pitch, that her control over herself threatened
to fail her. Nevertheless, she went into the fresh air
more, now that the flowers were fresh and blooming,
the trees displaying their most refreshing and attractive
garb.

With an immense effort to become philosophical, she
endeavored to live for the day, for the hour. Her love
of nature was profound, and she took a melancholy delight in burying herself amongst the trees, away from
everything that could be harsh or unkind, and where at
least no sound came to her except that of the birds she
loved so well, who seemed to be her friends, the only
ones she had. Of General Hourko she had lost count,
though he had assailed her again upon the old pretext—
her charity and pity for those of her race less fortunate
than herself.

On his part, Hourko certainly had her fresh in his
mind. While she was endeavoring to cope with the woe
that threatened to engulf her, he was in the old palace of
the Polish kings, immersed in business, besieged with

dissatisfied dispatches from St. Petersburg. They were calling his policy in question, even censuring it. Inundated by instructions, in dread of being ignominiously recalled, he could still quietly remark—

"This Jewess will not bite, eh, Popoloff? The avowed interest in Judaism won't do. We must think of some better bait."

"Excellency, you will have more time when——"

"Anyone else would be dismissed, Popoloff, for talking about time. How often am I to remind you that I am not a slave? Won't once do? I am sick of the sight of papers, each with a fresh string of suggestions, the last of which always proves more useless than the first. There is nothing tangible, nothing substantial about these accursed Poles—that's what it amounts to. I should like to hunt them out of their filthy dens, where they are knee-deep in plotting impossibilities, into the light of day, supply them with arms. and then, as a soldier, I could deal with them. Fighting with conspirators such as they are, is to me, what fighting with something invisible would be to any man. I am sick of it—just in that condition, in fact, when a pretty face would be a relief; and was there ever a man who liked one, cooped up and harassed as I am? All the same, I am not going to give up my Jewess. Who would, once they had seen her? This banker fellow is just the right man to find his way to Siberia, and then, in a gilded prison such as I could provide her with, my beautiful Sara would thrive and delight me. That's what it will come to, eh, Popoloff? But not yet—the time is hardly ripe. Have you had news from the palace this Hernani maintains?"

"Some of the money that is being steadily collected by the chiefs of the insurrectionary movement has already been supplied by him, sir."

"Ah! How do you know that?"

"Excellency—as I know everything." answered Popoloff, with some show of pride, and the shadow of a grim smile upon his inscrutable face. "He has already been guilty of that and of assault."

"Good; then we can arrest——"

"Anyone, Excellency."

"True, but I question; he is very rich and a leader amongst them—one of their head men. No, we will wait. Have you heard anything more?"

"The relations between Kasimir and his wife are less satisfactory, though the reason is unknown."

"Is that so?"

"Yes, sir; but this information about his monetary dealings is really important. His immense wealth at the disposal of these traitors to his Imperial Majesty makes a dangerous combination."

"His wings will need clipping."

"They will, sir."

"But at present we must be patient. Have you issued my instructions to the officers?"

"Yes, Excellency."

"Then there can be no excuse for brawls of any kind. What fresh signs are there? How are the streets looking? I must take a drive for the sake of some air."

"The streets are as usual, sir. No new symptoms. The women clad as for a funeral, the men ready for a wedding. The fools, to be strutting about like so many peacocks! Colonel Woronzow was insulted by one of them in a café this very morning, the young jackanapes who was guilty of the affront, displaying what he would be pleased to call the national dress, which, as you know, is as bright as that of our Circassians. Top boots, embroidered shirt, and red fur-brimmed hat—nothing short of it. The numbers who take to this absurd attire, appear to increase every day, making the general mourning of the women more noticeable."

"Yes, I know—I have remarked that. But how did Colonel Woronzow act?"

"He was patient under the insult, sir."

"I am glad of that. The names of those officers or men who are not so, under such annoyances, must be reported to me. I have strict injunctions to avoid more bloodshed or disturbances, though such leniency will only foster arrogance and produce dissension. The rifle and the knout are what is required. Any reports from the provinces?"

"Excellency, the provinces record no fresh outrages or disturbances; the rule of our Holy Father the Tsar is maintained in unbroken quiet. The peasants, one and all, know which side their bread is buttered. They have been well counseled and will obey, as good subjects should."

"That is gratifying."

"Most gratifying, sir."

"If they observe that attitude, there will be nothing worth calling a rebellion."

"They will do as they are told, Excellency. They are so simple and ignorant, as you know—just like overgrown children; and it is only necessary to remind them of the tyranny their Polish masters practiced, of their indifference to their sufferings, of the way in which they enslaved and used them as beasts of burden—to rouse them to fury and knit them to us."

"And has this been done thoroughly?"

"Thoroughly, sir. And our judiciously-selected emissaries are devoted in their endeavors to instil into them an exact idea of their position. They are unwearyingly reminded not to anger the Tsar, of the submission they owe to him as the head of the kingdom, and on account of his tender solicitude for them. The treacherous character of the Polish nobility, and the hollowness of the promises they make, are duly set forth, and they are exhorted to stand firm for the sake of their own interests."

Hourko smiled grimly.

"In short, the work is being done well." he exclaimed.

"I trust so, your Excellency. Every day my labor increases. I have spies in every hamlet, village and town, and so great is the correspondence and intricate the detail, that, mindful of your permission, the large staff of officials and clerks has been increased. Soon there shall not be a single family of any consequence of whose most private actions I am in ignorance, and when the time comes, what power must remain on the side of law and order, in consequence of such important information! They will not know us, but we shall know them."

"Yes, yes—you are wonderful—an enthusiast, Popoloff," answered Hourko, with a look of weariness upon his face, as though, despite his interest, something new would please him better.

Considered apart from Popoloff's ideas and schemes, the fact remained that there was nothing of the diplomatist about Ivan Nicholaevitch. Intrigue and detail, fine shades of thought, of feeling, or of policy, were never conceived or understood by him. In his opinion, there were only two things fit for a soldier to do—to fight and make love. He was brave, some said brutal, and he liked to come to downright blows, or, if there were none to be exchanged, console himself with what, in his opinion, he could well appreciate—a fair form and face. Women and the peasants might be considered in the same breath. The peasants were meant to be ignorant, to remain ignorant, that they might till the land and minister to the needs of those who were not so. And women—well, women in the concrete were a shade better than the peasants, but the end for which they were created was the same: to crown with comfort and delight the existences of those superior beings—men—the lords of the soil. For virtue he entertained respect and admiration in the dim recesses of his mind. But then, could virtue be found? Certainly his wife had never deceived him to his knowledge, but then his wife was such a fearfully attenuated specimen of humanity, and where there was no desire or temptation, there could be no virtue. There had been a time when he was savage in his hatred of a lie, but that time had never outlived his cadet's uniform. Some sorts of lies were of the first necessity, though it was a pity, and truth was best, though dull, and only endurable at certain seasons.

For instance, Popoloff was so conscientiously truthful in the way in which he bored him with a lot of things he might just as well have kept to himself. It was a pity, too, that he was so ugly and not the least little bit of a roué. It was so odd for a man to have a mind like iron, to possess a perfect memory, and to work, work, work always, never seeming to remember that a little relaxation, a little amusement in the shape of feminine society, would be consoling as well as refreshing. But then experience might have taught Popoloff that the fair sex would have none of him, and, after all, he was invaluable.

"Popoloff, you should marry," he suddenly remarked, surveying that strange personage with a half ironical, half comical grin, fancying the while that the man seemed even longer and thinner, more cadaverous and more knock-kneed than he had thought he was. Without a word in answer, feigning deafness to perfection, Popoloff gravely submitted some papers for his chief's signature, and when it had been affixed in the usual sprawling hand, and Popoloff was going off limping on his heels, Hourko added—

"You are cut out for a chief of police; you might emulate the deeds of a Fouché, but to follow Benedict's lead is not in your line, eh?"

Popoloff brightened.

"That's it, Excellency."

"Oh! you heard, you dog."

"Yes, sir; but these important dispatches and—and many things being on my mind, diverted my attention."

That Popoloff was unscrupulous there could be no doubt, otherwise he would not have remained a day in the position he occupied. It was something for the obscure tchinovnik to be patronized by Madam; so he had readily adapted himself to the situation into which he had slid—that of the master's trusted servant and the wife's confidential spy. He had to please them both if he meant to remain where he was. And Popoloff, it so happened, was ambitious of climbing high, the road to this great end apparently being much like Hourko's, a blind belief in the orthodox faith and in his Imperial Majesty the Tsar. Clad in such sound and shining armor, it only remained for him to come to the front, to distinguish himself; and here again the way seemed clear. Jewish troubles loomed ahead as well as Polish ones, and deep down in his heart there was hidden the desire to become a great Jewish scourge. The ripening insurrectionary movement was only the looked-for opportunity which would enable him to attract the Emperor's notice. His ability would insure this success for him, and this once done, there would be no limit to his ends and aspirations. It followed therefore, that in a degree he discountenanced Hourko's attitude towards Sara. Though again it might be the means to an end. She was one of the accursed race, by his desire to exterminate which he was to obtain consideration in high places, and in addition, wealth, which to him meant everything, avarice being his crowning vice.

The position he had assumed meanwhile was that of watching and awaiting events. Perhaps the lynx-eyed and jealous Madam Hourko might become exasperated, and he might quietly lend her a hand in exterminating the whole Hernani brood, for his hatred of Jewish blood was so inveterate, that instead of Sara's beauty producing admiration, or assuaging his feelings in the very least, he would have had her stripped in the market-place, and flogged through the streets in the light of day, before a sea of eyes.

With these rancorous sentiments within him, how masterful had been his control over himself, and with what consummate tact had he acted, even to the point of sup-

plying ideas, and with his own hand writing letters, in
furtherance of his master's desire to develop an intimacy
with this Hebrew woman, quietly chuckling as he received smiles and expressions of approval in return for
his services. "He had been clever, he had done well"—
though after all, in establishing spies and gaining all
possible information, he had done no more than he un-
failingly did. Meanwhile, if driven to grind his teeth
and bide his time, it consoled him to reflect that such
people as these Hernanis would finally be consumed in
the general conflagration approaching, as would many
more pestilent Jews who encumbered the ground, and
upon whom his glance of hatred was fixed. He could
well afford to wait, so great would be their confusion in
a little while, and at present it was his policy to be all
things to all men. So he played with Madam Hourko,
as he did with the General, both being unconsciously his
tools when it pleased him, for both were blinded by their
belief in him; Madam Hourko, the only one in a position to see through him, attributing all his actions, in a
measure, to his gratitude for the notice she had taken of
him, the preferment she had gained him.

Her idolatrous regard for Hourko, which, owing to
his actions and temperament, took the form of the most
insane jealousy conceivable, left her no time and no in-
clination for thinking of much else. But it was this element of jealousy that rendered her capable of becoming
extremely dangerous to a woman born and placed as
was Sara. Her exalted position invested her with limit-
less power. What could she not do, or cause to be done
to a Jewess, and one, moreover, whose audacity she believed had led her to trifle with her husband, the General's, affections? For in Popoloff's skillful hands, the information supplied her was just such as to arouse and
develop indignation, without causing her to overstep
the bounds he had at present mentally fixed for her. He
could easily make her do that when he wished. And it

was interesting to watch how tigerish she became when her appetite was cunningly whetted. Of course she unhesitatingly blamed the woman. Eyes were being made at her husband, whose position and splendid appearance had completely dazzled and subjugated this Hebrew banker's wife.

"But what is to be done?" she screamed to Popoloff, in the course of one of their talks.

"Nothing, Madam; and it is because these people shall be sent off to Siberia by étape one fine day, that I say, Nothing. If you took any step now, his Excellency's suspicions would be aroused, his indignation excited, and he would put protective measures in force which would probably baffle us both. We should be outwitted, and furthermore, he would be certain to suspect me. You would not wish that?"

"On no account."

"Then trust me, Madam. You may do so implicitly. You will find me equal to the occasion."

So in blissful unconsciousness of the storm that was gathering beneath his own roof, Hourko took long drives round the town, even along the Avenue, under the pale arching foliage of the limes, down into the beautiful park of Lazienki, always keeping a sharp look out, yet scarcely ever catching a glimpse of this woman he was hunting for, who seemed so absurdly unapproachable, and who was, in fact, more anxious than ever to avoid him. When he stopped his carriage, and alighted to speak to her on one or two occasions, Sara had received him with nervous and chilly reserve, he the while taking no pains to conceal the admiration he entertained for her.

No kind of social intercourse between them was possible on ordinary lines, his nationality, if not his rank, erecting obstructive barriers of iron. He knew that, yet "she must come to the palace and talk with him. Much good might come from such conversations. He was prepared to be as good as his word and to befriend her co-religionists in all ways that were feasible and prudent." But the great man pleaded in vain. Having heard as in a sort of misty dream all he had to say, and been well stared at for walking with so important a personage, Sara thanked him courteously, but politely excused herself, with pretty but undeniable dexterity.

In reality, her heart was too full, her brain too actively engaged in unhappy reflections, to give a thought to him, and the policy she had but so recently deemed desirable.

Far from disheartening Hourko, this resistance to his wishes, and indifference to his advances, affected him as might have been expected, seeing that he was a strong-willed, obstinate man, to whom the sensation of being repulsed was distinctly refreshing. He was so powerful and influential, accustomed for many years to being courted and made much of, even by those who were themselves of some importance; and here was this Jewish woman setting herself up against him, ignoring his advances, unaffected by them, apparently only desirous of being rid of him. This opposition at once set her upon a higher platform in his mind. In proportion to her difference in appearance, so was she purer in mind and in virtue than those other women, who had been, one and all, only too glad to accept his favors and caresses, pleased if they might thus buzz about him. Yes, this Sara was evidently of rarer and more precious material, worthier of a true and lasting love than of a simple passing fancy. But, all the same, was he not Ivan Nicholaevitch Hourko, and had he not always obtained what he had coveted? To think that he had stooped to, and shown himself attracted by a woman, who if not nameless, was in the eyes of some people lower even, by reason of her blood. There came moments when he was dangerously piqued, though these were when his thoughts were lowest and most passionate. Still his *amour propre* had received a shock which at such times made him feel al-

most vindictive. She had better take care, or she should
rue the day in which she began to trifle with him. As a
woman she must have seen all along how he had been
affected. Perhaps she had laughed at him. A thousand
furies! He would bring her to her knees, she should beg
her honor and her life from him, the little fool. Did she
think herself free to do as she pleased? She should discover her mistake, and that soon. There was no such
thing as freedom in the land for her or her race. Pish!
she was very beautiful, but she had her price, and if not,
it was in his power to make her take, and be glad to take,
what he chose. Do what he would, he found it impossible to shut her image out of his mind. She was always
rising up, disturbing and seductive. There was something in her lithe and easy carriage, in the milk-white
nape of her neck, with its curling auburn locks, something in the liquid depths of her wonderful eyes, which
inflamed his passions and bewitched him, as he had never
thought to be bewitched.

Titus Prokofievitch Popoloff, and those beneath him,
had a bad time when such visions presented themselves,
and Ivan Nicholaevitch grew irritable, because he was
no nearer those perfections than on the day when they
had first met his gaze, besides seeing no way to approach
them either by strategy or force. Considering the state
of the political atmosphere, if he were guilty of any extraordinary step, Warsaw might be ablaze, and a leakage
of news would at once get through to St. Petersburg.
He would be talked of, injured, with such fine capital in
the hands of his enemies. No; he was not going to be
such a fool. He must fret and fume and wait; lose sight
of his purpose, never.

And in ignorance of the deadly enemies she had so
unconsciously created, Sara sorrowfully dragged through
the days that were now not the least bit like what the old
ones had been, and would, it seemed, never come round
to right themselves again. Such a hope seldom glim-

mered in her mind, and when it did, she wondered how
it had come there, since there was no shadowy ground
even for its existence. And as though to sadden her,
and remind her more forcibly of the mourning that had
taken possession of her heart, when she went out, every
woman she met—even Russian—was like herself, attired in deep black, and could not have walked the streets
in safety otherwise. In addition, all places of public
amusement were now completely abandoned, even the
mildest form of recreation being as sternly tabooed in
private circles as though the most solemn season had
been entered upon, and each house sorrowed for its beloved dead. The churches were crammed and ringing
with the sad and tender prayerfulness of the national
hymn, while no great day in the annals of Polish history
was suffered to pass unmarked.

After the municipal elections came fresh demonstrations, and these were indulged in, until one fine day, an
official declaration of a state of siege was proclaimed.

In all this there was nothing to cheer, not one flash of
light to illumine, and Sara felt her spirits at zero, in spite
of the unflagging efforts she made to forget herself by
means of the old recipe of taking interest in others. As
a proof of the genuineness of her attempts in this direction, she busied herself in gaining information, going
into really minute calculations over the revolutionary
question, finally by drawing up a plan with much labor
and thought, in which she succeeded in setting down
with admirable lucidity—considering the conflicting
statements made in the materials at her disposal—a vigorous résumé of what should, in her opinion, be done to
cope with the difficulties of the political situation. She
was inspired to do this by the decision she had arrived
at, to damp Hernani's patriotism no longer, her innate
conscientiousness demanding that she should at least
learn all she could of a cause, which, if not warmly ad-
vocating, she at least countenanced; the undertaking

being an attempt to justify herself for the course she had adopted. When she had finished it, she showed it to Hernani.

"Why, what is this?" he inquired, pushing some papers aside and unrolling the scroll she had handed to him.

"A plan of campaign," she answered rather seriously.

"Drawn up by Joan of Arc?" he asked with an amused smile.

"By poor Sara Hernani," she replied wearily.

"Why poor?"

"Oh, I don't know."

"A woman's answer—but let me see. You must have spent a lot of time, and taken any amount of pains over this."

"Yes, it gave me some trouble."

"And why did you do it?"

"Because the subject is of vital importance."

"Quite true. It is very clear and ingenious. Do these figures represent the number of male inhabitants between these ages?"

"Yes, that is the total; and, even supposing that half the peasants refuse their assistance, there remains a sufficiently formidable body upon which to count. The two greatest difficulties will be to supply arms and teach even the most rudimentary discipline. To feed them I imagine would not be quite so hard a task."

"No, I should say not; you are right there. Many friends would be met with, and supplies to a certain extent would be assured." He was surprised at the clearness of her ideas. "But to rely upon half the peasants, to begin with, would be a mistake. Men have long memories where grievances are concerned. They will—in bulk—probably forget a kindness; they always remember an injury. The wrongs of centuries have brought them to the pass they have arrived at. In addition to flogging and imprisonment, the Polish noble occasionally took it into his head to deprive his serf of life, his

only punishment for the savage crime being a fine of a
few livres. I need not say more, to convince you that
the peasant has a heavy account to get settled, and will
not forget to demand payment when the chance offers.
But all this you know as well as I do."

"Yes, I suppose I do."

"As for the importation of arms, something has already been done, yet very little, and for every rifle that
reaches its destination, three are lost. Discipline to any
extent seems out of the question."

"Your views are not usually so gloomy."

"Perhaps not, but it is well to err on the safe side.
Leave this with me to look at. I'm glad you are so much
interested. In all your calculations remember this: the
Russians will yet suffer for doing what we, the Poles,
have already done, and are suffering for now. The
worm will turn and so will the peasant, wherever he may
be enslaved and ill-treated. The Polish noble is paying
now for the tyranny practiced by his forefathers; the
Russian noble's turn will come."

How cold and business-like was his manner, how stri-
dent his voice—so woefully changed from that of old
days—and he had as good as dismissed her without the
warm kind kiss so common once, now, alas! a luxury;
and yet, knowing the turn of his thoughts towards her,
she dare not say, "What is amiss? Come—let us be
again what we have been." Such a request was impossible; there could be no putting matters right, and she
must just drag on her life thus, thankful that she might
see and speak with him, conscious that ere long she
would be deprived of even that consolation.

It was at such times as these that she felt like going
mad—moments when his actions flung her face to face
with facts. She was in a regular trap. To think that she
loved this man more than her life, yet dare not reproach
him for his altered conduct, for fear of hastening the
catastrophe she dreaded, and had silently to contemplate

overtaking her any day. What ill-luck had come to her, when by mere chance she had overheard his terrible disclosure to Bloch—Bloch, before whom she now felt shame-faced and awkward, as though she had no right where she found herself, and was only there on sufferance. And to keep up appearances she had been compelled to meet him. It was too cruel. If, instead of making the discovery she had, the space of but a few yards had separated her from that detestable doorway, then at least her existence would have been tolerable, since she then would have accepted some such excuse as his oft-repeated, "Pooh! you don't understand—I have much upon my mind—I am busy," as a sort of reason for the complete transformation her affection detected. Besides, she would have invented; there would have been business anxieties which told upon his health and temper, the shadow cast by the great stir in the country, like the increase of wind, the sighing of it, and the accompanying distress and gloom heralding the storm; all sorts of excuses would have been made for him, and so she would have lived a little longer in the fool's paradise she had been so contented with. Anything rather than the load she now bore. Sheer nervousness, too, made her confident that other people besides Bloch and Riva Krein were aware of the state of affairs—scandal traveling far and furiously. She saw it in their eyes and in their manner to her, and was forever imagining that she had detected some fresh symptoms of pity or thinly-veiled contempt. When such fancies as these laid hold upon her, she was beside herself with mixed feelings of indignation and annoyance. A pretty figure she cut, supplying food for gossip; being ridiculed unmercifully, no doubt, for endeavoring to hang on where she was no longer wanted. When despairingly appealed to, Riva Krein had expended her tears and her eloquence to no purpose.

"What ails my lamb? It can't be; make your mind

8

easy. The thing is impossible. The dead are not more silent than I have been. Not a soul knows."

But Sara refused to be comforted.

"Oh! that I could rest somewhere," she would sob, her spirits at the lowest ebb. "Do you see how he has changed—what a different man he is to me?"

"The Holy One will curse him unless he takes care, for it is written, 'Men should be careful lest they cause women to weep, for God counts their tears.'"

"Hush! Riva."

"Well, my lamb, is it not so?"

"Hush! I say. You must not say such dreadful things. He is not to blame—it is I. I should never have been born. Such women as myself, who are incapable of fulfilling the duty for which they were brought into the world—that of child-bearing—only encumber the ground. I speak plainly that you may understand what I feel, Riva."

"Oh! I understand; but, dear heart, to hear you, one might think there were not enough of us already. See what a time I've had; there's never been a place for me, though I've looked hard for one. Now I'll tell you, this is my belief—that there are too many of us, and that good store should be set by those who just come and go, without making misery by multiplying. If a man knew when he was well off, he wouldn't look for sons to blacken his name and worry him into the grave, as many a son has done before now. If the Holy One gives him no children, he should say, 'Well so,' and be content. I've no patience."

"But we all expect children, Riva. It's only natural."

"Well, so we may. I've expected a lot of things, but as soon as I found I came no nearer getting them, I stopped expecting. It's best so. We're only happy when we've got nothing to hope for, and what we get comes to us as a surprise."

"Must we indeed become embittered?"

"Things bitter to the tongue are sweet to the stomach. A good few of us would be happier if we didn't expect so much. Look at the master—the Lord preserve him! What a lot he has to make him happy—if he wouldn't look for more, and so work hard to spoil what he has."

"Riva, you don't know his troubles, you can't feel as he feels; therefore you must not judge him. No two of us are constituted alike. I can fully understand that I am a disappointment to him, but I would have had him come to me and tell me so, not talk about me to others."

"I'll hear no such thing as that you are a disappointment to anyone. If you are, it's because they don't know how to value you. Was anyone ever so beautiful?"

"In your eyes, Riva."

"No, not in my eyes alone. Doesn't the whole street turn to look at you when you pass? Haven't I seen it many times? In Cracow, when we were poor, wasn't it the same? It was the joy of my life, to see the fine ladies with fortunes on their backs, envious of you, whose whole outfit would not have fetched twenty gulden. And you are good and charitable; could anyone be more so? Haven't you given your time and money for others, and thought of them more than of yourself, risking health and life many a day when the fever and cholera's been raging? Don't I know? Ah! to have been a man, and to have been loved by you, would have been a foretaste of bliss. And I have had my love; I know about it—what it is to feel one's limbs palsied, one's heart as though it would stand still, faint. weary unto death. I loved like that, and it was all useless. I have never loved since."

"My poor Riva."

"Don't sorrow for me—I'm past needing it; for, though I used to know what it was for the days that kept us apart, to seem like years; for the warmth and

light of the sun to be in my heart as well as about me;
though the thought that we were to meet—and the sight
of him made me tremble with a joy I can't tell of—think
of this; I am never to tremble again, not even for death.
No, don't you sorrow for me, because you are all I have
to live for in the world, and you're enough."

"I know it, I know it, and you will come with me
if—if——"

"Come with you to the ends of the earth. We two will
journey along together; and what is it after all—it will
soon be over; the journey along the rough ways and
through the night, will soon be done, and the Holy One
—blessed be He!—will have us in His arms, safe, somewhere." Tears stood in Riva's black eyes, and her
wrinkled skin was drawn into a web of puckers as her
feelings worked in her face. Sara could not speak, and
the old woman, with her peaked and shriveled breast
heaving tumultuously, gasped forth: "Ah! it has been
a weary fight, a weary fight, my lamb; but courage—
we shall go to rest when it is time." And a seraphic
light shone in her face, as though the land she spoke of
lay illumined before her earth-worn eyes.

"But meanwhile," murmured Sara, controlling the
emotion that threatened to master her—"meanwhile we
must keep on fighting. You will help me, you will be
with me, and what a comfort you are!"

"Am I, my love—am I? Then I am happy. To
hear you say that, from your heart, is what I've lived for
this long while past. The riches seemed robbing me
of you, and in my heart I cursed them."

"They will have taken to themselves wings and fled,
soon enough. But can you understand what I suffer,
Riva—I, who was so happy that the days were never
long enough? I seemed to walk on air, to breathe the
breath of heaven, and now—now——"

"I know, my lamb, I know. But you must conquer
and crush these feelings, or soon you will cease to

struggle at all. It may seem hard, but it must be done. The master loves you—that's what you have to go upon and look to. With my own ears I've heard him tell you that you are his first real love, and woe to him if he cleaves not to you. Is it not written, 'Tears are shed on God's altar for the one who forsakes his first love'? The man who forsook me never prospered. And it was just; he robbed me of all I had to give, and then fled. The Eternal reckons up these things, my love. Lay yourself out to keep the master, and you must succeed; what man could resist you?"

"If only he had not said what he did, Riva."

"Perhaps he was angry and did not mean it. Men are like that."

"How could that be? Bloch was with him by appointment. He had arranged to meet him to tell him about me."

"Go and ask him, then."

"Ask him?" repeated Sara passionately. "How often have you suggested that, and how often have I said I would rather die than do it! If I needed proof to convince me that his words were neither angry nor idle ones, I have it in his whole treatment of me."

"Then be patient," answered the old woman sagely. "It is written that 'to be patient is sometimes better than to have much wealth.' Ah! how should I have come through my life, if I had not remembered and treasured up these blessed sayings? We fail to value what we have at its worth. When one is famished, how one relishes a crust, when each blast of wind blows through one, what warmth and cheer is to be found in a gleam of sunshine, and when one hungers for sympathy, how the chance word of a stranger even, yields consolation."

"Then you think I make too much of my troubles?"

"If you were to count up the mercies more diligently, you would be able to bear them better, my lamb. And

after all, the Lord can give, and He can take away. He
may wish you to begin a new life, and for such as you,
how many men there are in the world!"

"You are wrong, Riva; for me, no men exist. I
shall never love again." And Sara turned sadly away,
wondering why she had talked so long, and at the end
of it, had found so little comfort; though it happened
so always, no matter how often she found herself listening to and confiding in Riva.

Sometimes it occurred to her that she was too much
alone, and that if she cultivated the numerous friends
or rather acquaintances she possessed, and resumed the
old habits with which she had broken, she would be
able to forget herself and her misfortunes more, and
endure her lot better.

It had come to this: she, who used to be so busy, with
never an idle moment on her hands—visiting the poor,
tending them in sickness, cheering and inspiring them
always, even reminding them of the hard, sad life she
had once lived—could now contemplate recontinuing
this renunciation of self, yet for the moment felt herself too weak to do it. The painful sensation of nervousness which caused her to shrink from meeting anyone, and which strengthened every day, partly prevented her. And besides, how was she, in the midst of
sickness and misfortune, poverty and oftentimes death,
to bear up with unruffled composure and cheerful placidity, when the hand of sorrow lay so heavy upon her?
How could she speak words of consolation and tenderness to others, when at the bare thought of it all, her
own grief blinded her? No; she was prepared to admit
that she was incapable of such an attempt, and rather
than make it, preferred to wander about the garden and
the house, a prey to the melancholy reflections which
had laid such firm hold upon her. She even avoided
the little shopping excursions, which had once been a
recognized portion of her daily duty, availing herself of

every possible pretext for sending Riva instead, and the drive or walk beneath the centenarian lime-trees of the Avenue, or to the left, amidst the plane-trees and sycamores of the park of Lazienki, was fraught with the possibility of encountering Hourko and his passionate glances, and so a thing to be avoided.

After she had scrupulously attended to her household tasks, however, there was the one spot—the garden—in which she felt herself safe from intrusion, and where she could indulge in her mournful reflections without dread of being disturbed, since in it she could escape from the gaze of the curious, from the admiring glances which persecuted her once out of doors, and from being forced into conversations which were without a particle of interest for her, in the mood she had become reduced to.

Here, on pretense of reading, she would retire, for hours, the book unopened, it is true; but when, after moments of mental distress, comparative calmness had come again, she would surrender herself to the enjoyment of admiring with the eyes of a true lover of nature, if not of an artist, the soothing and beautiful effects of light and shade, as the sun streamed through the great dark boughs of the cedars, and danced upon the sparkling waters of the fountain where the gold-fish lurked, motionless in the shade of the Flora whose image was flung upon the waters, and from whose sculptured fingers the crystal spray descended upon them.

It was here, amidst the soft cooing of the doves, the hum of insects, and the multitudinous but more distant sounds of the great city surrounding her, that she gave the rein to her thoughts; pacing amongst the flowers, admiring their delicate and brilliant faces, delighting in the odors that arose from them, and never wearying of it all for one moment, only wishing herself less sad, less lonely.

When the weather was fine, it had been a habit of Hernani's to join her there, to take tea from her hands in an arbor within sound of the fountain, and after an hour or so spent in this fashion, it had been his custom to return to his bureau and finish the business of the day. She could count on half the fingers of one hand, the number of times he had done so latterly, and even when he had so condescended, his going had been rather a relief, so awkward had been the turns the conversation had taken. Once, when he had joined her in this way, she was on the point of telling him of her visits to Hourko, and all in connection with them, but she refrained from doing so, as she reflected that they were a little happier together for the moment, that most assuredly he would be dreadfully angry, and finally, that to explain her reason for having gone, she would have to sound her own trumpet, since it had been her desire to help others that had prompted the step. Better not, she thought; better let the past be past. So she had turned from the subject, deciding not to speak of it, little dreaming how closely she had approached the happiness she sought and seemed to have said farewell to. It is often so in life; a tiny spring or wheel awry, even a grain of dust, and the whole going of the machine is altered, spoiled.

But to retrace our steps a little. The plan of campaign—as Sara had jestingly entitled her written attempt to comprehend clearly, the prospects, and probable line of conduct, of the insurrectionary leaders—produced effects that could never have been conceived as possible by her, once her back was turned.

Hernani unrolled the manuscript again and examined it attentively, a shadow, dark as a thunder-cloud, slowly gathering in his face and completely distorting his fine features during the process. At length with an angry exclamation he dashed it upon the floor. What was this insane piece of paper calculated to do? Mislead him, beguile him into believing her true to the cause he had at heart, and, in consequence, an enemy to the death of Hourko's, when the last thing he had heard was that she had been seen walking with him in the Avenue, the two of them evidently exchanging confidences, with heads bent low like lovers, while the coachman followed them at a respectful distance, in readiness to whisk his master away to further acts of villainy. Was she pleased to think, then, that nothing that was done by her was known to him, and that she could career about the town as it suited her, receiving attentions from the most prominent of the Government chiefs, without it so much as reaching his ears? He, Kasimir Hernani, wealthy, respected, and he had every reason to believe, beloved —he, the pillar of his party, the strongest prop and most trusted follower of his persuasion in all Warsaw! Was there ever anything so absurd? He, who employed spies, who was known to everyone, and could not stir without stumbling across an acquaintance, not to know of such shame-faced behavior! For there was no use in mincing matters, casting about for fine phrases; shame-faced it was, and he would call it so. Of course information reached him through circuitous channels, but then information of such a kind naturally would. And it would be retailed as fine gossip, repeated as a good joke, and told to him from cynical as well as meddling motives. People would wonder what he was about, what strange move he was authorizing and quietly calculating the effect of. He would be discredited by those in whose trust he stood high. Was he employing his beautiful wife, as a decoy or a go-between, for the further development of some subtle ruse, some carefully-thought out machination, the result of which would be startling? Was he preparing some Russian nest, in which to ensconce himself snug and safe when the strife ran high?

For without doubt he would be credited with knowing all she did, since they were looked upon as a model couple, who had made a love-match and had found it

answer.   Of course this was the light in which people
would look at it.   And it was the condition under which
they had lived, their love and perfect faith, upon the
genuineness of which he could have staked his life, that
had produced his proud, suspicious, and jealous decision
to remain dumb.   Sara's conduct had, by its apparent
infamy, electrified him into silence, and reduced him
into awaiting with agonizing interest, a further development of the situation, under the growing impression
that she had suddenly shown herself in her true colors,
leapt out of his control, and was no longer worthy of it.
Thus, the appalling nature of the spectacle he had set
himself to watch, had gradually enchained him, breathless and spell-bound.   What was the use of speaking
to her, he had argued scores of times?   If proofs were
needed, they were to hand in plenty, and if he doubted
his own ears and eyesight, he surely could not mistake
the meaning of her altered conduct toward him.   She
was another being.   In a few weeks her affection for him
had steadily dwindled to nothing, his own manner and
actions during the time having, he imagined, been ex-
emplary.   For like many a man, he believed himself to
be a good actor; and in reality, had played well enough
up to the point at which he had become too much interested and incensed to conduct himself consistently.
When the news of the fresh and further meeting between
Sara and Hourko had reached him, he had received it
with the tact he deemed suitable to the occasion, being
in the highway with the broad glare of day upon him;
but, once under cover and alone, the change became
startling.   His anger was terrible, his despair pitiable.
Such an outburst was natural to such a man, and in
the heat of it he suddenly seemed to be capable of over-
stepping all bounds.   The silent walls of his bureau rang
with menaces and imprecations, he goaded himself into
a fury as a newly-caged tiger might have done, dashing
himself against the bars, as it were, in an impotent at-

tempt to escape from this galling persecution. If
Hourko had not been altogether unassailable, then he
might have extricated himself from this trap in which
he was caught, and in which he seemed doomed to suffer
in silence; he would have struck at him as man to man,
and his life would have paid for his rascally temerity,
but such a step was impossible. The chosen representative of the Tsar, incased in the iron support of the realm,
Hourko was invulnerable, and the knout or transporta-
tion to Siberia would have been the result of any rashness. Since this was so, the only solution to the difficulty, was the one he had arrived at long ago, and so
boldly spoken of to Hermann Bloch. But when it came
to this crucial point, he found himself too weak to act.
His own near relatives were dead; Sara was the one
being upon earth about whom he was entwined, the
very sight of whom made his pulses thrill, his heart leap:
for whom he had toiled to increase his reputation and
his wealth, before whom he had taken an almost childish
pleasure in displaying his abilities. He could sever
himself from her no more easily than the monarch of
the forest could break from his roots.

And if he steeled himself to endure the wrench, what
about the effect upon her, given that her love for him
was dead? Once adrift, he well knew that she would
take no money from him; and since she did not possess
a penny of her own, how was she to exist? Upon the
charity of others; or yet, more terrible to contemplate,
the sale of the virtue and perfections he had prized more
than all his worldly possessions. And should he be the
one to drive her to such degradation—to that or to
death? An heroic idea darted through his mind, and
as its soothing influence stole over him, he ceased his
impatient walk to and fro; the hands that had severed
the air with indignant gestures fell listlessly to his side,
the muscles of his forehead relaxed, the stern expression
of his mouth softened, and he sank into a chair. Out-

side, in the square upon which the lofty windows looked, a scene of peace presented itself. Three or four palaces the size of his own encompassed it, while in the center was a smiling garden, in which bright patches of color were revealed, and surrounding these flowers, the light foliage of acacias and plane-trees, silver birches and sycamores, waved in a cool refreshing breeze, in which the birds took delight in twittering. Overhead, soft fleecy clouds floated through a sky of azure blue. His eyes sought to pierce the depths between these gently-drifting ridges, that presented themselves wave on wave like the waters of the incoming sea. What filled those deep blue distances, and what had he done to merit a home up there, where the choiring angels should sing the praises of their Creator? It was true that he had fought, that he had been galled by persecutions and restrictions, and in many a moment of his strange life, in his travels and in his work, had encountered the gibes to which his despised race were universally subjected. But what of that? Had not the Eternal blessed his efforts, crowned them with success, made him rich, in spite of the malignity of his enemies, smiled in love upon him always? In return for all this, could he do nothing—nothing but build some synagogue or scatter some alms, to give which he had to deprive himself in no way, make no personal sacrifice? It had been the wish of his life to do something great, to confer some lasting benefit, to leave some fair imperishable record; now here, close at hand, was something greater than a universal bank or a successful steamboat venture. Should circumstances favor him, the development of such schemes as these would be easy; but the thought that had entered his mind was the father to a gigantic task, and one, moreover, for which he would receive no public recognition, no reward at all, too probably.

It was this. To return what seemed to him to be good for evil. His wife had sinned against him. Instead of driving her out, acting toward her as he had intended and as the bulk of men would have done, could he not continue to keep her near him, influence, shelter and protect her in all ways?

Given that she was guilty of all he deemed possible and dreaded most, there had never been a period in her existence in which she had stood in so much need of guidance, consideration—in a word, of friendship—as the one she had now reached. But was he capable of such an effort, of such complete abnegation of self, such almost heroic charity, and could he curb his anger, which he knew to be at times both hot and sudden?

It appeared to him to be a tremendous undertaking, and he doubted himself sorely, but after long deliberation he decided in favor of making the attempt.

This decision and the further desire to adhere to it, to pledge himself in fact, occasioned an almost immediate change in his conduct, and though he went cautiously to work to begin with, so keen was Sara's power of perception where he was concerned, that she noticed the alteration at once; yet with his ominous threat expressed to Bloch ringing in her ears, she very naturally thought that something had pleased him, that he was in an unusually amiable frame of mind and no more.

However, since his kinder words and actions continued, she slid into wondering, soothed and pleased, doubting the evidence of her own senses, yet with fluttering pulse, longing to leap into his arms, and be again to him as she had once been.

In this mental condition, nearing each other imperceptibly, almost on the verge of spanning the chasm that separated them, an event found them out which was to work its will upon both, developing, changing, affecting powerfully.

They were together in the quiet of evening time; objects were already of an uncertain size and color, the birds had talked themselves silent, and a few marvel-

ously bright stars were to be seen, when with quiet tread
and voice, Riva entered to tell of the arrival of two
strangers, a lady and gentleman, who wished to speak
with Hernani.

"Show them in here," was his answer to the demand,
and in a few seconds a young man, handsome as a picture, accompanied by a young girl who resembled him
in many respects, entered the apartment.

"Count Dorozynski!" exclaimed Hernani, almost im-
mediately.

"And my sister, too," the young fellow replied, bowing; and then after a few courteous expressions, glancing round the room suspiciously, he added, "May I
speak?"

"Freely. Only my wife can hear you."

"Well, then, we are fugitives, compelled to seek shelter somewhere, or otherwise I should not have presumed
to intrude at such a late hour."

"Don't give that a thought—but—fugitives——"

"Yes."

"How? What has happened?"

"Oh! the usual thing."

"The police——"

"Took it into their wise heads to visit us by day
instead of night, and having searched the place—or, as
I might better describe it, tumbled everything upside
down in spite of assurances and entreaties—how should
I catch them, but in the act of satisfying themselves as
to the color and delicacy of my poor little sister's skin."

"Hush! Andrew," interposed the girl, her cheeks rosy
with blushes.

"No necessity, my dear child—we are with friends and
married folk; besides, I am still savage about it, so let
me speak out. They were actually stripping her in the
garden—think of that!—a lot of dirty Cossacks pulling
my little sister about, when by good luck I, who had
been out shooting, arrived upon the scene. Grasping

the situation at a glance—and who wouldn't?—I clubbed my gun, and after the display of more strength and energy than I believed myself capable of, I succeeded in rescuing her and escaping into the woods at the back of the house. Since then we have been hiding and maneuvering like so many thieves, and at last here we are."

"Where you are cordially entreated to remain, and in perfect safety, at least for a time."

"That's what I thought. Amongst my own people——"

"You would naturally be sought for, but here, in the house of a Jew, no one would ever think of looking for you."

"True; but I am ashamed of myself. I shall give you a lot of trouble, and I hate putting people out."

"Now, my dear Count, you must dismiss such ideas from your mind. My wife and myself in our joint names bid you both welcome. Is not that sufficient? This is a time of trouble. The greater part of this house is empty, so you see you are not disturbing anyone, but merely occupying space for which we had no use. You can repay me by discussing at greater length those subjects upon which—so far—we have only written. We shall be able to exchange ideas much more freely upon all points. The unjust treatment you have experienced, together with the brutal insult offered to your sister, occasions me no surprise, simply because nothing does; but it is certainly one of the worst cases I have heard of for a long while past, and the effect of it should be to unite us; for since Poles and Jews are persecuted alike, strength to resist the common oppressor of both, must be sought in union. Out of a seeming evil much good often springs. It may be my turn to be ill-used next —who can say? But if anything can knit us firmly together, it should be the existence of such lawlessness as prevails."

Dorozynski's eyes flashed, and his well-drilled, symmetrical figure, seemed to straighten and swell with pride and patriotism as he thundered—

"It must be so. We shall be one united body, and the result will be that again the Polish eagles will flutter in the breeze. Ah! how I long to take the field, to engage the scoundrels and exterminate them. And as I have, perhaps, told you, I am not without knowledge as well as practical experience. I have studied in Paris, served in Hungary, and in the army of the kingdom of Italy, so that I am fitted to play my part, and, like a good many more, am only consumed with the desire to begin."

Hernani gave vent to a satisfied laugh. Dorozynski was so refreshingly full of life and fire.

"But we cannot be too cautious," he replied; "above all things, when the time comes, we must act in concert."

"Ah! but when will it come?" inquired the young fellow with a long-drawn sigh, which was full of meaning—"when will it come, that's what I want to know. Meanwhile one must wait, while one's sisters are insulted before one's very eyes, one's parents driven into the grave. Would you believe it, at this very moment I have no idea what has happened to my father. When I returned in the manner I have tried to describe, my first thought, naturally enough, was to save Deotima here from the ruffians in whose clutches I found her. I saw no sign of my father, and had I done so, doubt if I could have been of use to him, my hands were too full. Now what I dread, is the effect the shock may have upon him. You see he is very old and feeble, and if they would touch a girl, they would not hesitate to handle him roughly. However, there is little use in talking, and now that my sister is in a place of safety, for which I shall be eternally grateful to you, I must

not remain idle. It won't take me long to ascertain
how the land lies, and I shall start at once."

"To my mind, if you would be wise, you will not go,"
answered Hernani gravely; "after the resistance you
have made, the country will be scoured for you. You
risk almost certain detection and capture."

"Risk? I love it!" laughed Dorozynski with flashing
eyes.

"Yes, that's all very well; but picture yourself a prisoner, locked up in the Citadel, or some more isolated
fortress, incapable of escaping, of helping your father,
your sister, or your country's cause, and simply because
you chanced to be a little hot-headed."

"But I have no choice."

"Why?"

"I love my father and cannot leave him to the tender
mercies of those brutes."

"I sympathize with you entirely, but in all probability
the whole of their spleen will be directed against you.
You are the only son, the heir, the hope of your father's
old age. Do you think they are unaware of these facts?
Ten to one, they will have left him uninjured and in
undisputed possession of his house, his sole anxiety at
this moment being his ignorance of the fate of his children. Now take my advice; remain here, enjoy the
rest you stand in need of, and in half an hour I will
dispatch a messenger in whom I have implicit confidence. Mounted as he shall be, he will soon return
with all the information you require. Don't you agree
with me, Sara?" he added.

"I do. In my opinion the Count would be very wrong
to go," answered Sara, with a kindly glance at Dorozynski.

"Oh! well, I give in," laughed the Count. "When
so advised, how can I do otherwise?"

And there the matter rested, the returning messenger

9

proving to the hilt the soundness of Hernani's predictions.

He brought word that, considering the shock he had received, the old Count was well, and since his son and daughter were safe, as contented as he could hope to be while thus torn from them. They were not to trouble about him, but to be sure to keep him well posted as to their health and movements.

In quite a short space of time the brother and sister settled down in their new quarters, where they found themselves treated with such kindness that, had it required an effort on their part, they could have done no less than strain every nerve to please their protectors. But no such effort was needed. The two women had taken a great fancy to each other at sight, and this feeling, so instantly awakened, developed with speed. As for the men, Hernani found in Count Andrew a patriot, and a brave one, a mixture of intelligent sagacity and headlong courage, almost boyish in some respects, hopeful always, and invigorating to a surprising degree. Some people would have argued that the companionship of such a man, at such a moment, was a danger to be shunned. Hernani, alive to the risk, courted it as befitting the hour.

Here was one who was to play a stirring part in his life, some still small voice within him insisted; well, he was disposed to offer no resistance; he might be the man for the moment, and together they might accomplish much. To be able to influence a young officer of tried valor and intelligence, might be of great advantage to him in the future. Besides, the Count's condition aroused his interest and sympathy, the mental sketch he had rapidly drawn of him, if rough, being vigorous and of this type.

His mother, dead of a broken heart, in consequence of the failure of the 1830 affair; his father, half ruined pecuniarily, and wholly so mentally; his sister, the apple of his eye, but just insulted in a singularly brutal way; he himself, a fugitive from the home of his childhood, and in momentary peril of arrest, because of a natural display of promptitude, spirit, and right feeling. The galling sensation of belonging to a conquered and down-trodden people had been his birthright, and to resent such oppression had been the one great lesson, taught him so effectually that his whole being had become impregnated with it. The Count had freely told him, how in his earlier days he had dreamt of, and revelled in the doings of those from whom he had descended, and in his later ones had burned and panted to eclipse their gallant deeds, to lay down his life for his country, and win it back again from the cruel, gray-coated, stony-hearted Muscovite. Hernani knew that, with this aim in view, he had strengthened himself by means of all manly exercise—practicing thrift, rigid economy, working early and late—the result being that when at the Ecole Militaire he had signally distinguished himself, and when in the pay of the Austrian and Italian Governments had shown such aptitude and intelligence, that he had been twice decorated for his services. With a few clear touches such as these, he sought to outline and appreciate Count Andrew Dorozynski. In his sister, Deotima, he considered that he saw a more impulsive, if possible, more patriotic figure; warm-hearted, affectionate, truthful, a sister worthy of such a brother, and one in whose heart an admiration, amounting almost to adoration of that brother, ranked before her love of her country, even before her hatred of the Moskals.*

These were the sort of people who, in Hernani's opinion, had come beneath his roof; and in so considering them, he thought of them merely as types of well-bred Poles.

---

*Russians.

Meanwhile political events developed with speed, appearing in hot succession, shaping to one great end.

People who had filled the churches, and, in spite of threats from the authorities, remained there praying in honor of the national hero, Kosciusko, had been arrested and carried off to the fortress in large numbers.

The declaration of a state of siege had checked many of the outward signs of rebellion. The hymn or prayer for liberty was no longer borne upon the breeze, there were no more discontented gatherings and political celebrations, and apparently the Government were masters of the situation.

Yet, though the Russian chiefs were for the most part ignorant of the fact, the hidden machinery worked smoothly; the engines of agitation, well fed, were grinding at top speed through the darkness of night. The funds of the Moderate or White party were steadily swelling; the Reds or extreme men of the party of action were marshaling their forces, levying taxes, printing and spreading over the country a secret journal, establishing a National Committee, which was to develop into the Central National Committee, and thence into the National Government. Nothing was suffered to stand still, the great cry of "Forward" having gone up.

And in the midst of this energetic, arduous and daring movement, glance at Hernani's great banking machine.

Every tiny wheel worked well there, by not so much as a few grains of dust was that huge money mill affected, though the external confusion was actually terrific. Business was not suffered to languish, the sinews of war did not stiffen, and were kept oiled by what seemed magic, and people who knew the real condition of affairs hurried into the square, only to find all quiet and orderly, smiling and prosperous as the faces of the intelligent and hard-working clerks, the polite and methodical cashiers and heads of departments, strong, and apparently unassailable as its calm and resolute chief—Hernani.

Early and late he labored, with a perseverance equaled only by his untiring strength. After the arduous business day, when under other circumstances he would have sought complete relaxation of some kind, he discussed fresh schemes and attended to obligations already incurred, and of a varied nature, or with Dorozynski disguised so that the old Count himself would have failed to recognize him, penetrated into a new life, a new world—that of underground Warsaw, where he controlled, advised, received reports, issued instructions and inspired, as many had grown to think, he alone could inspire; for since the affair of the square, where he had seen defenseless people indiscriminately slaughtered, he had ceased to hold himself aloof—had, in fact, become a ruling spirit.

With so much upon his hands, it followed that Sara was thrown into Dorozynski's society, and piqued by the chill courtesy with which Hernani treated her when alone, she rather encouraged the young fellow's evident admiration for her, with the dangerous object of kindling Hernani's jealousy if she could.

In the presence of a third party, his treatment of her was that of a dignified but sufficiently affectionate husband, but when on several occasions she had attempted to break through the reserve he affected when alone with her, she had endured the mortification of having her advances repelled.

"I don't know when I've laughed so much," she told him upon one occasion, having been listening to some amusing stories of Parisian life which the young Count had related admirably.

"You think him entertaining?" demanded Hernani sharply.

"Very."

"Charming, in fact?"

"Yes."

"God of Israel," he roared, suddenly beside himself with rage, forgetful of his good resolutions and remembering only his fancied wrongs, "such women as you ought never to be married! Any foolish boy can possess himself of all the trumpery affection you are capable of."

Sara heard him in speechless amazement. Was he mad, to talk so? Then, quickly as a woman would grasp it, the real meaning of his behavior flashed upon her. He was jealous. Then he loved her still. With her beautiful eyes luminous with the light that shone in them only for him, she extended her arms as though to encircle him, to lay his head once more upon her bosom. Her lips parted with an enraptured smile, and

"Kasimir, you love me—you do love me!" escaped her.

For one brief instant she was on the verge of regaining him, and could he for that instant have remained dead to thought, her marvelous beauty must have triumphed, and they would have been sobbing deliriously in each other's arms. But, alas! poor Sara; disappointment was upon her swiftly. The very means she had employed, the coquettish effort on her part to stir his feelings, to say to him, "See, young and handsome men spend their time with me and are at my feet," coupled with the voluptuous abandon of her attitude, were to him at that moment only fresh proofs of her shallow unworthiness, possibly infidelity. All men were one and the same to her, the heartless hussy! But he would be fooled no longer. It was time he broke adrift from such snares, snapped such worthless ties. To do so would be a victory for him. With ill-suppressed wrath he just contrived to hiss between his clenched teeth—

"I—love you? Oh! do I? Ha! ha! No: I did once, but that piece of experience was enough." And turning his back upon her, he left her standing watching him, until the door he banged behind him hid him from her sight, and she, cold and bloodless as marble, sank nerveless upon the soft rug spread beside her bed.

After such words and so little deserving them, some women would have begun to dislike, to become revengeful, to keep the wound his bitterness had inflicted raw and gaping; but upon Sara's loving nature, absorbed in and devoted to him once and therefore always, they only acted as the whip does upon the dog, and had she been a dog she would have pined for his caresses; as a woman, she longed for him more, and last thing fell on her knees and prayed to God to give him to her.

"The master is jealous," said Riva, who was shrewd, and kept her eyes open always, where her mistress was concerned; "he is jealous, so he loves you still, my lamb. Is Riva right?"

"No," answered Sara, with a pain in her face.

"Then what is amiss with him?"

"I do not know."

"But I know, my love."

"There is nothing fresh."

"But there is, and it is just what I say. He is jealous of Count Dorozynski, and I don't wonder. What a figure and face, and mad for love of you."

"You're a fool, Riva!" screamed Sara, for once exasperated beyond control, longing almost to strike the woman, so much did she suffer.

With a cloud of reproach darkening her face, and without one word, Riva just gazed at her reproachfully, then left the room.

CHAPTER X.

Another day had ended in quietness, and the evening
had come on with a gentle and refreshing breeze, in
which the trees in the great quadrangle, where stood
the Hernani palace, rustled and waved pleasantly. Overhead, the stars were flashing distantly, in tremulous submission to the fuller light of a cloudless moon, in the
searching rays of which, the houses and pavements appeared dazzlingly white.

All at once, the silence, which had been that of a city
resting, was broken by the heavy and regular tramp of
a little knot of strong, stout, great-coated figures, who
entered the square and deliberately marched along one
side of it until Hernani's door was reached, when their
leader stepped forward, and with a cautious knock demanded admission. Scratching his uncombed hair and
blinking furiously, the tired and startled dvornik*
crossed himself and opened to the summons. An instant's pause while a few words were whispered in the
man's ear, and the fortress was stormed and won. The
compact little body of gendarmes and men in civil dress
clanked up the steps, to the right and left of which
stretched Hernani's business premises, and, passing
through a massive inner door which the dvornik unhesitatingly opened for them, stood in a warmer atmosphere, amongst the exotics, beneath the great dome,
where stood the fountain with its silvery imagery of
the oasis and the tottering form of the parch-stricken
Arab dismounting from his camel.

A slight departure from the usual proceedings was

*Porter.

now noticeable. Instead of dispersing over the house, securing the screaming women and alarmed men in their very bed-chambers, in obedience to an order from their chief, who was accompanied by a red-bearded and bulky personage, whose behavior was that of a spectator, the party halted where it stood, appearing like 'a body of bronze statues in the pale silver refulgence which streamed through the arching glass above them.

Meanwhile the dvornik, frightened and wondering, had dashed up the main staircase and communicated with Hernani, who quickly arrived upon the scene, calm and self-possessed, though in reality disturbed, even much alarmed by the unusual occurrence.

"You have a warrant for this intrusion?" he demanded in a firm voice.

"Undoubtedly, or we should not be here."

"Have the goodness to show it to me."

"It is unnecessary. You are Kasimir Hernani?"

"I am."

"Very well; we will proceed with our work. We shall make a search. You will give us every assistance."

Knowing the uselessness of remonstrance, the absurdity of threats, or a display of the indignation he felt, Hernani took out some keys, and passing down the marble steps into the vestibule, entered the banking portion of the establishment, followed closely by the police; one man alone remaining motionless beneath the dome, as if on guard, watching intently. This was the personage whose conduct throughout had been that of an onlooker.

Abruptly aroused from what, for a wonder, had been a refreshing sleep, and agitated as any woman would be under such trying conditions, Sara at once thought of Dorozynski and Deotima. The search must be for them. The police had discovered their hiding-place, and had come to arrest them. With speed and deftness she thrust her little bare feet into slippers, coiled her

hair into a firmer knot, and, enveloped in a long loose
wrap which effectually concealed her night attire, hurried to Deotima's room, with the result, that in a couple
of minutes, Count Andrew and his sister were descending into the garden, by one of those spiral iron staircases
not uncommon in old Polish houses.

Consoled by the reflection that she had done her best
for them, and that in the quaint old garden, favored by
the hour and the dense shadows, they would have a fair
chance of escape, Sara next went to reassure some of
the servants, who were three parts panic-stricken, and
then, anxious about Hernani, and feeling that her place
was at his side, she hastened to join him, and was in
the act of gliding noiselessly between a clump of feath-
ery-leaved bamboos and the fountain, when from out
the shade of the plants a figure advanced and a voice
said in low but authoritative tones—

"Madam, a word with you. Let us go in here." And
stepping up to the curtained door of the very room in
which Sara had overheard Bloch and Hernani talking,
the man opened it as though the place belonged to him,
and she followed mechanically, thrown off her guard by
the strangeness of the situation, the suddenness of the
request made by this stout, military-looking personage,
whose face was hidden by the large flat-topped cap he
wore in defiance of all courtesy, whose shaggy red beard
looked savage and repulsive, and, strange to say, whose
voice, it flashed upon her, she had heard before. She
could not divest herself of this idea, and also for the
first time she remarked that the whole place was lighted
up; this room into which she had been invited being
illuminated like the rest. An expression of irritation stole
over her face. Her fears, then, were about to be real-
ized. She would be forced to look on, while the sanctity
of her home was violated, her beautiful rooms dese-
crated, her Lares and Penates defiled by the hands and
feet of coarse strangers. This great unwieldy brute, this

clumsy Cossack in front of her, how dare he come there at dead of night and march her about, addressing her as though he had a right to do so! The thought exploded in speech.

"For what reason have you invaded us in this manner?" she demanded, both voice and bosom betraying the emotion she strove to control. The red-bearded man smiled, calm and secure in his official superiority.

"Does your conscience not tell you that, madam?" was his stern yet half amused reply.

"My conscience? No."

"It is possible that it should. However, you have lived here long enough to understand the meaning of this visit. The police wish to satisfy themselves that all in this house are loyal and devoted subjects of my master, his Imperial Majesty, the Tsar."

"No cause for doubt upon the subject has been supplied to them."

"You take a grave responsibility upon yourself when you say so."

"I believe in my household as in myself."

"Misplaced confidence too probably."

"I have never had cause to doubt them."

"You may have; and, madam, we, the police, think differently to you, though by all the Saints I hope wrongly, or we should not have disturbed your slumbers. But accept my assurance that there is no desire to annoy you or anyone, only to do what duty demands, quietly and well."

The soothing effect of the last few conciliatory words was somewhat marred by the entrance of the chief of the search party, who, with an apology for the interruption, delivered a little bundle of papers.

"These documents may prove important, sir, and I would draw your attention more especially to this one," he remarked, with an air of respectful deference. Then, receiving no reply that detained him, he retired.

"This one? Ah! let us see. Why, what have we
unearthed? There can be no doubt. Some statistics
and remarks concerning the insurrectionary movement.
Some value may attach to this." Then, fixing his keen
eyes upon Sara as though he would read her very soul, he
continued in an easy, chaffing voice, "You see, madam,
the police are not always wrong. Would you guarantee the good conduct of your whole household now? I
think not, I think not. Ah! the police are cunning, very
cunning, I assure you. Their scent is keen, and sometimes it enables them to seek so well that they find all
sorts of queer things. But what is this? A signature
quite carelessly scribbled in the corner. Another surprise! Madam, it strikes me that this is not a case of
answering for your servants, but for yourself. This
document is signed—Sara Hernani. I have reason to
believe—are you that lady?"

"I am."

"That is unfortunate, decidedly. May I inquire
whether you are aware of what the discovery of this
means, what kind of fate will probably be yours, in consequence of having written such words and figures at
such a time? Your beauty will not avail you any better than your prayers. Your own handwriting con-
demns you. You thought to help set a trap, and you
have fallen into it. It is a pity."

Sara was alarmed, greatly so, but her fears were not
defined. They had yet to strike her with all their benumbing force. Besides, it would be foolish to give
way; she must be brave and make a good fight of it.
Pointing to the paper, she said, though with ·a hand
that shook—

"It is ridiculous; those remarks cannot harm me;
they are merely my own private views."

"Private opinions reduced to writing, and of sufficient
importance to be placed in your husband's custody are
dangerous. However, you know best, madam."

"But I have done nothing," she gasped, led on by this cunning allusion to her judgment.

"I have told you what I think. If these opinions of yours leave my hands, nothing can save you. In Russia we have strange and summary methods of dealing with such offenses. People guilty of them are generally never heard of again, and I repeat, that should I see fit, nothing can save you from the punishment I have described."

White to the lips and tongue-tied, Sara clutched a chair for support and sank into it. Under the lash of such brutal allusions she gripped the situation with terrible distinctness. She would be torn from her husband and her home there and then. Her body would be mutilated with the awful knout. She would be dead, and yet alive, a prisoner for life in Siberia. So colorless did she become, so like dying on the spot, as these appalling thoughts leapt upon her, that her tormentor, who had evidently miscalculated his strength to endure the sight of her anguish, sprang to her assistance, his arm upon her shoulder, his threatening tones gone.

"But listen, madam; it may not come to that—there should be no necessity. Those who know, can be silenced. They are my slaves. It shall be for you to decide. I can—ah! I will keep up this farce no longer. We shall be disturbed, and then—— Open your eyes and look at me. Do you hear? See—this beard is a false one."

Sara did just hear, could just open her eyes sufficiently to see that the man bending over her was his Excellency the Governor-General, who, as if to leave no doubt of the fact, added—

"I am General Hourko, and no one knows it but yourself and the chief of the gendarmes; so you see, on your part you have a little secret to keep, which I will help you to do by assuming my disguise. Come—don't be alarmed. I had no intention of betraying myself, but

you would have fainted, and I have no wish to give you
pain. As I have told you all along, I take an interest
in you."

Hourko had stepped back to readjust the deceptive
tuft of red hair, as well as to survey Sara, and gloat over
her beauty. Having sunk back nerveless in the large
chair, her slippered feet were half exposed to his roving
gaze, and at sight of their tempting whiteness, passion
gleamed in his eyes, while his large, strong-jawed face
reddened as the blood leapt into it.

Recovering herself with a great effort, Sara saw the
look and understood its meaning.

"You," she said feebly—"you take an interest in me?"

"A great one, believe me. You need fear nothing
from this document. It will be perfectly safe in my
keeping; you have only to be a little more considerate
for me. This descent upon you was my planning. I
wanted to see you, to hear your voice, to feast my eyes
upon you. And I had pictured you just as I have found
you, in this charming dishabille, only you are a thousand times lovelier than my imagination had painted
you. See—now I have explained, you have no cause
for alarm. You must have confidence in me, that is all.
There must be a perfect understanding between us. I
would bring pleasure into your life, not pain."

A growing sense of dread and distrust stole over Sara.
Her limbs trembled from the unwonted excitement. Her
whole body shook with nervousness. She was conscious
too of anger mingled with disgust. The meshes of this
strong man's net were closing around her. In spite of
her struggles she was more completely encompassed
than ever. And he had dared to approach her at dead
of night, and beneath her husband's roof had poured
poisonous words into her ears. The desperate situation
in which she found herself, suddenly acted like a tonic.
She was not only strong again, she was reckless. If
her life was at this man's mercy, if it was to take what

shape he pleased, and drag to its close in pain and suffering, at least there need be no degradation in it, since her honor would remain to the end unblemished. She stood up erect.

"You would give me no pain—then leave me. There can be no understanding—as you call it—between us, since no honest woman could listen to the language you have used without feeling insulted. There are some women who prefer death to dishonor. I am one of them."

Hourko's face was swept by emotions. Was it possible that he, the Governor of Poland, the Tsar's representative, should be so spoken to, snubbed, taught the meaning of the word honor, and by a Jewess? His ears tingled. How absurd; he was not going to accept such a ridiculous situation. She was acting, going into heroics, playing the highly virtuous rôle, so as to increase her value in his eyes. All through his life his experience had taught him, that this exalted twaddle, ran skin-deep only—was, in short, mere gilding.

"You misunderstand me," he said insinuatingly.

"Unfortunately I do not."

"You are mistaken. We shall come to know each other better, and then you will regret your words."

"May the God of my fathers forbid"—and then, overwrought, in despair: "Your Excellency forgets that for the oppressed there is the grave; but as a Russian officer you cannot forget that your presence is an infliction to an unprotected Jewess."

"Cannot forget what! By all the Saints, you shall have cause to regret these insults!" exclaimed Hourko, placing the little bundle of papers in his pocket, and half turning on his heel to go. "But, no—I won't get angry with you. If I left you in this way, I should only blame myself five minutes after. I have a quick temper, which luckily does not last long. But, as I have said, you must treat me with a little more consideration. It is only reasonable. Because I admire you, and in a weak moment, when you were terribly distressed, told you so, boldly, bluntly, if you like, I don't see why you should jump to the conclusion that I wish to wrong you. Why think ill of me without a cause?"

His sudden change of front was admirable. He was tender but respectful. Paying homage at the feet of beauty, imploring only to be heard. And he had calculated the effect of this alteration in his manner to a nicety. Sara was partly disarmed at once.

"I think ill of no one unjustly. God forbid," she murmured in a low and quivering voice, that told how she longed to find a friend and kindness, rather than an enemy and strife.

"But have I ever injured you in any way? Tell me that."

"No—not that I know of."

"Then dismiss the idea that I am capable of such unkindness from your mind, and judge me as you have found me. You will recognize the truth of what I say, when I tell you that you stand in much need of friends, and that events ahead will render that need constantly more pressing; is it not so?"

"It is true."

"Then count on me a little. You tell me that there can be no understanding between us; my reply is that for your sake there must be; otherwise, who is to keep your and your husband's head above ground. Supposing that I do not suppress this document, but allow the law to take its course, your arrest and his would follow at once."

"His? Why?"

"He is guilty of many things. And those things are all known. Everything is known. The walls listen, and we know what they hear. Do you understand me? Now let the commencement of this little compact between us, be your silence as to my visit and my words. Mind, tell no one, or it will be told to me again. Now I must go;

be easy at heart. I shall find means to communicate with you when it is advisable."

"But——" stammered Sara.

"Hush! It must be as I say," he interrupted, and without giving her time for more words, with a quick movement he seized her hand, pressed it firmly in his strong grasp, and then, like a dark shadow, left the room.

"So her husband is her weak point," he muttered, as without word or order he clanked down the entrance steps, and, with the old dvornik bowing low from fear of him, emerged into the night air; "the fortress must be stormed from that side. I thought so, I had my suspicions, but I had to be cautious in alluding to him; now I know, and it is always good to know. This intrigue grows in excitement and interest, and without excitement of this sort I should die. How lovely she is, and what a fright she was in! Perhaps I was an ass to let her know who she was dealing with—perhaps I have been stupid—but no matter. If I thought she was genuine now—virtuous—ah! if——" And with a yawn, expressive of the gravest doubt on that score, Hourko hailed a droshky and, jumping into it, rattled away in the direction of the palace.

Within an hour after he had gone the Hernani mansion became as dark as the grave. The police had disappeared as they had come, like specters. White and shivering, Sara had returned to bed, and the whole household had followed her example and that of Count Dorozynski and his sister, who had gladly exchanged their temporary imprisonment in the garden, for the comfort of their own rooms, where curled up in warmth, the Count fell asleep, firmly impressed with the belief that Sara was as cool and plucky as she was beautiful, and that to her courage and tact, he and Deotima were indebted for their continued liberty.

With one swift searching glance, the effect of General Hourko's strange visit can be grasped.

10

Sara herself felt prostrated, and with racked brain and wide open eyes lay staring into the blackness of the coming day. She had been in no way prepared for this last blow, and it seemed one calculated to stun the strongest. How could she summon courage to fight against such odds, and what was to be her end? were the questions she put to herself. Was she indeed doomed to be torn from her husband, to become the plaything of a human tiger, notwithstanding her efforts, her prayers? And then, was she to be lost in the mists of the Siberian night, to be thrust into that hideous country from which so few ever returned? How often had women of her persuasion met with such deaths. All the saddest and most terrible stories of cases told her by those whose word she could trust, recurred to her. The closed cells of her mind opened for the escape of harrowing details, until that moment forgotten for years. A sensation of helplessness and loneliness indescribable stole over her. She was like a hunted animal with the hot breath of her pursuers upon her, strength and heart failing, and no aid at hand. Sunk in this despair for hours, gradually she rallied, and as her mind cleared, the natural buoyancy of her nature asserted itself. With all the ills she had reckoned against her, what could she count on her side? There was comparative youth, health, and beauty, and in addition, courage; for forced into this critical situation, into this corner from which there seemed no escape, she began to feel the existence of this superb quality. Timidity would not serve her; the time had come, or was close upon her, when unaided she must either swim upon the turbulent waters surrounding her, or sink in weakness, perhaps misery. And after all, nothing that the future hid, could crush her as the sound of Hernani's voice had done. when he had thundered, "Any day I may have to divorce my wife." Those words still stood out with cutting clearness. Once again, for an instant, it occurred to her to go to him, to tell him the whole history of her dealings with Hourko, and seek his protection and advice; but her pride, hardening with the recollections of the things he had said and done, forbade the step. Had he not told her that he no longer loved her? What more did she want? She would say nothing.

If he did not know what had become of the paper she had covered with figures, and her own ideas, and had playfully laid before him, hoping to say to him by the simple act, "See—I am interested in whatever interests you," so much the better. She would cause him less anxiety. More fortunate still, he might never miss it, might have forgotten all about it, or believe he had destroyed it.

So when the two met in the light of day neither could read the face of the other, for Hernani did know, and was acting as cleverly as she was, though trembling for her the while. Signs of anxiety were soon apparent in the others. Dorozynski, naturally capable of grappling with difficulties, was silent and preoccupied, as though a problem had presented itself for solution; something he did not quite like to talk of, did not know how to talk of. Deotima, usually as blithe as the birds she had learned to love, in the woods and pastures round the old château where she had been born, evidently had some weight upon her mind. The coils of her fair hair were less carefully confined, and her cheeks were paler, while her large blue eyes were heavy from sleeplessness. As tall as her brother—Count Andrew being a small man when compared with Hernani—the young people presented a marked contrast side by side on the staircase, where they stood talking; she so fair, with snowy neck and hands, and with eyes like the sky after an April shower—he, lean, compact and soldier-like, with aquiline nose, and close-cropped, curly black hair.

"What shall we do, Andrew?" she asked for the third or fourth time.

"Oh! I'll think it over. Don't you worry, little one."

"How can I help it?"

"But try."

"It's impossible.   We must go from here."

"Why?"

"We must."

"But why?"

"Because it would be unsafe to remain."

"I'm not so sure of that."

"Andrew!"

"How can we move?   Besides, probably, they dare not arrest us—the brutes!"

"Dare not?   Why?"

"Because we are Dorozynskis.   That should be sufficient."

"Just why they should seize us."

"Well, don't distress yourself—leave it to me."

And then came a meal, during which the conversation was disjointed, each one having more than enough to think of, Hernani furtively devouring Sara, as though he were looking his last upon her, before the entrance of the police who were to tear her from him—this woman upon whom he doted, every particle of whose flesh was a thousand times dearer to him than his own, for whom he had lived and striven, and—if he might judge by the anguish he endured, and had endured for her—whose death would occasion his own—this woman was to be torn from him at any moment, wealth and personal standing availing him nothing.   Dirty-fisted, half-washed fellows, whose very breath was pollution, would lay hands upon her, revelling in the chance afforded them of handling and insulting so perfect a specimen of womanhood. His inability to prevent it would equal that of an infant. In some filthy prison she would remain unfed and unwashed; she would become emaciated and her hair would grow gray and fall off.   In an agony of spirit, he started from the table, abruptly excusing himself for his departure.   Then, after a time, when a moment served, with quivering lips and a tongue dry as though fire-scorched, he unburdened himself to Dorozynski—told him everything; how that this document was as damning as words could make it, under an unkind eye, adding his fears and reasons for dreading the worst.

"And now, what am I to do?" he finally demanded.

"Are you sure that she knows nothing and suspects nothing?" inquired the Count.

"Certain. How should she?"

"Then, my friend, cost what it may, you must keep silence, and should she ask about this precious paper, which, were I hard-hearted I might blame you for not having destroyed, be ready with the best lie and the smoothest face you can summon. Poor thing, she would be half dead with fright if she knew what we do. Keep her in ignorance—that is the only plan."

"But they may return to arrest her at any moment."

"Good heavens! I forgot that—and you too."

"Of course. For me it is all right; I can suffer. Ah! I am well used to it."

"But you forget—our country is in bondage for lack of men with heads and hearts like yours. You are a power. Don't let us think, much less speak of such misfortunes, such horrors. One thing is certain—flight is useless. Even with your experience it would fail, and by the simple attempt, guilt would be admitted. But, a word for one instant, if you will forgive me for talking about myself, which but for my sister I would not do. What should be my course? Shall I leave here?"

"On no account."

"I could hide in a score of dens, where I should be safe."

"And take your sister?"

"Ah! that's the difficulty. I don't want to drag her into roughing it, though she would glory in it. Perhaps Zamoyski would help me."

"Count Zamoyski can help no one—will not be able

even to help himself if Wielopolski has his way. Is it
not clear to you? The Marquis——"

"Whom no man loves."

"Yet who means well, I firmly believe, will stomach no
rivals. In his opinion, any more fingers in his pie will
spoil it; so with him it is—take them out or they will be
burnt. Besides, Zamoyski is too anxious to stand well
with the government, to be tempted into helping a noble-
man such as yourself, who, in the cold eyes of that government, is under a cloud—forgive me for the expression. No—be advised. Remain where you are. You
are welcome, you are wanted, and I firmly believe you
are safe, or I would be the last to say 'Stay.' This police
visit was not on your account, rest assured. Ah! our
talk has soothed me, set my brain working and nerved
me, so that I feel—even with all these troubles weighing
me down—strong as a lion. They have yet to discover
what it means to press and fight with a man like me.
Listen; we must arrange so that, should this house be
forcibly entered, we can escape through the garden and
the door in the wall I have shown you, into our good
friend Nikolay Brauman's premises, and thence elsewhere."

"But you may have spies amongst your servants."

"I don't think it."

"Or if that is not so, some of your employes will be in
touch with these accursed police. Would I had the
whole body of them by the throat."

"Again, I don't think it. I have selected them all with
the greatest care, and have treated them, without exception, generously enough to attach them to me."

"In that case, there may be ten spies where one might
have been looked for. Such is human nature."

"I disagree with you. If you would be trusted, you
must trust. I selected these people because I knew they
hated the existing state of things, and I've trusted them
because I have in part proved them to be worthy of my

confidence. No; I refuse to rake up doubts of this kind. We are not responsible for what we cannot help, and therefore should not consider."

"True."

"As a rule you are so confident, so cheerful."

"And so I am now, only our uninvited visitors have made me feel that caution of the closest kind must be exercised."

Hernani tugged at his long moustache unconsciously. Then, rising from his chair with an expressive gesture of approval, he exclaimed—

"Ah! now you have it. That is the lesson we must lay to heart. Caution. In addition, we want time—and if we get it we need not despair; we shall accomplish great things. My fear from the first has been that you were too impulsive."

Dorozynski smiled.

"And this has struck you, because occasionally, it is the greatest relief to me to give free vent to my feelings. I have got into a habit of talking to you as I talk to no one else."

"Keep to it; you shall never regret it. But in the midst of misfortunes here is some good news for you. I learn that we are doing wonders by means of our secret press. The country will soon be as one man, united, irresistible. Subscriptions for large amounts are pouring in, enlistments are frequent, and by means of widespread connections, arms, in fair quantities, are traveling towards us, slowly but surely. The day is not far distant when, if it seems well, we shall be strong enough to rise en masse, and then for a rush upon the Citadel. We shall overpower the troops, and Warsaw will be ours."

"I shall be in the front; you will see me in the front," shouted the Count, unable to restrain his enthusiasm.

"You are right, and in the front we shall both be, with a sea of good men behind us. The thought makes me ten years younger. But now we must do, not talk. Ah!

if I could only know what steps the police will take.
What a fool I was not to have destroyed that—in fact,
all the papers. Strange how it could escape me." And
Hernani heaved a sigh that shook his large shoulders.

Before many days were out, since no demand for admittance rang through the house, no visit in force at
dead of night was made, Hernani found himself growing interested in watching Sara closely. She seemed to
him unlike the same woman. Instead of the anxious
dependency upon others, the looking out for love, for
sympathy and attention, which he had thought to be a
part of her nature, and had admired, though latterly had
much ignored, she behaved as though she had suddenly
learned a lesson of self-reliance not to be forgotten. But
by whom or what was she inspired? Restless and rapid
in speech and movement, she was simply a masculine
edition of Sara, wound up to go at speed. Not an instant of her day was spent with her old tranquillity. She
was wearing herself out, in a high state of fever, and
what was the cause? Did she know of the action of the
police, and in consequence of the position she was placed
in, or more properly, they were placed in? But that
idea was no sooner thought of than dismissed. She
could not know; it was impossible. Much more likely,
he reasoned, that with the keen perceptive faculty of her
sex, she scented the nearer approach of the threatening
crisis. That was it. The conversations between Dorozynski and himself were sufficient; she had overheard
them and was agitated. For the future he must be more
careful, for though she had treated him ill, had secrets,
was even false to him as he feared, he had no wish to
alarm and harass her by constant allusions for which her
temperament was unsuited. And all the while Sara was
flitting about him, regarding him with the eyes of love,
longing to cast all pride to the four winds, praying God
that they might be reconciled if only for a day, and re-

garding with terror the future, in which it seemed to her their separation was decided.

Since she had had time to think, her fears were for him, rather than for herself. Over and over again, with sickening persistency and acknowledged weakness, she had recalled Hourko's threatening remarks concerning him. "He is guilty of many things," rang in her ears. And she had gone to him as soon as she dare trust herself to speak, and upon the basis of this domiciliary visit, had implored him to use all the caution possible.

"Already you are suspected," she had said.

"May be," he had answered gloomily.

"Your shadow upon the wall is watched."

"Possibly; I am not afraid."

"For that very reason you will be caught; foolhardiness will be your ruin."

"I don't want my womenkind to predict my ruin."

"Your womenkind? You mean me, I suppose?"

"Whom else should I mean?"

"But it is because they—it is because I care. Oh! Kasimir, in thinking of these things you little know how I suffer."

And then the big, strong, prosperous man, shook for a moment. His name upon her lips as of old, and her soft voice imploring him to be cautious for her sake. God—if she did but care! But then, that beast, Hourko —ah! she wanted to deceive him. It was another of her tricks. All the same, she was in jeopardy—she whom he loved—she might be wrenched from him—and yet—perhaps she was really safe enough. Hourko would see to that. He had scarcely thought of it that way. Ah! hateful thought; rather than owe her liberty to Hourko, better that she were dead—and yet—dead—it was difficult —his heart was so overcharged, his brain so strained, that without trusting himself to look at her, and in a husky voice, he could only just reply—

"The Most High—blessed be He!—has us in His keeping. We are safe now and always."

And he turned away, her eyes following him wistfully, her heart bounding to be at his side, her lips tremulous with the words, "If he would but be kind to me—if he would but be kind to me!"

Riva knew what was going on. If she did not actually see or hear, she imagined so accurately, from her long knowledge of those whom she served, that her mistakes were few. Near her mistress always when circumstances permitted, she had been the only one in the whole household who had heard her talking, while Hernani had led the way, and been occupied in his counting-house. What had been said, she knew not, but, lurking about in fear and trembling, she had seen Hourko's bulky form filling the half-open doorway, then disappearing with obsequious attention from the dvornik; and as friend rather than servant she had gone to Sara. Could she be of use? Was there anything she could get? Sara looked pale, faint—and no wonder. But seemingly with a great effort, coupled with a brusqueness altogether unusual in her treatment of Riva, or indeed of anyone, Sara had denied that she was ailing or in need of anything.

"Get to your bed, Riva," she had insisted. "It is the best thing you can do." And Riva, annoyed as a child might be, had gone, but with her quick wits at work, wondering vaguely. Since then, no confidences on Sara's part, scarcely an allusion to that night of nights—none as to whom she had spoken with, spy, gendarme or what not—and matters in Riva's mind were working furiously. For in addition came that change marked by Hernani—by Dorozynski, for that matter, though to him it was pleasurable in a sense. Forced gayety, unflagging energy, amounting to tirelessness, might deceive Dorozynski, whose knowledge of Sara was superficial, but the servant, the nurse, the friend, who with many failings was faithful according to her understanding, could not be so mistaken. Sara was in a more dangerous mood than she had witnessed, over all the long years bridging childhood and womanhood. But cunning as Riva was, she occasionally shot wide of the mark; and after casually recalling the deep male voice mingling with her mistress's silvery one, she set the matter aside, considering the man as a police functionary in pursuance of his duties. Sara was unhappy—she was sure of it—miserably so. More than that, her relations with Hernani were still the cause. How stupid it was! Why could not they have children to link them together like all other rational folk? A child—only one—would settle the matter. Riva was also as sure of that as that hens lay eggs; so she set to casting about, keeping her eyes open wider than ever, her ears distended under her lank black hair, so that nothing escaped them.

"Time sends it to sleep," Sara remarked to Deotima one day, speaking of sorrow, and having for the moment hammered her mind into thinking so, though her heart bled as she spoke.

"True enough; but time sends everything mundane to sleep, and the unfortunate part of it is that we may sleep our last sleep, before the soothing specific benumbs or affects our minds as we would wish," replied the girl, whose soft fingers were at work upon some rough warm shirts for those who were to take the field, and as she believed enthusiastically, restore her country's greatness.

"Time has played tricks with our poor old father, so far," put in the Count; "with snowy hair he is now encountering his greatest grief, since the mother died."

"Which is the enforced absence of both of you, I suppose?"

"Yes; Andrew means that."

"Of course I do. It makes me savage to think of him alone in that great house."

"I can understand and sympathize with you. But of

late you have had good news of him, haven't you?" Sara
inquired, looking up into the young fellow's face.

"Yes; the best that could be expected. Too good to
be true, I fancy sometimes."

"But papa would never deceive us," the girl insisted.
"Ah! I wish you could see him. No one could be hand-
somer. He is taller than Andrew—as tall as your husband, in fact, and straight as an arrow, with perfect features, snowy hair, and eyes like—like——"

"Yours," laughed the Count.

"Oh, mine are not half so blue. He is a dear. I only
wish I could kiss him."

"Do you remember how you used to tease him by kiss-
ing him on the neck, eh, you rogue? You are no light
weight, and once on his knee, he could only laugh,
though you tickled him frantically."

"But he liked it."

"Did he? I'm not so sure."

"Then, for saying such horrid things, you shall receive the same punishment." And, flinging her work
aside, she gave chase to her brother with the abandon
of a child of ten. "How foolish we are," she panted, after
a minute or two, the Count laughing at her futile efforts
from the other side of the table. "Oh! I am out of
breath."

"Yes, you must take care, sis. Why you are quite red
in the face. Really, you are too big for such frivolity."

"Don't be rude, sir."

"Do you remember when you fell into the pea-field
fish-pond, and I pulled you out with all your pretty
white clothes covered with duck-weed?"

Deotima blushed deliciously.

"Isn't he a tease?" she said, appealing to Sara, who
was amused in spite of herself.

"Would you believe it," pursued the Count, brimful
of mischief, "when I roared with laughter at the figure
she cut, with mud, weed, and feathers sticking all over

her, she drew herself up like a Duchess, and just shouted, 'Don't be rude, sir!' That was all I got for saving her life."

"Really, Andrew, you are too absurd. Saving my life! Why the pool was only about three feet deep."

"That's all you know. Three of water and three of mud would be more like the thing."

"Besides, ladies don't shout."

"Don't they, by Jupiter. If you didn't shout, you screamed. I thought you were being murdered."

"Oh! you are simply incorrigible. Come and hold this flannel and behave yourself, if you can."

"I'm not quite sure that I want to; but—shall I try? Very well. Those—ah! yes, those were jolly times," he added, subsiding into a chair, with a cigarette between his brown fingers, and a dreamy far-away look in his dark eyes.

"Jolly because they are past?" suggested Sara.

"Well, I'm not quite clear about that. We were young and thoughtless, I suppose."

"But don't you think we live too much for yesterday and to-morrow, and too little for to-day?"

"There's something in that," replied the Count, opening his eyes wider and becoming attentive, as he invariably was when Sara spoke.

"We are not philosophical when we do so, are we?"

"Perhaps not. I scarcely think so."

"We don't do justice to to-day. What work we have on hand is less thoroughly done, and our pleasures are less keenly entered into. We weaken our efforts by thinking of the wrong things at the wrong time."

"But then we are not mere machines," observed Deotima.

"That's exactly what we are, little stupid," answered the Count.

"We cannot control our thoughts," insisted the girl.

"Perhaps not wholly, but to some extent, and we can

guide them; at least I have brought myself to think so," said Sara deliberately.

"Oh! I agree with you; but though a weakness, in a vague sense, this groping in the past," the Count observed thoughtlessly, "you probably like to hark back to your own childhood—to live in it again mentally. Then you hadn't to think for yourself. There was nothing to trouble you, and you breathed and dreamed through every hour, half unconsciously perhaps, but yet delightedly, feeling it to be so very good. Was it not so?"

The allusion was too much for Sara. A film hid her sewing. She could scarcely see, and to hide her feelings got up and rummaged in the deep well of an inlaid worktable. Her childhood! Rough words, friendlessness, and her playing-ground the damp or sun-scorched pavements, or places where mud and filth lay thick; her greatest delight a flower that struggled in a pot. Later, the anxious, anæmic, storm-worn face of her hollow-chested father, playing his own part, and that of the faithful wife and mother, who had fallen asleep in a city whither the Russian Government would permit no return, having driven them from her grave with whips. Later again, the torn and shabby books the worn-out father could get by hook or crook, seeing his daughter cared for such things, and longing to teach her all he could, before he too was hustled gravewards. She could see it all, plainly as ever. But what a heart! How brave he had been, bidding her hope—always—with the tears in his eyes and the phlegm in his throat. With blue, bloodless lips, choking through asthma at night, and weak and faint in the day, yet gentle as a woman—his first lesson, his last one—teaching her to be honest and virtuous. Her childhood! She had never been a child.

Sufficiently mistress of herself, the apparent thing she sought for found, she turned from the work-table. What a contrast to her thoughts—this room with its luxury, these two young people of noble birth, her guests, herself beloved, or rather coveted passionately by the great man of the country—the Governor-General; she, the wife of the richest banker in all Warsaw; in addition, threatened with divorce because barren; finally, in the power of the police if it pleased her admirer and persecutor.

With her mind harping upon these things, knowing them all, was it not wonderful that it kept its balance, and was it not still more wonderful that she should feel strong? Like the great Catherine, self-made Empress of all the Russias, of whom she had read, did she indeed strengthen when sore beset.

Turning to Count Dorozynski, she said sweetly—

"No, I think I was not clever then—in my childhood. I cried too much. I might have saved my eyes. It was foolish. But then we are all foolish—always. As children, only in the lesser degree. My prayer still is that I may be given faith and wisdom. It is terrible to have only such a little life, and to find all the time, on looking back, that it has been lived so stupidly."

"Oh! but you take things too seriously," exclaimed Deotima.

"Do I? Perhaps, if one were a little wiser, one would be enabled to live so that to scrutinize the past would give one fewer shocks. But let us talk of something more cheerful."

"There, that's your fault, Andrew, you stupid old thing! Why do you stir up unpleasant recollections?" remarked the girl.

But the Count, like a man, did not take the broad hint, though quick enough to detect the ring of sadness in Sara's voice, and fascinated by it, as he had been before.

What possible trouble could she have, other than the common one of oppression? he asked himself. She had married for love, and had got riches as well. She was clever, healthy, and beautiful. What more could she want? She was to be envied. More than that, he had

got so far as to think that there would be no hardship
in having to fill the shoes of the man who possessed her.
It was scarcely possible to be with her constantly and
to look at her for long without these thoughts arising.
He would have wagered that ninety-nine men out of
every hundred would have echoed his sentiments. Without heeding Deotima's thrust at him, he observed to
Sara—

"So you dislike to review the past? Surely, considering all things, you have been fortunate, just as you seem
to be now?"

"Appearances are sometimes deceptive," replied Sara,
unconsciously using the very words which Hernani had
addressed to Bloch, before telling him of the strained
condition of his home ties.

"It strikes me that we are either very frivolous or
ridiculously solemn," interposed the young girl, bent on
supporting Sara and stopping her brother's mouth.

Quick to avail herself of the alliance, Sara replied—

"Yes; and if we would do great things, we must not
be guilty of little ones. What precious moments we have
been wasting." And she set to work with renewed ar-
dor.

As for the Count, he contented himself with gazing
admiringly at this young wife, who, with nimble fingers,
was embroidering the white eagle in silk, upon a material
of the same substance. Where would it float, and under
what conditions? Mentally he drew a picture of the
thick woods which were a feature of the country. Amidst
the tall stems of the pines, but thinly mingled with de-
ciduous trees, the Russian infantry were retiring in confusion, amounting almost to a rout. The vivid flashes,
the rattling detonations, and the puffs of blue smoke, indicating where they faced about, paused and fired, then
scurried off again in full retreat. The triumphant shouts
of his countrymen rang plainly in his ears. Victory was
with the white eagle. Bullet-riddled and smoke-be-

grimed it would flutter proudly in the wind. That would
be the termination of the contest; the Moskals would
be thrashed all along the line. It was a foregone conclusion. So real did it seem to him, and so strongly were
his sympathies enlisted in support of the imaginary idea,
that he found his pulses beating wildly, his breath coming short and thick, as though, already in the forefront of
the battle, he inspired and piloted his men. Mastering
his emotion, he approached Sara, and gathering some
folds of the banner in his hand, remarked—

"Yes, you are right to be busy; and I have a fancy
that in every Polish home it will be the same. I should
condemn myself as a worthless fellow for standing and
watching you, but that for the moment my share is done.
To-night again I shall be full of work. Ah! I tell you, it
is interesting. Nikolay Brauman has at last lent us his
cellars. They are huge, and amidst the flickering of both
gas and torchlight, the drilling and instructing of squads
of fine fellows goes on. I wish I could paint. What a
subject! Imagine whitewashed walls, supporting low
cracked ceilings, on all sides, plenty of evidence of the
presence of wine, in cask and bottle. Then, some dozen
pairs of broad shoulders, supporting the anxious, determined faces of men, who feel themselves on the eve of
delivering their country from the hand of the spoiler.
But that is the serious side of the picture. Overhead
there is something amusing to be seen. There, with superb indifference, the police are tramping about with the
regularity of machines. We can almost hear them.
It is a splendid joke."

Both women paused in their self-imposed tasks. The
Count had a way of riveting attention when he spoke.
His voice was a musical one, and when he became really
interested in his subject, the charm of his manner was
not only apparent, but irresistible. The expression on
the attentive faces of both his listeners was one of un-
disguised alarm. They were aware, to some extent, that

11

such things were happening, but to be told outright was painful to a degree.

"What if you were caught, Andrew?" exclaimed Deotima.

The Count shrugged his shoulders significantly.

"Well, it would be rather a bad business, sis."

"You would be shot."

"Lucky at that."

"Oh! think of papa. If anything happened to you, it would kill him."

Sara had listened in silence, quaking and white to the lips, in the presence of this forcible reminder of the imminent perils which beset Hernani. For herself, perhaps, there were some loopholes. If driven to desperate straits she would have to rely upon her wits, and stand or fall upon her manner of handling Hourko, but if caught red-handed, as it appeared he might easily be, how could she hope to save him?

The Count had watched Sara change color, and regretting the thoughtlessness of his remarks, he hastened to reassure her.

"The risk we run is really very slight. It would take a big body of police to do us any harm; besides, we are on our guard and are much too artful to be caught. You may make your mind easy, sis—we shall have good news to send home, not bad."

Hernani entering the room with Hermann Bloch, the Count fancied that something had pleased him, and said as much.

"What is it, man?" he inquired, drawing him aside. "Come—let me into the secret."

"Only that Bloch here has brought news of the safe arrival of a quantity of arms and ammunition, long since considered lost." And the two men began talking confidentially, while the little fat notary, clad in his shiny frock coat, perspired and fidgeted in his efforts to be civil to the two women, with whom it appeared he made poor

headway. Sara had grown to dislike the sight of his
white bristly hair, and keen little pig's eyes half buried in
rolls of red fat, and wondered how his wife, who was
rather pretty, could have been induced to marry such a
man. It had become almost unbearable to her to have
him about the house, ever since Hernani had made the
mistake of talking to him about her. Sheer nervousness
induced her to credit him with knowing a great deal
more than he did; little gossip that he was, frequenting
the cafés on his own admission, and always to be seen at
street corners, talking with odd-looking acquaintances.
In her distrust of him, she decided that the very atmosphere of sharp dealing clung to his clothes, while his
manner was like that of a detective. When bad fortune
befell her, it would come from such a quarter, and here
he was haunting the place.

Quite unconscious of the sentiments he unluckily created, after a few minutes spent in struggling against the
tide of disapproval, Bloch respectfully took his leave,
and Sara, breathing more freely, was at liberty to direct
furtive glances at Hernani's face, and read there all that
it betrayed to her. Some time had elapsed since she had
had a good look at him, and it at once struck her that
he was thinner, besides being more excitable and restless in manner, as one working at high pressure. Otherwise, his finely-moulded features, set off by the bronzed,
healthy complexion she had at first admired, were just
the same, showing no signs of the attacks time was making upon him. The poise of his head and the spread of
his shoulders were unaltered; he was as erect and stately as on the day when he had entered the house where
he had found her in Cracow. No gray hairs seamed the
long curling moustache, and his splendid brown eyes—
not the least opaque, as common, and to be distrusted—
were as clear, fearless, and full of expression, as when
they at first made her pulses dance in the old time long
past. Watching him, thinking of the load of responsibil-

ity those broad shoulders carried, of the many anxious
and intricate thoughts passing beneath the smooth skin
of that spacious forehead, she felt thankful beyond the
power of her tongue to tell, that she had borne the weight
of her troubles, and not gone crying to him in the first
flush of her fears for her own safety. Had she ever discovered that Riva was right, and that his head was full
of another woman, her attitude would no doubt have
been that of the enraged tigress, rather than of the patient, burden-bearing ship of the desert. As it was, she
was charitable and gentle, and every petty detail of her
home life was dwelt upon and attended to, with scrupu-
lous care and unspeakable affection. Soon it would no
longer be her lot to have these duties to perform, for if
the projected revolt became a Russian defeat, her dismissal would come the quicker; that would be certain,
for Hernani, with time on his hands, would again be
Hernani, full of the failure she had been to him. Yes,
she was aware of it—he would sweep her aside, as the
wind hurls the autumn leaves. The Russians triumphant
—as she could never help fearing they would be—meant
that they would be fugitives upon the face of the earth—
their vast wealth confiscated—a price upon their heads
—or worse—Hernani in a fortress, en route for Siberia
or Kamtchatka, she in the power and at the mercy of his
Excellency the Governor.

So daily and hourly she seemed to take leave of her
luxurious home, every corner of which was so indescrib-
ably dear to her. To look at a picture, or with careful
fingers to dust a piece of china, was to examine and touch
a dumb friend, for her woman's heart was full of affection for these trifles, which to a masculine mind under
similar conditions would scarcely have appealed. Thus,
the magnitude of the issues at stake, did not prevent her
from considering the minutiæ surrounding her, though
she found plenty of time to think of the weightier matters, with a lucidity and grasp which left little to carp at.

The Governor's silence and inaction, so far as she was concerned, was a mystery to her. What was he doing? What was he thinking of?—cooped up with that subtle-looking villain, as she thought of him—Titus Popoloff. Perhaps he was too full of the political game he was playing to think about her. No doubt her turn for persecution would come during a lull, or at least, fast enough. Meantime she could only say to herself over the samovar, where it was so necessary to appear cheerful and act well, "If they only knew what I endure—Kasimir and these other people." And, with a sense of satisfaction that she could be so brave and bear so much, she would hand and sip the yellow tea that soothed and refreshed her.

There could be no doubt that she derived an immense amount of consolation from Deotima's society, though ignorant of the extent of the interest she already took in the young girl. Attracted towards each other by the common misfortune of oppression, the desire for freedom was at once an indissoluble bond between them, which was further cemented by Deotima's unvarying amiability. And then, the two men, Hernani and the Count, not only shared the same interests, but agreed so well over them, which was another tie.

So shut up in that luxurious house, where it seemed best for them to remain almost close prisoners, they worked and talked, casting anxious eyes into the impenetrable future.

At the end of a day in which Sara had been more than usually busy with household matters, in addition to having received a number of visits from so-called friends, the two women were once more together, having seen next to nothing of each other for hours.

"Did any of your friends see me?" inquired the girl. "I was afraid they would, and rushed out of the way in a tremendous hurry."

"I don't think so. I should have been questioned had

you been noticed. You see you are not easy to hide," Sara replied, surveying Deotima's large and ripening figure with the admiration women often bestow upon each other.

"That is what Andrew means, I suppose, when he calls me a great gawky girl. I would much rather be your height, and have your ruddy-brown hair, than be as I am, so fair, all pink and white, like a china doll. But I did not make myself, that's one consolation."

"My dear child, you are all that could be wished for. Any man would be proud of you."

"I don't think any man will ever get me."

"Why?"

"Oh! just because——"

Sara laughed at the naive simplicity of this deliciously fresh plump maiden. Then pointing some silk with her teeth, to thread it, she returned to the charge.

"But tell me," she entreated persuasively.

Deotima became grave, the blood mounted to her cheeks and her eyes flashed.

"This is no time for marrying or thinking of marriage. As her daughter, Poland claims me."   .

A little shiver passed down Sara's back. The brave words, so full of meaning, thrilled through her.

"But have you made up your mind not to marry?" she asked gently, repressing her feelings.

"No."

"And you don't care for anybody?"

"Not as I should. Why, I have been shut up; with the exception of a few brother-officers of Andrew's, I have never met anyone. You see, we have been too poor to entertain, thanks to the way in which we have been deprived of our land. And mother's death had a great effect upon papa, who was heart-broken and would see no one. But if I ever marry, it will be for love, and if I love, I shall trust implicitly. I can do nothing by halves."

"It is the only way," answered Sara, surprised and interested in the same breath. Deotima was over-young to speak so shrewdly. Had she always trusted Hernani? she instantly asked herself, the penciled eyebrows tightening into a painful frown, as without stopping to investigate, to accuse herself of her one piece of deception which had been so well meant, she told herself that she was not to blame, since, if only she had been fruitful, all would have been well with her. Her failure was through no fault of her own, and with another brave effort to ignore this constantly-recurring misery of her life, and the consequences which were yet to come of it, she thought to give advice. "Yes," she said; "if you marry, you must trust—place your honor in your husband's keeping and let it rest there; but, let him know and feel it to be so. You don't mind me saying what I think, do you?"

"Go on," said Deotima.

"You are sure we understand each other?"

"Certain."

"Well, I have heard it said that we all begin by believing implicitly, by trusting absolutely, but that too often our eyes are roughly opened. The man proves worthless. But jealousy and suspicion, the tendency to expect too much, to give too little, may make one think this. Let a woman first satisfy herself as to his worthlessness, and be sure that it is none of her doing. Is he so, then she had best fly from him. At least her happiness with him is over. But in nine cases out of ten she is not sure, she is a little put out, dissatisfied, jealous, always too ready to doubt. Then the weak moment comes when she flings her doubt in the man's face, with this result: if he be by nature bad, she feeds his vice; if really good, she has done her best to make him bad—to turn the materials given her to the worst account. All women understand how to secure the man they covet, few, that having got him, the struggle has but commenced. But perhaps this does not interest you?"

"Yes, it does—go on."

Sara stitched away silently for a few seconds, and then observed—

"If you distrust an honest servant you may make a thief. To be no longer believed in, no longer trusted, means that the grossest insult has been tendered. Let a woman trust, I say, and cling to that trust as to her very life. You may mend broken china, but the cracks remain. Whatever women say to the contrary, and I have heard some strange things said, men possess that delicate commingling of many qualities, termed honor. Place a man on his honor, and much more often than not, he will proudly maintain the right, inherited from his birth, to be called an honorable man. Trust is the only card a woman holds worth playing. When her interest and happiness have been irrevocably staked, let her always say to the man, 'See, I trust you.'"

Stirred by her subject, conscious throughout of her own unhappiness, the convincing tones of her voice, so round and soft, rose and fell, and at length ceased, and Deotima, who had never before beheld her so animated, could not take her eyes off her face. The extreme beauty of her complexion was heightened by a deeper flush, her wide expressive lips, ruddy and parted, revealed teeth even and fair as pearls, while in the bright shaft of light cast by the shaded lamp, the fine curves of her figure, the warm hue of her hair and eyebrows, shielding those eyes which Hernani loved so well, were seen in all their rare perfection. Dazzled by her beauty, Deotima could only repeat Riva's sentiments and exclaim—

"If I were a man, how I should love you—my goodness, how I should love you!"

Sara blushed like a child, and without a word, worked, stitched as though her life depended upon the quickness of her needle, for she was completely disconcerted by the girl's blunt expression of her admiration. After a while she broke the silence which had fallen upon them.

"And since we are both women and I am a weak one?" she inquired timidly.

"I shall love you less selfishly. But then"—and she pouted deliciously—"you will not care—I mean, every-one loves you."

"One can never have too much love, never have enough," said Sara.

•"But you are so rich."

"What difference does that make?"

"You have so many distractions."

"Of what kind? You know my life."

"Oh! but just now no one is gay. Such gloom as this will not last; people will entertain again, the theaters will re-open, mourning will be cast aside. The women in black, will be an historical feature of the past, and all will be bright and gay, thoughtless and happy. As for me, I am sure to be buried in the country with Andrew, so you will forget me, and, like the butterfly emerging from the chrysalis, you will leave this house——"

"A beggar!" cried Sara wildly.

Deotima paused in astonishment, but only for a second, Sara having quickly recovered herself.

"My word—a beggar!" she repeated. "Wherever did you get such an idea? I should not mind sharing your poverty and grief."

"Do you think I am happy?" inquired Sara.

"Of course I do," said Deotima.

"Then I ought to have been an actress," answered Sara, with a little smothered laugh; "how well I must play. Seriously though," she added, laying her hand upon the young girl's knee and looking up into her face, "should I ever come to you, homeless, with no money and no friends, weary, and with only the clothes I stand up in, will you—will you be kind to me?"

"As long as I breathe," replied the girl impulsively.

"Very well, I warn you. I may put you to the test.
Now let us change the subject."

"I have not annoyed you?"

"How could you? What have you done? Hush!
that was the door—someone is coming; your brother or
my husband."

But no one came. Sara's ears had deceived her, and
for a long while they were silent, both of them full of their
own thoughts.

Annoyed at having so nearly betrayed her feelings to
Deotima, Sara again began to criticise her conduct towards Hernani. She had plenty of advice to offer to
others, and yet had somehow made a mull of her own
affairs. Why had she not pocketed her pride and sought
an explanation, even after the conversation she had overheard? Ah! if only she had not heard him say what he
had. She would have credited no reports. But her own
ears! It was too much. And what would have been the
use? She would have knelt at his feet and he would have
said, "Get up; you know my feelings. I am disappointed, and I have said so, often." She would have hastened
her own downfall perhaps. Anyhow, it was too late.

And just then Deotima alluded to an oft talked-of
project—that of visiting home. Much as she loved her
brother, she would like to return, if only for a few hours.
Her father was old and lonely, and it would be so sweet
to get a peep at him, and the old place so full of memories. But Andrew opposed the step, and her father
appeared to be in league with him. So far as she was
concerned there could be no danger, and no one need be
the wiser, since she could easily go and return without
being observed. The distance was not great, and for the
time of year the roads were good; besides, she knew
every inch of the way. It was all very fine to say that
she was of most use where she was. She could not see it.
And what difference could a few hours make, either one

way or the other? Andrew was not a baby, and could
sew his own buttons on, if it came to that.

"Oh, you will go one of these days," Sara remarked
soothingly; "meantime, you are safer here." And with
a few more opinions on Deotima's side the conversation
dropped.

Sara went out one afternoon, accompanied by Riva.
She was obliged to go, but while the old servant babbled
of her own views and feelings and dropped her choice
bits of wisdom, Sara was intensely nervous. Every soldier or gendarme she saw—and the streets were full of
them—had been instructed to arrest her. This was to
be the outcome of General Hourko's long silence. She
did not like that silence. It boded her no good. He was
only maturing his plans for seizing her, and the delay
must have been a necessary one. Then, ashamed of her
own weakness, she held her head up, looked into the cafés
as she passed them, and thought, comically, of what an
immense amount of liquor, caviare, salted fish, and other
dainties, the great hulking fellows that filled them must
consume. Her fears returning, she struggled with them,
and again thought how absurd it was of her to imagine
that she really occupied a moment of Ivan Nicholaevitch's day. Such a great man, with so many compli-
cated affairs to attend to, could have no time to spare to
worry his head about her. He might even have forgotten about her altogether. But then, what would become
of that stupid document which might injure her so much?
She was in terror whenever she thought of that awful
night, and that great strong man towering over her so
threateningly. Would he do all he had promised, and let
no one see the paper? Her liberty was so insecure. Oh!
if he would only forget her and burn the hateful thing.
How often had such thoughts racked her brain.

When she arrived home, Riva tripping at her side,
with a cloak over her shoulders and a basket on her arm,

she found Hernani excitedly declaring that Hourko had
been shot—shot as he was driving along.

"Do you hear?" he added, addressing her, his manner
almost aggressive, his eyes, as it were, searching to find
some fault.

"Well, I am sorry," she answered simply, without
thought of what such news might mean to her.

"Bravo! I suppose you are."

"Who would not be? Murder in the public streets! It
is too terrible."

Hernani was baffled.

"You are right there," he agreed. "How these women
can act!" he thought. "Is it likely that she would ever
have admitted anything, had I asked her!"

Then he began to grapple with the news, while Sara
wondered at the strangeness of the reception he had given
her, and set it down to excitement or some such cause.

"Mind you, it will do us no good," he remarked to
Dorozynski.

"The man who did it must be mad," asserted the
Count.

"Well; but it is all the same. Fresh troops will be
poured in. There will be all sorts of rigorous measures
enforced."

"Stop a bit though; there is this chance—the rumor
may be a false one," suggested the Count.

"True; though my information should be good. It
occurred near the Hotel de l'Europe, I am told. I must
have been within a few hundred yards at the moment."

However, before nightfall it transpired that Hourko
had only been wounded, and that, it was said, but
slightly.

The next occurrence worthy of note came in the shape
of sad and startling news for Deotima and Count Andrew. A trusted messenger arrived at night, fatigued
and covered with dust, to announce that Count Dorozynski had died in his sleep. Worn out with disappoint-

ment and ill-usage, he had at length succumbed. There could be no doubt that the attack made upon his home was the immediate cause of his end. The shock of being so rudely separated from his children, added to his constant fears for their safety, had been insupportable to him. He had been unable to sleep or take proper nourishment latterly, and more than once, in a kind of stupor, had been discovered muttering their names, which had finally been his last words.

Count Andrew was on no account to return to the house, as such an act would be one of extreme rashness in the opinion of his advisers. It was thought possible, that with caution, his sister might attend the funeral, but if she could be restrained from doing so, so much the better, as the authorities were known to be deeply incensed at what they were pleased to consider as the outrages committed by Count Andrew. Deotima received the news speechless with horror and grief. She spoke little and few tears flowed; these were the worst signs. When the Count entreated her not to go, with quivering lips and all the affectionate influence he could exert, she replied by informing him that she was ready for the journey, and only awaited the necessary arrangements for it, which must be made at once.

On her return, when they were alone, her first act was to solemnly swear to dedicate her life to the destruction of those foes who had wantonly, and in cold blood, destroyed her father, and by way of answer, the steadfast exchange of glances, the quivering of lips, and the silent clasping of hands, was all that followed between them, but from that hour certainly, the Russian Government might have added two more names to its long list of irreconcilable enemies.

After that the Marquis Wielopolski was twice shot at. Then there was a little lull.

CHAPTER XI.

The General's wound was healing well. The doctors had gravely prescribed rest, and had been pooh-poohed for their pains. Relying upon his stout constitution. Hourko had politely sent them to the devil, and himself to work, with a grim will. Confined to the palace, his temper was said to be diabolical, and in truth a milder word would not have described it. He kept Titus Popoloff trotting about on his heels all day long. "Led every one of them a devil of a dance"—so said his perfumed and gorgeously-clad aides-de-camp—Petersburg dandies of the first water.

"Well, what do you want now?" was the reception the great man accorded his apparently indefatigable facto-, tum, Popoloff, upon one occasion, on his entrance into the same apartment to which Sara had been introduced.

"I have brought important dispatches, Excellency."

"Set them down—they can wait."

"But——"

"What are they about?"

"They need your consideration, sir."

"Consideration! I am sick of considering. If only I had a tent about me, instead of picture-hung walls, ceilings with fat-cheeked grinning imps, soft carpets, ticking clocks, and all the rest of the precious paraphernalia. The sight of brave Czengery and a cloud of Cossacks, the smell of powder—something to stir one's blood, that's what I want—not physic or rest; you can't make a silken, smooth-tongued puppet out of a soldier. What is it? Read them."

Popoloff wiped his eternal spectacles, and in a sing-song voice drawled through a long official report. Another followed, then several shorter ones, the General the while making some pencil memoranda, without speaking a word or ceasing to puff at his cigarette.

"That is all, Excellency," said Titus at length, clearing his voice, which had grown husky.

"All, is it—and enough, I should think! What will Wielopolski say to this? Does he know?"

"The Marquis has read the dispatches, sir."

"Has he? Oh! Well, all I can say is that these devils seem to be going ahead. So Nazimoff has found it necessary to declare Grodno, Kovno, and Wilna in a state of siege."

"Together with——" And Popoloff enumerated several less important places.

"The result, probably, of renewed efforts on the part of those ruffians Mieroslawski and Czartoryski, I suppose."

"You are not far wrong, sir."

"What—you know it?"

"Well, several fresh proclamations have been discovered and seized, Excellency, and the recent increase in the agitation is traceable to no other cause."

"The scoundrels! We'll hang them—we'll hang them yet; but meanwhile they are free to trouble us, and they are missing no chance. Have you been able to obtain the names of any more people who have been guilty of supporting this movement financially? For evidently large sums of money are being supplied."

"Yes, Excellency; I have a further list of those who are known to have done so, or who are suspected. They are mainly Jews, but in the forefront of their ranks stands Kasimir Hernani. I mentioned this to you some time back, and his guilt can be proved."

"I fancy you did. I remember something about it. To have arrested him would have been a useful step, but considering his influence, a false one, or it should have been taken long ago."

"He has, I find, afforded shelter for some while past to that young desperado, Count Andrew Dorozynski, who is accompanied by his sister."

"So I have understood. Watch them well, Popoloff; know where to lay hands on them, but wait for the word. I will consider the dispatches, to which I shall have answers later in the day."

These last decisive remarks were Popoloff's dismissal. He could remain no longer, for, enveloped in clouds of cigarette smoke, the great man had forgotten his existence. So with his colorless, unfathomable eyes blinking, as though from out of darkness he had suddenly been thrust into light, Popoloff shambled off to a room where a worse annoyance awaited him. Madam Hourko had sent for him. He could not remember when such a thing had happened. She had always awaited his appearance, which had been at night and in her boudoir. What did it mean? The General no longer trusted him—of that he was convinced. Never a word of confidence of late, not a single allusion to his mad passion for the Jewess, Sara Hernani, no matter how dexterously angled for. To declare himself overworked, worried, in the wrong box, or disgusted at instructions received from St. Petersburg, was one thing; to talk of his love affairs, quite another. He frequently did the former, never the latter by any chance.

Popoloff was agitated; he had noted the change for a while past, but, rack his brain as he would, he could not discover the cause. Had some of his side issues, his clever little intrigues been detected, and was he on the verge of being exposed, disgraced, banished? The Jewish and Polish gold, subscribed to support the revolution, and of which he had given so good an account to Hourko—was it known that some of it had found its way into his pockets? It might be. And yet—no, he would not think of such a thing. Plenty of accusations might be launched against him, but proofs would be

needed. He had gone to work with such care, his precautions were unique—bah! he was too old a fox to be
caught. It was impossible. He was all right. So in
this confident mood, patting his hollow chest as though
he cared naught for the whole world, and having actually surveyed his wrinkled, yellow-skinned face in a
mirror, he presented himself to madam, whom he found
in the same little octagon chamber, elegantly attired,
surrounded by canine pets, above all things, warm.

Olga Pavlovna had not altered one whit. She had
reached that age and condition at which people seem
loth to do so, and was still the little lady with sharpened
features and anæmic face crowned with straggling remnants of wiry yellow hair. Disposed upon a sofa, with
her dogs growling defiance from her skirts, she signed to
Popoloff to seat himself opposite to her, so that the light
fell full upon his face, and when he had done so, she
dropped one word interrogatively—

"Well?"

"Madam," stammered Popoloff, his guilty fears returning, his confidence shaken by this funny reception.

"What have you to tell me?"

"I, madam? Nothing."

"Oh, but you should have."

"But surely it is well if there is nothing disturbing to
relate."

"That may be—if nothing disturbing has happened.
Shall I tell you something?"

"If it please you, madam."

"His Excellency, my husband, distrusts you."

Popoloff's face expressed the greatest surprise.

"His Excellency distrusts me?"

"Precisely. I sent for you to mention that important
fact, coupled with some others which have occurred to
me. What I shall tell you, I have thought, for weeks
past. Now I have proof, and I hasten to give it to you.

12

His Excellency has visited the Jewess—Sara Hernani—at dead of night."

Popoloff felt himself in a dilemma, but he accepted the situation with the placidity of an innocent child. His pale eyes dwelt upon Madam Hourko vacantly, as though he did not comprehend, or was very tired, then an expression of surprise slowly awoke in them.

"Is it possible?" he ejaculated.

"It is true. It has happened, and you—you were in ignorance," replied madam severely.

There was nothing for it but to appear incredulous.

"But there is, perhaps, some mistake. I can scarcely credit it." Then without giving time for an answer, his elbows upon his knees, his long bony fingers pointed together, he put a cunning question: "Is the information upon which madam bases her statement perfectly reliable? I have a little doubt."

"It is beyond the smallest."

Baffled, he attempted to elicit an admission.

"Of course, if the source——" he began, and found himself stopped.

"We will pass beyond that, sir. I am content to believe—that is sufficient."

"Oh, well, certainly—then no more can be said.· Still, it is possible that his Excellency visited the house for some political purpose, or owing to some trivial accident of which he saw no reason to acquaint me."

"His Excellency visits no house by accident, disguised, and at such an hour. Whether he attained his object, that of seeing this base woman, I am unable to say, but before I have done with her I shall extract an admission of her guilt."

"Yes, yes, of course—that will be simple. You have only to will the thing, madam, and such a trifle as the humiliation or extinction of a corrupt and insolent Jewess, must at once follow. But I am sorry. *Bozhe* *moi,* * to think how I have slaved to be of service, and how in this instance I have failed! Ah! I am grieved— I am grieved. Yet there is this comfort, madam—you must feel that your interests are ever nearest my heart. I can never forget that I was the poor tchinovnik whom you——"

With a rapid and irritable gesture she interrupted him.

"I don't know—I don't know. Your protestations need testing. I am wronged, and I hate. Help me to be revenged—that is all I ask."

"But, madam, I would lay down my life——"

"So you say. But instead of words I require deeds, or I must seek for assistance elsewhere."

Popoloff was fairly alarmed.

"I ask time and your confidence," he whined. "Then you shall see, you shall be satisfied."

"Well, you know the price of my favor," she answered him, grudgingly becoming pacified.

"And I will pay it. Ah! am I not indebted——"

"We will not talk of that. I have trusted you, and I am content, so long as I may continue to do so. It rests with you to prove yourself worthy. I am resolved that if his Excellency plays me false, he shall have ample cause to repent it. I will spare no pains to make him know that he is wronging one who can right herself, or who at least is not such a poor weak fool as to accept just what he chooses to give. If you take trouble and display tact you will soon regain his favor. Do we understand each other?"

"Without doubt, madam. My one aim shall be to serve and please you in all things."

The heavy lids descended over Olga Pavlovna's eyes; the tired expression so habitual to her returned, and in silence she caressed the silky coat of her nearest dumb friend, who gratefully licked her hand, which was long,

---

* "My God, Good Heavens!"

thin, and white. Reclining there, she looked the indolent and jealous wife to the life.

Titus Popoloff shifted his great splay feet awkwardly. He was glad of a momentary respite, and he fervently congratulated himself, too, that no woman was tacked on to him, whose lynx eyes searched his paths, and counted his steps. For a moment he caught himself wondering what had become of Madam Hourko's pride, that in the midst of her brilliant life she should yet make a study of running after a man who took no pleasure in her. Owing to her position, she might have amused herself with many lovers. Could she not content herself? What was the use of fighting against the inevitable? His Excellency's ways could be changed no more easily than the satin coat of his favorite charger. In this way the pause between them lasted some minutes, at the end of which time, one of the little dogs toppled on to the floor, with a whine which became a snarl, as Popoloff ventured to put him in his place again, the noise he made rousing his mistress.

"Shall I tell you what his Excellency intends to do with this woman?" she demanded suddenly. "When these stupid people, these Poles, stand up to have their throats cut, in the uproar, he will take steps to secure her. She will disappear, with his assistance."

With a woman's intuition she had suddenly stumbled upon Hourko's pet plan. He had been silent and inactive, because he intended to make that move. He had not even hinted such a thing to a soul save Popoloff, yet his wife had found him out. Popoloff looked at her and admired her shrewdness.

"It is possible, madam," he answered her.

"It is so—I am positive; that is what he meditates. Now we must defeat him. I intend that this Jewess shall be in my power, not his. Do you understand me?"

"Perfectly——"

"We shall seize her; then when he arrives at the nest, he will find it empty. Can this be done?"

"With ease, madam. Trust me—that is all you have to do."

"Very well; but mind, let there be no bungling. Think —we have lots of time, and if this is a success, as it must be, you may count upon my gratitude."

Popoloff bowed and went away, but he was disturbed, not satisfied, and he told himself that it would be a fine thing if he could contrive to do without either the Governor or his wife.

CHAPTER XII.

In the whole course of her life, Riva had never felt so distressed, so miserable. It was not that her glances ahead told her anything—she had no mind for such things. Her trouble lay in the present, and was always with her—her Alpha and Omega—beginning and end of everything being—Sara. As she had said, apart from her she had no interest in life. And Sara was an altered being, as the whole household agreed. Her moods were incomprehensible. She was lively, and sad, and silent, and talkative within the space of one hour—though to Riva talkative, never. It was cruel to ignore her so. Could it be that she did it on purpose, shunned her systematically, and when they were together became strangely uncommunicative—reticent all at once? Riva preferred to think not, but her dark eyes grew dim, and her heart felt like failing her, when the smile or the word she had waited for so long, so seldom came, and at the best, was not the old smile or tender thrilling voice known to her from prattling babyhood. In vain she kept her eyes and ears open and preached patience to herself in her own quaint way. She got no nearer her goal—that of discovering what new evil ailed Sara, and relieving her, so that she should be again happier—more like herself. Finally, she set it down in strong language and upon the ground of her past knowledge.

"She is being killed by inches—destroyed—my lamb —and it is the master," she wailed, in the quiet of her own little chamber, where she sat doubled up in a chair —"it is the master, and the Holy One will curse him, sure enough—with such a wife—in the bosom of Abraham no lovelier could rest—what matters it—children—

the fool! To see, let alone touch her, should be pleasure enough for mortal. And here she is eating her heart out. The man is an ass, and thistles should be his food. The bat is not more blind, and cursed be the day when he first saw the light! I grow to hate him. The young gentleman, the young noble, he sees my lamb's worth; he is wise. With her little finger held up, all men would run to her; but this one—the one lawfully her own——" And as disturbed as ever, Riva fell to thinking.

That night Sara retired early. Hernani and Dorozynski were out as usual, and Deotima, under cover of night, awhile back and by stealth, had journeyed to some relatives to rouse them with her woman's voice, to pour into their ears her wrongs, their wrongs, to the end that the Polish eagles might be borne more bravely aloft.

Seated before her toilet-table, Sara wore a long loose wrap, like the one in which Hourko had surprised her, and behind her stood Riva ready to brush her hair. The chubby fists of two china cherubs grasped the lighted candles on either side of the mirror, reflected in which was the adorable face and figure of this apple of Riva's eye. The stove was lighted, but the bed, curtained and dainty, lay in gloom like the rest of the room.

For once Sara seemed disposed to talk a little, to be gay, despite the cold dead weight at her heart. Pin after pin was removed—jeweled some of them; Hernani's gifts time back—and then coil upon coil fell the fine soft rippling hair that Riva loved to brush.

"Mine is getting gray," remarked the woman, as she labored with deft hands.

"Yours! Well, but that is natural; you are no longer a chicken. Is not age the cause?"

"No—trouble. It was black enough awhile ago."

"But you must expect such changes. Mine will be white soon. Live for the day, Riva; it is the only way."

"As you do, my lamb."

"Oh! let me alone. I am past redemption—hopeless."

"Hopeless?" repeated Riva.

"Quite. Did you get those things I reminded you about?"

"Yes, that I did. But talk as you were beginning to. I love the sound of your voice always, but most when it rings and trembles, thrilling through me."

"But you hear it so often. And we must not be serious; I want to laugh."

"And I want to hear you, though there is little to laugh at."

"There is a comical side to everything. When you brush my hair to benefit it, you pull it out. The man who has been starving must not eat too much. Do you remember young Jacob—shot in the massacre? His photograph exhibited as that of a patriot and martyr; his loss bewailed by all. Well, the boy's heroic death was a good day's work for his brothers; it reconciled the uncle to the family, and his money will now go to them. There is something comical in a man dying and being sorrowed for, when but for his death others would starve."

Aware of the influence Riva could sometimes exert over her, Sara talked lightly, preferring to monopolize the conversation. She had not dared to open her lips upon the subject of her hateful nocturnal meeting with Hourko, and she felt the secret to be a barrier between them. "Everything is known. The walls listen, and we know what they hear," had rung in her ears ever since that night. How could she tell—what might come of confidences, living as she did. But Riva had made up her mind. There should be an understanding between them; she had things to say, and say them she would, while she had the chance, that her lamb might be the happier.

"All that you tell me," she answered, "may well be

I am not wise, and my head buzzes when I try to think. But about living for the day—let the book speak: 'Thy yesterday is thy past, thy to-day thy future, thy to-morrow is a secret.' So to live for to-day would be well."

"Don't tug so, Riva; I sha'n't have a bit of hair left soon."

"I, my lamb? You can't say I was rough."

"But I do."

"Then it was by accident. Ah! you have been cruel to me this while past. Do you know if you were happy I should say you had forgotten old Riva."

"Oh! I shiver—I must get into bed."

"Ah! it is because the dear feet are bare, and the pretty legs—such bits of things when I knew them first —just like satin for all the world. I remember—so well —so well. There, with that stool and shawl, no cold can come."

"Thanks—that's nice, Riva."

"And I'll not be long."

"Oh! I don't mind, only don't let us talk of distressing things. You like to, I fancy."

"Never, if you take it ill."

"Well, I do. I want all my courage. I have enough to bear."

"That have you. But it seemed to me, time back, that whatever came, we could meet it together. Never a thought apart from each other; it was Riva this, and Riva that, and it kept me alive."

"But I am the same now, Riva?"

"No, my love."

"How could I alter toward you?"

"But you have. May I die if it's not so."

"Not at heart, I tell you. Ah! can't you see? Sometimes I think I shall go mad."

"But—my poor darling."

"Don't, Riva—don't. I can't bear it."

"And all of a tremble too."

"It's nothing. Listen; will you do this for me? I have scarcely tasted food all day. No one noticed it, but I couldn't, my head was racked."

"No one noticed it! Surely the master——"

With a gesture of impatience, Sara interrupted her.

"Fetch me some fowl or something simple, and I'll eat it sitting here. I shall enjoy it."

Riva was away and back again with a tray loaded temptingly, and after a long pause, during which the click of the knife and fork and the fainter sound of mastication alone broke the silence, Sara looked up at her.

"Do you remember how you used to cook little things and bring them to me?" she asked.

"In Cracow?"

"Yes."

"That I do."

"And how I discovered that you were pinching and starving yourself?"

"No, no—I was given a few gulden. Besides, it's best to forget all that."

"We will speak of it only for a moment. It is often in my mind."

"Is it, my lamb?"

"Often. What do you think I'm made of, Riva? And then you say I've changed."

"Did I? I was wrong, and had better have bitten my tongue out. Forgive me."

Sara looked at her fixedly and smiled, and the smile was sufficient to reconcile them; it alone was enough. But Riva felt emboldened. She had things to say and the chance was a good one.

"The Russian," she began suddenly in a strained voice —"the Governor—have you seen him, my love, since we talked?"

Sara hesitated.

"Yes," she said at length, firmly.

"Ah! I warned you."

"Warned me of what?"

"I don't wonder."

"But what do you mean?"

"Well, he is a great man, the Russian. Has he kept the promise he made you? Has he been good to the poor and fatherless?"

"He made me no promise that he would be."

"No! Perhaps my old head fails me. He was to do something, though, I know—something for poor folk like the Bielois."

"Yes; but he has done nothing."

"Then he has broken his word."

"In a sense; and I hate him."

"God of Israel, could it be otherwise! What did I tell you, my lamb? An old head is better than a young one. Now the gentleman, Count Dorozynski, would never break his word, I'll warrant me."

"Perhaps not. I don't think he would. But what makes you speak of him?"

"Oh! my own thoughts."

"What are they? Tell me."

"It is best not. Silence is the fence round wisdom."

"But I wish to hear."

Riva leant over her, her black eyes glistening.

"Do you remember speaking of the gold and finery in the great Russian's palace, where you had been?"

"Yes; but you have told no one that I went there?"

"Not a soul. You were anxious then, and your heart was heavy. Is it lighter now?"

"What good can come of troubling you; you have your own load, my poor Riva, and I have mine, which I must bear patiently."

"But is it heavy still?"

"Heavier than ever."

"I knew it—I knew it all along. And I have been sleepless because of it. You must change—you must alter your ways, my love. Bound up in this house and the master, your beautiful young life is going. Why should it be so? No enjoyment—no pleasure. Slaving, seeing no one, and as a reward always, always, no thanks."

"Hush! There you are wrong, Riva."

"Wrong, am I? Fit mate for the Princes of the earth —and neglected—that's what's wrong."

"You have been with me all my life, but can be no judge either of what I am fit for, or what would be good for me. No other eyes see me as yours do. You are bigoted. If I know myself, then I say, I was made for quiet, and simplicity, and love; for some little home where the sea I have read of and never seen, murmurs against the rocks; where I might be free to go out into the fresh fearless wind, and feel it upon my cheeks and drink it in, and live, and laugh, and be happy amongst the flowers and the sunshine. Oh! my God—the flowers and the sunshine and love. Love that would heal the bruises, the scars, the gaping wounds within me, that would stanch the sighs and lighten the load of living, and by its purity—for God is Love and God is pure —lift one nearer and nearer, until the kind clear heavens absorbed one, and one rested with Him. I hate this rush and sweat for gold. I have hated it ever since I knew it, but anything was well that he loved, since he loved me. Is it too late yet—all too late, Riva? Would he, if I went on my knees, tear himself from this ambition and strife, and come with me to where in quiet he might know me really and we could be one? But what am I saying? The bright visions of what might be, swarm within my brain, yet there is no substance for them."

"Ach, no—that is all moonshine, my love," replied Riva brusquely: "the master will stick where he is, as long as his legs carry him. Excitement is to him the breath of his nostrils."

"I believe you are right."

"Ach! I know I am. You can get no old bear to dance to a new tune. His habits are formed just as his bones are set. But see now—if I were you, though the times are ill and unchangeable, I would amuse myself—I'd have people about me and lovers too. The master'd be jealous, and serve him right; but see the good of teaching him to behave! A fine strapping lover. There's no saying what would come of it. No father, no child. And there is the Count to your hand; following you with his eyes if his legs take rest; near always when chance offers; hanging upon your words; wretched out of your sight; ready to risk his life for kiss from you. Keep your own counsel and grant him his desire. Harden your heart that the sorrow of your life may pass and the master be at your feet again."

Sara started from her chair. Erect and threatening, the loose robe caught about her waist and clinging to her, with eyes flashing and hands tight closed, she looked the very incarnation of anger and outraged dignity.

"What!" she cried—"you would have me be false to my husband, false to myself and false to God? How dare you—how dare you suggest such wickedness?"

"Only that—there is the gett—and a child——"

"The gett! Another word and all is over between us! To save myself from the cruelty of man and the injustice of the law, you would have me fathom the depths of dishonor. You have astounded me. No; if because I am barren the man I love turns me adrift in the world, I shall walk through it starving and toiling, sweeping the streets, searching the gutters it may be, yet at least striving to remain as honest and upright as when I entered it. But that we have lived all our lives together I should hate and despise you. Despise you I must and do—but—— Ah! you may well weep—and yet—no—Riva, Riva, my old nurse and friend, listen—I shall for-

get it. Something is amiss with you to-day. It is not
you who has spoken—it is someone else. You meant
it well, but how could you think so ill—and so ill of me?
I am no Saint, and for love, some great love, I might
be tempted and fall, as better women than I have fallen;
but to save myself from all the wretchedness the mind
can conceive, I should never have thought of a thing
so vile, and could never be so guilty as to do it. I am
tired—tired; help me into bed—in many a worse one
we have lain together. See—I forgive, and time will
heal. Let us sleep. Sweet, clean sleep. We shall
awake purer and better. Good-night."

And Riva rushed blubbering from the room.

CHAPTER XIII.

If Sara knew how to love, she also knew how to forgive, and as soon as she had digested Riva's bold and even unscrupulous advice, she began to make excuses for her. She had spoken hastily and had not intended to be disrespectful or to wound her, but, having been desperately unhappy on her account, had seen but this one way out of the difficulty, and since she was ill-born, ill-brought up and ill-educated, had caught at it.

A lover might mean a natural child, which it would be so easy to foist upon Hernani. He would never be the wiser if she were cautious, and at one bound the chasm between them would be bridged. That was what Riva had meant, and had nerved herself to say, in the most intelligible language at her command.

Upon the suggestion itself, Sara bestowed scarce a thought. It possessed no temptations for her. In fact, when it stood out in all its repulsiveness, she turned from it with loathing, deciding that if she wished to look Riva in the face again, and treat her as she had been in the habit of doing, she must make every effort to forget it. In her ready good nature and kindliness of heart, she even went so far as to attach some blame to herself over the matter. Had she thought more of others, and less of herself, she would have appeared in Riva's eyes less unhappy, in which case the desperate remedy would never have been suggested. True, she had striven to be energetic and cheerful, but to avoid the chance of any impulsive confidences on her part, had put an end to that familiar intercourse which had been the one enduring joy of the woman's life, by so doing thoughtlessly rendering her existence intolerable. That was the cause of Riva's conduct. She, Sara, had been wanting in consideration and attention, toward one who had served her faithfully over the whole span of her life, and who, by her devotion, had made good to no small extent, the loss she had sustained by her mother's early death. What would have become of her in the Cracow days without Riva? What should she have done without her always? Yes, she had been thoughtless and bad. With such reasoning as this, she strove to gloss over defects, and find excuses for retaining Riva intact in her heart.

Of course these views took time to shape and arrange themselves in her mind, and were to some extent traceable to the abject penitence displayed by Riva, but the result was that she reinstated her in her favor, almost too rapidly, some would have thought.

Meanwhile the household routine continued unchanged. Hernani retired to his bureau for the purpose of transacting his business as of old. The hours for meals were the same, and between them Sara attended to her womanly duties, received an occasional caller, or went to the synagogue, while the Count busied himself as he saw fit. In the evening, the two men discussed their projects, or went out in furtherance of the absorbing and dangerous plans on hand, Sara singing, reading, or sewing the while, missing Deotima much, wishing for her return a good deal, but throughout, learning to bear the load of her own troubles with patience and fortitude. She thought it only wise and right to assume an attitude of reserve toward the Count, and while gradually doing so, was mindful to watch for any of those symptoms of admiration of which Riva had spoken of so boldly.

And so in this way time crept on, one day closely resembling another, except that, instead of discussing the effect and benefits to be derived from a petition to be presented to the Governor-General by Count Zamoyski, it began to be rumored that the Count would have noth-

ing to say to the project, and had even torn up the draft
of the document; then, that he had been interviewed by
his Excellency, who had decided that he must proceed
to St. Petersburg for the purpose of seeking audience
of the Emperor; and after a brief delay, a pause, during
which speculation was rife, came the crushing announce-
ment that his Imperial Majesty had ordered Count
Zamoyski to quit the country—had exiled him in fact;
and upon receipt of that piece of information—as is well
known—there arose in men's minds and upon their
tongues, a great clamor of indignation.

All these many and weighty matters Sara heard discussed and sifted by Hernani and Count Andrew, during
long hours of patient listening, until in place of them
arose the shadow of the long, dimly-threatened Conscription, to which it was affirmed the Marquis Wielopolski lent his countenance and support.

And it was beneath the lofty span of glass, in the great
hall, when seated before the silver samovar, that Sara
first came to know of the serious and disturbing nature
of this arbitrary project. In the warm atmosphere which
was due to partly-concealed and admirably-arranged
stoves, she dispensed her tea—the beverage so dear to
her—in delicate china cups, which Hernani and the
Count accepted from her hands and solemnly sipped,
amidst the cool green foliage of the tropic plants, the
refreshing odor of flowers, and the gentle soothing murmur of the fountain.

"This threat of the Conscription will be found to be
the last straw," announced Hernani, returning his cup
for replenishment.

"Upon whose back?" inquired the Count, though anticipating Hernani's answer.

"The people will not submit to be torn from their
beds, and whipped away from their homes and their
lawful callings."

"I don't know. Their courage seems gone, their

spirit broken. What about the massacres, the arrests
even in the house of God, the dissolution of the Agricultural Society—last of all, Zamoyski's cruel and insolent dismissal? They have borne all that, and only
talked."

"Well, you will see, you will find me a true prophet.
And, moreover, you forget that those events have
ripened their minds, slowly but surely, as the sun ripens
the fruit upon the wall. For the last two years their
protests have been gathering in volume and violence,
and if this iniquitous act be perpetrated, with one consent they will agree that the moment for an appeal to
arms has arrived. Are their sons to be dragged from
them by brute force, arrested in the public thorough-
fares, and compelled to serve in the ranks of their enemies? Many a peaceable and hard-working citizen in
this town would rather see his child under the sod."

"If what you say be true, God be thanked!" murmured the Count earnestly.

"He is already thanked, then, as you will see shortly
enough. The agitation, so widespread and so well sustained, has revived historical recollections, and made the
youth of the land patriots, just as much as those whose
pockets are pinched, and whose wounds still smart from
the failure of the '30 attempt. That the great nobles
may remain quiet for a time is likely enough. We, the
party of action, they say, have nothing to lose—disaster
to us would mean nothing. For them it would be different. They have proud names which might be black-
ened, and rich estates which might go forfeit, and they
argue, as we know, that Europe is tranquil, and so that
the time has not come. But after shamelessly hanging
fire for a while, they will join us to a man; then too we
shall be helped, as Italy was. France or England will
come to our assistance, as I have contended all along,
and in support of my contention, see how the press up-
holds our cause. We have only to leap to arms—that

is all. They know as well as we do that the ranks of our foes are torn by dissensions, that the Muscovite army is not what it was six years ago, that the soldier does not respect his officer, and that nothing but corporal punishment can make him obey; but they don't know what we do—that the bulk of the officials in this, the capital of Poland, have no real belief in a rising."

"But how do you know that?" inquired Sara.

"From a dozen reliable sources," replied Hernani promptly.

"Yes, that is true enough," the Count chimed in, "and it is a great point in our favor."

"Of course it is—one of vital importance; but hear me out. They—the public, you understand—know that, politically, Russia is in the throes of dissolution, that disaffection is rife throughout the land, that the students are unmanageable, the discipline of the military schools lax to a degree, and that incendiary fires in Petersburg are of constant occurrence."

"Yes, that is so—that is all right," assented the Count; "but," he added irrelevantly, "what a deep game that Wielopolski is playing."

"Ah! I believe you. He is a misguided man," affirmed Hernani solemnly, "and would sacrifice or sell anything and everything to obtain power."

"But is there really any truth in the rumor that he intends levying these forces, to the number of several thousands, from families of all classes, thereby seizing those best able to strike a blow for their country's freedom?"

"Yes—every truth, I believe."

Suddenly Sara interposed. No one would listen to her—it was really past a joke.

"Well, there, drink this tea while it is hot," she said; and the simple blow fell like a bomb. It was so ridiculous to descend to tea-drinking. Hernani could have dashed his cup down, but he replied by emptying it, and

clattering it in the saucer as he replaced it, in a way
which said as plainly as words could have done, "How
trumpery are a woman's ideas, at a moment when they
should be great!"

There was an awkward pause. Hernani was for
continuing the conversation, when the Count interrupted him.

"I am getting anxious about Deotima," he said;
"already it is dark and bitterly cold, I suppose. Let us
go and see if there is any sign of her"—to which suggestion Hernani silently assented, and, having carefully
wrapped themselves up, they left the house together.

Within the hour the Count returned, without Hernani
but accompanied by Deotima, who had arrived overflowing with health and spirits, having met with the greatest
kindness, and being thoroughly satisfied with the result
of her journey. She had been escorted into the town by
one of Hernani's trusted agents, and she was loud in
her praise of his forethought and attention.

When she had removed her furs, and stood up smell-
ing of the cold and fresh sweet air of the country, in an
uncontrollable outburst of brotherly affection the Count
took her in his arms, imprinting two vigorous kisses
upon her smooth pink cheeks; then he pushed the fair
wavy hair from her forehead, and stepped back a couple
of paces to examine her critically.

"Upon my word, you've improved vastly," he remarked enthusiastically; "you've grown, I do believe!
I feel smaller than ever alongside of you; and what a
fine figure! Many a fellow would envy me those kisses,
wouldn't they?" he inquired abruptly of Sara; "and the
two of you make a picture, to which this perfectly
artistic room is the frame. One dark and the other fair,
and both so charming. Even with my knowledge of
languages, I should find it difficult to describe quite
what I see and think." Then, since Sara did not appear
to relish his glowing compliments, he drew in his horns

a little. "Well, come and sit down and tell me your news. Did you receive a great deal of attention? How many conquests did you make, and how many duels have been fought over you? Come—I want to hear everything."

Deotima seated herself beside him, and with an irresisitibly coquettish toss of her fair head and pout of her full wide lips, said—

"Ah! then you want to hear too much, sir. You are not a bit changed—just the same impudent old Andrew. Has he been good—really good?" she inquired of Sara.

"Very."

"No trouble to you?"

"Not in the least," answered Sara, laughing.

"So that I may tell him a little of what I have done and seen?"

"Yes, I think you may. But here is some nice fresh tea. You had better have some first, since you must be cold and tired, then talk to him, and come and have a long chat with me when you have finished. I have missed you very much, so we must make up for lost time."

"Now that is sweet and kind of you."

"But it is better—it is true."

"Well, don't leave me—I am afraid of Andrew. Come and sit close to me and hear all I have to say, the bulk of it being serious matter. Yes; now we shall do splendidly. Well, Andrew, uncle and aunt send affectionate messages, and the girls forward kisses."

"Thanks—I'd rather have the originals."

"You hateful boy! If I thought you meant it!"

"I do."

"I refuse to believe you. What!—Cara with her projecting teeth and ugly gums—that is, when she laughs. Mariette with her pasty face, her freckles, and her red hair; and Barbel with her great feet, her snub nose, and chronic cold! Don't tell me; if so, your taste must be execrable. Well, all want to see you; more than that,

all want to marry you, and Barbel declares she will have
no one else."

"A nice lookout for me! Of course you reminded
them of my peculiar but unalterable opinions upon the
merits of single blessedness?"

"I told them nothing untrue, but I reminded them of
the fact that you're a naughty, fickle boy, incapable of
sticking to any woman."

"Ah!' What a jolly reception I shall get there—next
time."

"Listen to me and don't talk so much. Adam is as
precocious as ever, but Ladislaus has improved im-
mensely—he is charming. I am certain you would like
him. But come—we really must be serious. I can assure you there has been no such thing as frivolity while
I have been away. There, as here, one hope fills all
hearts—the resurrection of Poland. I bring nothing but
good news. The pamphlets and proclamations, scattered so cleverly, have taught the peasantry the difference between right and wrong; they are stirred up, and,
no longer asleep, are ready for anything. If this cruel
Conscription be resorted to, from the Baltic to the
Dneister, there will go up one great and unanimous
shout for Liberty."

The click of the door handle, and the sound of someone entering the room, prevented Deotima from saying
more, and, almost sobbing from excess of feeling, she
remained silent, as Hernani approached her. He was
pale, and from his manner, usually so calm, it could be
seen that something of importance had transpired. Recovering herself, she continued—

"We took long drives and walks; not a moment of
the day was lost in idleness; we were up and working,
early and late, and what I saw and heard has inspired
me with confidence rather than with distrust. My feeling now is that the supreme moment has arrived. I
should tell you also that Adam and Ladislaus, between

them, have got together a small but well-equipped body of horse, composed of their own friends and acquaintances, and have at the same time been successful in importing and secreting a quantity of arms and ammunition. They taught me how to shoot at a mark, and you would be surprised—I am quite an expert now."

Having exchanged a few sentences with Deotima and congratulated her upon her apparent good health and safe return, Hernani contrived to whisper to the Count—

"Come with me; I want a word with you."

"What is it now? Has something gone amiss?" inquired the Count as soon as they were alone.

Hernani closed the door of the apartment into which he had led him, and, glancing round as though to make sure that they were the sole occupants of it, he exclaimed—

"The efforts of the Rzad* have failed. Wielopolski has carried the day. The Conscription will be drawn. His threatened resignation as head of the civil administration of the kingdom, and the pressure he has brought to bear, will end in this raid upon the people; for it is nothing else. Already the police have received their instructions."

"But when will they act? What date is fixed?" demanded the Count.

"Ah! there my information is at fault. The strictest secrecy is maintained. It may be to-night. Upon that point, as also upon the names contained in the list, I am entirely ignorant. But it will be an attack upon all classes—merchants, schlacta,† everyone. I have something even more weighty to tell you, so far as I am concerned—sit down, here are some cigarettes—something

---

* Secret Committee, Government.
† Lesser nobility, without office.

that will put a rifle in my hands quicker than I had thought."

The Count began smoking and settled himself to listen.

"You know how gloomy and deserted the Saksonski Sad* is at this season of the year—not a flower to be seen—only snow or dead leaves and muddy walks? Well, I was crossing it near the café, where the trees grow thickly, when a man sprang on to the path, not five paces ahead of me. Absorbed in thought though I was, in an instant I had set the fellow down as a Russian, and a hired assassin perhaps; so with a bound I had him by the neck.

" 'Remove your hand from my throat, batuishka,'† he said quietly, without a sign of resistance; 'do you not see who I am?' The voice I did not know, but, uncertain though the light was, I thought I remembered the face, so I eased my grip.

" 'Who are you, and what are you doing here?' I shouted, in no mood for trifling.

" 'Easy, easy, batuishka; lower your voice, if you please, and pay good heed to what I am about to tell you. It is of importance. Who I am I shall keep to myself; on the other hand, who you are is already known to me, which is sufficient for my purpose.'

" 'And what may that be?' I asked.

" 'Bozhe moi,‡ batuishka, I will tell you! Nu,§ it is to furnish you with valuable information in return for a sufficient sum of money, upon which we will agree.'

" 'But how am I to know that the information will not be worthless?' I again asked.

" 'Because I do not desire payment until you have proved the truth of what I propose to tell you. On my part, I intend to trust you, because of the reputation you

---

* Saxon Gardens.   † Little father.
‡ "My God, good Heavens!"   § Well.

enjoy. Now answer me quickly, for I have no time to lose. If I can save your wife from peril, will you pay me well?'

"My fears excited, I instantly said 'Yes.'

"'How much?' Unhesitatingly I proposed a large sum. In short, we came to terms, my agreement being to pay him when he should seek me, and, as near as I can remember, these were his words: 'I have learned that your house is again to be visited by the police, and your wife, your beautiful wife, seized. You know what that means.'

"'When?' I demanded, trembling so with excitement that I could scarcely speak.

"'That is a question you must answer for yourself. Perhaps to-night—who knows? All I advise is, get her out of the way, or any day your hair may turn white with grief. Now I have told you. It is the truth. It now remains for you to act.' And the man slid away between the tree stems, with a peculiar shuffling gait I shall not readily forget, though not before I had crammed every ruble I had about me into his hand. Now what do you think of the whole story?"

The Count cleared his throat, took another whiff of his cigarette, and then spoke.

"That it is a true one," he said briefly.

"My opinion precisely. What object could be gained by telling me a lie?"

"None, of course. He was there to make money out of you, without doubt. What are you going to do?"

"The Holy One direct me! I have not decided yet. It is a terrible position to be placed in—just consider —one's wife. I was so distressed that I could scarcely speak when I came to tell you. Would they see—your sister or my wife—that something was amiss with me?"

"No, I don't think so," answered the Count, feeling bound to say something consoling.

"I am glad of that. I did my best to appear as usual.

Well, I must take proper measures, and to-night. This
is why the police have remained inactive. They have
waited for the eve of this Conscription, and, calculating on the commotion resulting, are prepared to take
steps which in quieter times would occasion an uproar.
The papers they seized are at the bottom of this piece of
cruelty. One thing is certain—I would rather shoot her
than see her fall into the power of these brutes, who,
like machines, are without conscience or heart. They
shall never take her alive. God of Israel—how long—
how long—what I suffer at this moment passes description!" And Hernani, completely overcome, sank into
a chair and buried his face in his hands.

After a while, growing calmer, he rose to his feet and
paced the room, censuring himself aloud. "This is foolish—this is weak and unworthy of me. Any man may
be brave when the current is with him. But—at a moment such as this—— Ah! what have we to fear? The
Holy One has us in His keeping." Then suddenly, as
though a good idea had struck him at last, he said—

"That is it—that will do. I have arranged it all. This
is the course we will take. Nikolay Brauman is indebted to me. I could not ask too much of him. We
will go with Sara and your sister and give them into
his charge. If an attack were made upon this house, he
and his sons would devise means for their escape, and
would resist to the death rather than yield—that is, if
I require it of them. And as yet the police have not
treated him with suspicion. They would be safe there.
I will see to it at once. Go and rejoin them and keep
them in good spirit. Say that I have gone out but will
return soon." And Hernani prepared to leave the
house. Later in the evening he again spoke to the
Count.

"Nikolay Brauman will do all I want," he said: "we
have only to retire with them through the garden: then,
once they are safe, you and I will come back, and unless

visited by these devils disguised as men, we will remain, perhaps—who can tell?—our last night for a while in this house. Above all things, guard these timid ones from alarm."

The Count simply nodded. Full of the gravity of the outlook, he could not even smoke for the moment. Alone with Sara, Hernani spoke so plausibly that at first she was deceived. He told her that in view of the Conscription, and not knowing when it might be enforced, it would be well to remove to Brauman's house. This was all the more necessary because the police had already made themselves obnoxious, as she was aware. With Nikolay Brauman they would be at ease, since he had no employes who might be sought on the premises.

To which reasoning Sara agreed, though not without flutterings of the heart, and misgivings which grew into shape, when Hernani, driven to it, suggested the expediency of taking with them many necessaries—which in his anxiety he began to enumerate—and, in addition, a good stock of clothing.

"What in the world for?" Sara demanded, facing him.

"Because it will be best," he answered nervously, still striving to appear unconcerned.

Startled by the expression of his face beneath her steady gaze, she seized his wrist and forced him to look at her.

"You are deceiving me. You are keeping something from me. Kasimir—I believe—ah! tell me for the love of God. Is anything wrong? What has occurred? How white and stern you look. You frighten me."

"Frighten you? How can you imagine such things? Do as I say, then it will be well with you," Hernani contrived to answer.

"But why should there be a mystery between us? Do you hope to save me pain by treating me like a child? It is true that when I came here, I was one, almost. But now it is different. I am a woman, old enough and

strong enough to know and bear the weight of all that
distresses you."

Her words sank into his heart and unnerved him. He
forgot his grievances—everything, but that Sara was before him, mingling her breath with his, her beautiful
head flung back, her hands upon his shoulders, her eyes,
so soft and luminous, looking into his, while her voice—
the voice he loved so well—thrilled through him as her
pleading tones fell upon his ear. Half suffocated with
emotion, he murmured—

"Don't, dearie."

Years seemed to have elapsed since he had addressed
her so tenderly.

"But my place is by your side," she insisted, pushing
her little warm hand into his; "and I ought to know
what steps we are about to take, and why we are taking
them. Won't you tell me? In any case—you want me
to be ready to go where you wish to-night. Well, you
may depend upon me."

Overcome by his feelings, the immense importance
and sadness of the situation pressing upon him, he was
about to reply to her, but the words died upon his
tongue. What could he tell her—that the police were
tracking her, and that for her sake this flight was necessary? A sweat broke out upon his forehead. He sucked
the hairs of his moustache between his teeth and bit
them; in his nervous anguish he even bit his lower lip
until it bled. Then—suddenly—he drew away his hand;
this was no time for weakness. Every instant was most
precious. On the point of leaving his home, of taking
up arms in a great cause, spies and police swarming, perhaps even about to lose his wife, he must be strong—
it was demanded of him.

"Another time I may be able to speak more plainly
to you," he said, the stern expression she had com-
plained of returning; for the present I can only say,
pack and be ready, and it will be well."

The calm, firm tone in which the words were uttered left no room for remonstrance; she could only regard him wistfully for a moment, her desires and her anxieties crowding into her mind—it seemed all at once—then she turned and left him.

They had been, it appeared, upon the verge of a reconciliation, which in her opinion rested with him to bring about, and which would have been so simple and at the same time so delightful. Would it ever come to pass? she wondered. Then she set to work. By ten o'clock she had made her preparations, her last act being to linger in the rooms she loved, and with a vivid recollection of the happiness she had felt, even on first entering them, to say to each in turn, "Good-bye, good-bye." It cost her a frightful wrench to tear herself away. Two or three times she returned, on each occasion discovering something she could not part with—some gift—some souvenir of Hernani's which they had bought together on their return from a day in the country—an outing—the memory of which would last as long as reason itself. Oh! those pure delights—how innocent, how delicious they had been. What had she done, what sin had she been guilty of, that all chance, all hope of a repetition of them should have disappeared, and left her still young and still hungering, for the joys, the consolation, she had known and lost? Poor soul!—it was heartrending to read the word despair written in her eyes, and to see her with her cheeks flushed, her lips dry and feverish, and her hands trembling, as she persistently wandered from one object to another. A little painted miniature of Hernani, when but twenty years of age, was discovered in an out-of-the-way corner where it had been placed to make room for newer treasures—this was the last thing she pounced upon and forced into her pocket.

Compelled to go at length, she announced that she was ready, and when the moon was riding high and clear above them, they crossed the terraced walks where the flowers had been so bright in the spring and summer, and lingering an instant near the fountain where the gold-fish had sported, they then passed on beneath the boughs of the cedars, together and in silence.

While the key was being fitted in the door which admitted them to Nikolay Brauman's premises, Sara glanced back, then swiftly into Hernani's face.

"We shall sleep in the old home no more, Kasimir?" she whispered softly.

Hernani bowed his head. She was right.

CHAPTER XIV.

That night, that historical night of the 14th of January, 1863, the police fulfilled their instructions. The youth of Warsaw—to the number of two thousand, it is said—went to swell the Russian ranks, and the new day dawned upon what appeared to be a triumph of ministerial policy. The attitude of the Government had been resolute. In spite of threats, it had carried its point. It had conquered; yet could the official eyes have penetrated to where the wheels of the revolutionary machine worked swiftly and well, enough would have been seen to occasion distrust, even alarm.

Never having once closed his eyes, the pale beams of that morning found Hernani patiently at work. He and Dorozynski had returned to the house as agreed, and though the latter had done little beyond consuming a quantity of cigarettes, he had been the silent witness of a vast expenditure of methodical labor.

Early on the previous evening, Hernani had arranged for the attendance of an old and trusted official, and since for so long he had been steadily preparing for the worst that could befall him, his actions fitted like the parts of a puzzle. The doors of the bank were to be kept open, and the business to be conducted as usual, though a smaller staff was to be maintained; while, so far as the internal working of the establishment was concerned, Hernani appointed this little, round-shouldered, wizened, though trustworthy official, in all things his deputy.

Thus having set his house in order so far as in him lay, when the mist was clearing and the white and azure dappling of the sky was becoming tinted and streaked with gold, amidst the twittering of the sparrows, and the steady drip, drip of the melting frost, pattering in crystal drops from the flat and funereal branches of the cedar trees, he turned his back upon his luxurious, almost princely home, and with a heavy heart, and a mind harassed with care, sought the shelter extended to him by Nikolay Brauman. To the Count, who was by his side, he made but one remark by the way.

"So the police have not troubled us after all. Do they know where to find us, and so are they strong in their silence? It disturbs me—we must make another move, I think."

And worn out for once, he went away to take a little rest.

It was Nikolay Brauman himself who was the first to rouse him from a deep and unrefreshing slumber, and to cause him to start up with blood-shot eyes, while he told the tale of the unresisted, bloodless Conscription. Hernani stretched himself, and greatly disturbed, got up; then for the remainder of that day, and for two more, he was in the city alone. He had assumed a clever disguise, at which the very chiefs of the revolutionary party, with whom he was closeted, laughed, being unable to recognize him but for his voice.

Upon his return, he poured startling news into Dorozynski's ears.

"I have seen my friend of the garden," he said—"the man who stopped me in the Saksonski Sad, as I told you. He—with a party of detectives—has been on our track. Ah! he has been useful, and in the future I count upon some services from him. The Holy One—blessed be He!—has sent me such a friend at such a moment, otherwise I tremble to think what would have happened. Now tell me—what of our two doves, my wife and your sister—do they bear up well? They say so, of course, but you, who have been with them and have no doubt observed them—you will know."

"You need trouble nothing about them. They suf-

ier, but no more than they must, and they are strong and
full of courage. Your constant messages reassured us
all."

"Good! Now let us smoke, and let me tell you all I
have done, and all that is to follow. As I warned you,
the action of the Government in the matter of this Conscription has set the match to the fire; within the space
of this week the country will be in a blaze. Nikolay
Brauman, my friend—we may speak without reserve—
no one will hear us?"

Nikolay Brauman assented.

"Very well; our foes not being prepared, and not believing in their hearts that we have the courage to fight,
it has been decided at a meeting—held now many hours
ago—to take the great step on the 22nd of this month.
Our couriers are already scouring the kingdom, and on
that day the people will rise en masse—Poland will be in
arms—and then, as you will see, France will come to our
assistance."

"Ah! if we could but count upon that," exclaimed
Dorozynski.

"In any case, it is certain that we can count upon ourselves," answered Hernani; "but hear me out. I am full
of news, good and healthy for the cause. Every Russian garrison throughout the land is to be attacked at
midnight on the date mentioned. Already there are
bodies of armed men moving in the woods on both banks
of the Vistula, and I am in receipt of special information
as to their numbers and condition."

The Count rubbed his hands.

"By heaven, this looks like business! We are really
about to do something," he exclaimed, with an almost
comical expression of satisfaction.

"You are right, my friend, and to-morrow night we
begin, we take the step. By nine o'clock, since it is so
dark, we shall have crossed the river, and if the roads
permit, in the early hours of the morning we shall have

14

met and mustered, five hundred strong. Each man has
been warned by me, and I think none will fail."

"But why was I left idling here while such work was
going on?" grumbled the Count.

"Because I judged it wise. Oh, you need not mind.
No slight was intended. When we are in the field we
shall depend upon you. What should I have done without you, since you have kept the women in good heart?"

The Count's face cleared. His generous nature was
free from the taint of sulkiness.

"That's all right," he said; "but what instructions did
you give the men? The greatest care should be taken to
get clear of the town without attracting attention, otherwise numbers of them may be arrested on suspicion."

"Of course I thought of that—it was one of my first
fears. They are to proceed singly or in parties of two
and three, riding or on foot, at any hour of the day they
may choose, but no arms are to be carried, and their
dress is to be their everyday attire. Now congratulate
me; there should be no hitch."

"With all my heart. No—none should occur so far as
one can see."

"We have a strong body of men, plenty of food, and a
fair supply of arms and ammunition."

"But is there to be no attack upon the Citadel?" the
Count exclaimed all at once, in tones of surprise, as
though the thought had but just struck him.

"None is planned as yet. We are said to be too weak."

"Then we begin by abandoning the key to the situation?"

"So I urged, but my representations were ignored."

"It should have been attempted, to my mind. A rush
should have been made. Look at the gain—the prize
was a rich one." And the two men continued talking,
with old Nikolay Brauman for an attentive listener.

The few hours which remained before quitting the city,
were entered upon by Hernani, in a spirit of feverish

excitement. He dreaded the police; their methods of dealing were, he knew, so subtle. Never in his life had he felt so anxious. He could abandon his business and his home, he could risk the confiscation of the bulk of his wealth with the calm deliberation of a man who believes in himself, having learned to fight the world; but when it came to the thought of his little one, his wife, in jeopardy—her safety, her very existence threatened— his legs felt weak, his head spun round, and he tottered as beneath a weight too heavy for him. Perhaps the limbs of the law would move with machine-like precision and rapidity at the last moment—on quitting Brauman's house, or on stepping into a droshky; on the way to the river, or when about to cross it. Now that his plans were made, his business complete, he could not bear her out of his sight. He caught himself eyeing her with melancholy tenderness, making up his mind to part from her, as it were, since at times, the disaster overshadowing them seemed as black as a thunder-cloud on the point of bursting. He was affected by fits of hilarity and confidence, depression and fear. Like a child he would start up and peer out of the windows, or stand still and listen for sign or sound, of the ubiquitous, iron-handed functionaries of the law. As for the time, it seemed as though the hours refused to pass. He examined his watch, tugged unconsciously at his moustache, thrust his long thin fingers through his dark wavy hair, and was incapable of remaining seated for more than a few minutes. The chiefs of the Central Committee, remembering his vast wealth, and consequent importance, favored him with long and inspiriting messages, to which he paid little or no heed. To such a pitch of distress was he reduced by his affection for this woman, whom in his darkest and most jealous moments he still believed to be untrue to him, that old Brauman's sons spoke of him as a bear, and even went so far as to touch their foreheads significantly, thereby indicating to each other that perhaps he was a

little mad. Of the men about him, the Count alone
pitied him, knowing the exact condition of affairs; and
Hernani, who occasionally encountered and understood
his sympathetic glances, said to him, more than once, as
though ashamed of his weakness—

"I shall be all right when we are clear of the place.
Ah! my friend, there is no need to tell you." And he
smoked and paced about the room, this old tried traveler,
this man of iron will and approved courage, in an apparently inconsolable frame of mind—waiting—forced to
wait; the unendurable suspense killing him.

Sara and Deotima, too, for that matter, were carrying
their separate loads of anxiety, but then, being women,
they bore them more patiently.

CHAPTER XV.

Shut up within his palace, protected from cold and discomfort by stout walls and innumerable luxuries, Hourko found himself alternately gratified and perplexed.
Wielopolski's coup d'état, the attempting of which he
had strenuously opposed, had deprived him of excitement
on the one hand, while supplying it on the other.

If the sons of the leading citizens of the town could be
arrested in their beds and in the streets, and tranquillity
be maintained, then obviously the Marquis Wielopolski
was right and there would be no revolution or rebellion
of any kind. And that was well, so far; still, there would
be no fighting, nothing out of which to obtain kudos—
and he loved fighting and kudos, and he hated the Poles;
besides, if there were to be no disturbances, what was to
become of his long-cherished passion for the Jewess—
the adorable Sara—which, if controlled or laid aside tem-
porarily owing to his wound and to absorbing demands
made upon him, was by no means abandoned. As he
had considered all along, with the whole kingdom in
arms, and Warsaw in a state of uproar and confusion, the
wife of a traitor and Jew might have been easily account-
ed for, but, with the loom of tranquillity and the growing
prospect of it, the realization of his desires might be difficult, in fact unattainable. For obvious reasons he had
not the smallest intention of using the criminous document, the possession of which had so alarmed Sara and
influenced Hernani. Sara, surrendered to the tender
mercies of the law, would be Sara out of his reach, lost to
him in fact. The idea that she was virtuous occasionally
forced itself upon him, and dimly, deep in his heart, he
felt himself capable of respecting such an admirable quality, though the teaching and experience of his whole life

was opposed to a belief in its existence. Whatever the temporary direction of his thoughts, however, upon all such points as concerned her, he invariably returned to the main one—his decision, fixed and unalterable, to have her within his power, hazard and trouble to be unconsidered trifles. So, though slowly, having so many distractions, his wits were at work, shaping out this problem he had set himself.

In another wing of the palace, that is to say, in one of the suite of rooms Madam Hourko appropriated to herself, a short scene was in progress, which would have occasioned the gallant Ivan Nicholaevitch no small amount of additional perplexity and also some surprise. Olga Pavlovna sat palpitating and furious, while before her stood Popoloff, cringing and crestfallen.

"So again this woman has slipped through our fingers, and again you have failed me!" she well-nigh screamed, in her thin, irritable voice.

"Do but hear me, madam," whined Titus, shuffling his feet, and unconsciously cracking the knuckles of his long bony fingers, in his evident distress—"do but believe me, when I assure you that to have done the thing would have been madness, and upon my head your censure must have fallen. Well was it that the house was empty, or what an uproar would have followed."

"Silence, sir," Olga retorted—"you were only born to obey!"

"Let me beg, let me remind you that the Jew is a great man in his own way, being rich beyond count; how then could this woman be seized without inquiries resulting? A little patience, a little waiting would be well; still, if you desire it, a commotion being nothing, we may have her yet. The tricks of the town are well known to the men I employ. She can be caught—oh! yes; there can be little doubt of that. I think I could go near to where she is in hiding at this very moment."

"You could? Then how can you lose time?"

"But, madam, I have despatched the detectives. To-night they will make their report to me."

"Oh! these delays—these delays."

"Madam, there must be reasonable ones."

"But they are maddening. Did you bribe the men sufficiently?"

"Yes—with a due attention to reason."

"But there is no reason in the matter. I may be alto-gether unreasonable in my hatred of this woman, since but for her I might be forced to hate another. That does not matter. I hate her. See—take these rubles; spend them; scour the town, every hole and corner of it, but let me know that she is under lock and key. That is all I ask of you."

"It shall be done, madam."

"Promptly and well?"

Popoloff smiled sarcastically.

"Madam, the detectives I have employed may be reck-oned on."

"And you will let me know the result on the instant?"

"The instant I know it, madam."

"One moment—there is one thing more I have to say to you. Should you fail—I may as well tell you frankly —you may count upon me as your worst enemy."

Popoloff ventured no answer; he merely bowed and shuffled out of the room, muttering to himself—

"Of what use to reason, to point out that the time is not ripe! Reasoning with a woman in love, is like talk-ing to a mad dog."

Later still, that day, it might have been said that he was employing his own wits oddly, since he was myste-riously engaged with members of the Central Commit-tee, in return for what he would have described as a "sufficient sum of money."

CHAPTER XVI.

At length, for Hernani, the supreme moment had arrived. With a view to attract less attention, the Count and Deotima had gone on ahead in a sauki,* intending to proceed over the Praga Bridge to the rendezvous, which was to be at a given point on the river bank.

All that remained to be done was to bid farewell to old Nikolay Brauman, and step into the street accompanied by Riva. Hernani's disguise was perfect, a long thick beard adding twenty years to his age; as for Sara, she was muffled up past all recognition. The door of the old Jew's house closed behind them as they descended the steps. A sauki came up in search of a fare, they engaged it, seated themselves, and in perfect Russian, Hernani gave his instructions. They were off. Sara's pulses beat wildly, and her beautiful eyes, appearing black now that the pupils were dilated, flashed anxious glances on all sides. Would they be stopped? What would happen? Every dusky figure approaching in shuba, military great-coat or other attire, was assuredly a foe to be reckoned with, and when at a breakneck speed their driver swept them round a turning, almost into the center of a group of mounted Cossacks, her distress was complete. She uttered a nervous stifled cry. Surely they were lost? Leaning back in his seat, his broad shoulders expanded, a couple of loaded revolvers in his pockets and a good cigar between his teeth, Hernani appeared at his ease. His utterances were monosyllabic, and he contented himself with firmly gripping Sara's arm at the moment when he heard her weak expression of fear; otherwise he sat motionless. In this way they

---

* Small sledge.

swung round the angles of the streets, miraculously, it seemed, escaping collision with other vehicles, until, with a jerk which threw the horses on their haunches, they at length drew rein within a few paces of the river. The little passage over the ice was nothing, and there in the gloom, awaiting their coming, were the Count and Deotima, while close at hand was a sani* and pair, and a couple of saddle-horses. A few remarks exchanged, even a joke thrown in, and they were off again, Hernani and the Count riding, the two women tucked up warmly in the sledge; above all things, Warsaw was behind them, and the open country and the woods ahead.

Throughout that drive the sensation was strong upon Sara that she was entering upon a new life. She experienced a feeling of sleepy contentment as the horses tore along and the sledge labored and creaked. Now and again they rumbled and oscillated over a bridge of pine trunks, the interstices of which were stuffed with branches and soil, pounded and moistened by exposure and usage to the consistency of clay. When she looked out she could see nothing but the dim outline of a white-walled cottage, a fence, or the straight dark stems of trees disappearing into interminable gloom, and this, thanks alone to the side lamps, athwart the light from which, the rapid breathing of the horses struck in pointed shafts of vapor.

Hernani and the Count rode ahead or in the rear, the road being for the most part too narrow for them to keep abreast of the sledge, and she occasionally caught herself judging of their position by the dull rhythmic thud of their horses' hoofs. These monotonous sounds created by this passage through the silence of the night, succeeding the protracted anxiety and nervous strain to which she had for so long been subjected, caused Sara to sink at length into a deep and placid sleep, during which Deo-

---

* Large sledge.

tima remained awake without attempting to speak, the Count and Hernani scarcely exchanging a word, except of advice or caution.

And so they journeyed on, hour after hour, through dense woods and occasional open spaces, until, as in a dream, Sara was conscious of alighting and entering a long low house with a wooden porch, of receiving the kindest welcome and some much needed refreshment, and then, still in a pleasantly tired and happy state, of hurrying into bed, thankful to rid herself of her clothes and nestle beneath the cool soft sheets, with the abandon of a child who is weary and wishes but to stretch its limbs.

In the morning, she was awakened by the muffled noises made by people moving and busying themselves within and without the house. As she lay on her back wondering where she was, and yawned and stretched her soft round arms above her head, slowly she became conscious of the cheering and appetizing sounds and scents of a country house. She, who in her heart loved such simple things, discovered that the air was fresher and purer, and that stored herbs and fruits, such as apples and pears and preserves, mingled their perfume with the more subtle fragrance of wood smoke, hay, and an occasional puff of a stronger odor, caused by the presence of cattle and the roots necessary to them. Gradually becoming more alive to sounds, she distinguished the low, monotonous, but soothing coo-coo of wood-pigeons, the twitter of sparrows and linnets, and the more prolonged and agreeable notes of mavis and blackbird. With a little shudder she drew her arms beneath the bed-clothes, which she collected about her ears, despite the increased cold, taking pleasure in moving her limbs into the cool parts of the bed, vaguely wondering and listening still, but dimly conscious that she breathed and was refreshed. Finally, in response to the dull rumble of wagons, some shouts rising above the hum of many voices, the crack of a rifle and an occasional command in sharp decisive

tones, she flung the bed-clothes aside, hung her little feet
over the edge of the bed momentarily, then boldly stepped across the floor and cautiously raised the milk-white
linen blind. The sight she beheld enabled her instantly
to appreciate her position.

Before her lay a drive and a flower-garden, separated
from an orchard but thinly planted with fruit trees, by a
rough wooden fence. On the edge of this orchard a long
line of farm buildings appeared, built upon a scale suitable to an estate of several thousand acres, situated in a
country where the climate and method of farming necessitated a great storage of produce. Upturned carts,
ploughs, and other implements of husbandry, were to be
seen mingled with all the litter of a space, where through
open doors, cows were standing gently swinging their
tails. As a setting to this scene, as well as a serviceable
protection from fierce gales of wind, imagine the dark
brown trunks and feathery crests of an apparently interminable forest of pine trees.

A fresh fall of snow had occurred over night, but the
dampness of it was totally ignored by groups of men
scattered over the orchard or gathered around the out-
buildings, where horses were being groomed, arms and
equipments examined and cleaned, the arrival and un-
loading of wagons attended to. Occasionally, rifles were
being discharged over the heads of young animals, with
a view to accustom them to the sound of firing; this pre-
cautionary measure being carried on at some little distance to the right, near the pine wood, on the fringe of
which the Count might be discerned instructing a little
squad of men. And upon the whole picture, the sun was
making attacks in amber shafts, dispersing the mist and
flashing light upon every piece of shining metal—bits,
gun-barrels, implements, every particle of snow, ice, and
dripping moisture.

But where was Hernani, and what had become of the
usually attentive and devoted Riva? Why had they

allowed her to sleep so late, for evidently it was late? It
was too bad, and made her feel desperately guilty. She
should have been up and doing with the rest; it was
disgusting, lazy of her at such a time; and, thinking thus
ill of herself, she was in the midst of hurrying, when in
reply to a knock, Deotima had to be admitted. And the
young girl came in looking the embodiment of health,
her lips and cheeks ruddy as ever, her eyes clear and
sparkling, though her hands were somewhat cold and
blue, owing to the low temperature of the water in which
she had been splashing about. But it was easier to get
Deotima into the room than out of it, brimful as she was
of strange news, rumors, positive facts, actual occur-
rences; for already she had been out and about, having
run down to explore, like a child, naturally curious and
keenly interested in a new place.

Deliberately seating herself on the edge of the bed, her
skirts spread out, she showed rather a large though shapely foot and ankle. Then she began to talk. Had Sara not
enjoyed the long drive? To her it had been delightfully
swift and romantic; and what a complete change of existence it had brought about. Had she slept well? She
looked as fresh as a flower. Oh, yes; she would let her
get up in a moment, but there was really no occasion to
hurry, and she must just say her say before leaving her
in peace. Sara rolled the bed-clothes about her and sat
up, clasping her knees, listening with amused good nature and interest to this breathless account; and Deotima continued. Several sturdy and fine-looking young
fellows who had not been expected, had already dropped
in amongst the rest, who in many cases were really well
mounted and good riders. Andrew had expressed himself much pleased with their appearance. Then wagons
were rolling up, as she surely must have heard, filled
with hay and straw and any amount of provisions, so that
the place would soon be converted into a camp on a large
scale. Their host, old Sicinski, was a charming patriot,

ready to spend his last shilling for the cause, and his two
sons were most civil and obliging—but of course Sara
had seen them. Oh, and Andrew had promised to
further her instruction with a rifle and revolver, and—
but how stupid of her—that news was stale. Very well;
since Sara was so anxious to dress, she would be off and
would not forget to send Riva, whom she had already
encountered downstairs; and away went this fine, simple-
minded specimen of maidenhood, in such spirits, that
Sara scarcely recognized her. Then the dressing recommenced more soberly, and with the conviction that she
was hopelessly behindhand.

She had slept well, and no doubt under the influence
of the keen frosty air, sweet with the resinous odor of the
pine woods, her thoughts flew swiftly. She became conscious of freedom from gloom and anxiety. It was as
though she had been suddenly relieved of a heavy incu-
bus by an unseen hand, and, surprised at this lightness
of heart, she put the question to herself more than once,
"What has happened—what has happened?" And she
actually sat down, the better to enable her to analyze her
own feelings. "Why do I feel so different?" she inquired.
"I am like a new being. Let me think." With a towel
over one arm, her hair escaping over her shoulders, she
raised the fingers of her left hand and began to enumerate her ideas; then, after a while, she again commenced
her toilet, her mind still at work, though in a less methodical fashion. For instance, that snake in the grass, that
little fat oily pig, Hermann Bloch, was no longer near
to work mischief. Besides that, Hernani must have a
warm corner for her somewhere in his heart, and, as if in
support of this idea, had she not surprised him in the act
of regarding her with something of the old interest and
affection? He had certainly been more sympathetic and
tender in manner. As for the magnitude of the step they
had now taken, her belief in him was prodigious, absolute. Over again she was the young woman who had

clung to him in the old Cracow days, wondering, rever-
encing, adoring. No matter what he might do, he would
be lucky. Her fears had been groundless, the overwhelming obstacles she had at first discerned had existed
only in her imagination. The cause he had espoused
would assuredly triumph—the Russians would be worst-
ed and forced to come to terms, and once again Poland
would be free. But even while she so arranged the termination of this death-struggle, through her window a
spectacle presented itself which upset her. Out there
in the orchard, a tall, slim young fellow, with a white
face—one of the new recruits—was being shown how to
hold his rifle. She recoiled a step. What material!
Was there not something wrong, something worse than
a forlorn hope about this revolutionary effort? There
were thousands of splendid troops in and around Warsaw; in some instances, the flower of the Russian army.
She had seen and heard them march, and the precision
and thunder of their disciplined steps, rang again in her
ears. A sensation of emptiness, even sickness, over-
came her, and she passed her hand over her forehead as
though to disperse such unpleasant reflections.

"It is all right. He knows," she at length had courage
to murmur, and she shrugged her shoulders as though to
say, "It is thus I banish such ideas."

At the close of that first day the greatest progress had
been made. To begin with, more than the number of
men expected had joined, and these had been questioned
separately, with a view to ascertain their special capabili-
ties. Quarters for the whole force had been found in and
around the farm-buildings, which in case of attack were
to be defended to the last. The thick woods in rear of
the position, were to be retreated into, only in case of extreme need. The best mounted and most trustworthy
men had been thrown out as scouts, having received instructions how to act in case of emergency from the
Count, who in reality was in command of rather more

than five hundred men, in good health and in the best of spirits.

Word had been received from Deotima's cousins, Counts Ladislaus and Adam Goroski, that they were joining with all speed, and moreover, not single-handed. All the peasants thus far encountered had proved friendly, though that, it was thought, might be due to the influence of their host and his two sons, who, jointly, were the proprietors of an immense stretch of land.

Up to the hour at which they sat down to the evening meal—a sort of homely tea—five-and-twenty of them at a long table which extended nearly the length of the room, no news of any kind had been received from Warsaw. It was not yet known whether the Government was aware that they had taken up arms, and Hernani was anxious that the fact should be disguised as long as possible. To be let alone for the next few days would be of immense advantage, he urged. Their friends would have time to join them—perhaps one, if not both, of the two bodies of men reported to be within twenty miles, would come in to swell their ranks; the men would be better accustomed to the weapons they were about to handle, and, more important still, the result of the grand attempt on the 22nd, would be known—after which it would be so much easier to gauge the situation accurately.

The appetites of all these people, these young fellows met together for so desperate a purpose, appeared to Sara to be really enormous. Some of them had never been a day's journey from home, yet they were laughing and chaffing, eating and drinking, as though they were accustomed to such work—behaving like veterans, in fact. She caught herself wondering whether this mirth was not too loud to be natural. It was all very well, but what a noise! Beneath the surface were there no shadowy misgivings such as she herself had been troubled with? Unused to hardship or exposure of any kind, without reckoning the enemy's bullets, a great many of them would

never see parents or home again. And to think that
Hernani had staked life—everything—just as they had.
At that thought she must have looked intensely serious,
for Deotima, who had been watching her, could not help
exclaiming—

"What are you thinking of?"

Disturbed, almost startled, Sara could make no other
answer than a very commonplace one, which was—

"Oh, nothing."

"But the expression of your face was quite tragic."

Sara shook herself and with affected surprise said—

"No—really—did I look so disagreeable? What a
mistake. But I was dreaming—that was all."

"Are you feeling well?" inquired Deotima sympatheti-
cally; and Sara declared with energy that she was. All
the same, her spirits had somewhat evaporated, Hernani
being in a measure at the bottom of it. He had not
escaped her notice through the day—in fact, when it had
been possible, she had spoken to him and had been de-
pressed by a slight, but to her insignificant, alteration in
his manner towards her. He seemed rather to avoid her,
she imagined, and by way of an additional annoyance,
for the sake of space, it had been decided that she and
Deotima should occupy one room together, so that her
much cherished desire to share whatever accommodation
there was with Hernani, was at once destroyed. It was
irritating in the extreme; however, having decided to
make the best of everything, she laid herself out to
be charming, with the result that before bedtime she
had succeeded in winning the hearts of all those with
whom she came in contact. Last thing that night Riva
joined her as was her wont, and the gossip she delighted
in, having been missed latterly, she was overflowing
with her own simple ideas. In her servant's voice she
began by grumbling at their change of quarters.

"This is no place for you, my lamb. What could the

master be thinking of, to leave a beautiful home and all the comforts of it, for a hole like this?"

"You don't understand, Riva," Sara answered gently.

"Then it's no fault of mine. I ask, and I obey; now, don't I? It's Riva do this and that, and I'm to be found trotting about, here, there, and everywhere, always on my legs. Tell me—did the pan* here lose his wife? Pity for him; a house without a woman to look after it is no better than a pig-sty."

"It does make a difference."

"I should think so indeed."

"But you are well treated, Riva."

"Oh, as for that, yes; I have nothing to complain of. But the place is going to ruin. If I were an obyvatel,† with land by the mile and money by the sack, I'd have my ceilings white and my windows and walls clean. And those great strong sons of his—what do they do all day but smoke, smoke, smoke."

"Ah! Riva; you are in the wrong mood to be pleased."

"What do I see to please me, my lamb?"

"Well, make the best of it."

"Oh, as for that, that's all right; but I wish we were back in Warsaw again."

"Don't."

"Why?"

"Because it is useless to wish such things."

"Where are we going, then? Shall we be here all through the cold?"

"I know no more than you do, Riva."

"How strange; and does the master?"

"Not as yet. A day or two may decide."

"And you will tell me?"

"Yes."

"Well, from what I can see of it, there is no rising

---

* Mr.—Sir—Owner.　　　　　　†Landed proprietor.

15

throughout the land. Only ourselves, stuck fast in the midst of woods. If the great Russian, the Governor, move against us with his host, may the God of Israel fight for us, I say—we shall need him."

"That must be so always. But He is on our side. Our cause is a righteous one."

"Yes, that is so. Well, the master knows what he is about, I suppose. He has a long head, and fortune pursues him. Ach! How grand he looks in his great-coat and boots, like as in Cracow when he came to us through the snow—eh, my lamb?"

Sara nodded her head with the pleased expression Riva was on the lookout for.

"Not one of them here can make his shadow."

Sara fairly blushed and did not answer. She was as simple as a child in aught that concerned Hernani, and never knew what to say when his praises were sung. In her eyes he had no faults. All this Riva knew, but, shrewdly judging enough to be as good as a feast, she slid on to another topic.

"Well, have caution for yourself, my lamb. When you are out of my sight, what is to be done if you are not careful? And the draughts here are awful—think of that! Ah! what a night I had—never a wink of sleep, what with the ache in my teeth and the pain in my shoulder. Is there enough on the bed—are you sure? Ach! The more comfort one has, the more one wants. There, now, someone is coming. For the life of me, I can never get you to myself." And Riva retreated precipitately, just as Deotima entered.

Evidently the young woman did not share Riva's horror of cold or draughts, for her first act was to make for the window, which she flung open.

"What a relief to get a breath of fresh air, after the heat of that room downstairs!" she exclaimed, filling her lungs with a sigh of satisfaction. "Really it was insufferably hot; I felt like fainting. Come and have a

peep. A lot of them have decided to camp out. I joked
them about being hot-house plants—told them they
would catch cold if a leaf stirred, and this is the result.
They declared they had tents and meant to use them.
Come; it looks quite pretty in the light of the huge wood
fires. You won't catch cold. It is dry. There is a sharp
frost."

Sara joined her, and the two of them rested their arms
on the window-sill. A sudden thought struck Deotima.

"Let us put on our furs and go out for a few minutes," she said; "the house is not shut up and it will do
us good."

Sara objected. It was late.

"But not too late," argued the girl; "for my part, I
never felt less like sleeping—come."

Sara yielded—the two of them skipping down the
staircase as though they were escaping for some fine
fun. In spite of remonstrances from Riva, who had
heard them and begged them not to be foolish, they followed the curve of the drive as it wound through the
garden into the orchard, Sara firing a last shot at Riva,
who stood shivering in the doorway.

"You stupid old thing—it will not hurt us. We shall
be back in a moment."

But it was all very fine. In a few minutes they shivered, the keen air having chilled them.

"Let us go back: Riva was right," said Sara.

"No, no—come on," urged the girl; "I cannot sleep
to-night. Can you guess why?"

"Yes, I fancy so."

"Why, then?"

"It is the great night—the 22nd."

"You are right, and I shall never be able to close my
eyes. Think of what will be happening now and within
an hour. It is already past eleven. At this very moment they will be stealing to the places of meeting,
avoiding the police or the troops. May the Blessed Vir-

gin watch over them and endow them with strength—
courage, I know they have. The old and infirm—the
parents—will be praying for the young and active—the
children—who will be arming, and in their hearts praying too. Ought not we to pray—we two—here, with
only the sky between us and God's throne? No one
will see; it is so dark. Let us."

And at the edge of the wood, whence came faint noises
of the night, at the foot of a huge pine tree, which cast
its drooping branches encrusted with frozen snow almost over them, they lifted their eyes to heaven, and as
their different religions prompted them, implored the
Divine aid for Poland and her sons. Then, in a silence
which both felt to be good at such a moment, they skirted the fringe of pines, passing near the watch-fires recognized and unchallenged.

Over their heads not a star was to be seen, mist even
floating through the summits of the loftiest trees, driven
by the cool wind. Once they distinctly heard, far up
above them, the measured flap-flap of some great bird's
wings, as in mystic solitude and impenetrable gloom it
beat its trackless course southward. And the same
thought occurred to both at the same moment—what
strange and terrible scenes might those tireless pinions
hover over!

The remainder of that night passed away in peace,
though in a large village near at hand, manifestations of
friendliness to the Polish cause were freely indulged in,
much to the wrath of the Russian burgomaster and tax-
gatherer. This was entirely due to Hernani's efforts,
supplemented by the orders he had issued to cultivate
the goodwill of the peasantry and to pay the price demanded for any supplies obtained.

As the new day dawned, the thoughts in the hearts of
all were, What has happened—when shall we receive information? The Count had advocated an attack upon

Siedlec hours previously, to which Hernani had objected.

"I promised to come here, and to do nothing until I received instructions," he had answered. "Let us act as I agreed; it will be for the best." And there the matter dropped.

For Sara the event of the day came early. There were a few gleams of sunshine, though the air was damp owing to a thaw, and she and Deotima stood in the wooden porch sheltered from the wind, enjoying the feeble warmth and watching the puffs of blue smoke curling away from the Minié rifles, as the men in their simple gray uniforms practiced at a mark. Neither of them had slept well, and both were in that frame of mind, when to think little, is as great a relief as to talk little. The large rambling house of one story in height, the garden, orchard and outbuildings had all been explored—even the frozen pond which supplied fish for the Lenten fast, had been looked at and walked round; there was no new sensation to be got by a further exhibition of curiosity, and since there was no immediate cause for uneasiness, they abandoned themselves to a momentary sensation of comfort, blinking there in the sun, dropping monosyllabic remarks without being conscious that they opened their lips. A perpetual hum of voices came from the direction of the outbuildings, where most of the men were assembled, only a few of the rawest of their number being out, burning the powder which was so precious. So there were the bulk of them, lolling about, amusing themselves, smoking, singing, playing cards, telling each other how the Russians were to be made short work of, while only those who thought more and talked less, washed, hung out some clothes, mended the fires, or groomed their horses.

Amidst this jumblement of sounds, came the clang of the iron gate at the bottom of the drive, the latch rattling as it swung upon its hinges.

A little old woman with a basket trudged up to them. She wished to see Hernani. For what purpose? Oh! for that matter, she had two fowls, plump and white, and some fresh eggs. She wished to give them to him, and had walked some three miles to do so. Why? Why? Because he had been the salvation of her son, who had been lazy and given to drink. He had found work for him at a time when the world had tired of him. She knew of others who could tell the same story. Yes, it was a long while since—before she had come to live in that part of the country, but she had not forgotten—she should never forget. She had been assured that he was close at hand, and she had come to see.

Sara turned to Deotima.

"Take her to him," was all she could say.

Ah! what joy, what unspeakable joy to hear him spoken of with such affection, to know that he was beloved as well as respected. No wonder that she loved him. It made her quiver with delight. To think of it—in the country—miles from home—his good deeds blossoming in such a fashion. Then she remembered. The woman was poorly clad and it was cold. She was only copying him, it was true, but, with her heart throbbing, she rushed upstairs. She had few things to choose from, but there was a shawl, a soft woolen one which would be just the thing. Riva should take it. Ah! it was delicious to be kind, she thought, as hidden away she stood and watched the little bent figure limping along, looking bigger and warmer for the extra wrap, her empty basket hooked upon her arm, her heart evidently strengthened by the treatment she had received, if one might judge by the laughter that marked her passage through the ranks of the well-meaning young patriots.

For a little while—and for the first time for years—Hernani experienced the sensation of being out of his element. Count Dorozynski was a soldier in the true sense of the word, that is, he had seen active service.

Hernani was a traveled civilian of large experience, a shrewd business man and born financier, but he could claim to be no more. By a retrospective bound, which recalled old days minutely, it seemed to him that he would have felt more at home amidst the wild freedom of an Arab encampment, than surrounded by the discipline the Count did his best to enforce. Amidst the rifle practice, the drilling, the exercises of various kinds by word of command, he was forced to look on while the Count stepped into the position habitual to him in all he undertook—that of chief. Chief he was to many of the men, his own employes and those who knew him, and chief he might be again when it came to the turmoil of a fight, but amongst military red-tapism he felt out of place. It was only by degrees that this feeling passed and he began to make headway and to be conscious of it. Possessing the rare power of inspiring others with the confidence he felt in himself, he had only to throw his whole heart and soul into his new duties to make the most astonishing strides in the right direction. His practical, penetrative and logical mind, was so capable of grasping and advising quickly and wisely, that even where technical knowledge seemed to be required, his counsel was useful. He won the hearts of those of his following to whom he had been but slightly known, and in the eyes of those who thought they knew him he displayed fresh qualities. It was as though he had started a new business, which at the outset required every moment of his time and attention. It was the master mind at work again. Even the Count was not prepared for such an exhibition.

"You should have been a soldier!" he could not help exclaiming.

As for the men, they talked amongst themselves, sifting, discussing, measuring him accurately and assigning him his place in their midst. "Let the chief alone; he's all right; he's got a head on his shoulders," they were in the habit of saying. "To see him shoot, one would think he had been born to the business." Then they would allude to his wealth. It whetted their curiosity; it awed them. How much had he got? Ah! that was a question. One thing was certain—a man with so much money was a man worth respecting. And all sorts of fabulous stories were circulated about him, the things he had done, and the things he had not done but was credited with, when added together, making a heavy total. However, there could be no doubt that he was warm-hearted and generous, as well as enormously wealthy—that he had traveled everywhere awhile back, and that his linguistic attainments were unique. Then, too, there was his wife—could anyone be more gentle and charming, or quicker with a kind word or a good act? And the more intelligent added that at times she looked thoughtful and sad, an expression, they contended, which softened and enhanced her surprising beauty. A button sewed on by her, was fingered with respect, by the soft-hearted fellow thus favored. A few simple words falling from her lips, made the pulses of the recipients flutter with pleasure. And was it to be wondered at, when to her beauty, goodness had been added, and to that, affability, an irresistible combination with which to assault poor susceptible humanity?

So these two, Sara and Hernani, were in a fair way to be thought much of, and this not less because they were both unconscious of the subtle charm of their own individuality.

At length, when it became known that a mounted courier had arrived bringing important information, what gossiping began, and what signs of excitement were visible upon each face; what conjectures were hazarded, and what speculations indulged in! Some of the poor fellows talked of getting news of their parents, though how it was to come to them was not quite clear. It was true, they had only been absent a little while;

but their position was a perilous one, and they were un-
accustomed to being out of sight of their own house-
tops.

Actually in receipt of a direct communication from the
Central Committee, Hernani and Dorozynski proceeded
to discuss it with closed doors. None of the subordinate
officers they had appointed, not even Counts Ladislaus
and Adam Goroski, who had by this time arrived, were
to be told anything until they had carefully decided how
much to tell.

The despatch proved to be a lengthy one which occasioned pleasure, but also indicated the necessity for
energetic action in the near future. The tale it told was
that the secret of the rising had been faithfully maintained to the last moment, with the result that it had been
general and singularly successful. The whole country
was in arms. Isolated bodies of Russian troops had
been overpowered, their weapons and ammunition
seized, the military chests carried off, the towns and villages they had garrisoned occupied. The peasantry favored the cause, and were arming or quietly rendering
every assistance while appearing in the villages in open-
mouthed innocence and apparent inactivity. Capable
and trustworthy officers were spreading themselves over
the country to organize and lead the insurgent bands
forming on all sides. Furthermore, it suggested that a
junction should be effected with one, if not both, the
other insurgent bodies in movement on the right bank of
the Vistula, and it added—and this was the alarming
part of the despatch—that a force of three hundred Russian infantry was shortly to leave Warsaw for the purpose of attacking the position occupied by Hernani and
Count Dorozynski. Hernani folded up the paper, then
tossed it to the Count, and both men remained silent for
some minutes, Hernani twice muttering audibly, "So
they are coming," a third time adding, "Three hundred
of them, and they are about to march. Very well, my

friend, we shall meet them—eh? That will be the plan, and there are some nice places for the purpose between here and Warsaw. There is also another advantage we shall have over them: we know them, they don't know us. We understand what we have to expect from disciplined troops, they will look upon us as a rabble, a collection of silly ignorant peasantry, or a lot of townsmen who for fighting purposes are no better than babies. We are civilians, and regular soldiers turn up their noses at civilians. They will come strolling along, their pipes in their mouths, so to speak, and without a scout thrown out, and we shall await them where there is a morass and a thick wood just beyond. You remember my remark as we passed it? That will be the plan, eh?"

The Count demurred. What would be the use of abandoning their strong position? What if the enemy were not careless and felt them first, then encountered them on even terms? It would be foolish. No, no! the thing would be to remain where they were. But they must think. The situation had become serious.

"Ah! But you don't understand me," retorted Hernani, returning to the charge. "Abandon this position? On no account; it is a strong one. These farm-buildings, loop-holed, the rise in the ground, and the woods, not too close in our rear, will suit us well."

"That is my opinion," agreed the Count.

"But this is mine, my friend, and you will forgive me for pressing it upon you, since I am no soldier. Let us divide our force. With a hundred and fifty to two hundred men we will waylay these Moskals,* choosing ground to our liking. We make this place our base, and the remainder of our men with the supplies and ammunition must remain here; then, if the worst comes to the worst, and we are defeated, we can make a final stand upon this spot."

---

* Muscovites.

"Well, we must think it over," conceded the Count, brightening up.

"But we must be prompt," urged Hernani; "every moment is precious; at such a time there is much to be done."

"The scheme has its good points," mused Dorozynski, lighting a cigarette and puffing at it vigorously. Then they began to reason and argue afresh—they could not quite agree—there was so much to be considered; finally, after a long discussion, the idea was practically adopted. Counts Ladislaus and Adam Goroski, who had joined with over a hundred men, were to remain behind, Sara and Deotima being committed to their charge. And in spite of all Dorozynski's representations to the contrary, Hernani insisted upon going. What—it was dangerous—and there was no need—and he was wanted where he was. That might be true, all of it, but he had always loved danger, and time back had gone in search of it—danger in life was like the spice in a pudding: it flavored it. As for being wanted—others would fill his place very well. Sara would be anxious—true, he was sorry for that—but what was to be done?—she must get used to such things. Of one fact there could be no doubt —he must go. It was, he felt, his duty. So the necessary preparations were at once commenced; the taking of the step itself depending upon further information as to the movements of the Russian forces.

CHAPTER XVII.

To follow the course of events accurately, and to understand enough of their working, the inmates of the
palace, Titus Popoloff and the Governor-General, Ivan
Nicholaevitch, must be glanced at quickly.

The apparent intention of the former, which was to
spirit Sara away, had been upset by the stranger's desire
to serve Hernani (he of the Saksonski Sad*), as previously related, this failure of course having its direct
effect upon the General, since he soon knew of her escape; also, though he little thought it, upon madam,
his wife, as well.

Having given no fresh orders, but having trusted to
Popoloff's watchfulness, Hourko was distinctly offended
by the display of clumsiness, of which he considered he
had been guilty, in allowing the whole brood—as he
thought of them—Sara, Hernani himself, Count Dorozynski, and Deotima, to get clear away from the city.
His faith in this obsequious servant, latterly on the wane,
had thus drawn closer to a breakage. The matter of
Sara, and the handling of it, had been a special charge,
a delicate trust emanating from a whim of his, it might
be, but all the more important because of the value he
chose to set upon it. As for madam, henceforth, as she
had said of herself, she was Popoloff's enemy. So that
the storm that personage had drawn upon himself, partly by his lack of promptitude and partly by the betrayal
of his trust, could do no less than gather until it burst.
He had been completely outwitted, so it seemed—how.
he appeared not to know; in addition, he was certainly

---

* Saxon gardens.

fast exhausting all his resources on the score of other irons still held in the fire by him. That was the position.

The eventful night of the 22nd once over, with a space added for the press of events and the arrival of news, and Hourko was able to find time to order the step alluded to in the despatch forwarded to Hernani by the Central Committee. Three hundred infantrymen, commanded by the well-known Major Suroff, were directed to be in readiness to cross the Vistula, and reduce to submission Hernani. Count Dorozynski, and the insurgent band under their joint leadership; such instructions being supplemented by orders delivered privately to Major Suroff, which were as follows:—

The Jew Hernani, and the Pole known as Count Andrew Dorozynski, with such subordinates as might be with them, were to be captured alive if possible, but with regard to the two women known to be in their following, the wife of the Jew and the sister of the Count, no pains were to be spared to take them alive and unharmed. This order accomplished, Major Suroff was to communicate, and await instructions wheresoever he might chance to find himself.

CHAPTER XVIII.

A kind of pause had come in the life at the hastily-formed camp. So thought Sara. A pause during which it seemed that she had grown to know it all, and that what was at first novel and interesting, had in it a vein of monotony. When relieved of extreme doubt on the score of safety, surely it should have been pleasant enough to be with Hernani, to watch his tall form, to see him advising, encouraging, inspiring; to look into his face when the chance offered, and try to read there all that she would have had him tell her. And yet she was not at ease, not as she had felt upon that one morning, her first one there. Ever since that day her old feelings had steadily caught her up again, returning in force, though one by one. The notes of suspense, anxiety, positive dread, sounded loud and ever louder in her ears. In her weak moments she felt as if all the preparation and practice, the drilling and maneuvering, could not avert the coming of the crash, though by such means it might be stayed for awhile. Danger was gradually stalking upon them, walling them in, encircling them. They were in a false position. Then, too, her mind was awry. In nothing did she resemble what she wished to be. A constant thought with her was, "What have I done? What am I doing?" Even when conditions seemed to favor her, she could but play the prosaic part of simple housewife. With the desire so strong in her to do something heroic as well as useful, something to win back her husband's affection, and worth exchanging for the youth which was passing from her, the beauty which was decaying, she could discover no outlet, no opening. All her struggles were against a death in life, an existence in which individuality dwindles and becomes lost in a mere nihility, accepted placidly by millions of wives.

Conscious of vast stores of energy and affection, it was becoming a daily and hourly grievance to her to feel that her place in the world was a sinecure, that she was not useful, not necessary to anyone. And this sensation strengthened, because, to her consternation, Hernani's conduct had—after the excitement of the escape from Warsaw—reverted to the lines with which she was so familiar. He was amiable and polite, even attentive, but never by any chance sympathetic or affectionate, and the hopes she had entertained of the possible advantage to be derived from their altered fortunes, were disappearing fast. With indescribable suffering she again began to understand that his attitude towards her was an inexorable one. Yet she was fain to admit to herself—and she hated her weakness—that she loved him with a love which grew rather than diminished, as might have been expected. The fact that he did not pay her the compliment of confiding in, or consulting her in any way, was another misfortune which made her feel still more a cipher. It was so ignominious to receive news from Riva, which Riva had picked up second-hand or by keeping her ears open. And to be thankful for that—how humiliating! There could be no doubt, she considered, that she was being disgracefully treated.

So the morning of the start to intercept the Russian advance, suggested by Hernani and acceded to by the Count, found her in an unenviable and unhappy frame of mind, though apparently cheerful and obliging.

The information Hernani had waited for had arrived, and within an hour or so from the receipt of it, the little force was drawn up under arms, each man having volunteered, quarrels even having taken place as to who should go, for there was scarcely one who was not eager for the adventure. It was to serve their country, it would put an end to staying in the camp talking, and the first blood would be drawn.

Before mounting his horse Hernani approached Sara and kissed her on the forehead. The others were standing round—Deotima and Dorozynski, the two brothers, Ladislaus and Adam Goroski, even Riva was close at hand. And this cold farewell took place in the front of the old farm-house, near the wooden porch, while the men stood to their arms in the orchard, amidst the stems of the apple trees, with the huge farm-buildings in their rear. Hernani was smiling, chatting right and left, and he held a lighted cigar in one hand when with the other he finally grasped Sara's fingers.

"We shall only be away a few hours, and you are in good hands—so cheer up," he said quite lightly. "You must think of us in this way—we have food, ammunition, and are in health—so there must be no worrying or anxiety on our account. Do you promise?"

Sara's hand rested passively in his. She dared not trust herself to look in his face. She could not open her lips.

"Very well," he muttered, and his voice shook perceptibly as he added, "Good-bye," and to Ladislaus Goroski, "Take care of her, Count."

A moment after they were off with a ringing cheer, marching amongst the stems of the trees, lost to sight of the farm and its inmates, none of them knowing that two dark figures, two women, followed them quite a distance, further than was safe, to obtain a last glimpse, and with the anxiety, the sorrow in their hearts that women wrestle with when husbands and brothers go out into danger. No one knew either, that in the dusky shadows of the woods Hernani brushed away more than one tear, while affecting to be in the best of spirits, and breathing nothing but confidence and encouragement upon all sides. Throughout the whole of that day they marched—those young fellows, jubilant, cutting jokes, behaving as though they were tramping to a wedding, a carouse, or to meet the girl of their choice, rather than in the cold, with spare food, over rough country, to their first engagement, their first blood-letting, as it proved to be.

No event marked that long, wearying, machine-like movement along the flat ground, amongst trees, through open glades, and past an occasional hamlet, farm, or isolated hut, until the waning light and the deepening shadows made faces and forms gray and indistinct, and at that hour, just as some of the weaker ones were flagging, and rest was being thought of, a shout re-echoed along the line, and a dark mounted form drew rein in their midst. What was the news? It was this—so this man, their scout, would have it—the Russians were at hand and in force—two to three hundred infantrymen, if one, and he could lead the way to where he believed they would be found camping for the night.

A halt and a meal was ordered, then with the greatest caution an advance was commenced, orders being given that not a word was to be spoken, not a sound made; and in this deep silence, throughout the blackness of these amaranthine shades, following the cautious movements of their guide, they stepped along without exchanging a syllable, obedient as children, their hearts beating, their eyeballs strained, feeling that at last something decisive was to happen, and that blows were to be struck for the possession of the soil upon which they stood, the beloved country in which the oppressor had dared to make a home.

Within a mile or so of where their foes were believed to be, they were again halted, with instructions to remain quiet, to kindle no fire or light, to make no noise, but wrapped in their coats, to seek the deepest shadows and patiently await orders. Hernani and Dorozynski both spoke to them, mindful that many of them were of good blood, serving at their own discretion and by free

16

will, therefore meriting greater consideration and gentler handling. A subordinate officer was left in charge of them, and Hernani and the Count went forward, treading in the footprints of the scout as nearly as they could, bent on reconnoitering the Russian position, and, if feasible, on making a prompt and telling attack upon this nest of enemies, at once so near to them, so dangerous to their very existence and to the cause they so ardently supported. Less than a mile of this stealthy work absorbed more than an hour of time, but with eyes well accustomed to the darkness, at the end of that short period, which had seemed like an eon, a fire was discovered, and soon afterwards, what appeared to be the figure of a soldier, erect and motionless upon the watch.

So they were not going to have it all their own way, and the Russian chief had been too wide awake to neglect the common precaution of posting sentries. Retiring and edging to the right, through an open glade, they at length got a better view of the hasty bivouac, carefully noting the strength of the place; then, withdrawing to a distance, they consulted as to the move to be made. Darkness favored an attack; the time would be ripe enough towards midnight, but the only sentry they had come upon was in the wood through which they must advance. With a quick grip of the situation Hernani decided.

"Leave him to me," he said; "he shall be disposed of or his mouth shall be stopped, whichever suits best. You go back and bring up the men so as to be here by twelve o'clock. That will give me time enough, and by then our friends yonder will have grown sleepy. You will find me waiting for you upon this spot."

"Ah! But if you fail to kill or capture the fellow," objected Dorozynski very naturally, "the alarm will be given and we shall have the whole force upon us. Besides, look at the risk you run. As a younger and an unmarried man I am better suited for such work. Your life ought not to be hazarded."

Hernani was speechless for some moments, as though the objections raised were hard to digest. Then, without even noticing the remarks about himself, he said coolly—

"Leave all that with me, my friend. The first thing for us to do is to have confidence in each other. As for danger"—and he gave a little laugh—"a man can die but once. Come—go along—be back here at midnight. You will find me waiting for you. Meantime I shall have turned Indian, to suit the occasion, and experiences in my early life have taught me how to do it. Go along, you skeptic, you can't fancy a banker, a business man, knowing aught of warfare, much less how to muzzle a Russian sentry, eh?"

"He is probably a picked man," grumbled Dorozynski.

"So much the better," retorted Hernani firmly; "be off!" And in that firmness there was a resolute ring which told the Count to go; so he went, though with many misgivings. Left to himself, Hernani's first action was cool, if extraordinary: in a sheltered spot where he deemed it safe to do so, he lighted a cigar, and there, crouched upon the ground, watching the red glow come and go as he inhaled the fragrant smoke, he became conscious of thinking with great clearness and vigor. The track of his life stretched in a long thin line behind him. He could see every inch of the way back. He had schemed, toiled and made love, and to what end? There was his deserted business and his home to which he could never return, unless all went well. There was his wife who had taught him to love her, and then deceived him as he thought. Nowhere could he discern anything worth living for. It had come to that—it was a mistake, and he knew it at that moment, having topped the hill and being half-way down the slope that led to the foot. Assuredly he was the man for some mad act of

daring—he knew that too—as a vision of the foes of his
race, the oppressors of his forefathers, arose before him.
Perhaps it was his turn—his, the Jew, since these enemies, these heavy task-masters, were so near, and it
might be, delivered into his hands.

Then, as though to control and balance the harsh and
bitter thoughts, kindlier and better ones crowded upon
each other. The Most High had been good to him all
his life through. Though myriads of beings covered the
earth, had it not pleased Him to create him one of the
chosen race, which, though scattered and trodden down
for a while, would in the end unite, and triumph, as one
people under one God? Health and riches and honor
had been given him over long years, and though the
love he had treasured had changed and was fast growing
gray and colorless, there was a reason for life and living,
which the one word Duty described. He had a duty to
Sara, to the country of his adoption; also and before all,
if he could but remember it always—to the God who
gave him breath. Then why despair or yield to depression? Was it not fair and manly to measure the rough
against the smooth, and was it not pleasant to feel, and
hear, and breathe; to see the flashing stars, the moon,
and the glorious sun, and to know that the Maker of
them was his Maker, the Supporter and Controller of
them, his Helper too and friend? Of course, in common
with other human beings, it was not given to him to
understand much of these mysteries, but while the soft
winds rustled in the tree-tops, and the dappled clouds
chased each other in the wondrous sky where the warb-
ling voiced birds found echo, could it ever be too hard
to live? Even in those sad and serious moments—Sara
being at the root of such gloom—Hernani thought not.
Then he bestirred himself, and having shivered a little
and buttoned his coat about his throat, he noticed that
the moon peered through the trees, and that a broken
scud sailed swiftly over it.

For a few moments he remained thinking—thinking as though painfully disturbed; then producing a pocket-book and pencil, aided by the light from his cigar, he made this simple inscription in the Hebrew tongue: "I have loved you always, Sara—always," and he added a date. "Should she ever see it she will understand," he muttered, replacing it in his pocket; and then, as though conscious that he had rested and thought enough, he set his face towards where the Russian infantrymen lay snoring round their flickering fires, and where—in a little log hut or hovel, seen as the flames had crackled and leaped—he had no doubt the officers would be found, enveloped in tobacco smoke, playing cards, and drinking wine or vodka.

Bearing to the right as before, after a slow and tortuous movement, in which he dreaded the snapping of a twig or a false step, he again lay at full length, looking down the glade, which at the point of the camping ground widened perceptibly. At first there was no sign of life, only dark masses, recumbent forms, piled arms or food and forage upon which uncertain shadows were cast; then a soldier arose, and with his heavy boot kicked the burning logs together, heaped on fresh ones, and took a bit of blazing wood between his fingers to re-kindle his pipe. There was only this straight glade passing through the encampment, the hut or hovel, which might have belonged to a wood-cutter, being to the left, and as far away as the shadows would permit of seeing. In the intense stillness Hernani could hear the sounds of voices and laughter proceeding from it, and light gleamed through the chinks of the logs and door.

Smiling grimly to himself as an idea struck him, he began to drag himself along the ground, keeping within the shadow of the trees, and never pausing except to be sure that he was unobserved, until he judged himself to be between the sentry and the camp. Then he turned and began an advance upon where he felt sure the man

was posted. After a while, and to his delight, he found
that he had not deceived himself. There, ahead, stood
a motionless figure. Availing himself of a line of tree-
trunks he stood up, shook a powdering of crisp snow
and dead leaves from his heavy coat, and, with his hand
upon a revolver hidden in his pocket, waited for a moment of dense gloom. In such obscurity, favored by
the length and cut of his great-coat and flat peaked cap,
he could, he thought, play the rôle of officer well enough.
With caution he approached the man. Within five yards
he did not stir. Was it a man? The outline was odd
and irregular. He stepped up, and to his amazement
discovered the stump of a tree, thicker than a pine and
covered with ivy. How astounding—but what good
fortune—and how stupid he had been—the scout and
Dorozynski would never be able to trust their eyesight
again after such a mistake!

He had meant to ignore the danger of a challenge
coming from the sentry or the camp, to take the risk
and in Russian say authoritatively to the fellow, "Follow me, my man"; then when at a safe distance to turn
upon and cover him with the revolver, adding the threat
that if he spoke, he might consider himself dead.

Perhaps it was a mad scheme, perhaps it would have
failed, although executed with the complete confidence
he had felt.

One thing was certain—the Russian officers were bent
on enjoying themselves, and, as he had by chance pre-
dicted, were not going to put either themselves or their
men out to keep watch, when opposed to such canaille
as stupid civilian insurgents.

"The fools," said Hernani to himself—"they have yet
to learn that it is well to conquer a foe before despising
him! It only remains to show them what those they
scorn can do."

After stumbling about in the gloom, sinking deep in
snow, damp earth, moss, and leaves, and knocking his

shins many times, he again arrived at the spot fixed by him for the rendezvous.

Dorozynski was awaiting him, and after a few hurried sentences in which they exchanged ideas and agreed upon a plan of attack, they proceeded to spread through the wood; the men having been again warned that success depended upon silence. Dividing the force, Dorozynski was to advance upon one side, and Hernani, crossing the glade or ridge at a higher point, to close in on the other, when, without cover to protect them, the Russians would be exposed to a cross fire. The signal for action was to be a shot from Hernani's own rifle.

About to be pitted against regular troops said to outnumber them—under conditions highly trying to the nerves, sleepless and after a long march—the men, or in a few instances boys, as some writers have called them, stepped out with precision, caution, and pluck. They were patriots in arms against oppression, there to fight for their parents and their homes, about to wrestle for the glorious liberty their forefathers had enjoyed. They represented their nation; keen human interests warmed the breast of each one, and being educated for the most part, proud memories stirred and strengthened them. Such feelings, backed by the might and splendor of right, would atone for their youth, their lack of experience and discipline—all their defects—there should be no flinching—they would triumph.

Pale with such thoughts, but cool and confident, they groped their way midst the trunks of the pine trees, until at length, and almost simultaneously, both little bands looked upon the Russian camp.

The scene there had changed. There was a stir; some shouts issuing from dark hurrying forms told that they had been discovered. Then, at that critical moment—by good fortune or the will of God—came the solitary shot for which they were to wait—the signal which boomed through the silent night-enshrouded woods,

only to have its echo drowned by the sharp crackle of
the Minié rifles, as slowly advancing, loading rapidly
and aiming low, Dorozynski and Hernani led them to
the attack.

Even under these disadvantages, surprised, exposed to
a galling fire from foes whose position and numbers they
could judge of only by the flashes of the shots which
struck them down, the dogged but phlegmatic Russians
moved like machines. They tried to arm, tried to form
up, and did so, back to back, in two separate bodies.
Charging amongst the trees they attempted to dislodge
their enemies, the disturbers of their slumbers, who,
scarce yielding an inch, met them with clinched teeth
and the warm steel muzzles of their rifles which belched
forth a deadly hail. They were veteran troops, but they
found it hot, too hot, and stumbling down the slight
slopes into the camp again, disconcerted, it looked as
though they were beaten. But after all it was a mere
check, and again they rushed into the gloom.

At this stage Hernani thought that Dorozynski was
being driven back; his fire, it seemed, was slackening
—he himself was hard pressed. Obeying a sudden impulse, he shouted, "These men have fired upon your
women! Remember the massacres, remember the Conscription"—and almost point blank, he discharged his
revolver at the head of an officer, who sword in hand,
would have cut him down. A wild yell greeted the encouragement. Still they were pressed. Dorozynski was
at his wits' end. Oh! for regular troops and the steady
coolness born of discipline. In despair he cheered and
charged, in his loudest voice shouting a stave of the national hymn, the prayer for liberty. The effect was
magical. ·There was not a man there but pressed forward or stood firm with the strength and the courage
of ten, the strange, grand, soul-stirring music ringing
in his ears, and lightning-like thoughts, evoked by it,

flashing, quivering through him—for his women, his old mother, his sister, his wife or girl-lover.

Before that nervous vigor, that heroic front, the Russians wavered and again recoiled. They were not used to face and fight with men who strove for the ties that make life dear and ennoble it; it was too much for them at such an hour and under such conditions. With shouts which became cheers, footing in the camp was gained; a few dropping shots like the crackle of burning wood followed, and the fight was won, the last of the heavy gray-coated figures had disappeared into the gloom.

Unobserved and in pathetic silence, Hernani and Dorozynski wrung each other's hands. The struggle had been a sharp one, and throughout it, their all had hung in the balance. Without speaking, they understood each other, and Hernani's wish was accomplished, confidence between them was established.

Having collected an armful of rifles, a little ammunition and some provisions—all that was to be found—with their dead and wounded—four men had been killed and more than twice that number injured—a swift retreat homewards was commenced, another weary march begun, footsore, hungry, and with alarms, but in repayment for the anxiety and exposure, at length there came the arrival unharmed at the camp.

Thanks to the rapidity with which news travels—whether of good or evil—rumors had reached Sara even in advance of a message which Hernani had despatched as soon as he could. Aware that amongst the peasants through whom such reports filtered, there were those who took a delight in lying, she knew not what to believe, and until she was again gladdened with a sight of Hernani—the one man in the world who belonged to her, and the one of all others most blind to her good qualities—her anxiety was well-nigh unendurable.

In spite of the victory won, the price paid for it occasioned a gloom. Of this Hernani was unconscious. His mind was too full. In the presence of fresh news from the Central National Committee, and of several reports which he knew to be trustworthy, he shut himself up with Dorozynski. The information received from the Committee clashed with that supplied by his own agents, whom his connections as an influential business man made widespread, and whom his wealth enabled him to pay well.

"What does this mean?" he asked, laying the papers before the Count. "Read for yourself. This one from the Committee is a catalogue of success from beginning to end. The tenor of the others is dubious, and gives details which are distressing. Because we have been brutally treated, should we in return be guilty of downright cruelty? Read the thing."

Without a word, the Count sat down and did as he was bid.

The scene was a striking one. These two careworn men, closeted in this farmhouse room, which bore signs of having been used for stores, and odds and ends for which no use could be found at the moment. A couple of chairs and a table without polish or cloth, were grouped in the center of a bare plank floor. Bunches of herbs and paper bags containing seeds, lay amidst dust upon shelves or hung pendent from hooks driven into the walls, while a hammer and some strips of cloth for nailing up fruit trees, lay near a stove, within which roared a fire of split pine logs. It was a poor place in which to decide questions of life and death, and added to the general discomfort, the cold that morning was intense, the frost thick upon the window, which was dirty and looked upon the cheerless ice-coated fish-pond.

Hernani paced the room with heavy step and long stride, keeping the table between himself and the seat occupied by the Count, who read to the end and then laid down the papers.

"Well, what do you think of it?" demanded Hernani, seeing that the Count had finished. "Give me your opinion."

"I think that the official suggestion to join Langiewicz* and co-operate with him, is a good one, if we could carry it out."

"If we could carry it out?" repeated Hernani.

"Yes; it would be difficult, I admit."

"We should have to risk being intercepted and forced to fight, perhaps in the open, and we both know how near we have already been to defeat, though everything was in our favor at the time."

"Yes," assented the Count.

"And then, what about supplies, which are already running short? We should have difficulty in collecting sufficient to keep us going on the march—but these are all questions which, though of the first importance, we are not called upon to decide in haste. What has upset me is this. In the dispatch from the Committee, the peasants are alluded to 'as arming and supporting the cause generally.' Now our own experience latterly has taught us quite the reverse, and this information from private sources, upon which I can depend, contains no such reassuring statement. In addition, atrocities which chill one's blood, are boldly spoken of."

"But let us consider one subject at a time," suggested the Count; "the atrocities——"

"Ah! let us speak of them," interrupted Hernani excitedly. "Can good come of capturing a Cossack and beating him to death with the butt of a rifle? Can good come of burning Muscovite soldiers, because they have barricaded themselves and can be overcome in no other way—and what about murdering them while sleeping, setting fire to their barracks as though to hide the crime? Can good come of that, I ask you, and I say 'No' without waiting for your reply?"

* A leading General, and for a few days Dictator.

"But if these deeds have been done——" began the Count.

"Unhappily, no doubts upon the subject are admissible," interrupted Hernani.

"Very well, then; they have simply been retaliatory acts. The Muscovites have behaved as monsters. You may depend upon that, or——"

"Oh! I know, I know—proofs of that are not wanting. But such an argument will not suffice. As I have said, because we are ill-used, should we be cruel? Fair fighting is what I had hoped to see, and for a fair cause had come to support, but such accounts as these make me sick. We are not barbarians. Is it charitable, is it noble? I am disgusted. I had hoped to do good with the rifle, as I have tried to do with the ruble. For this I have toiled early and late, and this I know—that rather than have connected myself with a cause so conducted, I would have fled from the country as a criminal does, under cover of night. Oh! I tell you, my friend, I am incensed."

The Count bowed his head. What could he say? Hernani's sentiments were, in the main, his own. At length, however, his face brightened and he looked up.

"Well," he said, "there is this consolation. To whatever straits we are driven, we at least may make ourselves known for our fairness and mercy. We are not responsible for the actions of others, whom we cannot control, but of our own doings we must be prepared to give an account."

"Yes, that is true—we can control our own actions," muttered Hernani absently, as though thinking of something else; then resuming his naturally energetic utterance, he added, "But there is a more serious aspect to the affair, and it is this: such dealing will be prejudicial to us in the eyes both of peasants and proprietors. As it is, they are hanging fire, ready to rush to the winning side, or are watching, without a policy, too timid to act.

Ah! what fine patriots. Shall I tell you something? If these proprietors, these land-owners, were decided and united, success would follow without doubt. Poland would be free. There could be no other result. As matters stand—I fear—I have my fears."

"Langiewicz* is doing wonders," said the Count, trying to appear hopeful, even confident. "It says here"— and he glanced at one of the letters—" 'that already four out of eight chief towns are in his hands.' That looks well. And some of the peasants are also friendly, and the priests are with us to a man."

"Yes," assented Hernani.

"And the news from Paris is not disheartening. Czartoryski† speaks with confidence, and is not only capable, but may be counted upon to do his best. The fact that a few Frenchmen are already scattered over the country, may also have its good meaning."

"True," murmured Hernani, and then he walked to the window, staring through its frosted panes at the pond, for full five minutes without speaking. Young Sicinski, the son of the owner of the farm, of whom Riva had spoken as "smoking, smoking always," had flung a stick for his dog to retrieve, and as the beast, having made a rush, slipped helplessly upon the glassy surface, barking furiously the while, the young fellow laughed until his face reddened. Some fowls scratched and clucked upon a manure heap—four hens and a jaunty little bantam cock—and the contented but disagreeable grunting of pigs could be distinctly heard occurring with monotonous frequency.

At the distance of two fair-sized fields, through the straggling branches of some leafless walnut trees, a number of the men could be seen jogging along on their

---

* General Langiewicz was in the government of Radom, and had done this.

† Prince Ladislaus Czartoryski, then in Paris, representing Polish interests.

return from a foraging expedition. On seeing these
young fellows earnestly fulfilling their duties, an intensely serious expression stole over Hernani's face. The
dog sliding over the ice had made him smile, though unconsciously, and the vigor with which the fowls sought
for food had not escaped his quick eye, but the glimpse
he had caught of the men who believed in him and had
followed his fortunes, made him reflect. In the event
of a disaster what could be done for them—what could
atone for their loss to the parents whom he had persuaded them to leave? Perhaps he had been wrong—
Perhaps—— With an irritable shrug of the shoulders
and a twirl of the fingers which drew his moustache to
a point, he turned on his heel.

"It would be well for us if we could join Langiewicz,"
he recommenced brusquely; "in small detached bodies
scattered over the country, we cannot have the weight
and strength that combination would give us. We
shall be annihilated in detail—that will be the end of it.
Divided we are weak, united we should be strong."

"But to join the General, even with regular troops,
in the teeth of the opposition certain to be encountered,
would be a dangerous and difficult operation."

"Therefore one not to be attempted with the force at
our disposal."

"I think not. We are not fit to run the gauntlet."

"Well," said Hernani, "you must be the judge upon
such a point. Your opinion is a practical one. But we
must consider."

"Yes, we must give it thought. A hasty decision
might be a fatal one," replied the Count, lighting a cigarette—which, he contended, soothed him always—and
emitting some little rings of smoke.

After a pause, during which both seemed lost in reflection, the conversation drifted into other channels,
and they talked of the scarcity of supplies, of the ever-
increasing difficulties encountered in obtaining them, of

the amount of ammunition their one successful engagement had cost them, of the quantity still left; and Dorozinski was deep in such matters, when Count Adam Goroski burst in upon them, and in spite of the grave outlook, sent them into fits of laughter, by mimicking the manner and expressions of one of the young fellows who had played his part in administering to the Muscovites the defeat they had sustained, and who had been foolish enough to brag of it in no mild terms.

After Dorozynski and Goroski had left him, Hernani was disturbed by Riva entering with a message from Sara which necessitated seeing her, and so the day wore on. Having attended to innumerable details, and given instructions of a varied nature, in the dusk of the afternoon he found himself alone for a few minutes, and during that time the whole of his conversation with the Count again recurred to him. He felt keenly what he had said on the subject of the atrocities, yet had not said a tithe of what he had thought. It cut him to the quick to think that any member or portion of the party with whom he was allied, and for whom he had risked all a man can risk, should be guilty of acts at once ignoble and blood-thirsty; and it weighed nothing with him, as he had said, that the Muscovite oppressors should in the first instance have been guilty of even more desperately brutal outrages.

His thoughts straying a little, other ideas floated before him—oft recurring recollections of the difficulties he had met with always, of the indignities to which he and his race had been subjected; of the well-nigh superhuman efforts he had put forward before the business he had conducted had become great.

And then of how hard it was for him to think that the police were in possession of his premises, that his splendid home was shut up or overrun by strangers, that he himself was an outlaw in the eyes of that Government whose rule, had it been an equitable one, he would

so gladly have upheld. Harder still was it for him to
look upon his wife, to see her placed in the thick of dis-
comforts and hardships, and hourly in danger of life
and limb, after the luxury lavished upon her, the love
which he had given her, and of which in his heart, he
at times felt that death alone could deprive her. What
was to become of her if the peasants would not rise in
defense of the soil to which they were heirs, if the land-
owners—the men of substance—continued to present a
timid and vacillating front, and to blow neither hot nor
cold? Dimly he felt that it might soon be beyond his
strength or resources to protect and save her from the
unscrupulous and cruel hands of those enemies whom,
in his dark moments, he thought of as closing in on
him upon all sides. Then too came visions of his home
life as it had once been, of the days which had been
sweetened by labor and love—perfect love, but for his
one great grievance, his one regret—that no children
had come of it. And it never occurred to him that he
had been at all unreasonable in forming and adhering
to the decision at which he had arrived in the cafés at
Warsaw, when he had drunk so much vodka, after having tracked Sara to the palace and watched her leave it.
He had always told himself that her manner towards
him—considered apart from her actions—had of itself
proved her guilt. He even took some credit to himself
for his forbearance, in having so unswervingly befriended her in spite of her behavior, as he had resolved to do.
So, after all, he was very weak, very stupid, very human,
in spite of his great abilities and the gift akin to genius,
of knowing what he could do best, and doing it with his
whole might. Such was the substance of his reflections
in the chill winter of that afternoon, during the last lull
he was to know for awhile.

As usual, when she could be near, Sara was not far
from him, but the steel-blue glitter of the stars, far away
in the frost-bound sky, found her bending over the

wounded sufferers who had come in; forgetting her own
anxieties—forgetting even Hernani—as she strove with
gentle touch and kindly word to lessen the pain they
endured, the injured ones being grateful beyond description; and though she tried to check their utterances,
telling her so, while overhead the stars still gleamed
coldly down, flashing as proudly as the eyes of a cynical
worldly woman to whom nothing seems romantic or pathetic.

They had witnessed so many struggles, those distant
twinkling worlds of light; they had seen so many dark
forms totter forth upon the earth, supporting burdens
too heavy for them, all the while exhibiting the courage
and indomitable will of the tiny insects upon which they
also looked—the ants—yet only ant-like to disappear beneath the hard ground, when with dull thud it came to be
heaped upon them. It was pitiful. So haughty, ma-
jestic and marvelously distant was their scintillating silence, that it might have been taken to say, as it played
upon the roof of that lonely farmhouse and peered into
the pallid faces of the afflicted ones, "Why are ye not
now content to depart?—it will save you much trouble."
But of such icy ideas Sara knew naught. She had found
objects worthy of her attention, beings with hearts of flesh
and blood like her own, upon whom she could pour all
the pent-up womanliness within her. The instincts of a
mother were so strong in her, and her imagination was
such a restless and vivid one, that while handing a cooling drink, a dose of medicine, or smoothing a tumbled
pillow, the tearful faces of the anxious and lonely parents left in Warsaw arose before her, and her heart
warmed and expanded, and she told herself silently that
she would try her best to fill the places of the absent ones,
and that the sick men should be to her as her children.
Then too a sense of duty influenced her. Was not Hernani, or perhaps Count Dorozynski, responsible for having persuaded these young fellows to bear arms in the

17

cause which they supported? Had they remained quietly in Warsaw, possibly they might have escaped harm.
So it was in vain that Riva pleaded and whined.

"What will become of your beauty, my lamb? Take
sleep or it will vanish. One is young but once. It is a
sin to destroy youth. See, now—you will get gray, your
eyes heavy, and wrinkles will come to remain. Do as I
tell you. I will sit up, and in the morning you will be
fresh and a joy to all eyes. For me it does not matter;
work was the portion allotted to me."

"And what was my portion, pray?" Sara inquired
comically.

"To be careful of yourself, and by so doing to care for
those who love you," replied Riva.

"But if I cared for myself at the expense of others, I
should be hated. No; you must let me have my way.
You are more tired than I am."

"Let me sit up," interposed Deotima, who had overheard Riva's expostulations; "it would be a change for
me. I am as strong as a horse—stronger than either of
you."

Thus beset, Riva gently obliged Sara to give up some
broth she was carrying, and muttering half audibly,
"Victuals prepared by many cooks will be neither hot nor
cold," she disappeared into the sick-room. But in spite
of such appeals and the display of so much decision on
Riva's part, the end was the same—Sara invariably did
as she wished.

Owing to the strain upon her nerves, occasioned by
the uncertainty and danger of the position she found herself in, added to the anxiety about Hernani, all of which
sensations became aggravated by loss of sleep, she began
again to live at fever-heat. It was as though she existed
in momentary dread of the police once more, though,
now that that fear had passed, it seemed trifling when
compared with the morbid terror which stole into her
heart and left her face colorless, whenever the danger to

which Hernani was exposed occurred to her. A sudden
sound made her start and shudder. Her beautiful eyes
shone and dilated with feelings which crossed her mind
with the rapidity of those variable cat's-paws which skim
the otherwise placid bosom of the sea. She would talk
with careless vivacity, appearing tireless in her activity,
but when alone, overcharged and overwrought, she
would pay the penalty in floods of tears. Nothing escaped her. She was like an instrument screwed to its
highest pitch—to that of breaking. She had even arrived at the point of imagining that the responsibility of
the whole situation rested upon her shoulders. And
just in the midst of this trying period, when most in need
of support, she was disappointed and saddened by the
fullest consciousness of isolation and loneliness she had
ever experienced. Riva even galled her by the manner
in which she dropped her wise sayings, borrowed and
stored up to fit any occasion. For instance, the faithful
and shrewd old servant grasped the situation so cleverly,
that, while trotting on her legs all day, and racking her
brain to save Sara either labor or anxiety, she must needs
say to her—

"Take things quietly, my lamb, or you will wear yourself out. What says the Book? 'The sun will set without thy assistance.' "

Sara was irritated. The remark was meant well, she
knew, had she stopped to think, but to her ears just then
it seemed ill-judged.

"Don't prate, Riva—I hate it!" she exclaimed angrily;
with the result that, feeling it best not to say more, Riva
stole out of the way.

Deotima too had proved a disappointment. In the
time of trouble she was not sympathetic, and Sara had
been disgusted at the callousness displayed by her when
told of the deaths of those who had fallen in the fight.
The tender and gentle qualities in the young girl appeared to be dried up, and in place of them had come a

hard and stony desire for revenge. The injured ones were looked to by her with care and attention, but when strong enough to bear it, she took occasion to fire their blood with the repetition of wrongs inflicted and insults endured. To Sara this seemed to be a needless stirring up of strife. She herself hoped to be courageous when necessity demanded, but she pitied the Muscovite rank-and-file, thinking of them as poor uneducated soldiers, who were only obeying orders when they received or inflicted wounds or death. If they were brutal, it seemed to her that it must be because they knew no better. All her indignation and hatred she reserved for the chiefs, who instigated or directed movements which necessitated what she dimly began to understand as the horrors of war.

Sometimes she would try to imbue Deotima with her own milder views, to which she would once have listened; but Deotima as she had been in Warsaw, and Deotima face to face with Russian foes, were two different persons.

"Ah!" the young girl would exclaim, "you have not suffered as I have."

"But you do not know!" urged Sara, thinking of her early life and of her dead parents.

"Know what?" inquired Deotima with startling energy. "To what extent I and mine have been injured."

"How should I? You do not tell me, but I am sure you can't have gone through what I have. Your wrists have never been bruised by the vile hands of filthy Cossacks, you have never been dragged into your own garden, and there made to stand, amidst jeers and obscenity, while being stripped of your clothing. Such insults I have not forgotten or forgiven, and never shall. No—never as long as I live. And what would have happened but for Andrew, I tremble to think. Besides, you seem to forget that, not content with hunting us from our

home, by their barbarous conduct they killed my father."

At that point she broke down, the mention of the dead
Count invariably reducing her to tears. Of course Sara
ended by sympathizing with her, as any woman would.

Being thus, as described, keenly on the alert, it at
length came to Sara's ears that a great move had been
decided upon; in short, they were to make an heroic effort to join General Langiewicz, who at the moment was
known to be successful in all directions. This step being
deemed wise, though bristling with danger and difficulty,
preparations for taking it were at once begun.

In the noontide of that very day, and within a few
hours of the time at which the decision had been arrived
at, a mounted patrol returned to camp at a gallop,
breathless and having been fired upon. Hernani, prepared for anything, received the news as composedly as
though it were a mere business communication.

The Russians were not five miles distant, and were
advancing swiftly upon the position. The whole force
was composed of infantry, and if the peasants were to be
believed, they were the men upon whom the night attack had been made. The idea of co-operating with
General Langiewicz was instantly abandoned. Fresh
orders were issued, a plan of resistance long agreed upon
adopted, and in a few minutes after the instructions were
given, every man was armed and at his post.

"Go and ease the minds of the women," said Hernani
to Dorozynski; "go to my wife. You will do better than
I should. She can read my face too well; besides, being
a soldier, she will attach more importance to what you
say."

Though his faith in Sara was so shaken, Hernani's
first thought was of her.

"Go to her," he repeated, and Dorozynski, though
conscious that his mission was a difficult one, went.

In attendance upon the sick men, calm and self-possessed, Sara bore some resemblance to a patient and beautiful sister of mercy, as in her black dress she ministered to their wants.

"You see, I learned how to make myself useful when I was very young and very poor," she said gayly, adding playfully, "Hush! you must be quiet, or I shall turn you out instantly."

The Count smiled. What could he say to this nervous creature, who was so kind and so adorable in her simple dress of mourning, symbolical as it was of the sorrow of a nation for its enforced captivity? Seeing his embarrassment, she came to his assistance.

"You want to tell me something," she said; "don't be afraid. I am not easily alarmed."

"Well," he blundered like the soldier he was, not the diplomat he wished to be, "some stupid Russians are in the neighborhood. We may have to drive them off, so don't be surprised if you hear the sound of firing."

"Who sent you?" she inquired abruptly.

"Your husband," he answered.

"Why did he not come himself?" it was on her tongue to say.

"Tell him I don't understand what fear is," she replied, her face crimsoning.

"May I say that?" he asked, admiration and satisfaction marking his utterance.

"Of course," she said, with a laugh; "and add that he is to take good care of himself."

"If all our hearts are as stout as yours, we shall do," murmured the Count below his breath; then he went off, after some casual remarks, in which advice to Deotima figured.

So Hernani had thought of her, Sara reflected. True he might have come himself—yet she was pleased.

One by one the pickets were driven in, though without the firing of a shot. as powder was so precious, and soon afterwards the head of the Russian column came in sight.

The next move made by the enemy was to send a flag of truce, which Major Suroff—for he it was, in command —mindful of the instructions received by him from General Hourko, ordered as a cautious and possibly effective method of obtaining his ends—namely, the possession of the women, the arrest of the chiefs, and the dispersal of the force.

If he entertained such hopes seriously, however, they were quickly destroyed. In answer to the proposition of an unconditional surrender, coupled with the vague promise of fair treatment, Hernani and Dorozynski tendered a brief but resolute refusal. It was of course expected that an attack would soon follow this absolute rejection of all overtures, but, strangely enough, during the remainder of that day no such attempt was made, though through the night the watch-fires were seen burning brightly, while at intervals shots were fired, and there were constant alarms. The Count and Hernani were of one mind in a decision they formed to act entirely on the defensive, and to further this object, Sara and Deotima, with the wounded, were made as comfortable as was possible in the out-buildings, the stout walls of which were better adapted to stand a siege than those of the farm itself. The old house was strongly garrisoned however, bags stuffed with earth being stacked up to the height of a man at all weak points, such as the windows, the rifle barrels being thrust between and through them, the glass having been carefully removed.

All that night no eyes were closed, and, shivering and sleepless, the questions were often put—"Do they mean to starve us out? What can they be waiting for? Is it the daylight, or are they fatigued with their march?" To such remarks many answers and suggestions were made, which again were as often upset by new ideas and opinions. The morning brought no relief, only the informa-

tion that the attacking force had encamped snugly
amongst the pines, and with boughs torn from the trees
had erected shelters, which for hardy soldiers, warmly
clad and well fed, might serve for days.   In addition, the
weather seemed to favor them, the atmosphere having
turned warmer by several degrees.

In consultation with the two Goroskis and Count Dorozynski, Hernani expressed the opinion that Major
Suroff meant to tire and weaken them, before hazarding
an attack.

"Otherwise, why this delay?" he demanded.

"Perhaps reinforcements are expected," suggested
Count Adam.

"They probably think mere rifles insufficient against
stone walls, manned by men who are desperate," observed his brother.

Hernani made no answer, since it was evident that
nothing was to be gained by talking, but, as if to prove
the soundness of such haphazard conjectures, it was
found impossible to convey supplies of any kind into
camp.   Small detachments of Russian infantry disputed
the passage of all the roads, and in face of the fact that
powder was so scarce, temporary orders were issued to
prevent skirmishing, unless it was found necessary to
engage in it.

At the end of forty-eight hours the position had not
changed, but near about that time a sudden alarm furnished at least one reason for Major Suroff's silence.   A
few shouts were heard, a few flying shots indulged in,
as like a flash of lightning, a little cloud of mounted
Cossacks dashed right through the camp, leaping their
horses over all obstacles, and escaping clear, but for the
emptying of two saddles.   An hour later safe dragoons
were encountered on one of the roads, and then another
night dragged itself out into the gray of the new day,
in the early light of which Suroff, thus strengthened,
commenced the attack.

The dark outline of the fir-trees could just be seen through the mist and fine drizzling rain, the long straggling branches, heavy with moisture, hanging sadly, like sepulchral ostrich plumés, pendent and motionless, there being no wind. The snow had melted or been trodden into dirty gray patches, and as the eye traveled along the level ground which separated the farm with its out-buildings from the belt of wood, and finally rested upon the stems of the trees, from between their straight trunks flashes of flame spurted, and little white clouds of smoke curled ominously.

As the sounds of the firing became continuous, Riva's black eyes gleamed, and as she stood in the great barn which now sheltered them, she unconsciously drew nearer to Sara's side. On her own account she experienced no sense of fear, having in her time witnessed too many fierce fights of the Ghetto to be readily intimidated—it was for Sara that she was distressed—so she felt for a keen-bladed knife she had hidden in her bosom, and with consummate coolness began to reckon up the odds—for and against—in the situation which she rightly judged to be one of life and death, freedom or captivity for all concerned. Only once, as the volleys rattled more fiercely, and a storm of lead struck both brick and plaster with dull ominous thud, did she hold up her worn fingers and call upon God to witness the dire distress of her mind.

"May the Lord of Hosts fight for us!" she murmured in a broken voice, to which Sara, who was assisting in bandaging the arm of a fresh victim to the Russian rifle fire, answered below her breath—

"Hush! Riva. Take heart—He will."

It seemed that that was all Riva wanted—just to hear her mistress speak—for she said no more, though eyes and ears worked the keener for her silence.

She saw Hernani and the Count, and for that matter, the two Goroskis, redoubling their efforts, behaving like men, unflagging in their determination to win or die, and she could not help rubbing her bony hands together with a sort of fiendish joy, as taking the rifle of a young Pole who rolled backward in the death agony, Hernani himself pushed the barrel through the loophole whence the fatal shot had come, and waiting his chance, disposed of at least one more foe.

If this state of things, this tumult and danger found favor with anyone, apparently it was with Deotima. Her manner became animated, her actions brisk, her eyes sparkled and the color in her cheeks deepened; the impression she would have conveyed to a disinterested onlooker would have been that she had triumphed in some great purpose of her life, and could but enjoy with keen relish the full flavor of her good fortune. And, after all, was it not in a measure natural? With the hereditary enemies of her house and of her race, the rude ruffians who had shocked her girlish modesty and threatened her maidenly virtue, within arms' reach, striking distance, was it strange if her blood was up, the expression of her face determined, and her heart as hard as that of a man who after years of patient waiting at length confronts the foe of his life? Of course, with Deotima it was possible to hate; to some natures it is not so. However, the young girl of her own accord suddenly developed into an experienced vivandière, fulfilling the duties which become such a rôle like an old hand. She had hunted up a little wooden cask and had filled it with fine old vodka, and, while pressing upon the men she knew best a tempting drink, she stepped from her pinnacle as a young girl of birth and position, and became at once a friend, an equal.

To induce them to fight with every nerve in their bodies, she struck those chords which she knew lay deepest in their natures; she even went so far as to whisper, "If I am to esteem you, you must fight as your forefathers did in times past." With such words confidentially spoken, with all the charm of manner which was natural to her, she restored confidence and rekindled enthusiasm.

At one end of the great clumsy old barn, with its ponderous doors and massive cross-beams and rafters, there was a sort of loft, approached by a short wooden ladder, and up this Deotima climbed unhesitatingly in pursuit of her purpose. Here the noise of each discharge seemed more deafening, the smoke as it ascended thicker, the gloom more intense. Still, a clearer view of the enemy could be obtained, and a few of the better shots had appropriated these higher loopholes, from which posts, with praiseworthy steadiness, they were giving a good account of themselves.

Under cover of a hot fire, Count Andrew had headed two sorties, with the object of driving the enemy from their position, but in both instances had been repulsed with loss.

Choosing what she believed to be a favorable opportunity, Deotima singled out a young fellow who lay flat upon his stomach behind some hay, and bending over him said—

"Pick off the officers if you can, Ladislaus." Then receiving no answer, she stood upright, and glanced stealthily into the gloom on all sides of her, the nauseous fumes of the powder making her cough; finally her eyes became riveted on a small strongly-made trunk of wood, which, had she not known where to look for it, she would never have discovered, thrust aside as it was in a corner near the eaves. Deotima unlocked it and lifted the lid, then, as though doubtful or nervous, she closed it, and, stepping back, touched the young man on the shoulder, addressing him by his name. Still receiving no reply, she shook him gently, and then a benumbing sense of horror took possession of her. Sinking on her knees at his side, she supported herself upon her hands, the sensation that she touched some warm liquid substance making her start·back and examine them. They were cov-

ered with blood.   In another instant she knew the truth.
A bullet had passed through his forehead, and he was
dead.

"Blessed Mother, this is too horrible!" she gasped.
"Ladislaus dead!"—and white to the lips, for some moments she felt as though about to faint.   Recovering herself by the strongest effort of which she was capable,
with solemn reverence and a heart-breaking expression
of despair, she made the sign of the Cross, and with a
sigh that was almost a gasp, exclaimed in a broken
voice—

"Poor dear Ladislaus!"

It was Count Ladislaus Goroski.

Returning with deliberate steps to the little trunk,
where in the feeble light amidst the dense blue smoke no
eye could see her, she stood erect, and with fingers tremulous from excitement, not nervousness, began to unbut-
ton her bodice.   This done, she next freed herself of her
skirts, substituting in place of them a pair of soldier's
overalls, which she tucked into high leather boots.   Then
she put on a braided tunic, which fitted as though made
for her, which indeed was the case.   Beneath a large
flat-topped cap she hid her hair, drawing the peak well
over her eyes, and adding, as a finishing touch to her disguise, a long military great-coat which had a strap at the
back, she stepped up to the body.   Exerting all her
strength, yet with infinite tenderness, she dragged it away
from the loophole, and taking up the dead man's rifle,
lay down on the floor that was yet warm.

"Poor Ladislaus!" she again sobbed.   "So they've killed
you—you whom I loved best—and it was to be near me
that you came here.   Very well, poor darling, you shall
be revenged—we will both be revenged."   And fairly
choking with emotion, she prepared to fire.

Below, in the body of the great barn, amidst sound and
unsound implements, quantities of hay and roots used in
feeding the cattle, on the shaft of an upturned cart, sat

Hernani. From time to time he would exchange a few words with Dorozynski, or satisfy himself as to the movements of the enemy through a slit in the wall. Hope was still strong within him. It was not his fate ever to be beaten. Notwithstanding the reinforcements of dragoons and Cossacks, Suroff had made no headway, and must have lost many men. If only there had been plenty of food and powder, protected by such stout old walls, his chance against the whole Russian force would have been worth a good round sum. As it was, his marvelous fortune would not forsake him. Something favorable would happen. His turn would come. They would be able to beat a retreat, having crippled their foes. The Central National Committee were aware of his critical position—perhaps they had already despatched assistance—or a turn of cold would be a fine ally. There were a thousand and one chances. Suroff would see. He would receive another lesson, and this time a decisive one. Revolving all these possibilities with astounding cheerfulness, amidst the strong smell of the place, which, mingled with that of burnt powder and human beings, was almost sickening. he encouraged those about him, the strange influence of his personality remaining as yet unimpaired, and causing the poor fellows surrounding him still to think, "It will be all right—he knows—we shall see."

Amidst the uproar of the fight, the rattle of the firing, an occasional shout of triumph or scream of pain, the frightened lowing of the two or three oxen yet unslaughtered, and the shrill neigh of dragoon and Cossack horses, he remained calm and self-possessed as though in his great counting-house at Warsaw. Judging by his manner, the band of men around him—sweating, dirty, and worn out—might have been his sleek, well-fed staff of clerks; the huge beams and dust-covered rafters above him, his own roof-tree; the corner of the place in which Sara was huddled with the wounded, a handsomely furnished apartment in the splendid home he had left. The

might have been did not affect him; he was himself even
with what was.

It was the master mind still at work, the man of huge
possibilities, hemmed in by difficulties. All at once, and
as though in grim derision of such amazing equanimity, a
chorus of exultant shouts pealed through the damp,
smoke-laden air, after which came a pause of some minutes, broken at the end of that time by the sullen roar of
a heavy weapon, a Krupp cannon. At such close range
the round shot crunched through the wall, knocked a
shower of splinters from the opposite one, and rolled and
spun almost to Hernani's feet.

Such a shock moved even his stout heart. Of what
use brick walls with a well-served Krupp playing upon
them? He turned the shot over with his foot, and for
the first time despair seized upon him.

So there was to be no relief of any kind, either from the
distant French, upon whom he had cast such patient,
hopeful glances, the lukewarm nobles, of whom he had
expected such great things, or the Central National Committee, who were, he had believed, to be counted upon.
However, the strife might go with others; all—all—had
failed him. His grand schemes were at an end. He
would never deepen the Vistula, so as to accommodate
a large carrying trade, or start his great banking scheme
which was to have crowned him with the name of universal benefactor. The game was up. He was caught in a
trap from which there was no escape. Very well; he
was not of the sort to languish in some foul prison or rot
by inches in a mine—they should see how he could die.
As though reflection even were denied him, at that instant Dorozynski rushed up to him, and with breathless
eagerness, though in a voice inaudible to anyone else,
said—

"You see how it is. Again they have been strengthened, and if we can't take that gun, in my opinion we are
done for."

Hernani nodded; words failed him.

"Shall we try?"

"Yes," he said huskily; "you get the men together. This is the moment to show what we are made of."

Still sitting upon the shaft of the cart, his right foot planted upon the ground supporting his weight, he drew out first one, and then another revolver, to assure himself that they were ready for use; being satisfied, he was in the act of replacing them, when a terrible thought entered his mind. What about Sara? He had promised himself that she should never fall into Russian hands alive. He had told Dorozynski so. His hope of protecting her was as good as gone, the chance of returning to her side a worthless one. The moment for action had suddenly arrived. What was to be done? Could he take her life? Could he deliberately shoot her—his wife —in cold blood? Would it be right of him? Could any extremity justify such an act? There she was, not ten paces from him, her profile clear cut against the dirt-begrimed wall of the barn, and though as pale as death she was as beautiful as ever. The thought was too horrible. For a few seconds, which seemed like a lifetime, he paused in doubt, turning one of the weapons in his hand, his eyes gleaming, fierce lit like those of a madman, the muscles of his forehead contracted, a frightful expression of despair and irresolution disfiguring his fine face; another shot crashed through the roof, and shrieks came from the direction of the farmhouse. He could hear Dorozynski addressing the men, imploring them to be brave—to do their duty. That brought him to himself. White to the lips he put away the weapon; then, scarce knowing what he did or how he came to do it, he flung himself upon Sara, his arms upon her shoulders, choking with the terrible nature of his feelings.

"The Holy One," he exclaimed—"the Holy One—He will have you in His charge!"

And before she could reply, further than to try to hold

him, he had wrenched himself clear of her, and passed
out into the light drizzling rain, almost side by side with
Deotima, who had descended from the loft, and who, un-
noticed by anyone in the excitement of the moment, took
her place in the ranks with the men.   Again Dorozynski's voice rose high.

"My countrymen, my comrades, remember what we
have been.   What our forefathers did we can do again.
Let us strike for our beloved country and for our homes."

With the speed of despair, and the recklessness of a last
hope, the small but solid phalanx of heroes answered
him with cheers, and by bursting upon the Russian position with a wild hurrah that made even Suroff admire
and wonder.

"Take them prisoners—don't cut them down!" he was
heard to shout, as his Cossacks and dragoons rode
through and through them.   "Spare all you can!" he
yelled, well knowing it to be too late.   Yet, despite the
fire, the charge, they were at the gun, amongst his men,
Hernani and Dorozynski still living, still heading them.

Pressing forward—all that remained of them—as
though the spirit of ten were in each, they were hidden by
the smoke, the mist, and the brown stems of the pines,
Sara with strained eyes watching them, as dazed with
dread of what might happen she stood out in the open,
stray bullets whistling round her, and old Riva, wild with
fear for her, clinging to her skirts and dragging her back
under cover.

Borne upon the heavy winter air, the shouts, the uproar, the melée of horse and man and clanging weapons,
soon told its tale of widowhood and woe, soon lessened,
and slowly died upon the ear.

In minutes swifter to pass than to tell of, it was over,
and Dorozynski, in the thick of it, had gone upon his
knees beside a form he had thought to be a gallant troop-
er, fighting at his side throughout, and had recognized
to be a woman and a sister only as a fatal bullet had sped,

and the large confederatka* had fallen, setting free her golden hair. Blind to danger, ignorant of what fear meant, deaf to everything but that it was his sister, Deotima whom he loved, he knelt there, his heart benumbed, his tears falling as a woman's might have done upon the long slim hand, so soft and white, so powerless, and so heavy.

God! How he longed that she might speak—that word of his might wake once more some spark of life and light within the glazing eye that had so often looked with warmth and love into his own!

Could he survive such bitterness as Deotima gone? A shout was all his answer, a rush of horse and man upon him. To stagger to his feet, to try to ward the blow was all he did, and all he did was not enough to save his life. Pierced through and through, he rolled upon the ground, the cries of those he hated most on earth, ringing above him as his life blood ebbed.

They might have spared him, so young, so brave, and fighting for his native soil; yet such a death was his that all, since born to die, might covet.

Recovering as from a sort of swoon, the new sight that showed itself to Sara's gaze was that of Riva, struggling with a large, clumsy-looking Cossack, her keen knife buried in his arm, the great barn filling with men not of their side, soldiers, helmeted dragoons, with mud-bespattered boots and uniforms, and swords yet stained with blood; Cossacks rough and dirty; infantrymen, snub-nosed, fair-haired, and furious like the rest for plunder and a grip of the foe they had vanquished at last. Look as she would, there was no sign of Hernani, of Dorozynski, of one friendly face to lessen the horror of the feeling that, weak and unprotected, she was at the mercy of those who to her, at such a moment, seemed fiends in the garb of men.

* Confederate cap.

Springing to assist Riva, the Cossack caught her by the neck as he would have done a rat, and with a cuff on the side of the head, sent her reeling backwards against the boards, upon which the wounded were stretched.

The huge fellow's triumph over his feminine antagonists was, however, short-lived, for his hands were scarcely quit of Sara, before a shower of blows descended upon his broad back, delivered with a will and the flat of a sword, and, turning to defend himself, who should he face but Suroff, accompanied by several officers and evidently in no mood to be trifled with.

"What! you hound, you would set upon women, would you? As though there was not enough men about for you to practice upon! You dare to answer?"—as the man attempted to speak. "Here, Bazaroff—where are you?"—turning to a handsome young officer of Cossacks. "I hand him over to your tender mercies—he is one of your fellows." Then stepping up to Sara, he addressed her with an unclouded face and a slight but captivating smile—"Madam, are you the wife of the Jew, by name, Hernani?"

By this time Sara had recovered herself, and now stood erect before him.

"I am," she answered simply, though with dignity.

"I guessed as much. Well, I regret that I was not in time to save you from insult, though I managed to do so from harm, I hope. You need be under no further apprehension, I assure you; though a prisoner for the time being, you will be treated with every respect and consideration while in my charge. Beyond that I have no power to promise. In a little while I shall ask you to confine yourself to one of the rooms in yonder farmhouse, where I suppose you were living until I was forced to disturb you."

This rather long speech eliciting only a mute assent from Sara, Suroff fell back a few paces amongst his brother-officers, his fair complexion ruddier with increase of color, as though under their critical glances he experienced some awkwardness in addressing a woman.

"The devil!" he muttered to himself under his fair moustache. "So that is his Excellency's fancy—and no bad one any way! What eyes, and what a figure! A Persian's idea of perfection, being plump and white. She is very handsome—but—faugh! a Jewess." Then to the officers around him, with a significant smile—"One must always be civil to women, but of this one we had better see as little as possible, or it will be a case of trespassing upon other people's property." Then in response to an amused, almost comical exchange of glances—"Oh! don't mistake me; I mean the observation for myself as much as for Bazaroff, or any of you."

"Well, sir," ventured Bazaroff, who was a licensed favorite and knew it, "since she is a prize, taken in warfare, it——"

"Matters very much sir," interrupted Suroff with well-assumed severity, straightening his muscular figure, and looking large and important in his loosely-cut greatcoat, heavy boots and clanking spurs.

Within an hour of Suroff's brief remarks to her Sara found herself locked up with Riva, in the very room Hernani had appropriated, and from the window of which he had smiled as the young Sicinski's dog had slid upon the ice-bound pond in pursuit of the stick thrown to him.

"Oh! my lamb, my lamb," groaned Riva, after a dead silence, which it seemed to her would never be broken, "what is to become of us—what is to become of us? Not a bone of me seems in place, and I ache—oh! how I ache. That unclean beast of a man shook me as the whirlwind would. The teeth in my head rattled, and I thought my hour had come."

Sara stood before the window—her back to Riva—her mind far from the sodden cheerless landscape upon which her gaze seemed fixed. Snow in large flakes descended with that sliding zigzag motion peculiar to it, and the drip, drip of moisture from the branches of a tree, which in the fitful puffs of air occasionally rubbed against the window panes, was plainly audible. There were no tears in her eyes now—they glittered with a hard cold light—and her lips met tightly, as though she suffered, while her face was deadly white.

"To think of it all," pursued Riva; "it's terrible—terrible, and half my time I can't believe I'm Riva and not mad or dreaming."

Still Sara remained silent, Riva regarding her long and wistfully, with an expression of acute anguish in her face. For some minutes she too contrived to remain speechless, then she broke out again.

"This is beyond me to bear—this is awful! In Cracow it was bad. Times were hard. In Warsaw I was miserable towards the last, but to be shut up here like sheep in a slaughter-house—I wish I were dead, for I'm hopeless, and to be hopeless is worse than death."

"Hopeless? I am not!" Sara suddenly exclaimed fiercely. "They've not killed me yet!"

Riva sprang to her side, and clinging to her skirt groveled at her feet, an unspeakable joy illuming her thin dark face so seamed with wrinkles.

"I am not," Sara repeated. "Is this the time to grumble—is this the time to despair? Oh! I feel distracted."

"At last you speak. The Holy One be thanked! That is what I wanted and waited and talked for—to hear the sound of your voice. Never a word have you spoken for five hours, judging by the light, and with it all, cold as an icicle, and never a tear. I grew to be frightened, for what do I live for but you? I could——"

And Riva fairly broke down, her pent-up feelings escaping in hysterical sobs. Impelled by the woman's almost idolatrous affection, Sara laid her hand firmly upon her shoulder and in a gentle though decided tone said—

"Hush! That will help neither of us. We have got to think and act and be brave."

"And— who— would— not— be— with— with   you?" quavered Riva.   "Oh! it does my old heart good to hear you—and—what—courage——"

Sara laid her finger upon her lips and turned her head in the attitude of listening.   The sentry grounding his rifle outside the door occasioned her no surprise.   Something more unusual had disturbed her.

"What can it be?   There it is again!" she exclaimed in an excited voice.

Riva passed her bony hand across her wet face and listened attentively, scream after scream reaching them at length, though faintly, owing, no doubt, to the thickness of the walls.

"It's nothing, my lamb—nothing that need trouble you," she declared with languid indifference, well knowing the necessity of soothing Sara.

"You are wrong, I am certain.   It is the cry of some man in pain," answered Sara in awe-stricken accents; and then there followed, sweeping through her mind with lightning speed, her recollection of that land in which she had spent her life; of the cruel scenes she had herself witnessed, and the barbarities of which she had been told. Troubled beyond the power of words to describe, she clutched Riva's arm convulsively, and in a voice which excitement reduced to a whisper, gave vent to the thoughts which had been upon her mind, but which until that moment she had lacked the courage to put into words.

"What of him—where is he—what can have happened?"

To such questions it was not in Riva's power to make answer.   Her own concern for Hernani was neither deep nor warm.   Any consideration she might have felt for him had been swamped by jealousy in the days when her mistress had been happy, and since then by a growing dislike, he to her mind being the absolute and unworthy cause of all Sara's grief.   Besides—had he not got them into their present plight—the fool—as she thought of him? Therefore knowing the nature and staunchness of the heart he had won, and fearing to wound by some ill-judged word, she took refuge in silence.

"What of him, I say," Sara repeated, still gripping her arm, till Riva could feel the little nails cutting into her skin—"is he dead, or are they torturing him?"

"No, no, nothing of that—it cannot be," the woman ventured, thus driven to say something. "See the charity he has bestowed upon others, the schools he has built, and the synagogues, and the money he has cast about him on all sides. He will not be forgotten of Him who rules the world, and who knows the hearts of Kings. The master's good fortune will not fail him even in such straits. Take heart—you will see."

"Do you think so, Riva? Is that what you think?"

"I know it here, my lamb,"—pointing to her heart; "though what says the Book? 'When the ox is down many are the butchers.'"

Riva knew nothing of the kind, and thought quite the contrary. That signified nothing. Sara must be comforted; to her mind the circumstances warranted her words.

"Bless you for saying that!" murmured Sara. "But, oh! the sight of him as he disappeared—I shall see him always." And she hid her face in her hands.

"Why were you silent before the officer?" Riva now took courage to ask. "He was the man to speak to, and then was the time. When he said, 'Are you the wife of Hernani?' I made sure you would say 'Yes; and what of him? Is he unhurt?'"

"How could I, Riva? You forget how I was surrounded by men, all staring at me as though I were a savage, and at the time my head ringing with the blow I had got."

"The brute! I wish my knife had entered his heart instead of his arm," Riva blazed up. "No—you did the best," she added, pursuing her subject; "but when you see him again you can ask him questions. He will answer them. I saw him look at you, and I know what such looks mean. You can ask him about the young lady and her brother, the Count, and the other two gentlemen. I never saw them towards the end. I never set eyes on her—did you?"

And the two women went on talking, occasionally fancying they heard the strangest noises and were perhaps about to become the victims of the foulest of plots, yet with it all striving to take heart, comforting each other as best they could, but securely guarded, as the heavy and monotonous tread of a sentry outside their door constantly reminded them.

CHAPTER XIX.

In pursuance of his instructions, within an hour of his victory, Suroff had despatched a courier to his Excellency, General Hourko, and with his prisoners secured and the wounded looked to, awaited the reply, which, when it came—after a lapse of more than forty-eight hours—was, in the main, what he had expected.

The whole batch of prisoners were to be sent to different specified fortresses—with the exception of the two women, with whom, after giving over his command, he was to hasten to an address situated within a few miles of the Chateau Villanov, and upon the direct road to Warsaw.

Suroff well knew that the place mentioned was a villa owned or rented by General Hourko, said to be of comfort, even elegance, and to possess conservatories, where notable specimens of orange, pomegranate, and other beautiful trees flourished.

"So his Excellency meditates a little relaxation, I imagine," he told himself upon the receipt of these orders. "Well, I don't think I blame him, though his sharp-visaged wife will, if she gets to know of his doings. He can trust me, he knows. My pay will come in medals and promotion, and I shall get both for this clean bit of work." And Suroff stroked his moustache, and allowed his thoughts to wander to some of the fair sex in Petersburg for whom he owned to a leaning, and then, soldier-like, set about carrying out his instructions without delay.

In receipt of a curt order to hold herself in readiness for a journey, Sara, who was still in ignorance of Hernani's fate, and felt the impossibility of leaving the farm without doing her utmost to obtain news of him, seized the opportunity to address the bearer of the message—a soldier—whom she saw for the first time.

"I wish to speak to the officer in command," she said mildly, and in her most persuasive manner. "Will you please give him that message for me?"

The man turned upon her half in astonishment and anger at receiving such a request from a prisoner, but remembering that for some reason she was treated with distinction, the oath and the point blank refusal upon his tongue, were changed for a civil assurance that the desire should be communicated, the result being that after a while, Suroff himself came to her.

"I am told that you have something to say to me," he said, barely allowing his eyes to rest upon her as he spoke, but seeming rather to prefer to look about the room, or at Riva, who, with the best intention, had withdrawn to the furthest corner, and there appeared deeply engrossed.

"Yes; I ventured to send such a message," answered Sara, inwardly agitated and nervous, now that she really faced this man whose power over her was so absolute, and who was, she felt, intentionally impervious to an appealing glance or a trick of the voice.

"And in what way can I be of assistance to you?" returned Suroff, in tones which before Sara preferred her request, impressed her with the hopelessness of it.

"You can tell me what has become of my husband," she said, with startling abruptness and energy, as though convinced that with Suroff, plain speaking would weigh the heaviest.

For the instant he appeared slightly confused, as though the directness or nature of the assertion, for which he should certainly have been prepared, placed him at a disadvantage. Then he said—as if to gain time for reflection, or to soften the refusal he meditated—

"How do you know that?"

"Common sense tells me. Ah! if you knew how I suffer, you would not hesitate; and what harm could it do to anyone?"

"Probably none."

"Then let me entreat you," urged Sara, vaguely conscious that if he would but look at her she could win her way to his heart.

Inclined to doubt himself under the circumstances, feeling that to hesitate was to be lost, and that he had to choose between a chivalrous desire to be lenient to a woman and a grave doubt as to how far wisdom would support him in the act, Suroff said firmly, though evidently against his will—

"Duty does not permit me to grant your request. If it seemed wise, I would. There are few harder tasks in life than to know when to be silent."

"You refuse?"

"Absolutely, madam."

"Then that is all I have to say, sir," answered Sara calmly, though in truth despairingly.

Suroff bowed as politely as though quitting the salon of a Duchess, simply because it was natural to him so to do when dealing with a woman, and Riva, in the depths of her corner, thought, though with strange laxity of reasoning considering the looseness of her own tongue, "The young man is right; that he should know such things is why he is where he is, for the Book says wisely, 'Silence is the fence round wisdom.'"

In a little while after that, conscious of being crestfallen, down-trodden and unfortunate to a degree past any previous experience or conception, and yet dimly sensible that since she breathed, all was not lost, Sara found herself seated in a conveyance not more comfortable than a perekladnaia, being of rough country build, muffled in wraps, with Suroff at her side, and Riva following in a cart packed with prisoners, guarded by an escort of Cossacks.

In the greatness of her grief, as she was thus forced

away from the Sicinski farm, and as she looked long and
wistfully upon it, it seemed to her that in leaving it she
was leaving him, severing the last link that bound her to
him—Hernani, whose voice still rang in her ears, whose
hands, when she shut her eyes, were yet upon her shoulders—and that if not dead—and the awful thought would
come—they were dead to each other, and that on earth
they had spoken and touched for the last time. Through
the driving sleet, as it swept over her in gusts, she could
dimly discern the little window at which she had stood
on that first morning—hopeful, strangely so—and the
memory of it, and that then she was not alone, was so
cruel, so heartbreaking a mockery of the suffering she
endured, that, proud though she was and determined to
be brave in the presence of her victorious foes, in silent
woe she hid her face.

Throughout that long sad drive Suroff made no attempt to speak to her, but muffled to the very tips of his
ears seemed ignorant of her existence, save when the
clumsy vehicle lurched in the deep ruts, and threatened
to pitch them bodily into the snow, when he evinced interest enough to rouse himself, and support her with a
strong hand until the danger was past.

A roadside inn sheltered them for some hours while
the storm was at its height, and there the horses were
changed and a less comfortless conveyance, a sleigh, obtained. When a fresh start was made, part of the escort
with the half-starved prisoners in charge, branched off in
another direction, and soon after, they had rumbled out
of sight, jolting in the carts, and some of them screaming
with pain, Sara began to think that certain features of the
landscape were familiar to her. Occasionally she felt
positive that a tiny church with its gilded cross and green
dome, a group of cottages, multi-colored from dilapida-
tion, the shape of some fields, or a certain peculiar curve
in the dusky outline of a pine forest, were not new to her;
but at such points, exhaustion, mental and physical, pre-

vented her from troubling her head more than to wonder. Of what account was it where she was going, since in all directions she was equally friendless and forlorn?

The bitter wind and driving sleet had chilled her to the bone, her feet were like icicles, every joint in her body seemed to have stiffened, her head itself was benumbed and like lead, with a dull throbbing ache in it almost insupportable. The severe jolting she had sustained had shaken her to pieces, and she was so tired that she could scarcely sit upright.

In such a condition despair might well lay hold upon her, the limits of her endurance having been reached. Feverish and overwrought, her mind seemed in too weak and excitable a state to deal lucidly with any one idea, and yet ideas swarmed. Visions of damp and noisome dungeons, such as she knew existed, where huge and loathsome rats alone could thrive, were succeeded by recollections of her beautiful and costly home, which presented itself instantaneously in all its details—of Hernani—of her barrenness—of the divorce she had lived under the shadow of—of that terrible paper in General Hourko's hands—of his passionate glances on that night so like a nightmare to her—of the burning words he had poured in her ear; and then with startling irrelevancy she leapt backward over years—she was again in Cracow—a slip of a girl; there were the streets she knew so well—the door of her home ajar, revealing the form and face of her father, and between the paroxysms of his terrible cough she could hear voices, lifted in altercation, as he repeated his oft-told story of the fortune his knowledge and discoveries would one day bring. The very tunes popular at that date pealed from the street organs, and voices shouted the doggerel lines of songs just then the rage. Oh! they were all so cruelly fresh and clear to her, those myriad recollections of that long and fitful dream which was her life. And then, as though at last worn out, her troubled mind became a blank, and she no longer

possessed the power to conjure up those panoramic pictures, and was only dreamily alive to such monotonous
sounds as the creaking of the sleigh, the crunching of
the snow, which had become crisp with frost, and an occasional clear ring of the horses' hoofs as some hard substance was struck.

Suroff was still impassive; he had lit a fresh cigar,
which glowed as he smoked, while a great clear moon
peered down upon them, and a bird croaked as it was
disturbed. A couple of turnings were taken, the last a
sharp one, and through tall iron gates they swung into a
drive, overhung with leafless trees, arriving at length before high stone columns, flanking the entrance to a villa,
from the doorway of which a blaze of light streamed upon
them. Two bulky figures in somber uniforms stood to
their arms as, shaking the snow from his furs, Suroff rose
to his feet, and then Sara understood that what she had
dreaded throughout—yet would not hint to Riva—had
come to pass, and that she was in General Hourko's
power.

A few words from Suroff, spoken well out of hearing,
relieved him of his charge, and with a "Good-night,
madam," and a careless lifting of his fingers to the peak
of his military cap, Sara saw him disappear, as it proved,
for ever out of her life.

With Riva at her side, and in silence submitting to be
conducted, a broad flight of stairs was ascended, a corri-
dor traversed, and a suit of rooms entered. Here there
was warmth at least, and luxury and tempting food at
hand; better still, there was privacy for the instant,
though, as Sara sank into a chair with a furtive glance
round the walls, she suppressed a shudder as she thought
of how those walls might yield to a practiced, unscrupulous touch, for aught she knew, and discover her helpless as she was.

"Riva," she said, when she had recovered a little from
her exhaustion, and the heat from the stove had warmed

and set her blood at work—"Riva, did you see anything
at the head of the staircase facing the statue holding the
lamp and upon the wall before it?"

"Ach! Yes—a picture in a big gold frame. What of
that, my love?"

"That is a portrait of the Governor—of General Hourko."

"The Holy One protect us—of the great Russian—
then——"

"You know where we are."

"God of Abraham, Isaac and Jacob—in his hands! He
of whom such things are spoken, and who has shed the
blood of the innocent! Is it so? Can it be? Then evil
has indeed overtaken us. Oh! My lamb, my lamb—
and I knew it all along. What did I say—have none of
him—that was my counsel."

Ignoring the censure, strong in her innocence, Sara
remained silent for a few seconds, and then in her low
sweet voice told of Hourko's night visit, concealing
nothing, even to the paper in his possession, ending with
the demand—

"What do you advise? Can you see any way out of
this trap? What is to be done?"

"What can you do?" answered Riva, after having com-
mented upon the disclosures in her own quaint way.
"Here, as in the world, might is right. He will lay hands
upon you—you will be sacrificed——"

"Lay hands upon me!" interrupted Sara, with the indignant gesture of a very Queen of Tragedy. "I can
strike him dead should he dare." And as though to draw
some hidden weapon, her hand sought her bosom.

Riva now appeared calmness itself, but it was the calm
born of terror. She laughed hysterically and spoke fast
as though without control.

"Oh!—ah!—strike him dead—that is good! But not
here—and for you—you would be taken and cut in pieces
with the knout, and your body—think of it—your body

would be flung to the dogs of the street! Strike him
dead? No—there must be nothing of that. What says
the law? 'All that a man hath, will he give for his life.'
And you—you are young, without a wrinkle, beautiful
and with the plumpness of youth. Ah! life is sweet, my
love."

"Not to me, Riva. Every hope that it contains is centered in—in——"

"Ah! yes—the master. I know—I know."

"You are right, and as though to punish me for loving
aught but God so much, here am I without news of him.
Even now, at this moment, he may be lying dead in some
vile pit into which these monsters have flung him; or,
if not dead, immured in some foul dungeon, where is
neither warmth nor light, and where the atmosphere
breeds death. But this is yielding to weakness—help me,
Riva—help me to take heart, like a good soul, for upon
me everything depends; in me the last hope—our last
hope—his and mine—is centered. So you thought me
strange when I kept my own counsel, and pretended that
I was happy."

"You never deceived me. To my eyes you were
wretched."

"Ah! you know me so well. You understand. But
the tide of my life sets from bad to worse; this is worse
than that, for that was happiness compared with this. Yet
I felt strong then, as though, were I put to it, I could do
much; yes, then at the worst I felt strong; now I know
that I must be so, and what I have to do seems shaping
in my head. When beset, I should be brave; else it were
better I were nothing. Riva, how strange life is, and
how many are its lessons, in the forefront of them being
contentment and endurance. We would give something
for the old Cracow days at this moment. I had not suffered then, and yet I thought I was a martyr; but then,
too, I had not loved. Ah! a physical ill is nothing to a
mental one; remedies may mend the one, but a genuine

sickness of the other is incurable. But we must face all
this and fight through it. I feel my spirits rise at thought
of struggling more. Riva, look to the door—the one
with the spring—you will find it locked, I think. They
will shut us off from the rest of the house, and confine
us securely by means of it. How tired I feel, and sore
from head to foot, as though I had been beaten with
sticks. Well—is it locked? I thought so. Now for the
walls. A while back I should never have thought. of
making a mental plan of a house in mounting a staircase, or of examining a room, as though each chair or
cupboard concealed a bomb, each picture or panel a secret door; but now my inquisitiveness must be humored
if my eyes are to close. It cannot be called taking precautions, for what precautions are possible? Still, it
eases one's mind to peer into cupboards, beneath beds, or
behind curtains; all of which proves one, after all, to be
but little better than an overgrown child. No; so far as
I can see, there is nothing suspicious, and yet the very atmosphere is charged with evil. Now listen to my sum-
ming-up of the situation, Riva.

"We are in one or other of the Governor's summer
residences, not a great way from Warsaw—I am sure of
that; there is an armed guard outside, and within, a man
and woman—man and wife, I should say, who are faithful
and discreet, and who have been told to supply our wants
and prevent our escape. We have apartments en suite—
a luxuriously-furnished sitting-room and two bedrooms,
the smallest of which, I should say, has done duty as an
ante-room. In all probability, in fact, these are his Excellency's private apartments. We now await the great
event, his Excellency's approach, which——"

"Ach! you are clever," interrupted Riva.

"Clever? No; I am stupid to a degree or I should not
be here."

"Stupid! The mind wears the body out, and it is so
with you, my lamb. All this talk comes of excitement;

though who can blame you? You need rest, or you will
be ill. Ach! your hand is like a live coal, your cheeks
aglow, and your eyes aflame. You are in a fever. I
know it—I know it. Am I not your nurse, your own old
Riva who has rocked and sung you to sleep in the days
when your mind was a blank? Ah! you can tell me
nothing. You must have rest and warmth. Come, let
me see you get it; let me ease you of the boots and the
clothes. The little feet will be cold, like unto stones, and
must be chafed, and I shall watch by you that no harm
may come near."

"It is good of you, Riva, but how can I rest? I can
recall too plainly the face of the great Russian, as you call
him, and that strange visit at dead of night, of which I
have told you. How I hate him! People talk of beauty
and sigh for it; it is easy for beauty to prove a curse."

"Yet, if you were like me, wrinkled and yellow as a
skin ill-cured, where would this night have found us?"

"One may pay too dearly for safety, Riva."

"Ah! well, my lamb, then such a price must never be
paid."

And there in those big rooms, bearing the subtle
marks, not so much of wealth as of refinement and culture—in loneliness, with the shadow of unknowable dis-
asters hanging over them—they gradually ceased talking, Riva flitting about as though of india-rubber rather
than of flesh and blood; attentive, gentle, seeming alike
unconscious of ill or of fatigue, so long as her love, her
lamb, the apple of her eye, was beside her. And so the
hours sped, and the cold increased, and the snow fell
pitilessly, no news coming to them whether of good or
ill.

To demean herself by questioning the stern-visaged
attendants, never occurred to Sara, and no good could
have come of it, seeing that they were a sour-faced pair
—it seemed, fanatically devoted to the interests they
served. So there was little else to be done but wonder

19

and wait, and try to shape plans and actions for that future which seemed profoundly dark and even terrible in its obscurity.

As for the manner of her conduct towards the Governor when he should burst upon her, at one moment Sara fancied she saw her way clear, and could handle him to a nicety, holding him at a good arm's length; but in the next hour, ignorance of the man, doubts of herself, of her will and wit, doubts of all things concerning her condition, clouded her mind.

Some days thus sped, in bewilderment, monotonous speculation and torturing anxiety—at least to Sara, for whom it had been well, had her mind been duller, her nerves less sensitive—at the end of which time, and unheard by her or Riva, isolated as they were, came a tinkling of silver sleigh bells over the crisp white snow, as, drawn by coal-black horses of that famous breed of which the Orloffs were so proud, the Governor, Ivan Nicholaevitch himself arrived.

What a bustle there was, what a running to and fro, and homage and hypocrisy on the part of all concerned; in return for which the great man replied with placid indifference or harsh contempt, a flinging aside of his furs, and an imperious call for tea with lemon shredded in it, after which came an appeal to the eternal cigarette. The tea would stimulate and create warmth. He would recover himself from the chilling effects of the drive, then he would dine well, and then—he would send for Sara. That was the programme he sketched out, as in a cosy arm-chair, drawn close to the stove, he warmed himself, stretching forth his hands, stamped by the time which had whitened his hair and grizzled his moustache.

He was in a triumphant mood, as well he might be, according to his reckoning of things; for had not his wife —the jealous and exacting Olga Pavlovna—disgusted with the increased cold—shivering, hating it—disgusted with the failure of her schemes for capturing and humil-

iating Sara—disgusted also with Popoloff's imbecility or
perfidy—at length beat a swift retreat towards the sunshine, the flowers and the swallows; trusting to the bitter
cold of the forests, to exposure and want, for that ven-
geance upon one whom she chose to consider as an insolent and unscrupulous rival. And had not Popoloff been
detected in the committal of acts of long-suspected
treachery, and was not the General, Ivan Nicholaevitch,
waiting and watching patiently, until it should seem good
to him to punish his unworthy servant; above all, was not
Sara actually under the same roof with him, and could
he not summon her or go to her, as might please him?
And as to that, he would eat well and then he would see;
but upon that frost-bound winter evening, he was certainly master of the situation upon all points, and none
could have disputed it.

In such a mood there was danger in Hourko, it would
be thought—danger in any member of that large class
described as unscrupulous. So as the cold increased, and
the stars flashed clearer as the night aged, with heavy
curtains drawn and fuel fresh upon the stove, the General sat erect in his chair, his fine chest eased by the loos-
ing of his tunic buttons, his decorations glittering, not a
hair awry in his waxed moustache, and upon his face a
benign smile of satisfaction.

Before him were the remnants of delicacies, while a
costly wine sparkled in his glass. He was not rich, and
his debts were huge, but he lived as his rank demanded;
moreover, for him a gala night had arrived. He hic-
coughed a time or two and finished his wine, then he
drank his coffee, and, having lighted a cigar, addressed
his servant harshly, as though that servant were a mu-
tinous dog. In that stately, masculine language, the
Russian tongue, he gave some orders, then with dignified carriage he passed beneath the half-drawn folds of
an embroidered curtain and entered another apartment.
He had sent for Sara.

When the message came to her, Sara bit her lip and turned pale, and old Riva stifled a little scream and protested.

"See him here, my lamb, and you will be wise. I am but an old woman, yet should you wish for me I am at hand."

But Sara knew better. For the weak there could be but one course—to appear strong. So, woman-like, looking to her beauty even at that pass, she followed at the heels of her conductor, appearing on her way down the staircase, and upon her entry into the General's presence, refined and dignified, as suffering will refine and dignify, being God's own marking of His creatures' faces. What if the simple black dress which had protected her from jibes and insults in Warsaw, and done service at the Sicinski farm, were worn and shabby? Does the light of the eye, the sheen of the hair, and the delicate tinting of the fair cheek, need a fine setting or ornamentation? If so, Sara had none, but stood before Hourko with the simplicity and easy dignity, which, coupled with her beauty, had attracted him at first, when, with Popoloff and the aide-de-camp on either side of her, she had been brought before him at the palace.

The General looked imposing and substantial, as he stood with his back to the stove in his favorite attitude; for his years he appeared even handsome, with his keen blue eyes, his red square-jawed face, and heavy cavalry moustache. But in Sara's sight these perfections did not exist. She only saw before her a rugged unscrupulous soldier, to whom the shedding of innocent blood was easy, who had pursued and hunted her down—a tyrant, in short.

It was Hourko's passing intention to avail himself of all the advantages and power of his exalted rank, and from that lofty pinnacle to impress and bend Sara as he wished; so with this idea he greeted her sternly with a—

"Madam, we meet once more, and this time beneath my own roof."

Without reflecting a second Sara answered boldly, "The shelter of which has, I need scarcely remark, been forced upon me."

"True; and had it not been so you would have starved in the forests, as others who have revolted are doing, or been left to languish in a fortress. You will remember how I told you that you would need a friend; well, it is so now more than ever, for——"

"I believe you, sir."

"For the account against you and yours has swollen."

"Excellency, I am aware of my condition, but could a wife do less than I have done?"

"You have judgment, you——"

"I have used it. If my debt to the Government of this country is so heavy, my liberty or my life must go to discharge it."

"That is what will probably happen," replied Ivan Nicholaevitch grimly; "but," he added as he looked down upon her, seated as she was in a chair, "it is my desire to prevent such a reckoning."

"Then I may look upon your Excellency as the friend you said you were," she answered, eager to gain a point.

"I am proving it."

"Will your Excellency be good enough to tell me how?"

"I have rescued you from imprisonment."

"But only to imprison me here."

"Only to keep you out of harm's way. Are you not supplied with every comfort? You have only to ask to be satisfied. Are my people attentive to you?"

"I cannot complain."

"Then what is amiss? In the present disturbed state of affairs, safety is worth having. There are thousands who would give sacks of rubles to be in your place. You are not thankful enough."

"Excellency, it is not for me to argue with you. I am only a simple-minded woman, loving honesty and candor, and being untaught in the ways and windings of the world. I understand nothing of finesse; therefore this I frankly tell you—if, as you assure me, you are a friend to me, I have cause to be grateful, and shall not forget to be so, but I must beg you to prove it, and satisfy me that your sentiment towards me is nothing worse. I hold that——"

"By all the Saints—such spirit and such language——"

"Sir, my language is not meant to give offense and is merely a straightforward rendering of my thoughts; as for my spirit, it is not yet crushed. Would you have it so? The punishment with which you have threatened me—Siberia——"

"Punishment—Siberia—pooh! Let us talk pleasantly. With your beauty——"

"Better women have gone and died there."

"I'm not so sure of that. But you need fear nothing, only you must be reasonable."

"I can only be myself, Excellency."

"And a very sweet self—a self to which I am inclined to be devoted."

"Words will not hurt me, sir."

"No; but I'm prepared to prove mine."

"I will ask you rather to prove your consideration for me by modifying them. In addressing you Excellency, I shall always remember that a strong"—Sara would not say brave—"and honorable man cannot take advantage of a weak and defenseless woman, but as a test of the friendship that your Excellency has professed for me, will you favor me with news of my husband—of Kasimir Hernani?"

Hourko took a turn or two in front of her, his steps always bringing him back to the same point, the stove; then unconsciously, though feeling disappointed and irritated, he lighted a fresh cigarette. Had Sara cringed before him, or shown sign of fear or weakness, his course would have been simple. He would have taken good care to work on and develop such symptoms, but by her simple self-reliance and confidence, springing perhaps from the love and consciousness of the right she professed, she disarmed him. A twinge which had hurt him before pained him again, the twinge being the thought—not new—that in the flesh, before him, there was an upright woman, upon whom, moreover, rank, or wealth, or bribery of any kind would pass as the water over the coral of the deep sea, leaving it fairer and purer for the contact. In his young days he might have dismissed such reflections successfully—he had silenced his conscience so often—but to his annoyance he now found them difficult to get quit of. As to Hernani—why should he not tell her the truth, watching her face so as to estimate the depth of her affection for him, now that his ruin was complete?

"He was taken prisoner," he said slowly, stationing himself before her with his eyes fixed upon her face.

"Yes," said Sara, without eagerness, as though listening to a pleasing story, and wishing him to proceed—"yes," she repeated softly, for she instinctively divined his intention, and was guarding even the quiver of an eyelash.

"He was found to be wounded, and——"

"Is he dead?" she asked, in a perfectly natural voice, which actually startled Hourko into thinking her either indifferent or the most perfect actress he had ever met. He reflected for an instant. If her affections were not involved, as he had thought, to threaten or promise to aid Hernani would avail him little.

"No," he said, removing his gaze to knock the ash off his cigarette, and as quickly glancing at her again, in the hope of effecting a surprise—"no; his wound was slight, and when I last heard of him I seem to remember

that he was doing well. But I may be mistaken. There
are so many things to think of."

"God of my Fathers, how I thank Thee!" Sara thought,
but with only a natural pause she said—

"Was that long ago, Excellency? Can you remember?"

"Quite recently, I think, but I will inquire if you wish
—which is another proof of my friendship."

Sara smiled, and the smile thrilled through Hourko,
who, as he felt the sensation, half cursed himself for the
weakness.

"And yet," he argued silently, "the woman is mine.
She can never escape me now. Still, if——" Ah! he
was irritated.

"Thanks," murmured Sara. "Where is he, sir?" she
ventured to ask a moment later.

His temper ruffled, Hourko turned upon her savagely.

"Madam, he is safe in a fortress, where he is likely to
remain, and where it seems you would like to join him.
You can easily be accommodated, I assure you. There's
lots of room—at present," he added darkly.

Feeling that her only chance with this man was to
show no sign of fear, Sara said boldly—

"If it should be my lot to be immured in a prison, I
shall hope for the courage to endure it, though it has
pleased your Excellency to tell me that I am too good for
such a fate."

"And so you are!" exclaimed Hourko, for the instant,
as frank and simple as a boy.

"Then I will not think of it just now," answered Sara
calmly. "Will your Excellency give me further details,
and tell me of the fate of Count Dorozynski, of his sister, and of the two brothers, the Counts Goroski?"

Hourko hesitated momentarily. In reality he was becoming more and more astonished at Sara's bearing.
"There is no understanding these women," he thought

to himself. "I might be the delinquent in some measure, by the way she speaks. By all the Saints, she is
taking me to task; but then, she is beautiful, which is
a free pass to such license." Aloud he said, "I will endeavor to do so. According to the report made by Major
Suroff, one-half of the force opposed to him was destroyed, the remainder were taken prisoners. Count
Andrew Dorozynski was killed, and so was his sister.
She was shot while masquerading in a man's attire,
which was brave, in one sense, but foolish in another——" Sara interrupted him with an exclamation of
wonderment.

"What! you are surprised?" he inquired.

"Very."

"You did not see her in such disguise?"

"No."

"Where were you?"

"Excellency, I was attending to the sick and wounded."

"Which more womanly occupation probably saved
your life. Do you know that I was anxious about you,
and that, had I known what was going on, you would
never have left Warsaw. You were in my thoughts
when I despatched Suroff with the troops. Do you believe me?"

"Excellency, I do not know."

"You doubt my word?"

Sara thought a moment. She was playing a desperate
game. She might anger the man. Was it wise to risk
so much? In an instant of time she weighed her chances
and formed her decision.

"Has your Excellency given me no cause?"

Ivan Nicholaevitch was electrified. No one ever dared
to question him; yet within his own walls—helpless—
in his power, this Jewess as good as told him that he
had lied to her. His eyes flashed dangerously, but they
encountered Sara's truthful and steady gaze, which never

quailed before his angry glance. He was going to ful-
minate threats on the instant, the words actually trembling on his tongue. But somehow he could not—he
hesitated—this was a woman—and one who had never
lied as he had; whose purity compared with his was
what the driven snow is to the dust-heap—who, in fact,
in all ways, was different to his Petersburg women, who
had always flung themselves at his head. Besides, he
had lied to her systematically; his conscience, which was
not dead nor sleeping at this crisis, told him that. She
was right enough to censure him, since he had placed
her in a position to do so, but it was intensely annoying,
and, after all, whatever he had done had been for her
sake.

"What do you mean?" he stammered.

"Excellency, I will tell you. You found out, or else
you knew, that my sympathies were enlisted in favor of
those of my persuasion; that among them I had labored
in my small way, and unasked, you promised me your
support."

"Well?"

"And you had no intention of giving it, or showing
any favor to my co-religionists."

"No."

"And, Excellency, you expect me to credit your statements after such an admission?"

"Yes, when you know that all I did then, and all I
have done since, was because of my regard for you. Yes,
I put it stronger—my love for you, Sara."

"Oh! I am to understand, then, that the sentiment
your Excellency entertains for me is love, not friendship?"

"Yes—love," repeated Hourko; and before Sara could
prevent him he had his arm about her, and would have
pressed his grizzled moustache to her lips, had she not
sent him spinning backward with an energy that astonished him.

"Listen to me," she said, sinking again into her seat, breathless but calm—"listen to me. Is that the way an officer, representing his Imperial Majesty the Tsar, should treat a woman, who in the first place, is dragged into his presence for the sole crime of having tried to succor the starving?"

"By the God above us, you will madden me!" cried Hourko, in a voice like the growl of a wild beast. "I have but to ring this bell and——"

"I shall be on my way to Siberia by étape," Sara interrupted with reckless courage. "Do so—I am not afraid. I have already been there mentally—and, I may add truthfully, through your threats. You have deceived me by word, and in writing; you have tracked me, and had me spied upon; at dead of night I have not been safe from you; to further your purposes you have had me smuggled beneath your roof, and now you offer me physical insults under assurances of friendship. There is a right and a wrong, as the God whose name you have used is judge, and because I am right and know it, I have had the courage to speak to you as I have done. Leave me alone, Excellency; lay no hand upon me; drive me forth into the snow as you would a dog, rather than doom me, a woman, to that most fatal degradation, loss of self-respect."

Colorless as though dying—having risen to her feet in her agony of excitement—Sara stood with flashing eyes and parted lips, panting for breath.

Never a word was spoken for some seconds, and in the room, there was never a sound, save the ticking of an ormolu clock, a crackle in the stove, as the fuel sank, Sara's breathing, and at length, the creak of the General's varnished boot, as he moved slightly. Then, he spoke—dropping his words like bullets.

"Madam, there can be no doubt that you are a singularly fine person. I will say more—a remarkable one; also, that you have the best of the argument, if I may

so style it—women usually have—on the other hand, I,
Ivan Nicholaevitch, have the best of the situation. I
admire your views, and they have a certain weight with
me; but you are so delightful, so adorable, that you
will have to adopt mine, otherwise, the chances for you
as suggested, are much in favor of Siberia by étape. But,
what's up? What's the matter? Are you ill? By all
the Saints——!"

In the heat of his fear, without reflecting, he sprang
to the bell and sent peal after peal through the house.
The servants rushed in. Sara looked ghastly. Like
fools, these menials stood inactive—looking.

"Go and get some restoratives, wine, cognac, anything," roared Hourko. "Do you hear—you sheep
heads?"*

The sound of his hated voice, distant and singing in
her ears, though it seemed, made the alarm a false one.
With the aid of her pride and a prodigious effort of will,
Sara recovered herself, and Ivan Nicholaevitch, thinking
that he had been too harsh, and being, in truth, more
affected by Sara's words than he cared to own, tried to
make amends and headway, by what he deemed attention and kindness. With all the wit he had, he turned
the conversation into other channels, and finally, having exhausted the last moment of leisure at his disposal,
he resumed his furs, flung himself into his sleigh, and
more intoxicated than ever with the passion her beauty
had inspired in him, tore back to Warsaw, telling himself that he had obtained a clearer insight into her character that night, and that he would conquer her by kindness, if not, by threats, but that conquered and his, she
should be.

Other food for reflection and speculation, as well as
occasion for energetic resolutions, if not actions, would
have been supplied to him, had he, Ivan Nicholaevitch,

---

* Russian expression.

paid a visit to his villa at noon of the next day; also his eyes would have opened wider had they lighted upon the ungainly figure of Titus Prokofievitch Popoloff; Titus himself, who was there with his colorless, inscrutable face, polishing his spectacles leisurely as of old, and using them to peer at his, Ivan Nicholaevitch's, trusted dependents, with whom he appeared to be on the best of terms. This in itself was curious, but then, Mr. Secretary Popoloff was, in his way, a curious man, and had so many strings to pull to enable him to keep in touch with, and know everything, as was his proud boast, and then also, officialism has occasionally proved corrupt.

When Sara rejoined Riva, no sooner had the door shut and left them alone together, than Riva's old arms were extended at sight of her mistress, and so great had been the strain upon Sara that she straightway fell into them, exclaiming as she swooned:—

"Riva, he is alive—he is alive!"

CHAPTER XX.

The beginning of Titus Popoloff's loss of influence had dated from the—to him—unlucky day when Sara had been brought before Hourko. His attempt to serve two masters had begun to fail from that moment, and one is bound to admit that it could scarce have been otherwise. However, acting unscrupulously as was his wont, he had made money for himself throughout, and if destined to lose prestige with Hourko at the rate at which it had of late deserted him, he had decided that he had a mind to pursue his old tactics.

If kudos and the advancement he coveted were as far off as ever, it was still open to him to employ his talents in the acquiring and storage of rubles.

In Cracow, awhile back, adherents of the revolutionary movement had agreed to the establishment of a Dictatorship, and as a fit occupant of that post, had nominated General Maryan Langiewicz. It had followed that Langiewicz had become Dictator, had won a battle or two, which had helped his cause in no way, that the Russian Government had offered fifty thousand rubles for his head, finally that his force had been dispersed, and he himself imprisoned in an Austrian fortress, having crossed the frontier into Austria in the company of his romantic and beautiful aide-de-camp—so styled by courtesy—Miss Pustowoitow—daughter of a Russian General. These historical facts were ancient history to Popoloff. His knowledge extended further, for he knew that with the setting of General Langiewicz's bright particular star, the back of the revolution had been broken, a death-blow to it dealt. He knew that the peasantry had been converted by the government into a kind of brutal police, armed with bill-hooks, axes, any weapon that came to hand, that he himself had borne his part in bringing this about, and that in consequence, the landed proprietors—without whose support the revolutionary movement would dwindle and die—were actually being brought into the towns in their own carriages, their hands having been tied by their own peasants. With affairs at such a pass, what was to be done? His—Popoloff's—pay, was a mere pittance, compared with what he could earn by the judicious sale of information; so he promptly continued the selling of it. He had audiences of that mysterious group of personages, who, after General Langiewicz's overthrow, had hastened to resume the supreme authority, calling themselves the Provisional National Government. Thanks to his villainy and that of others, resolutions were made known, while the ink upon the paper recording them was scarce dry. The disposition of the Russian forces, the convoying and safe conduct of arms and provisions, were thus anticipated and intercepted.

It had now come to pass, that Titus Popoloff, in the restlessness of his mind, had conceived a fresh project, which stood commended to him, by reason of its easy accomplishment, the slight risk attaching to it, and the money it would bring him. In furtherance of the scheme, he had appeared at the villa, and there sounded the minds of the Governor-General's servants. His next step was to present himself at the Citadel, where, as he well knew, Hernani was confined. It was perfectly easy to him to gain admittance to that strong fortress, and with a little judicious bribery, to effect an entrance into the cold damp cell which doomed Hernani to inaction and despair. Once within it, and by way of answer to Hernani's mute expression of inquiry, he said abruptly: "Come—I have news for you."

"News?" was the tired reply from this man, who had been all fire and energy but awhile back.

"Yes, news, and of a pleasant kind, if you choose to

make it so. Ah! I see; the damp walls and the solitude
are already having their effect. Your face is as colorless as that of a ghost, and your hair is turning white."

This was true enough, but there being no friendship
between them, and not trusting his visitor wholly,
though they had had dealings, Hernani answered sharply enough:

"Pass on to your point. Give me the news."

"Fifty thousand rubles is a good deal of money,"
mused Popoloff.

"What of it?" inquired Hernani, irritated by the familiar manner and brusque bearing of the man.

"It was offered as a reward for the person of General
Maryan Langiewicz."

"With what result?"

"That he—I won't say owing to the reward, though
—is safe in an Austrian fortress."

There was something terribly pathetic in the dignified
silence with which Hernani received this crushing blow
to what remained to him of hope that his cause would
prosper, but it was not until some seconds had elapsed
that he found the words and the courage to answer
quietly.

"Is that the news?"

"No, I am coming to it," answered Popoloff with provoking calmness.

"Well, I am listening."

Popoloff carefully removed his spectacles, then, with
the habitual rub from his silk handkerchief, set them
upon his nose again. There was no trace of his usual
obsequiousness. Hernani was no longer the influential
banker and merchant prince, but, to his way of thinking, a ruined man. So he could afford to be curt and
brutal, as is the way with such people.

After a dead silence of some moments he again spoke.

"Tell me," he said, "since the information I gave you
in the Saxonski Sad concerning your wife, coupled with

other little transactions, your faith in me is established, is it not?"

Hernani almost smiled as he riveted his eyes upon his questioner.

"I have faith," he smiled grimly, "go on."

"That is well."

"Why?"

"You will have need of it."

"How so?"

"Because, without my assistance, you are lost, doomed."

"That is a pleasant assurance."

"It is a true one—is it not?"

"Perhaps; as yet I am unable to judge. How do you propose to help me, and so avert this doom?"

"You are brave, my friend."

This time Hernani did smile.

"I can lay claim to nothing more, now," he replied bitterly, "but," he added, recovering himself quickly, "to be helped would be interesting. Let me hear what you propose to do."

"I will tell you. It depends upon you. First, you must have faith in me, and must do as I direct; in addition, you must have one hundred thousand rubles."

The mention of business kindled a little animation in Hernani's face; for the instant, he forgot what he had come to, and remembered only what he had been.

"How am I to lay hands on such a sum, shut up here?" he enquired.

"There is no necessity for you to touch it. I will undertake to do that," replied Popoloff facetiously, "your hand set to paper, will be sufficient. You Jews help each other so well. You have but to write to a friend, and that friend through a friend's friend, will bring me good hard cash, to our little spot in the gardens, at any time and date we may agree upon. Is it not so?"

"Possibly. But what am I to obtain in exchange?"

20

"Your liberty."

"Is that all?"

"Is that all, my friend? Take care; what do you mean? Is that not enough for such a sum, may I ask?"

A listless expression stole over Hernani's fine face. He was weary—intensely so.

Confinement and the breakage of his hopes had already told upon him.

"No," he said bluntly.

"Why?"

"Because the bargain does not tempt me."

Popoloff was silent. He coughed violently, patted his chest as though confident of his strength and proud of its hollowness, and then, with his thin knees touching, and his pale shifty eyes searching Hernani's face, he decided regretfully to play his big trump.

"Suppose I throw in your wife?" he said slowly.

"My wife?" repeated Hernani, excited enough now.

"Yes."

"What do you know of her?"

"Everything."

"Everything?"

"Yes."

"Where is she?"

"Within twenty miles of you."

"Is she unhurt?"

"Yes."

"And in health?"

"Gently, my friend; let us go gently, and above all, let us be business-like. You will appreciate me, I know, being the soul of business. I repeat, suppose I threw in your wife?"

Hernani was silent. The animation had fled from his face as quickly as it had come. Popoloff watched him inquiringly. Shrewd Russian though he was, he was puzzled. Then, after a little reflection, he thought he understood. He would probe.

"She is quite near to you," he repeated.

"Starving in some foul prison, I suppose?" said Hernani, turning pale at the thought.

"On the contrary, she is living in luxury."

"What do you mean—a prisoner and in luxury?"

"A prisoner! I never said so."

"What have you to say then?" demanded Hernani, struggling to control his rising anger.

"As little as possible until we come to our bargain."

"Bargain—is that it? Don't trifle with me, upon such matters, or by the God of Abraham, Isaac, and Jacob, you will drive me——"

Popoloff retreated a step before Hernani's advance and threatening air.

"All right," he said. "I have no desire to trifle. You shall know all I have to tell you."

"Where is my wife? In whose hands is she?" thundered Hernani, as dread and suspicion laid hold upon him.

"The Governor's."

"The Governor's," he repeated as though he did not understand, though the vague and horrible fear of such a calamity had already entered his head. Recovering himself with an exclamation of rage, he leaped to Popoloff's side.

"What do you mean?" he again thundered, while if his glances could have slain, Popoloff had been dead.

That astute individual backed a pace or two, murmuring, "Ah! as I thought—jealous," as placidly as though ordering vodka in a café.

"What did you say?" stammered Hernani, as though the man's knowledge of his thoughts deprived him of breath.

"It is all right, my friend. You need say no more. I will save you the trouble. You are jealous of his Excellency the Governor, who has no doubt given you cause. I will explain. Mind, it may be mere conjecture

on my part, still, you may credit me with being neither
blind nor deaf. From your manner a moment ago, I am
convinced that you are offended with your wife, that a
man is the cause, and from what I know, and what I
don't know, but assume, I give it as my opinion that the
man is the Governor himself."

"And if so?"

Popoloff was silent, "Unless I say all I know about
the woman," he thought, "and I know nothing against
her, my plan will fall through. He will do nothing, con-
sequently, there will be no money to be got."

"Well, if so," he exclaimed at length, "it happens that
I am in a position to clear her character completely.
You wrong her."

"Oh, that I had shot her in the barn," thought Hernani.

"You wrong her," repeated Popoloff, "His Excellency,
it is true, was mad about her, but she loathes him as I
am a witness, having been present at their first interview, and knowing what has happened since."

"You present, you know what has happened?"

"Yes," said Popoloff, and told the whole story, sticking to the truth, where it suited him; finally adding,
"now what are you going to do, that's the question?"

"I must think. Give me time. You have sprung so
much upon me. Let me think. Why did you not tell
me this when I was free? I would have made you rich.
How long has she been in the power of this man?"

"Oh! not long."

"Not long—how long? Was she taken there by
force?"

"By the neck, as you were brought here."

"How am I to know——"

"Oh, suspicious again, eh! Curse suspicion. Put it
away from you. You need have none of it."

"My good man," exclaimed Hernani, irritably, "you

imagine too much. To be suspicious of you, would be natural enough. There my suspicion ends."

"You were green with jealousy a moment ago. What does that mean? Jealousy and suspicion are pretty close friends. But there—I am not here to argue. Splitting hairs does not interest me and is fatiguing. I am off. Your dainty morsel may stay where she is. Is that the way of it? She won't long remain dainty."

Hernani raised his hand, the veins in his forehead swelled. Popoloff very nearly received his fist full in his face. But he controlled himself once more.

"Will you swear to the truth of what you have told me?" he asked as soon as he could speak calmly.

"Yes. I swear it. On your part, will you swear that the sum of one hundred thousand rubles, shall be paid me by your agent, on condition that I effect your escape and that of your wife?"

"Yes. It shall be paid to you, once we are clear of the frontier."

"No, no."

"Once we are clear of the frontier," repeated Hernani. Popoloff smiled craftily.

"Very well," he said, "we won't quibble over trifles. I will come to you again shortly, and we will decide upon a date for the money to be paid over. The place shall be where we met in the gardens. Will that suit?"

"Perfectly."

"Good! Then meantime I will arrange matters; passports, disguise, horses, everything. Wait patiently. That is all you have to do. But I was forgetting. Here is ink and paper; write to your wife instructing her to obey me. I am going to her at once. She might deem me an impostor and perhaps raise an alarm, unless my credentials were clear."

Hernani took the paper, and looked at the pen which Popoloff had taken from his pocket and pieced together. It was a terrible moment for him. What should he do?

An hour ago he had not known that Sara was alive. He had been tortured by the most cruel doubts concerning her. Now he was told that she was well, within a few miles of him, yet in Hourko's power; and suddenly he was asked to write such a paper as could proceed only from his hand, that she might do whatever the bearer of it might direct.

Popoloff saw the look of perplexity, of hesitation, even of dread, which Hernani at that instant took no pains to conceal; and he gave vent to a harsh little chuckle, which said plainly enough: "Look here, my friend, I understand your feelings. But I have no sympathy for you—you only amuse me."

Amidst a dead silence, Popoloff snapped the spring of the pocket ink bottle which he held in his hand, a time or two; then he put it down on the wretched bed that was all Hernani had to sit or lie upon; finally, he took to cracking the knuckles of his thin bony fingers, in a manner habitual to him; at length, tired of that trick, he exclaimed irritably—

"Look here, my friend, you seem to forget that not content with keeping me waiting, you openly doubt me. You are a business man, and a shrewd one, let me put it to you. I want one hundred thousand rubles. You are willing to pay the sum. I mean to earn it. That is the only bond between us. That we are not total strangers may appeal to you, but there is the plain sum and substance of the contract. Were I in your position, I should jump at such a chance, and so would anybody."

Hernani dipped the pen in the ink. He had decided how to act, and stooping down began to write. Yet, as the words were swiftly formed, he reflected that Popoloff's visit, offer, and suggestion, might be a ruse of Hourko's, for some purpose not clear to him. However, with him, a decision was final, so he signed the note with a term of endearment, invented by, and known to Sara, then handed it to Popoloff, who took it, and after a remark or two not worth recording, left him.

Once clear of the Citadel and alone, Titus Popoloff's real feelings cropped to the surface. He held soothing converse with himself as he went his way, "one hundred thousand rubles. I shall get it, but they will not get their liberty. That is how it will be. Jews! faugh!— how I hate them!"

CHAPTER XXI.

Meanwhile, affairs at the palace shaped painfully. The Governor-General, Ivan Nicholaevitch, had begun to think himself an ill-used man. The reasons for such feelings being that his responsibilities were varied and irksome, that the insurrection still flickered on, and could not be got to go out, its broken character and hydra-headedness rendering decisive action a lengthy and difficult business; also that as is the case with exalted personages, Ivan Nicholaevitch was fenced about by jealousies, intrigues, Petersburg instructions of conflicting purport, and Petersburg doubts and suspicions. There was some talk of the great man's recall; not that such talk was new or meant more than it had hitherto done, but amidst all this clamor of tongues, one thing was certain, that Ivan Nicholaevitch's temper was not on the mend. Domestic affairs were growing to trouble him more, and might be said to be straining towards a breakage, since his wife, Madam Olga, wrote threateningly from out the sunshine to which she had fled, and was aided and abetted in so doing by a strong band of relatives, who, being in high favor with his Imperial Majesty the Tsar, had it well within their power to do him injury.

Then, too, in the matter of Sara, he had made no headway. For a spell of weeks, he had patiently pursued the kind tack, under the impression that with a woman of Sara's temperament, coercion would be useless. He had torn himself from his duties, and had rushed to her side at headlong speed, assuming the attitude and conduct of an ardent but honorable lover; the result being, that after such interviews, he had galloped back, disturbed, inflamed, disappointed, but no nearer the pos-

session of his baffling paragon of beauty. When the
urgency of his business had prevented his personal attentions—which had happened for days—scarce one had
passed without some recognition from him of her near
presence and his interest in her. Flowers, delicacies,
even jewels, had arrived at the villa, and had been received by Sara with indifference, coupled with a fear,
which was accentuated by the sight of each package or
costly bouquet—for were they not signs of the deep-
rootedness of the man's evil passion, of the unalterableness of his resolution concerning her? Poor Sara! she
saw them with pallor and a beating heart, an inward
sense of sickness, swimming of the head, positive loathing. Each one seemed to say aloud to her, "I have come
to remind you that as a woman, born of woman, you
must yield and be dragged to the depths. Circumstances
are against you. In the end, you will succumb, you will
see." Even Riva, being of commoner clay and looser
morals, dreading doubt and danger and coveting luxury
and rest, had begun to hint at the justifiableness of
weakness under given conditions, and to remark, that
Ivan Nicholaevitch had his good qualities, as his conduct latterly had proved.

At which dark suggestions, after ignoring patiently,
then with gentleness correcting, Sara had grown angry,
and forbidden the mention of such matters.

Such being a brief summary of the situation, Ivan
Nicholaevitch, though at a critical pass, state telegrams
thundering upon him, consigned them to the devil, and
himself to the road, his historical team of blacks clattering beneath the now budding lime trees of the Avenue
at top speed, bearing him to the villa, and what in his bad
mood he had resolved should be an understanding with
Sara.

As though to foster and compel this inevitable crisis—
Sara, though in reality pale from lack of exercise and
fresh air, and sleepless from anxiety—had, to Hourko's

mind, never looked lovelier. In describing her afterwards—for he had good reason to remember that interview—he affirmed that her beauty was such "that it deprived him of speech."

He had dined as was his custom. Sara had sung to
him, exercising herself the while, as to how to wear the
time away until the moment of his departure. From the
corners of her eyes she had watched him as he had hov-
ered about her, and had shrunk and shuddered as he had
caressed her hair, laid his hand upon her shoulders, and
with firm fingers encircled her arm. So nervous had she
gradually become, that being able to endure his distressing proximity no longer, and in obedience to a sudden
impulse, she ceased playing and sprang off the music-
stool.

"What did you do that for?" he asked instantly.

"I am tired," she faltered.

"Nonsense, play a little longer."

"I cannot."

Hourko's pent-up wrath found outlet.

"But you must."

Standing there facing him, Sara opened her beautiful
eyes wide, wonder and alarm shining in them. Her attitude displayed the grace and symmetry of her figure
to perfection, and in that lightning-like instant, the sight
of it increased Hourko's disappointment as well as his
passion.

"Curse it," he went on, brutally, losing all control over
his tongue, "you shall do as I tell you. Do you understand? I have played the fool long enough. Do you
suppose I am going to keep you in luxury, load you
with presents, and dance attendance upon you into the
bargain, for nothing? I can be kind and considerate
enough and listen to all your fine ideas—whereby you
keep me at a distance—so long as they do not weary me;
but I will have my way with you, as I have given you
to understand."

Still in front of him, still standing, Sara's attitude was so haughty and repellent, yet withal, so womanly—as though she were grieved as well as shocked—that Hourko, regretful of his anger on the instant, softened his speech.

"Come," he said, "I did not mean that, quite. But I am harassed on all sides, and from you I expect a little kindness."

"Excellency; gratitude, which I have a right to give, is yours."

"But how far does it extend?"

"To thanking you for——"

"To shrinking from me."

"Certainly not to obeying you in the matter of playing, with all due respect to you; though such an unreasonable attitude strikes me as being a little like a man."

Hourko winced and was silent, while Sara prepared herself for the mischief which she instinctively felt was coming, and waited for him to speak. There was to be a struggle, very well, it should be of his making."

"A little like a man; why should you sneer at men?" he at length asked.

"Excellency, I do not."

"Then what do your words imply?"

"That I know what is unreasonable and must be amused when I encounter it."

"By all the Saints, I shall be unreasonable in a way that will not amuse you, if you goad me to it."

"I goad you; I have no other wish than to please you."

"Then do so."

"But I cannot hear you speak of gifts and attentions, without reminding you that I ask for neither of them. My only request is——"

"What? Don't let it be unreasonable."

"It is that you will grant me my liberty. Let me leave this place, as I entered it."

"For the streets. To beg?"

"Yes."

"Unprotected?"

"No one would harm me."

"You think that?"

"I am sure of it."

"Oh! you have droll ideas."

"I should find friends, or at worst, should die."

"Highly romantic, but, pardon me, distinctly absurd. Why should you die? When people consider themselves unfortunate, they invariably talk of dying. My experience is, that when worst off, they live the longest. No, you would not die, and you would not even be allowed to beg, but you would be arrested and locked up, you would be at the mercy of men who would neither befriend nor pity you at a time like this. No, make your mind easy, I know what is best for you too well to let you go."

"It is cruel."

"Cruel! you don't know what you are talking about. I should be brutal, were I to do as you ask. Listen— during those moments when you have spoken most considerately and our thoughts have mingled best, you have hinted at being unhappy with your husband. Is it not so?"

"No."

"Then what am I to understand?"

Sara hesitated. She had feared lest, having Hernani in his power, he should seek to influence her through him, in some way, so had, wisely as she thought, though vaguely, alluded to the tie between them as a slight one. She did not know what answer to make, being directly taxed, and Hourko repeated his question without taking his eyes off her.

"Nothing," she said at length.

"Nothing; a regular woman's answer. However, I think I understand you. Still, I am in a generous mood, and I want you to be clearly aware that my affection for you is a genuine one, that you attracted me from the first, that I have risked a public and private scandal as well as other dangers on your account, and that I have never changed in the slightest degree towards you. Have I?"

"Excellency, you are very good, and I am indebted to you for such homage, you who are surrounded by so much beauty, but——" Sara paused, despising herself for her attitude towards the man, for dissembling, when she so loathed him.

"But what?" he demanded.

"How can I compel myself to like you, when——"

"Well?"

"When I should hate you, were our relationship what you would wish?"

"Nonsense! My devotion to you would win the day; and, Sara, believe me, I am devoted. I would sacrifice ambition, relatives, everything, for you. I recognize the fact that I shall never again meet with a woman capable of inspiring me with affection as you have done."

"But, Excellency, we are neither of us free."

"That does not lessen my power to protect you. I can offer you safety, comfort, even luxury—all that you need wish for."

"No honest woman would accept such a position."

"Accept such a position! Wouldn't they! Now, by all the Saints, you try my patience. I have stooped to plead, now hear my other argument. You have not forgotten the paper found in your house?"

"No!"

"I have it still."

"I thought so."

"By your own handwriting you prove your treachery to his Imperial Majesty's Government. Is it not so?"

"So you say!"

"Very well; that paper shall be handed to the police,

and with it yourself, together with what comments it may
please me to make, unless—well—unless you consent to
my proposals."

"Then, Excellency," answered Sara, wrought to such
a pitch that she was calm, "you had better label me with
that paper and your remarks, and hand me over to your
myrmidons."

"You still refuse?"

"Absolutely!"

"At the same time, be it understood, you doom your
husband either to lifelong imprisonment or ignominious
death."

"How?" gasped Sara, horror-stricken.

Hourko saw his advantage. He had cunningly kept
his strongest argument, his worst and most cruel threat,
until the last.

"If you accept my offer, and are to me all I wish, you
cannot suppose that those who have cared for and protected you, shall be allowed to suffer as I have described.
Be all I ask, and I will take it upon me to see that your
husband shall go free. He shall be escorted over the
frontier, and shall write from a place of safety in such
a way as to prove the worth of my promise. Now think,
and think well, for I am not to be trifled with. You
have it in your power to save your husband from death,
or worse, a living death in the mines. What is it to be?"

Confident of his advantage, by reason of the effect of
his words—already anticipating her reply—his eyes
gleaming with passion, Hourko stood over her.

It was a terrible moment. In the death-like stillness
of the room, terror and despair seemed to deprive Sara
of the power of speech. She could hear the loud full
beat of her heart, and her tongue clung to her mouth.
What should she do?

To that terrible frightened heart-beat, there was suddenly added another sound, and that one audible to
Hourko, nay, growing more audible each instant. It

was that of a horse stretched out at the gallop; in fact, approaching the villa by way of the avenue.

"Hark! What is it?" he exclaimed. Then as it drew nearer, "Ah! an aide-de-camp; and at this hour. Something has occurred. I shall have to go. Come! your answer before I leave. When we meet again my promise will be fulfilled—and he will be free."

As in a mist, half swooning, deprived of the time and strength to think clearly, Sara could only repeat to herself, "I have it in my power to save him—from awful suffering—perhaps from death. Can I hesitate? He may not love me, but I—it is the chance I have longed for always—to prove my love. Let me think?"—and Hernani's last words, so often repeated by her, rang in her ears, "The Holy One, He will have you in His charge."

The clatter of hoofs had stopped. A bell pealed through the house. Hourko left the apartment, and re-entered it with a dispatch in his hand.

"Come, your answer?" he repeated, inexorable to the last.

Sara's lips moved, but no sound came.

"What do you say?" he asked, bending over her as she sat.

Again her lips moved, and this time he heard distinctly, for the words rang through the room as in bitter defiance of fate. She had consented.

"This seals our compact," he exclaimed; and before she could move, he had kissed her passionately.

His touch, and the horror of the situation, deprived her of speech, and before she could give utterance to the words which rushed to her lips, Hourko had left the room and set out for Warsaw, the dispatch safe in his pocket.

It was a sign of the Tsar's displeasure, and of the triumph of his enemies—it was his recall to Petersburg.

CHAPTER XXII.

Armed with Hernani's note to Sara—which, by the way, he carefully opened, suspecting pitfalls—though delayed for days and by a dozen matters, Popoloff lost the least possible time in making for the villa. The arrangements for the double escape and flight complete, he waited only until he knew Hourko to be well out of the way, then he set forward. With lavish bribe of rubles he satisfied unscrupulous and avaricious hearts, and with mock show of halting, and many cautions from these people, he got himself conducted to where Sara, terror-stricken at a sound, by reason of her dread of Hourko's return, anxious and restless to a degree scarcely to be understood, awaited with old Riva the turning of events.

Imagine Sara's surprise and consternation, when this man of whom she thought so ill, arrived upon the scene to add to her complications. Though she had never exchanged a word with him, from the first, her repugnance for him had been complete. Was this some sudden move of General Hourko's? What was about to happen? What was he there for? She put this last question to him politely, when she had stayed the beating of her heart and knit herself for the occasion.

"I shall tell you, madam, with much pleasure if you will dismiss your woman."

This was a shot at Riva, whose presence he had discounted, but whose keen black eyes displeased him.

Riva looked at Sara questioningly, and after some slight hesitation on her part received a sign to go. Meanwhile, with his seemingly vacant glances, Popoloff took in the situation, noting with a curling lip the presence of freshly-cut flowers, even a case of jewels, collected on a side table, thrust into a corner. They were presents from Hourko he felt sure. The General had evidently hit upon that plan of laying siege. Then he looked at the object of such attentions, meeting the gaze he challenged frankly enough, but thinking with characteristic duplicity, how he would have the lovely creature stripped, that her soft body might writhe beneath the blows of the shabby old tasseled cane he carried! "A Jewess, faugh!" That was how he would have treated her. And he had a paper in his pocket to make her respect and obey his injunctions. He could have laughed; the more as, reading Sara's thoughts, he said to himself furiously, "I am ugly, so the minx has the impertinence to dislike me."

The silence becoming embarrassing, Sara was again driven to address him.

"You have some message or note for me from——"

"His Excellency? No, madam."

"Then may I again ask you to tell me the object of your visit?"

Ingenious in the rapidity with which he decided to amuse himself, even at the risk of being obnoxious, Popoloff answered promptly enough—

"Madam, my answer is that you have the best right to do so, since it entirely concerns yourself. I am here with a view to induce you to consign yourself to my safe keeping, and with that object before me, I have encountered innumerable obstacles and dangers."

"Can the man be mad?" thought Sara, "or in love with me, or what?" But being able to decide nothing, she stammered—

"Is his Excellency, General Hourko, aware that you have come here?"

"On the contrary, were his Excellency, my master, to know that I am here, my place would be forfeited and my person seized."

"But he will be told. His servants are——"

21

"In my pay. Ready to do my bidding. When it is
done they will pass the frontier."

"You cannot mean that you——"

"Precisely; that is what I do mean. For the moment
the General and I have parted company. Oh! when you
know me better you will see how many-sided I am. Experience has given me a large head and heart. I have
learned to live in any climate, hot, cold, or variable;
therefore, I can expand or contract as necessity may require. Let me beg of you not to judge me by my face.
That, I know, is all against me. But what can be more
deceptive than a face? True, in some cases the face is
the index to the mind, but in few only. Neither is it
safe to judge a man by words, for to my mind, you judge
a man, not by what he says, but by what he does not
say. Oh! it is very mystifying. I know it. But acts,
they are what we want. You should judge by acts. Now
listen to me, for my advice is sage. I want you to prepare yourself for a change. To have what you may have
—though it were well that that should go in a handkerchief, so to speak—collected and ready to take in your
hand, so that you may follow me from this house. It
is an extraordinary request you will say. I agree with
you; but you must bear in mind that the times are out
of joint, and that for one of your persuasion, this is a
queer place to be in. Do you comprehend me, madam?"

Sara was speechless. The last remark or two she had
not heard. Her thoughts were confused. Out of it all
she seemed to have but one clear idea—absolute distrust
of the man who addressed her.

Popoloff spoke again, and so spurred her into speech.

"Will you do as I wish!" he demanded, in a voice
which, when he pleased, was pleasant enough.

"No!" answered Sara energetically.

"I thought not; but what if your husband wishes it?"

"My husband?"

"Yes!"

"What can you possibly know of him?"

"A very great deal. There! now your face changes. Never judge by a face. A moment ago you could have shot me. Now, if you could only bring yourself to believe that I can give you news of your husband, you would kiss me, ugly though you think me. Well, I have never counted much upon women so that kisses would not move me——. But, I forgot, time is precious, therefore without a kiss, I will give you this note. There —now you will understand that you must do as I tell you."

Sara took the letter with tremulously eager fingers, turning both red and white even at the feel of it.

"You would be alone, I see," continued Popoloff, more from the desire to vaunt his own perspicacity than from any wish to be civil, "I wonder what this love is," he added to himself, as, deaf to his remarks, Sara stepped aside to read the letter. "One thing is certain; clogged with such sentiment, the mastership of oneself surrendered, one would sink rather than rise. Such silly weakness is not for men."

Flushing with a happiness bred in the last few minutes, wild with delight at the thought that Hernani was not lost to her, and that she would be saved from a fearful existence with Hourko, yet chilling fast, as her fears of the man in whom she was told to confide, again got the better of her, Sara finished her reading of those few sweet lines, and then said, with as much composure as she could summon:

"Whatever my personal feelings, sir, this letter would decide my actions. I cannot but be filled with misgivings, but you may depend upon me to do as you may desire."

Popoloff directed his gaze towards the door through which Riva had obediently disappeared.

"That is well," he remarked, "we shall get along now; but what about that woman? When you have gone, there will be a fine hue and cry after you. She will be questioned—flogged perhaps. Can you depend upon her?"

"How do you mean?"

"Is she to be trusted?"

"Absolutely. She would sacrifice her life for me."

"That is good."

"But she will be with me. We shall escape together."

"It is impossible. She is old, and her presence must increase the difficulties. She must remain behind and shift for herself. That is all I can suggest. She has no place in my calculations."

Sara looked at him steadily and with scorn.

"Then you must leave me out of them also. Not a step do I go without her. She has befriended me all my life, and at her age, after such service, would you have me desert her?"

"It is necessary. You must abandon her or give up the chance of escape."

"Very well, then, I have done with it. Riva goes with me or I don't stir." And as though to emphasize the unalterableness of her decision Sara sat down in a chair.

"What is the use of making a fuss about a paltry servant?" remonstrated Popoloff.

To which remark Sara deigned no answer.

"Very well, I must see about it. More money must be paid me for the safe conduct of such cattle, that is all," he added, fairly exasperated.

No reply coming from Sara, he continued in milder tones, as though he considered himself ill used:

"But, after all, I was prepared for this, as I am for anything. If you knew the difficulties you have to contend with, you would agree that you are foolish. However, I shall arrange. Now, if you will give me a few minutes' attention I will tell you my plans. According to my calculation, your husband should escape from the

Citadel to-morrow night. There should be no difficulty —doors and gates will simply be opened. Once clear of the walls, he will be met by my paid agent, who will travel with him over the frontier to the little town of Wieletzka where you are to join him. To do this, I propose that you should also start to-morrow night, and at nine o'clock have arranged for a conveyance to be in attendance. You will simply place yourself in the hands of the woman here who has waited upon you, and the more you hide your face, and the less you open your lips, until you find yourself in your husband's arms, the better."

Sara began to thank him—she could not help it—her gratitude would be lifelong—her prayers——.

Popoloff cut her short with a grim smile, and what he meant to be the most cruelly cynical, nay, brutal words he had ever uttered.

"Heap your blessings on your husband when you see him and are free."

Then he left her.

CHAPTER XXIII.

Affairs had shaped as Popoloff had wished. In no solitary instance had his plans miscarried. The risk he had incurred and the sum at stake, had guaranteed the working of his wits to good purpose. Bribery had unbarred the strongest gates in Warsaw—those of the Citadel—without a hitch, and Hernani had set out for the frontier, safely escorted, safely provided with passport and instructions warranted to work.

At Ivan Nicholaevitch's villa, the patient sentries—automatic, and there for military show and stiffest ceremonial—watched over empty quarters, so far as Sara was concerned—she and Riva having been got clear away, by aid of those in whom Ivan Nicholaevitch had placed such faith.

Popoloff had even received a telegram from his agent. as agreed, stating that Hernani had crossed the frontier en route for Wieletzka, and on strength of this and as also agreed, he in his turn had communicated with old Nikolay Brauman, fixing an appointment in the Saxonski Sad, for that very day, at nine of the clock. So far all went swimmingly. Friend Popoloff felt sure of his money. He had as good as got it. With such a sum added to others put away, he would be above the reach of want, for life, luxuriously placed even, to his way of thinking. It would be a nice nest egg, should his business of secretary, tchinovnick, spy, or what it might be called, fail him. From that pleasant aspect of the picture, he turned, as was his cruel nature, to gloat savagely over a choice termination to this adventure scheme of his.

He chose to think, with rare inventive devilry, of the blessings that would be showered upon him by the eager

Hernani, and by Sara, expectant, eager too; both brimming over with love, speeding towards each other with whole skins and palpitating hearts; believing their troubles ended or nearing that felicity; the confidence in each other rekindling, and the whole world before them it might seem. Popoloff dwelt upon these details with singular relish, yet with even keener appetite hastened on to others, which when dovetailed, should comprise a finale of surpassing merit, and irony of grimmest intensity.

He knew the little inn at Wieletzka where Sara and Hernani were to be again united, and since Hernani's sagacity had prompted him to pay only on clearing the frontier, this was the denouement, he, Popoloff, had deftly planned.

He would hasten to the Saxonski Sad, he would pocket his money, and that safe, by a judicious and' prearranged appeal to Austrian officialdom,* he would cause Hernani and Sara to be re-arrested, and flung into some vile hole where they could await his pleasure and further developments. By such an arrangement, his keen nose scented other Jewish moneys, perhaps rubles from Hourko, who might swallow some cunningly thought-out concoction, and prove grateful into the bargain.

Such was Popoloff's masterpiece of treachery, warranted to be steel-jointed and to fail in no way.

But Popoloff had forgotten that a lie cannot last in a race with truth, but must be outstripped, fail, and in its hideousness, be at length exposed to public gaze ablaze with wrath.

He had forgotten that if his plans were to triumph, to the undoing of others, for him too there must come a reckoning day.

However, with a light heart and an itching palm, he

---

*The Austrian officials aided the Russians throughout the revolt.

finished his business for the night, tidied official papers committed to his charge, closed his private bureau with cunning look and sharp eye, and set out with quick step and eager expectancy for the gardens.

At the hour he had chosen, they were deserted, as he had calculated; plunged also in deepest gloom, and moisture of copious spring rains which had left the paths slimy and unpleasant to the foot.

Arrived upon the spot, and seeing no one—nothing but straight stems of trees and shadowy stretching of dim alleys, he paced to and fro. The lights of an hotel, and of a palace, once royal and Polish, shone pallidly.

He began to grow restless—to stamp irritably—to wonder and to talk to himself angrily. Patience, friend Popoloff. The virtue of it is at all times great, and could you but see ahead, you would be glad of a respite, of Time, and all that Time confers.

At length a step was heard by him, a form seen to approach, seen also by three other forms hard by, intent on watching, befriended also by the darkness and the many tree trunks.

Popoloff coughed; which sign was answered, and the two dark figures came to a halt.

"Have you the money?" he inquired.

"It is here, as promised," was the answer, with additional suggestion to "count it at a café," where they can be quiet.

"It is unnecessary," replied Popoloff, "I can trust you. Have you anything further to say?"

"Nothing."

"Then I will wish you good-night."

The money safe within his grasp, consigned to his tchinovnik's portfolio of especial safety, once again he stepped out at quickest pace, with even his old heart beating fast in wicked delight. A few steps only did he take, or was suffered to take it would be well to say.

Then, no further could he go. Two men blocked the narrow path, one also closed on him in rear.

"What do you want?" he exclaimed.

"You," answered one.

"Say your prayers, old man," mocked another. "Aye, aye, pray if you can before you die the death of a traitor."

Popoloff was no coward. He would have fought or shown firm front, could he but have done so. But, alas, where now was Time for him? At last it was no more, but had deserted him for ever.

The third man, at his back, was not seen by him, and there lay the danger, for without fresh chance of speech, and with lightning stroke, a blow from keenest steel was dealt him between the shoulders; rough hands smothered his cries. What mercy had he ever shown, and what mercy did he now deserve?

His pockets rifled, bathed in blood, his foes beside him, till his evil heart ceased beating, that was his end, and that end the one he most merited.

CHAPTER XXIV.

The weather was magnificent, the sun shone in cloudless splendor, warming, cheering, and beautifying the
charming scenery which skirted the town of Wieletzka,
where stood the Inn at which Popoloff had decided that
Hernani and Sara should meet. He had selected the
spot because it was, to his mind, the sort of place at
which anything might be done without attracting great
notice. It was true that the spring had come, that the
varied tinting of the trees was admirable, that the lake
and the woods invited picnic parties, and that the vil-
lagers for miles round availed themselves of the charms
of the district and the cheap comforts of the Inn, and
trooped there with their women, bent upon eating, drinking and love-making; all these facts scarce counted, since
the peasants were calculated to sip their liquor with
sleepy-eyed indifference, while anything short of murder
was being committed.

So there stood the little white-walled Inn, begirt by its
pretty garden and bright green palings, its whole front-
age a bower of shade, thanks to a number of chestnut
trees, the tops of which had been pruned to pancake-like
flatness, to give light and a view to the upper windows.

In these pink chestnut trees, whole colonies of birds
chirped, twittered, and fought, while beneath them
strong wooden tables, painted green like the palings,
were grouped conveniently.

Coarse white cloths were spread upon these tables,
which were further garnished by cheap blue crockery,
black-handled knives and forks, and cruet stands, containing oil, vinegar, and French mustard; the salt, with
a knife to help it, being set in a separate bowl. All these
tables were filled to overflowing, and from each and all of

them came peals of laughter, coarse jokes, and the occasional fumes of bad tobacco.

A solitary waiter, clad in greasy black, ample shirt front and low cut turned down collar, perspired freely, and with unctuous good nature struggled to attend to every one at once.

Watch that brown-skinned, plump-fingered woman, lighting a cigar for that jolly, fat, peasant fellow who is her lover, and then travel with the blue smoke as it leaves his lips, through the tender green of the sun-kissed chestnut leaves, slowly and upward, until it curls into a little room, before the open window of which stretched wood and water in perfection.

The occupants of that room, two in number, have interest of their own, being Kasimir Hernani and Sara.

Titus Popoloff's emissaries, weary of waiting for instructions, and thinking that none could be forthcoming, had taken the road to Warsaw. Alone and together, the hearts of husband and wife had overflowed. In impassioned eloquence Hernani had told of his first doubts and fears, of the perpetual strengthening of them, and had broken down and sobbed like a child in an attempt to describe what he had suffered; after which, a few words from Sara had been enough to clear the way, to the locking of arms and the meeting of warm lips.

"Dearie, dearie, then you do love me?" she had gasped.

"Yes."

"For myself, and even though I have brought you no children?"

"For yourself, and as I shall never love again. But you—you——"

"I—I love you like this," and with trembling lips, as though the horror of it all still made her quake, she spoke of Hourko and the suffering he had put her to at the villa.

"So then—in your turn, you love me—mind, we shall

be poor—very—comparatively, for they will take care to confiscate all they can lay hands on."

"I—love you—and we shall be poor—listen," and in a torrent of burning words, unable to restrain herself, the blood in her face, determined to lay bare her whole heart, she told him how that for him, she would have yielded even herself; her honor being nothing when weighed against his life.

"God of my fathers! you would have done that for me!" he exclaimed.

And she nodded, adding, moments after, when she could gain her voice—

"So that now we shall be one—always—and never part while life lasts?"

"Never," he answered solemnly, taking her in his strong arms, "the Holy One will have us in His charge, and it will be well with us."

And beneath them, through the green of the chestnut leaves, the smoke still ascended, the laughter rang out, and the birds talked to each other, while into their hearts stole the blessed thought that for them there was still hope, for there was love.

THE END.